D0722182

A Shot Rolling Ship

A Shot Rolling Ship

BY DAVID DONACHIE

First published in Great Britain in 2005 by
Allison & Busby Limited
Bon Marché Centre
241-251 Ferndale Road
London SW9 8BJ

http://www.allisonandbusby.com

Copyright © 2005 by DAVID DONACHIE

The moral right of the author has been asserted.

This book is sold subject to the conditions that it shall not,
by way of trade or otherwise, be lent, resold, hired out or
otherwise circulated without the publisher's prior
written consent in any form of binding or cover other than
that in which it is published and without a similar condition
being imposed upon the subsequent
purchaser.

A catalogue record for this book is available from
the British Library.

10 9 8 7 6 5 4 3 2 1

ISBN 0 7490 8241 0

Printed and bound in Wales by
Creative Print and Design, Ebbw Vale

DAVID DONACHIE was born in Edinburgh in 1944. He has had a variety of jobs, including selling everything from business machines to soap. He has always had an abiding interest in the naval history of the eighteenth and nineteenth centuries. The author of a number of bestselling books, he now lives in Deal with his partner, the novelist Sarah Grazebrook.

To the memory of
Mick Jailler
A good friend who showed in life
a level of bravery and tenacity
that few could match.
He also tried very hard,
yet failed, to hide his generosity.

'Welcome to hell, brother.'

The voice under the thick felt hat was gruff, neither friendly nor unfriendly, the face the colour of mahogany, pitted, lined and weary looking, the eyes deep pools of brown. It stood out from the rest of the ship's crew only because it was close to a lantern, so that all the others present were but seated shadows, eyes in the gloom, sizing up a newcomer. 'Happen there are those who told you Old Nick's lair was hot and reeks of brimstone. It ain't, friend. It goes by the name of *Griffin*, and it be cold, damp and the smell is of bilge and rotten timber.'

A voice from the gloom added his opinion. 'Pressing this lot ain't goin' to make it smell any better.'

John Pearce, half crouching, lowered the canvas sack that contained all his worldly possessions, the homicidal fury he had felt on coming aboard subsiding into a cold anger. That was underscored by a deep feeling of powerlessness, the natural state of mind for a man ensnared for the second time in a matter of weeks by the tentacles of King George's Navy. How could he get out of this? He had to get off this ship, but there seemed no way of doing so short of chucking himself into the sea and that would only lead to recapture unless, and just as likely, he drowned in the cold grey waters of the English Channel.

The sounds above his head were of a ship getting under way; shouts as sails were sheeted home, the groan of strained timbers, the creak of the cables that controlled the rudder. A sudden lurch as HMS *Griffin*, out of the lee created by the much larger East Indiaman, dropped sideways off the crest of a wave. That forced him to grab hold of a ladder rung, his muscles tensed as the bows hit another wave, sending a shiver through the entire frame. This was happening on a relatively calm sea, which made Pearce wonder what it would be like to be aboard in rough water. He had to acknowledge one speaker, the fellow in the felt hat, to be right about the smell, except he had left out the stench of packed and unwashed humanity, hardly surprising given the lack of space. Pearce had to crouch just to avoid clouting his head on the deck beams: even if the mass of bodies prevented him from seeing the exact dimensions of his new home, he knew it to be tiny. The deck he had crossed on coming aboard was that, no more than twenty stretched paces bow to stern, and less than half that dimension in the beam; what lay beneath could not be greater.

'Are you to move on, John boy, or are you wishing to leave us to freeze on this here ladder.'

Michael O'Hagan's Irish brogue was muffled because he was still standing upright in the well of the hatchway, through which ran a wide, thick-runged ladder. Behind him the others pressed out of the *Lady Harrington* would be on deck, no doubt watching, as Pearce himself had done moments before, that spacious and steady merchant ship sailing away towards the easily visible southern shore of England.

'Aside there, let me pass.'

The voice was that of Lieutenant Benjamin Colbourne, the man who had just pressed them, sharp and commanding. Rufus Dommet was the one who answered, the shrill voice evidence of both his youth and perhaps a degree of nervousness. 'There's no room to pass.'

'Shift I say.'

'But…'

'Silence. You are new aboard, man, and I forgive this once, such a response as being due to ignorance, but do not in future address me with such familiarity, and do not leave out an acknowledgment of my rank, or I will be obliged to discipline you.'

From somewhere in the darkest recesses of the deck came the sound of a loud and derisory mouth-made fart. John Pearce edged forward towards that raspberry and the men before him, by standing and moving back the barrels on which they had been seated, cleared a space. Michael O'Hagan joined him, even more stooped because of his greater height, mouthing a quiet, 'Mother of Jesus', as he realised how cramped it was. Behind Michael came Charlie Taverner, still confused, that state of mind rendering the normally voluble Londoner silent.

He was bustled to one side as the blue-coated officer squeezed by. 'Move back there, make some space.'

The mahogany face spoke again. 'Can't make what ain't there, your honour, 'cepting we stove out some of the scantlings.'

'Belay that, Latimer.'

If Lieutenant Colbourne was made angry by the interjection, a vocal complaint from what appeared to be a common seaman, he did not show it – the response had no animosity, more a weariness born of habit. Instead he turned and commanded the other pressed men still on the deck to come below, which required him to push even more to squeeze them in. He then raised himself onto the lowest rung on the ladder so that he, bent forward, could address an assembly crammed so tight it seemed that only the bodies held each other against the pitch and roll of the ship, and that was with a quantity of the crew absent, for there were men on the deck still, sailing the ship.

'Get your sodding dunnage out of my mouth.'

Charlie Taverner, the guilty party, who still had his ditty bag slung over his shoulder, reacted sharply. 'Happen I would rather leave it gob stoppin' than smell your breath, mate.'

'You'll be smelling your own blood, cheeky bugger.'

'Silence.'

John Pearce examined Colbourne closely as he issued that stricture, expressed in an absent-minded fashion while he was occupied, simultaneously riffling the pages of a book. On the deck of the *Lady Harrington* the man, as tall as John Pearce, though thin, had looked imposing, but after only a few weeks as an enforced sailor Pearce knew that the uniform had some bearing on that. The lieutenant looked less impressive now – hardly surprising given that with a book held up to his face, and an arm hooked round the ladder upright, he was forced to speak from a position forced on him by the lack of headroom, one that robbed him of all dignity.

'By the power vested in me by those executing the office of Lord High Admiral, it is my duty to acquaint you with those statutes so laid down by them to govern the behaviour of the officers and men of His Majesty's ship at sea…'

The voice became a drone in the background, partly for the fact that John Pearce had heard the words before, but just as much because of the dull way that Colbourne recited them. It hardly seemed possible that not much more than an hour before he had been discussing how to get ashore on the Kent coast in a way that would allow him to evade notice. Every fibre of his being longed for that; it had since he had been, three and half weeks previously, illegally and violently taken up and pressed for the first time.

The image of that night came easily, as did remembrance of the Pelican tavern, hard by the River Thames, tucked in the Liberties of the Savoy, a warren of streets and alleys where minor felons and debtors could live without fear of bailiffs and tipstaffs. Sought by him as a refuge from pursuit by a more powerful law, it had been full of humanity, smoke, laughter and argument, all perfectly normal until the door burst open and the Navy arrived in force, with cudgels and purpose, rudely interrupting his cagey conversation with a quartet of impecunious strangers who made their living on the riverbank. It had led to sudden mayhem and a near escape, but he had not evaded the press gang; instead he had experienced capture and received, at the end of a knotted rope, his first taste of naval discipline.

The course of his life had changed in that moment, his only desire to get away and to do so without attracting attention. To get ashore discreetly was essential, for he suspected there was a King's Bench warrant out for his arrest.

Obstacles to that aim had been numerous ever since he was taken up, yet he had somehow overcome them all to gain his freedom, but now, having fallen foul at the very last hurdle, he must start all over again. He looked around at the dimly lit faces of his new shipmates, at least those he could see. They ranged from the very young and open, of seamen who were little more than boys, to the man who had spoken to them first, a gnarled veteran who had clearly spent years at sea.

There would certainly be people in this tub that would seek to stop him deserting; he had learned in the last few weeks that a proper sailor's attitude to a pressed landsman rarely included much in the way of sympathy. The best he could hope for was indifference, a stance that would have men look the other way at matters which they thought to be none of their concern. One or two might be positively compassionate, but to balance them, in any group, there were bound to be those who would interfere from natural malice – men who hated to see others make a gain not vouchsafed to themselves – and that took no account of those with warrants and petty ranks, keen to protect their little shards of authority.

Such a thing did not apply to Lieutenant Colbourne; he was a known quantity. Having gone to the trouble of pressing them out of a passing merchantman, the ship's captain could be guaranteed to do everything in his power to keep Pearce aboard, so the nature of the man was of serious concern. The officer who had first pressed him, and given him that welcoming clout with a knotted rope, had been a blackhearted tyrant called Ralph Barclay. Was Colbourne the same? Was he as watchful, as keen to see his inferior officers use their fists, a starter, or the lash to maintain authority?

Chance had allowed him to outmanoeuvre Barclay and regain his freedom; could he do the same to Colbourne? What of the ship, this HMS *Griffin*; where would she sail, what were her duties? She had come up upon the *Lady Harrington* close to the South Kent shore, in soundings as

Colbourne had insisted, a fact that seemingly gave him the right to press seamen from any merchant vessel he encountered. Did her duty keep her in such proximity to the coast or would she be sailing into deeper water? Soundings. The word had a funereal ring to it, a death knell of hope. A lead line cast into John Pearce's soul not twenty minutes ago would have touched bottom quickly when he realised what was about to happen, realised that, in the end it was Ralph Barclay who had humbugged him and not the other way round; as he had contemplated his options, he was in near despair. That, he knew, was a useless emotion and it was not in his character to dwell in the slough of despond. Now, every nerve end was alive, his eyes and ears acute for any clue that would aid his cause. He would get off this ship or die in the attempt.

'Article Four. No man shall have carnal knowledge of any beast carried in His Majesty's vessels on pain of death…'

'He has a right way with a jest,' whispered O'Hagan, 'with no room here to swing a dead chicken. Sure he's fit for the fairground tent. If he was to lay out his hat I'd toss him a sixpence.'

Pearce felt himself smile, which made him realise how tightly clenched had been his jaw. It might be involuntary and the joke feeble, but it eased the angry tension and he was grateful for the release to a man who, in only a matter of days, had become a close friend. That was Michael's way, to see humour in every situation no matter how desperate. Besides that he had a great flair for deflating those who sought to command him, as well as the ability, gifted as he was with height and strength, to stand toe to toe with any man who thought himself cock-of-the-walk. He had faults, all men do, and was bellicose when drunk, the state in which Pearce had first seen him, but if there was anyone he would want by his shoulder when trouble threatened, Michael was that man.

The words being mouthed by Colbourne were no joke. Articles of War they called them, those Lord High

Admirals; articles of death more like, given the number of offences that attracted such a penalty. Ideas raced through John Pearce's mind, split-second scenarios; a long swim if they ever got close enough to shore, the theft of a boat, or, given that he had money hidden in his ditty bag, a bribe to some of the crew to aid him and get him ashore. So real did these ideas seem that he could almost feel the solid ground of Mother Earth under his feet.

The way the ship lurched disabused him of that particular reverie and it also brought on a stab of guilt as he realised that he was thinking only of himself, ignoring the needs of those who had been taken up with him. That brought forth several emotions on top of self-reproach, feelings he had harboured before; annoyance at the way these men sought decisions from him, almost forcing him to be a leader – to think for them all when all he wanted was to think for himself. Michael, Charlie Taverner and young Rufus Dommet had been pressed too and with just as much brutality; they had shared discomfort as well as adventure, had been threatened and had stood together. In the giant Irishman's case Pearce had grounds to believe he owed him his life. He was less beholden to the other pair, but still they had come to think of themselves as a group; the Pelicans, named for the tavern from which they were pressed. On first acquaintance it was easy to consider abandoning them and he had tried to do so. Then they had been strangers; it would be much more difficult now.

'I feel sick.'

Cornelius Gherson's whine, so familiar to those who knew him, coincided with a more telling heave of the deck, as a groaning *Griffin* lurched and steadied. Colbourne glanced up from his reading for a brief moment before carrying on. If he observed, from his close proximity to the complainant, that this newly pressed recruit was green around the gills it had no effect. Pearce could not see Gherson clearly but then he did not have to; the habitual pout on his almost too pretty face was common enough to require no imagination.

'Don't chuck it, mate,' cawed the mahogany-faced fellow called Latimer, 'lest you want to lick it back up like a dog.'

'Don't go down on all fours in front of anyone on this barky, lad,' hissed another sailor in Gherson's ear. 'It would be to some aboard like an invite.'

That brought forth one growl of dissent, but mostly suppressed laughter; it was the way Colbourne did not react to the interruption that mattered, for it told John Pearce a great deal. He would not claim to know the Navy in the short time of his enforced service but he had the ability to make and trust swift judgements on people he hardly knew, for he had grown up surrounded by them as he traversed the length and breadth of Britain. This had been done in the company of his father, a well-known radical speaker and pamphleteer. John had watched Adam Pearce harangue, cajole and control crowds in many a fiery speech, this while his son passed round the hat to get enough coin for bed and board. Rarely had they stayed long in one place, often no more than a day. It had been an unsettled existence in which the growing boy had been frequently subjected to new surroundings, forced to make new friends, as well as to spot quickly those who might be enemies.

He was naturally and without consciousness doing that now, but he had one quite specific model against which to match this Lieutenant Colbourne, and that was his previous captain. The choleric bastard who had pressed him out of the *Pelican* would never have stood for such murmurings, nor would his crew have dared to utter them in the sure knowledge that such behaviour would see them gagged at the very least. So perhaps Colbourne was no despot, but was the manner in which his crew behaved brought about by easy familiarity – such as one might find on a happy vessel – or by the man's lack of the attributes necessary to impose a rigid authority?

Pearce would know in time, but that thought served only to drive home the truth; that was the one commodity of which he had none, and that in turn edged his task from daunting to impossible. John Pearce had not only to get off this vessel but to cross a hostile homeland, at risk of arrest and seek the intercession of some of his father's old friends to get the warrant lifted, brought on by a vitriolic pamphlet damning the government, which had forced both father and son to flee to France over two years previously. Regardless of the outcome he would then have to take passage over the very waters on which he was sailing to land in a country now at war with Britain and seething with bloodthirsty upheaval. He must make his way to the epicentre of the revolutionary storm and bring away from Paris his father, old and probably too sick to travel, then get him back to England. Anyone listening to that outlined would say he was mad, and the man contemplating these thoughts reckoned they would not be far off the mark.

'Mr Short,' Colbourne called, as he slammed shut the list of statutes and returned the book to his pocket, 'the muster book if you please.'

'Aye, aye, sir.'

Pearce looked for the voice, and found it to the rear of the companionway, in probably the only person aboard standing to his full, insubstantial height. At first he thought it a youth, but a step forward into a pool of light showed a pallid, lined, adult face and a truncated squat body, dressed in a midshipman's blue coat. He was carrying a large leather-bound book, as well as a lidded inkpot, which he placed on one of the rungs beside his superior, before extracting a quill pen from his pocket. Beside him Pearce could feel Michael O'Hagan shaking with silent laughter, and it was several seconds before he realised the connection that his friend had made immediately.

'Sure, they named him right, John boy, there's barely half a pint of the sod. Jesus, he'd fit in my breech pocket.'

'Mr Short will enter you into the ship's books and allocate you the number of your mess. None of you has a rating, and you told me you are new to the service, so you will be entered as landsmen.'

'I ain't no landsman, your honour.'

Colbourne lent forward to detect the speaker, his gaze alighting on a sailor from the *Lady Harrington* who had been forced aboard to make up the number the lieutenant required. The crew of the merchantman had drawn lots and this poor fellow had lost. Pearce thought of him like that but had to acknowledge that he had accepted his fate, if not with enthusiasm, then certainly with a palpable degree of equanimity, his main concern seeming to be that any monies he was due from his merchant service, as well as news of his impressment, should go to the right place. The man was a sailor by profession, always liable to be taken up by the Press Gang and so perhaps accepted what had happened to him as just one of the hazards of that occupation.

'I should be rated able, your honour. I can hand and reef with the best of 'em, and I ain't no slouch in the tops, either.'

'Name?'

'Littlejohn, your honour.'

'Mr Short, enter Littlejohn here as able.'

It was not only Michael who got that one; the whole crew began to laugh, some of it suppressed sniggering, in a couple of others less controlled, outright guffaws. Pearce was taken by the way Colbourne reddened in undisguised embarrassment, since it gave him another clue to his personality; he too saw the pun and was brought to the blush by the fact. A quick glance at the midshipman showed the pained expression of someone who had been, many times in his life, the butt of such jokes.

'Carry on,' Lieutenant Colbourne mumbled, before spinning round to make his way, hand over hand, back on deck.

Book held in one hand, Short had entered the able seaman, his next act being to point his quill at Pearce, who stepped forward and gave his name in a loud and clear voice. He could feel rather than see the reaction of his fellow Pelicans, and he was close enough to Cornelius Gherson to note a look of disappointment that his action engendered. Such a response was understandable given the way he had tried to protect his name the last time this had happened. On being mustered into Ralph Barclay's crew aboard his first ship, Pearce had refused to give a name for fear that it would expose him as a possible felon. That subterfuge had not held; his real name, if not his reasons for withholding it, had soon become common knowledge.

'That was bold of you, John boy,' Michael opined, just after he had entered his own name, soon to be joined by Charlie Taverner and Rufus Dommet, who made the same point. Gherson, who joined the cluster, said nothing, just looked at him with deep suspicion. Being naturally untrustworthy himself, he would only see deep subterfuge in what was, to Pearce's way of thinking, common sense. And quite possibly Gherson had harboured a notion to use his knowledge for some advantage; for himself, of course, he not being given to thinking of any one else.

'Call it a benefit of experience,' Pearce said, dropping onto his haunches to relieve the strain on his back, the others doing likewise. 'I think we erred aboard *Brilliant* in the way we sought to fight not just Barclay but the whole crew. Given that he had caused most of the trouble it was Pearce's turn to feel a tinge of embarrassment, as he observed Michael, Charlie and Rufus agree in their various ways. Cornelius Gherson's expression did not alter, and a hard look from Pearce made him move away, for he was not really part of their group, having arrived in the same situation as them after being fished out of the River Thames. Experience since then had taught all of them to mistrust him and never to discuss matters of import in his presence. Once he was gone his three companions looked at Pearce with eager expressions, which brought forth a resurgence of his previous annoyance. What was it about them that they gave way so easily to his notions, even Michael O'Hagan, who would fight anyone taking the least liberty? It had been like that almost from the first; they made out that they wanted to get free of the Navy just as much as he did himself, yet seemed incapable of forming any method for doing so!

Right now, the looks he was getting forced him to continue. 'They were not all bad aboard *Brilliant*, were they? There were some good men among them.'

'None that I saw,' snapped Charlie Taverner.

Pearce knew he was wrong, and was sure Charlie did too; it was only his natural bluster that had him denying the truth of what was being said, for some of the men on the frigate, if they had not been helpful about the Pelicans deserting, had gone some way to alleviate their discomfort. One or two had gone further than that, and told Ralph Barclay in no uncertain terms that on one occasion, in the article of punishment, he was coming it too high.

'We must get some of the crew on our side,' Pearce continued, 'or at least to act towards what we aim to do with indifference.'

'I doubt there's many of them,' said Charlie, not willing to concede an inch. 'To my mind these tars are bastards to a man.'

'Amen to that,' added young Rufus, who tended to follow Charlie in most things.

Pearce's response was terse. 'Then let us, at least, lull them into not paying us too much attention. Look at Littlejohn and Gherson.'

The sailor was sat on a barrel, hugger mugger and chatting away to his new shipmates, no doubt looking for places and people that would make a connection, for the men of the sea were like a tribe. Cornelius Gherson, all tousled fair hair and gaucherie, was grovelling in front of another group headed by Latimer, which was his way, trying to ingratiate himself towards some kind of advantage. Hard to imagine in so crowded a space, but Pearce and his trio of fellow Pelicans had already managed to isolate themselves.

'You.'

The finger, poked really hard into his shoulder, made

Pearce look up, though he did not have to go very high to find himself in eye contact with Midshipman Short. Close to, the lines on the pasty face were more obvious, but it was hard to tell if the fellow was prematurely aged or suffering from some affliction that made him appear so.

'Quit your lazing about. You're not aboard your merchantman now, there's work to do, so get moving.'

The last word was delivered with another hearty jab of the mid's finger. The temptation to poke a fist very hard into that face was almost overwhelming; indeed John Pearce's right hand had balled ready to do so without conscious effort, and he felt, as he always did when tempted to physical violence, the tremors that affected his body. But he forced himself to smile, and even touched his forelock as he responded in a meek voice.

'Aye, aye, sir.'

Chapter Two

Not reacting to the cry from the masthead of HMS *Brilliant* gave Captain Ralph Barclay a small frisson of pleasure, particularly since his young wife, Emily, had looked up sharply from her embroidery at the muffled shout of 'sail ho' – muffled because of the need to penetrate the closed skylight above their heads. He enjoyed demonstrating to her the authority he held, one that did not oblige him to respond immediately to everything that happened aboard ship; let others do that, then report to him if they, given what they observed, thought it necessary. There was another feeling in his breast, that being relief; the sighted sail would be one from the convoy he had been tasked to escort from Deal to Gibraltar, fifty-seven ships he had deserted in the face of standing Admiralty orders to pursue a single French intruder, in a way that could only be called, even in the most benign interpretation, a pursuit for personal gain.

The knock at the door was anticipated; the person who entered when commanded to do so, his acting First Lieutenant, was not. What was he doing undertaking a task that was properly that of the lowest midshipmen? Henry Digby removed his hat in the regulation fashion and tucked it under his arm, nodded to the top of Barclay's lowered head, before turning to add a small bow in the direction of his wife, that acknowledged with a sweet smile. Her husband felt another frisson – this time less pleasant – thinking that Digby could only have come below personally to afford himself a chance of such an encounter. The thought made him speak in a sharper tone than he intended.

'We have come upon our charges, Mr Digby, I assume?'

'No sir, our lookout reports a three-masted vessel, we think a barque.'

'Not the convoy?' Ralph Barclay tried but failed to keep any hint of anxiety out of the question and even if he had achieved that the way he suddenly raised his head slightly to look at Digby directly, he was sure, gave him away. 'Flag?'

'None flying, sir.'

'Course?'

'The same as our own, sir, we are coming up dead astern of her.'

'What do you recommend?'

Digby was surprised by that; Ralph Barclay was not a consulting captain, even when, as in this case, the answer was obvious. 'Closing with them, sir, and obliging them to identify themselves.'

'Then make it so Mr Digby, and inform me when they are hull up so I may take a look myself.'

Emily spoke as the door closed. 'Young Mr Digby seems to be settling well into his task husband.'

There was a temptation to question the use of the word young, for there was little difference in their ages; if anything Digby might well be slightly the senior of the two. Odd that someone only approaching her eighteenth birthday should use such a word. No doubt it was the married state that allowed for such condescension.

'He had better, my dear. It hardly looks as though his predecessor is going to make a swift recovery.'

Emily threw him a look of sympathy then for, even if he would not admit to it, even if she was unsure of the true cause, she knew her husband to be worried. The events of the past week had seen his mood swing dramatically, starting at exultation when they had first sighted a French privateer – a potential prize – switching dramatically as he had been humbugged by a superior sailing vessel. Fury as that French dog had snapped up one of his charges, albeit one that was laggardly, and carried her into a seemingly unassailable berth. The losses the ship had suffered in finding out the meaning of impregnability had been frightful, and only a stroke of what seemed to Emily like pure luck had saved matters.

During that period – the ups and downs – Ralph

Barclay's aura of husbandly superiority had suffered and his wife had discovered that she had no need to be meekly obedient to his every whim; she had found to her surprise that she had power in their relationship, that he craved her good opinion and was cast down if that was withheld. Discovery of such a thing had been heady, but Emily knew that whatever strength she had must be exercised sparingly, and never more so in allusion to recent events. In short, she could not be open and merely ask him outright to voice his disquiet.

Concern over Digby's predecessor, the badly wounded Lieutenant Roscoe, lying pale and silent in the surgeon's berth, was unlikely to be the cause – that she did know, for her husband disliked the man and had made no secret of it even before the recent action. They had exchanged high words on deck about certain decisions and it was quite possible that a recovered Premier would demand a court martial to clear himself of whatever slights Ralph Barclay chose to put against his name. Uncertainty as to the true cause of these anxieties deepened the furrows that already creased her brow.

Ralph Barclay could not face what he interpreted as a pitying look and for the umpteenth time that morning he opened the ship's log and examined the loose sheets of paper he had stuffed in between the pages. These listed HMS *Brilliant*'s true position over the last few days; facts which he was reluctant to commit to the book, for once written up they could not be altered. One thing could be entered certainly, the removal of that damned pest John Pearce and his band of malcontents. The thought of Pearce made his blood boil; the palpable arrogance of the man, the way he had by insubordination driven a wedge between himself and his new wife, and even worse, engaged the sympathy of the whole ship's crew against its lawful captain. That he had shown courage and resource in salvaging the bind that Ralph Barclay had created for himself was small recompense. He had taken the same occasion, the sending home of the East Indiaman *Lady Harrington*, to rid himself of his wife's nephew, a useless young man who was, without doubt, cowardly to boot, thus removing another potential source of marital friction. The beauty of that manoeuvre was that he could make it look as though he was showing the boy favour.

The other loose papers were less cheering; not for the first time he damned an Admiralty, specifically Lord Hood, the man actually running the Navy, for saddling him with a set of officers who were strangers. Such a thing made life hard, for he could never be certain that the loyalty he had built up from men he had brought on in the service himself was there in the men imposed on him by Hood. The wounded Roscoe was a case in point; argumentative, unable to smoke his captain's methods and preferences, forever questioning orders, showing no faith in those he was obliged to obey. He had demanded a court martial after a particularly high-worded spat the day before the action in which he had been wounded. Ralph Barclay tried hard to suppress the hope that his Premier would die of his wounds, his Christian beliefs fighting a hard and losing battle against self-interest.

His anxiety to catch up with his convoy was many layered, not least the mere fact that it was quite possible to miss them completely, even if it did consist of over fifty ships; the ocean was vast enough to hide an armada. Roscoe was a problem that he could do nothing about. If his Premier recovered it would mean trouble, if he expired his complaints about his captain would go with him to the grave. A quite different but related problem presented itself in the case of Davidge Gould, the man who commanded the sloop HMS *Firefly*, the second protective vessel tasked to escort the convoy to Gibraltar, a ship he had quite deliberately cut out of the chase and the subsequent action. He would have Gould aboard as soon as he joined, with his own ship's papers, including *Firefly*'s log which, no doubt, would have been kept scrupulously up to date; then and only then could he decide what to put in his own, facts about courses, times and positions that would make his actions appear in the best light.

At some time in the future this book before him would end up at the Admiralty, and there was just a chance that some clerk, emerging from his habitual torpor, might cast an eye over it. So a little obfuscation would be necessary; not downright lies, for that would be too obvious, but just enough to ensure that should the two logs be read together, the facts would not, too obviously, jar. That was something of which he could be reasonably confident; the idea that such Admiralty clerks were eagle-eyed defenders of the nation's needs was, Ralph Barclay knew, a myth. They were idle, claret-swilling placemen more interested in their salaries, pensions and post prandial naps than in the misdemeanours or minor peculations of naval commanders. They would sit, these logs, along with the purser's accounts and myriad other papers gathering dust, very likely never subjected to more than a cursory look, but, should someone in authority, in the future, wish him ill, and seek for something in his background with which to damn him…

Another sharp tap stopped that train of thought, as Midshipman Farmiloe, tall, fair of hair and gangling, knocked and entered. 'Mr Digby's compliments, sir, the chase is hull up.'

'Chase, Mr Farmiloe? I was not aware that we were engaged in one.'

Farmiloe knew better than to respond. 'Mr Digby wished me to add that it's odd, sir, that they don't seemed to have smoked we are in their wake.'

Ralph Barclay sat forward, suddenly all attention. 'Say again?'

'Well, sir, if they have lookouts aloft…'

'Which they must surely have.'

'…they are not looking over their stern.'

Ralph Barclay got to his feet, and called for his hat. 'From which we can deduce, Mr Farmiloe, that their attention is on something more tempting.'

'The convoy, sir.'

'Precisely.'

The atmosphere on deck, the air of tension, told the ship's captain that everyone on watch down to the ship's cat had drawn the same conclusion. The midshipmen, normally content to remain snug in their verminous berth, were visible, as was the master, Mr Collins. Even the little surgeon Lutyens had come up and was now deep in conversation with Digby. That ceased as soon as his presence was noted, with everyone coming to attention and raising their hat. A glance aloft at the sail plan told Ralph Barclay that his previous instructions, to crack on, were being obeyed. A glance at the slate told him that HMS *Brilliant* was making eight knots on a steady wind that was coming in nicely over her starboard quarter, and a current that was aiding her passage. Taking a telescope from the rack he trained it on the ship in whose wake they lay, a barque as he had already been told, with a low freeboard and clean lines. Most obvious was the fact that she had reefed her mainsails – that she was not sailing at anything approaching her full speed.

'Mr Digby, I hope we have a weather eye out for French warships. I would hate to make the same mistake as our friend yonder.'

'We have that, sir, and since we are due west of Brest, I have given orders that one of our lookouts, on the mizzen top, should pay particular attention to that quarter.'

'Good.'

'Do you anticipate French warships?' asked the fish-eyed surgeon, Lutyens, in his high-pitched voice.

Everyone else stiffened. You did not question a captain on his own quarterdeck, and certainly not one as tetchy as Ralph Barclay. It was common knowledge that Lutyens knew nothing of the sea or naval life, just as it was common knowledge abaft the mainmast that his powerful connections ashore were such that it was a wonder he had chosen to serve in the Navy at all, never mind a lowly frigate. It was that which saved him from a bad-tempered blast. For a man with little interest to aid his career, Ralph Barclay needed to be careful with one who had so much that he could decline to employ it. The telescope never wavered, though the voice was far from friendly.

'The French Navy may be in revolutionary ruin Mr Lutyens, with most of its competent officers fled or dead, but there are still men who can sail and fight their vessels. It is also the case that these are their home waters, and Brest is their main naval port, so it behoves me to be aware of the threat.'

Lutyens whipped out a little notebook, one that he carried everywhere, much to the annoyance of all aboard and did what he always did, scribbled some note in it. Many aboard had speculated as to what that book contained and thoughts amongst the crew of pinching it and getting someone to read its contents were commonplace, for all were convinced it could not be laudatory.

Brilliant was close enough now to see the tiny figures on the barque's deck, all crowded in the bows on the weather rail. Ralph Barclay had no doubt that they were French, another privateer out on the hunt for an English merchant vessel. He had a sudden vision of the way the one he had previously pursued had humbugged him, not once, but three times; that and other considerations made him act.

'I would wish to alter course slightly, Mr Collins. Take us inshore a trifle. I want this fellow left with only the option of the open sea and an unfavourable wind when he wakes up to our presence. Mr Digby, a word to the lookouts, if you please, to cast their eyes well beyond our friend yonder. From our higher masts we should be able to pick out the convoy before we overhaul him.'

'Sir.'

One nimble young mid was sent aloft with the message, while Farmiloe was despatched to inform the captain's wife that there was something of interest for her to see. Her coming on deck, well wrapped in a hooded cloak, coincided with the slight alteration of course, which meant adjustment to the yards to take full advantage of the wind. It also coincided with someone aboard that barque casting a look over the taffrail, for their deck was suddenly a hive of activity, as the reefs came out of her sails and her speed increased markedly.

'Deck there, sail due south. Two sail. More.'

'Our convoy, my dear,' said Ralph Barclay, as he took Emily's arm. 'And between us and them a French dog waiting for nightfall to sneak in and snap up one of our charges.'

'Chase has altered course to starboard. And he has hoisted a French flag.'

'That means he is heading out to sea, my dear, into the wind and away from his home shore, hoping to outrun us, perhaps even that some French warship is in the offing to aid him.'

'I can barely make out what he is doing husband.'

'Mr Digby, I wish you to fire off one of the forward cannon.' That got him several discreet sideways glances, for they were well out of range of the barque. 'No ball, just powder, and keep firing. Let us alert those ahead of us to the presence of an enemy. If Captain Gould has his wits about him he will put up his helm to investigate, which will give our friend yonder something else to think about.'

'Now, Emily, my dear, let us see if I can help you to master this telescope.'

'Is this the time husband?'

'None better, my dear, given that we have something for you to look at.'

Everyone wanted to observe this event, for this was a gentler Ralph Barclay than they knew, but only Lutyens, with no notion of the discipline required on board a ship of war, had the ignorance to openly stare as Barclay put his arms over his wife's shoulders, and admonished her to steady herself against him and his well-spread legs to master the roll of the ship.

'Now put this to your eye, so, and your hand to the front part, then twist and extend it till the image becomes clear.'

'Sea and sky, husband, is all I can manage.'

Ralph Barclay put his head very close to that of Emily, so as to point the telescope in the direction of the chase, delighted with the squeal of pleasure that told him, however briefly, that it had appeared in view. He could smell his wife's musk, the odour of her body as a sliver of warm air escaped from under her cloak to fill his nostrils, and leaning against him as she was, with her body resting on his, induced a natural tumescence. He was aware of the attention their joint posture engendered and took pleasure in the jealousy of those surreptitiously watching them.

'We shall have him before nightfall my dear, especially if Captain Gould brings *Firefly* into play.'

The anxieties which had assailed Ralph Barclay in his cabin faded: the problem had not disappeared, but luck had presented him with an opportunity to palliate his second in command, the man who, barring the wounded Roscoe, could most threaten his position. Situations where lieutenants like Roscoe fell out with their captains were endemic, and a bane that the Navy suffered with reluctance, given that it was usually one man's word against a superior officer, with courts of fellow captains inclined to support the senior man. That was not the case with a man who ran his own ship, even if he too was only a lieutenant. The word of a Master and Commander would count as near-equal; in short he would be listened to with great attention.

Gould would hear the cannon fire – nothing carried at sea so much as that booming sound. He would come about to investigate and together they would snap up this fellow trying to run from them. A share in a prize, a bit of hard coin in the purse, was just the thing to persuade another officer that whatever actions had previously been undertaken by Ralph Barclay, however questionable they had seemed at the time, could be justified. For a man who held that fate had, throughout his life, been less than kind to him, Ralph Barclay, with a wife seventeen years his junior in his arms, on the deck of his own vessel, envied by all aboard and in pursuit of an enemy he was certain to catch, felt just for once like the luckiest fellow in creation.

There was little drama in the capture; it took time for the fellow kept running, tack upon tack, as far as he could. Collins brought HMS *Brilliant* around and into the wind with something approaching efficiency, which pleased a captain who harboured ambitions to be in command of a crack vessel. Quiet suggestions from Ralph Barclay adjusted the sail plan in minor ways that made the frigate sail easier, if not perceptibly faster. The wind now coming in over the bows blew back his wife's hood, ruffling her long, loose-worn hair, and all the while her husband clutched her close and helped her fiddle with the telescope.

The Frenchman, judging by the streaming jets, had started his water barrels and was pumping like mad to get it over the side and lighten his ship. Well aware that he was at the apex of a losing triangle, other ship's stores followed and finally the small cannon, trunnions and all – popguns really, designed to threaten rather than destroy, but telling in their weight nevertheless. But there was one thing he could not chuck over the side; the numerous crewmen any close-to-shore privateer must carry on board to take and sail into harbour a number of enemy merchant vessels. The idea that he might shift them into his boats and abandon them, which is what Ralph Barclay would have done, disappeared as his cutter and jolly boat were cast adrift to float away on the current.

Davidge Gould, in *Firefly*, had reacted as Ralph Barclay knew he must, coming about to investigate gunfire that might be in some way a threat to the convoy. In doing so he would have espied both the chase and *Brilliant*'s topsails and deduced what was obvious; the frigate cut the French privateer off from the shore; he must deny him a southing, his best point of sailing on the present wind, and force him to the open sea. He would also quickly smoke that it would be his ship, a better sailor on a bowline, not *Brilliant*, which would effect the capture. Content that all was in hand, and that nothing of import would happen for some time, Ralph Barclay and his wife could safely retire to their cabin and some privacy.

'Lucky bastard,' said one of the sailors close to the surgeon. He was not addressing Lutyens, but a fellow tar. 'Every man jack aboard horned up and Barclay's the only one that can ease it.'

'It is a matter of some curiosity to me,' opined Lutyens, to no one in particular, 'that sailors, who from their conversation and behaviour when ashore are a salacious bunch, do not travel aboard in quantity the means to assuage their lust. It would be better if half the crew were females.'

That got him several looks, not all benign, for he was an anomaly on board every bit as unusual as the captain's wife; over-qualified for his post, always prying into matters that were held to be outside his province, a stranger to the ways of the service, and scribbling in that little book that was ever with him. Those looks were sharply curtailed when a grinning sailor responded.

'We do, your honour. Ain't you never heard the term all hands to the pump.'

'Belay that,' barked Digby, 'and get on about your duties.'

Lutyens heard the parting shot as the fellow replied softly. 'There you go mate, only sinners aboard reside before the mast. It's all saintly purity in the gunroom with hands clasped in prayer.'

'Mr Lutyens,' said Digby, coming close enough so that only the surgeon would hear him. 'It does not do to excite the crew.'

Lutyens, surprised, looked even more like a fish than usual, his eyes larger and that thin curled hair blown back by the breeze. 'I was not aware that it was I who excited them, rather that it was the captain's clear intentions towards his wife. As to the means of release, which that fellow alluded to, it is to my mind an activity to be heartily recommended. I myself employ it frequently, as I am sure you do.'

Digby's cheeks were red from the wind; the deeper red-
dening that suddenly suffused his face had nothing to do
with that.

A half hour later Barclay came back on deck alone, keenly
examined by every one who could look at him without
being observed, though only the good Lord could say why,
for there was no discernable change in his appearance. He
picked up his telescope, trained on the quarry, then said:

'Bow chasers, Mr Digby.'

'Sir.' The order being passed on, Digby asked, 'Do you
wish to clear for action?'

'No. The fellow has ditched what little armament he has.
A couple of shots over his bows should bring him too.'

'Might I recommend we issue some muskets, sir?'

'The marines have sufficient, Mr Digby. Let's get them up
into the bows so our friend yonder can see what is coming.'

Firefly must have been waiting for the senior vessel to
fire. As soon as a ball from *Brilliant* left the frigate's larboard chaser, a great plume of smoke was seen to blow away
from the other escort's bow.

'Well, this fellow is no hero,' snorted Barclay, as the tricolour flag at the masthead of the ship they were pursuing
was immediately run down. 'Not even a musket shot for his
honour.'

Chapter Three

The routine aboard *Griffin* swiftly assumed a familiar pattern learned in only a week aboard HMS *Brilliant*, reminding John Pearce just how much such custom was one of the tools by which authority dulled thoughts of liberty in men who were not sailors by trade. The naval day was fixed by the tasks they had to perform, the naval week by the irritation of repetitive food and the odd ceremony like Divine Service. The other method of control was exhaustion, for moving any sailing vessel from one place to another was hard physical work, made worse aboard this ship because no amount of habit could inure a man to sleeping in the cramped circumstances which pertained aboard an armed cutter, a state of crowding that made life aboard a frigate, with twenty-eight inches of space and the odd bump into a nearby body, seem like slumber paradise.

Proximity to his sleeping neighbours had forced up the sides of his hammock, so that Pearce had felt himself to be in something like a tomb. He could feel the effect that ran down both sides of his body, which had been crushed between two others as the ship pitched, rolled and snubbed on every wave, the groaning of the timbers almost human in their tone of complaint. His neighbours, judging by the muffled cursing which occasionally emanated from their hammocks, had suffered as much as he. Pipes blew at the opening of the naval day, in darkness, to rouse the watch off duty to quit their hammocks and stow them. A ship of war in a time of conflict stood to every morning before dawn, boats over the side, ports open and guns run out as the light increased sufficiently to allow the captain to 'see a grey goose at a quarter mile'; really to ensure that no enemy had snuck up close to them during the hours of darkness to gain an advantage that could see the ship taken.

Sure of an empty sea the guns were housed, flintlocks removed, the shot replaced in their garlands, cartridges and priming quills returned by scampering powder monkeys to the gunner sat behind his thick, canvas fearnought screen, the standby slowmatch doused and the crew set to commence the cleaning of the decks, a task carried out eagerly because only on completion could they be piped to breakfast. Food was another tool of authority, for if it was, to many, unpalatable stuff it was regular, plentiful and in the case of HMS *Griffin*, reasonably fresh, got up by a cook that had to work on a jury-rigged stove that could not be set up until the captain was sure the ship was safe, the planking underneath his pitch the first to be cleaned. Such regular food was not gainsaid to a toiling labourer ashore, a fact of which sailors were wont to remind each other, as though somehow just having a square meal was a blessing.

For the Pelicans the comfort of their own table, which they had enjoyed aboard the frigate, was not vouchsafed to them on *Griffin*. Littlejohn, allotted to them as the leader of their mess, tallied off a pair to take the mess-kids and fetch the grub, but it was eaten where a space could be found, some choosing even on a calm but chill morning to take their victuals on deck rather than squeeze into the stifling hutch that passed for the crew's quarters. At the rear of that, guarded outside mealtimes and sleep by a marine, a canvas screen cut off a space roughly one third of the whole lower deck for the two mids and the captain. Pearce, looking along the deck beams above his head, calculated that while there was more space per body, there was no luxury aboard for officers either.

'Gunner's coop is in there'n all,' said Latimer, when Pearce asked about it. 'Berths opposite where the mids and the captain's steward squeeze in, afore Colbourne's screened off bothy, and he don't half come it high an mighty 'cause he has his private space, jeering at the others warrants. Puts a plank o'er his powder barrels and calls it a bed, 'cause there ain't the room to sling a hammock. He's a squat arse, is the gunner, have to be to get a wink.'

'I don't know where you're sitting, brother,' said Michael

O'Hagan, 'but I have scarce the space to swing my elbow.'

Another voice spoke, one whose face was well hidden by the crowded sailors. 'Happen God was having a special jest when he put you aboard this barky, Paddy. Might be he wants to cut you down to size.'

'Christ, Blubber!' exclaimed another unseen voice, to a ripple of laughter, 'he's near the size of you. Man could cut the bog-trotting bugger in two an' he still wouldn't fit.'

Pearce, sitting very close to Michael, sensed his body stiffen and saw the way his face closed up. The Irishman was not averse to being called Paddy as long as he granted the person naming him so the privilege, but he was dead set against anyone assuming the right.

'The good Lord might have put me here to shut some gobs that need it, and to gather a few teeth to sell whenever I get ashore.'

'Easy friend,' Pearce whispered. It would hardly aid things if the Irishman started belting folk, for he had hams for hands and they would do serious damage.

O'Hagan ignored the attempt at restraint, his voice holding no humour now. 'And if I can't find room enough to swing my elbows I will be chastising and laying out four at a go, which will not bother me at all, given the time it will save.'

Charlie and Rufus had stopped eating, like Pearce waiting to see if anyone would take up the challenge. There would be hard cases aboard, just as there were in every group of gathered males, at sea or ashore, men who commanded others with their fists. Michael had been obliged to deal with the bully called Devenow aboard *Brilliant*, and he was obviously quite prepared to do the same here, all it needed was for someone to declare themselves willing to accept the challenge. No one spoke, though Pearce observed some members of the crew throw glances at one or two of the larger specimens, men who might have laid claim to respect prior to the arrival of these latest crewmen. Those in question seemed very intent on eating their food, so it was

Michael who broke the silence.

'Now you will find me Paddy enough to break a smile and laugh at a joke, and maybe even one to give a helping hand to a struggling fellow. But I will have the proper regard I am due from all here.'

The canvas screen was pulled back and Lieutenant Colbourne, hatless and with his coat undone, appeared, ranging his eyes over the crowd. That canvas screen and the one behind it would have done little to muffle Michael's loudly proclaimed statement, and the hard look in his eye was designed to tell all present that he would not tolerate violence.

'Mr Short,' he said, addressing the hidden midshipmen. 'With the sea state being so gentle, as soon as the crew have finished their breakfast we will carry out practising board-ing from boats.'

'Christ in heaven,' hissed Michael as Colbourne turned away, steadying himself against the roll of the ship. 'Gentle, he says! Is that blue-coated fool resting his pins on the same bit of wood as me?'

Colbourne, back now to the crew, the canvas screen still held up in one hand, stopped dead. Given that he had come out to the sound of Michael's voice, he could hardly be unaware of the source of the comment, even if it had not been made out loud. Pearce reckoned that to call a ship's captain a fool when he could hear and identify you was a dangerous thing to do. Michael liked to debunk people yet this time he might have gone too far, but the screen dropped as Colbourne disappeared. That was when Pearce looked around and observed that none of the crew, at least those he could see, had been holding their breath.

'He takes a tease well,' he said to Latimer.

'Ain't bad old Coal Barge,' Latimer replied, 'as captain's go.'

'Who's Coal Barge?' asked Rufus.

'You don't look too bright, lad,' Latimer replied, peering into the heavily freckled face and the light blue eyes, 'so it be a bit of reassurance to know that you is thick after all.'

'Not thick enough to be sailor by trade,' snapped Charlie Taverner, leaping to the defence of his young friend.

Latimer responded with a slow smile designed to take the sting out of what could turn into an argument. 'Coal Barge be the captain's nickname, and as I say he's not a crabbed one. Christ knows, I served often enough under worse. Dislikes the cat, which is a bonus, for there are those aboard, like there be on any commission, who give occasion to deserve it.'

'Then how does he maintain discipline?' asked Rufus. 'I thought all captains were friends to the lash.'

Pearce was just about to point out that the best way to control men was with consent, but Latimer's swift reply left that as no more than a thought in his head. 'The right way, mate. He gets we's to do it wereselves. He's a bugger for stopping the rum of those that gets out of hand, and the whole crew if they don't mend their ways after the warning. Done it twice for a two day stint already this commission, which don't do him no harm. Lines his pocket a bit, that saved rum, his being ship's purser as well as captain.'

'Is that usual?' asked Cornelius Gherson, always quick to join a conversation that connected in any way to money.

'Never in life, but where on a ship this size would you put a robbing bastard of a purser that would see him and his stores safe? No, the powers that be have gifted the captain the job, happen to make up for him having such a shit posting otherwise. He ain't as bad as the natural breed, but I doubt he'll come out of the commission showing a loss.'

Pearce almost asked outright if he was aboard a happy ship, or even a contented one, for what Latimer had been saying had elicited nods from those closest to them, but the old sailor, dark-skinned face closing, carried on. 'Can't say I blame him, being fair. Ain't Coal Barges' fault that we's crammed like sardines in a barrel, with not the proper room to eat and sleep, that be the fault of those who reckon this a ship fit for the duty, which it is plainly not.'

'The duty being?' asked Pearce.

'To protect ships like the one you was nabbed off, goin' in an' out of their home ports. *Griffin* ain't no flyer, which she needs to be to catch Johnny Crapaud, for as sure as hell won't freeze they rarely come out from their home ports in laggards, and the sight of us and a deck full of cannon is enough to have them put up their helms and run for home or safety. An' putting double the hands aboard ship don't help neither. Looks a good duty on the face, this here patrolling the sea lanes lark, an' it would be if'n we could take one or two.'

'Prize money?' said Gherson, with a familiar and avaricious gleam in his eye.

'Fat chance,' sneered a man between them, 'the workhouse more like when peace comes. We's been out here near a month, barring a trip a week past to revictual, and though we might have seen plenty the only thing we's ever got alongside is some Dane or Hanse merchants, which being neutral ain't no use at all.'

Pearce was not looking at Latimer or the speaker, but at the rest of the crew, at least those he could see, nodding vigorously in agreement, or shaking their heads in wonder at the foolishness of an Admiralty that had sent the wrong ship on such a vital task.

'And to think we signed for this without a press gang in sight,' Latimer added. 'Buggers got a full complement without so much as a cuff round the ear.'

Charlie was quickly on to that. 'If you are volunteers, why press us?'

'Replacements, mate. We fell foul of a frigate going south short on numbers. Captain of that bugger whipped half a dozen men out, prime seamen too, which tells you all you need to know. We's at more risk from our own in these waters than them French sods.'

'They could press me out of this bugger any time.'

Pearce recognised the voice that had spoken up to rile Michael, a heavy set, but fleshy fellow called Blubber, who might have been one to challenge the Irishman. In looking for it he observed very clearly that it was a statement with which a great number of the crew also agreed.

'The Med will be teeming with well-laden Frenchmen,' said another sailor. 'The buggers that went will be lining their pockets in the weeks to come.'

'As well as warm with it, Matt,' said a third, 'with room to sling a hammock for a decent night's kip.'

'An' droppin' anchor at Majorca,' Blubber added, 'so it will be warmer still when the señoritas are boated out.'

The buzz of general conversation broke forth, for there was nothing like carnal anticipation to get a group of tars talking; but beneath the happy anticipation or tale-telling of Mediterranean beauties lay a clear discontent. These men had signed up to this ship for the prospect of quick prize money, no doubt on the promise that it would be easy; it always was on any poster John Pearce had ever seen. They would have accepted any hardship in food and space for enough of that and the dream that went with it; of a prize so valuable, or captures so numerous, that they could live in comfort for the rest of their lives. Latimer had turned away, to continue his talking with one of the men who had joined with him, allowing Michael to speak softly to his fellow Pelicans.

'Well there's consolation, we being miserable, that we might not be the only ones.'

'We'll fit in right nicely,' opined Rufus Dommet, getting a slight raised eyebrow from his mates, for the boy was not one to put an opinion above the parapet.

'Mr Short,' called a voice from beyond the screen. 'I think it time to pipe all hands on deck.'

'Heard us moaning,' said Latimer softly, turning back to them. 'Which he should too. Reckon he thought this a duty that would see him in clover just like us. Happen he believed what he had printed on his posters just as we did. Well, it is only right that if we have the hump, he should know it.'

Not a happy ship, thought Pearce, on either side of that canvas divide.

'That ain't gentle, is it?' moaned Rufus, trying to steady himself while looking unhappily at the endlessly moving grey-green waters of the English Channel.

'He must be joshing us,' Charlie replied, jabbing a finger at the choppy waters.

'No sight of land,' said Michael, 'nor the smell of it.'

Pearce had already spotted that but he was more attentive to the way a called for duty had tempered the moaning so evident between decks; whatever discontent these men harboured was laid aside as soon as they were given something to do. Those given the task hauled in the ship's boats, which had been towed behind, covered with tarred canvas to keep them dry, sent over first thing after they were piped from their hammocks for there was no room on deck to do anything if they were inboard; you could not work the guns or clean the deck lest they were sent astern.

'Line them up, Mr Short.' Colbourne called, 'then send them aft for their weapons.'

The second midshipman, a stripling called Bailey, stood with a burly marine, wooden swords, dummy hatchets and padded clubs at his feet, two others holding muskets to their rear, as his messmate walked along the lined up sailors saying, 'Attacker, defender, attacker, defender.' Before he got to him, Gherson, unseen, nipped round an indifferent sailor to ensure he got the deck. Standing next to Michael, Pearce got the boats, while the Irishman got the defence.

'Luck of the Irish, for them boats is set to be damned uncomfortable.'

'I'll try to make this deck uncomfortable for you, Michael.'

'Don't trouble, John boy, it is enough that already.'

Still in the same line they trailed the few feet to where Bailey and his marine stood, those early enough given the choice of weapon. Pearce took a sword and in weighing it, he realised that were it real, not wooden, he was close enough to the ship's captain, provided his weapon was sharp enough, to sever his neck with one swift blow. What would happen then? Probably the musket-bearing marines would lower their weapons and shoot him, but what he could observe did bring home the notion that a disgruntled crew inclined to rebellion would have little difficulty in taking the ship if they so wanted, a quartet of marines being insufficient to stop them.

He called to mind his reading of William Bligh's published narrative of the *Bounty* mutiny, how easy it had been for Christian and his fellow conspirators to take the vessel. Really, like Bligh, all that Colbourne had to protect him was the authority vested in him by his officer's commission and the threat of punishment that hung over any sailor who mutinied. He had a vision of casting this lieutenant adrift in one of the boats. At least he was close to home, unlike Bligh who had had to sail four and a half thousand miles to find a civilised landfall.

'Move along there,' the lieutenant said, and for the moment it took for Pearce to obey their eyes locked, Pearce holding the look for longer than discipline allowed so as to annoy Colbourne. The expression to which he was treated showed him how well he had succeeded.

'Defenders to the lee rail,' called Colbourne, 'attackers to the weather. Mr Short, take on board your grappling irons.'

Charlie Taverner had to push Rufus so that he went to right bulwark. As soon as he spotted Pearce moving in the same direction the boy joined him. 'I ain't looking forward to this Pearce, having seen the way those boats were heaving about as they was hauled in.'

'They will be a little more stable full of bodies, Rufus.'

The voice was tremulous as he replied. 'What if I tumble o'er board.'

'Then you have a choice, Rufus, swim for the ship or stay afloat till you are dragged back in.'

It was telling comment of the youngster's naivety that he seemed to give the twin notions due consideration. Then he brightened. 'You can always dive in to my rescue, you being a right good swimmer.'

'You got gills, Pearce?' asked the sailor stood the other side of Rufus. The face was friendly, bright blue eyes and a broad winning smile under blond, near white hair. Pearce responded in kind, eager to address the first crew member, barring Latimer, to call him by name.

'I'm a shark, mate, so if you tell me what you'd like for supper I'll slip into the water and fetch it for you.'

'Name's Sam, mate, and I is partial to a bit of cod.'

'You be too far south for that, Sam,' said the man on the other side of him. 'Water's too warm.'

'I'd like to hear you say that, Matt, if you was dipped in it.'

'Mr Short,' Colbourne shouted, 'to command the cutter, Mr Bailey the jolly boat. Tally off the men you need.'

The sailors preceding Pearce and Rufus dropped into the boat with commendable ease. Getting over the side was not so easy for either of them, though the former did not make as much of a pig's ear as the boy. Lowering yourself, even if only some ten feet, on a single rope wet from seawater, into a boat bobbing four or five feet up and down, with a wooden sword dangling between your legs, was not easy. While Pearce dropped into the boat with a thud, Rufus practically fell in from his second hand-hold, dropping the padded club he had chosen as a weapon in the process.

'Anybody still see that Indiaman, lads,' asked the sailor called Matt, 'for we will be wanting to send these arsewipes back.'

'No need,' came the reply. 'Next man o' war comes along we'll ship them out in that.'

'Not if I get first in line you won't,' replied Matt. 'I'll have my ditty bag shouldered and a foot over the side before they gets hull up.'

'You,' commanded a voice behind Pearce, 'sit here. Somebody get hold of Ginger an' get him holding some-thin' afore he tips into the briny. And make space for the first boarders.'

Order was swiftly applied and Pearce found himself holding the thick end of an oar, the wood wrapped with twine to aid his grip. The space between him and the opposite oar was quickly filled by those who would board first. Looking towards the stern he was facing the prematurely lined face of Midshipman Short, who had taken station on the tiller.

'Haul away,' he shouted, much louder than was truly necessary.

Pearce could not claim to be efficient on an oar, though that commodity was all around him in the ease with which the true seamen hauled away, but he had competence enough to outstrip Rufus, who could not get his blade into rhythm with the others, it being in the water when theirs were out and vice versa.

'We's all out of kilter,' cried one wag, 'Ginger is showing us how.'

'Happen we should gift him a short blue coat an' call him mister.'

Midshipman Short deliberately looked away at what was an obvious reference to the general uselessness of his kind.

'Miss more like, the useless bugger.'

One of the men set to board took pity, and using only one hand got Rufus dipping and raising in unison. 'You just watch the back of the man in front lad. Go forrard with him and drop the blade, then haul back hard and lift when he does. Never mind the oar, that'll do what your body says it should if'n you hold it right.'

Rufus did not get it right, but that mattered little given that they were not going far from the side. They turned to face the ship, oars now used to steady the cutter. To their left the smaller jolly boat lay likewise, bobbing on the green water as wave after wave ran under the counter. Short passed the tiller to one of the spare sailors, and with some difficulty made his way to the prow where, transferring his own dummy sword to a wrist lanyard, he gave the command to, 'Haul away.'

The boats moved forward, gaining speed quickly, oars in and out before Rufus or Pearce had got their sticks into the water. When they did manage they aided progress very little as the boat headed for the side of HMS *Griffin*, the deck of which was now lined with their shipmates yelling and swearing a blood-curdling invitation.

'Mr Bailey,' Short shouted, 'you take the mainchains, and I will assault them amidships, thus splitting the defence.'

Quick to obey, the oars on one side hit the water while the others were lifted and the jolly boat was sent towards the bow. Pearce, craning over his shoulder, could see little until they came off the crest of a wave, and not much then – the ship wallowing, the side lined by those still aboard yelling and screaming – but he did reckon that what they were about against a real enemy would be hazardous in the extreme. All advantage lay with the defenders, who had height and bulwarks to protect them, while those in the boats had nothing but a few muskets to keep the crew away from the side of the ship. Done for real it seemed like a good way to get a boat load of sailors killed.

Both Pearce and Rufus failed to react properly when the command came to boat oars. Luckily Pearce was on the seaward side, so did himself no harm, merely trailing a useless oar in the water. Rufus' stick clattered into the ship's side, and jumping out of its rowlock sent him flying into the bottom. There, as everyone else aboard reached for the ropes that hung from the now-thrown grappling irons, he was repeatedly stood on until Pearce could get to him and haul him to his knees.

'Come on, Rufus, time to show them our mettle.'

Not all the sailors were using ropes; a couple had their backs to the ship's side and, hands cupped, were propelling their mates up towards the deck. The way the boat was dipping because of this sent both Pearce and Rufus off balance and they were last to the side, the only people in the thing except those tasked to keep it pinned in place, faced with a series of lines and the command, delivered with a scream, that they climb them. The grappling irons had been thrown into the ship's shrouds, high enough so that anyone using them could get above the level of the deck. Pearce took hold, looped one end round his hand, and jumped so that his feet were on the scantlings. Lying almost horizontal he hauled himself up hand over hand until he reached the ladder of ropes that ran to the mainmast cap. There was a brief moment in which he could observe what was happening on deck, as men who were shipmates fought each other with real gusto. The false weapons were swinging hard, and the odd punch was being added to what was a joyous melee.

Looking aft he saw Colbourne, smiling at what was happening before him, taking no part in the actions of his men but enjoying their mutual pounding. Disinclined to join in the fighting beneath him he saw no reason why the ship's commander should be spared active participation, should be left to enjoy his sport. Dropping down onto the deck he found himself standing over Cornelius Gherson, who was cowering, hands over his head, in the scuppers. That earned him a sharp jab from Pearce's wooden sword which brought forth a pleasing squeal, which Pearce followed up with a telling kick that sent Gherson's head into the ship's side. But dealing with Gherson nearly did for him. Spinning round, Pearce just got his sword up on time to stop himself being hit with a soft sand cosh, the wood of his blade taking his assailant on the forearm, which must have hurt for his face screwed up in pain and the eyes took on a look of alarm at what was sure to follow, a clout round the ear.

'Sorry mate,' he called as he slipped by, looking for Michael O'Hagan, who would be bound to be in the thick of things.

The Irishman was not hard to spot, standing near the ship's wheel, head and shoulders above those trying to contest the deck with him. He had eschewed a weapon, and was merely fending off his attackers, one of them the blond fellow called Sam, with his huge open hands, causing no pain and laughing out loud, calling to them to come at him again.

Pearce's sword was required again, this time to fend off a fellow with a similar weapon. The sailor clearly thought himself a swordsman, for he took on a fencing posture. That lasted only a second as Pearce, who had been properly taught, whipped his weapon up, slid his underneath, and jabbed him in the solar plexus, a blow that, winding him, had him doubled over on his knees.

Pearce tapped the lowered head he as made his way towards Michael, who spotting him called out, 'Come on John boy, and see if you can better these spalpeen fools, not one of whom is of any use in a scrap.'

The truth of that was in the way that Michael managed both to say those words and continue to fend off four men.

'Michael,' Pearce said, coming close, weaving and ducking as his friend tried to slap him. 'I want you to fall away slowly, as though we are driving you backwards.'

One of the things Pearce liked about the Irishman was the way he reacted to a request without demanding to know why. He had done so before on more than one occasion and he did so now, making it look as though Pearce and the others were besting him. They, not aware that Michael was only pretending, got bold, which earned the blond Sam a head-ringing clip.

'I am going to push you, Michael, and when I do I want you to fall back until you hit something.'

Pearce got a huge open-handed slap on the forehead that stopped him dead, giving him some idea of how much O'Hagan could have hurt him if he so desired. 'As long as it's not solid, John boy.'

'No brother, it is as soft as you sometimes are in the head.'

Michael grabbed Sam and his other attacker, one in each hand, and lifted them bodily off their feet. They still tried to club him, blows which when they landed made the Irishman laugh. 'How can you say that and me not even had a drink?'

'Now!' shouted Pearce.

Getting both hands in between the struggling pair he gave Michael the heaviest shove he could manage. O'Hagan, laughing even louder, staggered backwards at increasing speed, taking his assailants with him. Colbourne, who had not really been watching those right before him, instead looking beyond to see how Bailey and his party were faring in the bows, was too slow to react. Michael's back hit him foursquare, and the combined weight of the trio knocked him right over to land on his back on the deck. His body tripped Michael and he and the others fell in a heap behind him. Pearce, yelling blue murder, had the pleasure of standing on and pinning to the deck his commanding officer as he repeatedly jabbed his wooden sword. Having despatched Michael in dumb show he stepped off Colbourne, put his wooden sword to the other man's neck, and looking directly at him, said breathlessly, 'I think we might have taken the ship.' Then with just the right length of pause to rob his accolade of any truth, Pearce added, 'Sir.'

'Welcome aboard, Captain Gould, on what I think you will agree is a most providential day.'

Davidge Gould, dripping water off the hem of his boat-cloak, raised his hat as the whistle blew to pipe him on board, surprised that someone as tetchy about prerogatives as Ralph Barclay should have come on deck in full uniform to greet him; he was, after all, only a titular naval captain as opposed to a real one. A rather small file of marines, with no sign of a marine officer, stamped to attention as his foot hit the deck, making him feel as if he were the superior, and vastly so, while Barclay was the junior. It was all a bit much, especially since he had not come voluntarily. Gould had been ordered aboard, cursing his commanding officer on receipt of a summons that obliged him to cross from his own ship to this deck on a stretch of sea disturbed enough to ensure he arrived damp.

'You know my acting Premier, Mr Digby.'

'Good day to you, sir.'

Acknowledging Henry Digby begged several questions, not least his acting rank and the absence of two of HMS *Brilliant*'s more senior lieutenants, that added to the observation Gould had already made that there was no marine officer. Looking for damage he could observe none, the frigate was in all respects sound. Full of curiosity as to why such men were missing, he was obliged to observe the courtesies and reply to Barclay's opening remark.

'It is a most auspicious day, sir. The sun not only shines on the sea around us but on our endeavours.'

It sounded crass in his ears, pure hyperbole, but it clearly pleased Barclay, who positively beamed at him. 'Nobly said, Mr Gould, nobly said. Mrs Barclay has prepared us a decent dinner. You are already acquainted with my wife, are you not?'

'I am that, sir, since you were gracious enough to

introduce me when she arrived in Sheerness. We last met at the Assembly Room dance the night before we weighed.'

'Quite. Captain Nelson informed me that you were most attentive.' Barclay's tone had changed as he uttered that, being close to a growl, and Gould got the feeling it was inadvertent, because his superior suddenly, in a forced manner, smiled again. 'You boarded the prize Captain Gould. Is she as fine close up as she looks from here?'

Both men turned to look over the ship's side at the barque they had just taken, wallowing on the waters of the Bay of Biscay alongside *Firefly*, beyond that the sails of the Gibraltar-bound convoy spread over the horizon.

'She is a splendid capture, near new. Her name is *Chantonnay*. I have taken the liberty of ordering my Premier to stay aboard, pending your approval of course.'

'Make it so, Mr Gould. How was she in the article of hands?'

'Stuffed to the gunnels, sir, so much so that I was at a loss to know where they all slung their hammocks.'

'Then I will have some of those bodies aboard *Brilliant* if I may. I am deuced short-handed, as you well know, and I am afraid to say in the recent recovery of the *Lady Harrington*...'

'Recovery?'

'The ship was taken, Gould, and by that very French dog you saw me chase. He...'

'But you took her back.'

If Barclay was disturbed to be so rudely interrupted by a junior officer he did not show it. Truly, Gould thought, this is a different creature to the one I first met at Sheerness.

'I did, as it was my duty.' Barclay looked hard at Gould then, as if challenging him to disagree. 'As I was saying, the action was not without loss, so let us get some of those French dogs on board so they can haul on a rope and earn their keep. You may take some aboard yourself, which will create room for your prize crew and relieve the anxieties of your Premier that so numerous a body of men might try to take back the ship.'

'I am to provide both my Premier and the crew, sir?'

'Why of course, Gould. Do you not deserve it? It would have been a damned difficult capture without you coming to my aid. I would have struggled to take her before nightfall in a stern chase.' Barclay, having delivered what Gould thought a palpable exaggeration, turned towards the doorway to his cabin, with his guest tripping in his wake. 'Mr Digby, you have the deck. Signal *Firefly* and the prize to resume their course, Captain Gould's vessel to take station at the front of the convoy.'

The smell of food wafted into Gould's nostrils as they passed the steward's pantry, and he had a brief sideways glimpse of chafing-dishes sitting in hot water to keep warm the food inside.

'Shenton, Captain Gould's cloak.' As his steward obliged, Barclay added, 'See that it is brushed and dried, will you, and send someone to relieve Mr Gould's coxswain of his ship's papers. I will look at them after we dine. Now Gould, a glass of champagne.'

'Thank you, sir.'

Emily Barclay entered from the side cabin as her husband was pouring the wine, giving Gould a radiant smile that made his heart beat a little faster. She was a beautiful creature, clear skin, set off by naturally rouged cheeks and bright eyes under a mass of shiny auburn hair. He could remember the touch of her hand as she had danced with him at the Assembly Rooms the night before they weighed from the Nore, as well as the gaiety with which she had undertaken the various routs and reels. With her husband away in London it had been possible to indulge in a little raillery, perfectly innocent of course – one did not try to seduce the wife of a fellow officer – but more fun than if dour Ralph Barclay had been present. Davidge Gould knew he was not alone in wondering what a young beauty like Emily Barclay was doing married to a curmudgeon so many years her senior.

'Captain Gould,' Emily said. 'It is so good to see you again.'

He took her hand to kiss it, feeling the cool skin, smelling the Attar of Roses she used as a gentle fragrance. 'And you Mrs Barclay. Might I be permitted to say the sea air obviously suits you. I swear, if it is possible, you are blooming.'

'Champagne, Gould.' Turning to face his superior, Davidge Gould was made very aware, by a rather pointed look, that flattering the man's wife was not a good idea. Barclay handed a second glass to his wife. 'And you my dear.' Picking up a third glass he raised it. 'Let us toast the success of our voyage which, though troubled, has, till now, been equally blessed.'

The toast was made in loud unison, accompanied by a wine that had been chilled in a bucket lowered into the sea, one which Gould observed held more than one bottle.

'I say, sir, this is a very fine. Might I ask the name.'

Barclay acknowledged the compliment to the wine, but threw his wife a somewhat curious glance. 'Supplied by the House of Ruinart, which I daresay will be deuced hard to come by now that we are at war with the makers. We have to thank Mrs Barclay for it being available to serve.'

The words 'as wise in choice as you are beautiful in the flesh' formed in Gould's mind. He was prudent enough to leave them there.

'The same will apply to the food we eat, all chosen by my wife from the very best chandlers in Sheerness, though I think she would acknowledge that she had some assistance from quite a few wives of the other officers.'

Those cheeks rouged by the sea air deepened a tad, with Emily Barclay declining to meet her husband's eye, leaving Gould with the impression that he was witness to some private dispute between them. Whatever it was, enlightenment did not follow.

'I think we should eat, don't you,' Barclay said, 'for I am sharp set. Nothing like a bit of powder and shot to give a sailor an appetite, eh?'

Gould sat down, wondering at Ralph Barclay; his moods had in the space of seconds swung from being hearty to being grizzled, then back again. The thought occurred that dining at this board he had better be on his mettle.

'Fish soup to start, sir,' said Shenton, as he led in a group of sailors, neatly dressed in checked shirts, with red bandanas tied round their necks, one placing the tureen on the table, the others taking station against the bulkheads. The steward, a lugubrious-looking fellow with bent shoulders, took station behind his captain.

'The fish are fresh of course, Gould, but the stock is a concentrate from that newly-opened shop in Piccadilly. What is it called, my dear?'

'Messrs Fortnum and Mason, Captain Barclay.'

'That's the fellows. Used to be valets to the King, you know.'

'Indeed.'

'Bit of a come down, what, from flunkeying at Windsor Castle to being mere shopkeepers.'

'I'm not sure, sir, that service in the royal household is such a good billet. I had the good fortune to attend a levee at Windsor Castle in the company of my uncle, and the way the royals treat their servants would make it a good place to seek volunteers for the Navy.'

Barclay had frowned again, but whatever was troubling him was not reflected in his words. 'Maybe you're right, Gould, what with Farmer George dipping in and out of being batty.'

That topic carried the conversation on; the King's disturbed mental state, in abeyance now but always threatening a recurrence, the difficulties that presented to a government trying to prosecute this new war with France with an opposition and an elder son, the Prince of Wales, desperate to force a Regency. That subject was treated delicately, for it touched on politics and it was a tenet of naval life that there were two subjects best avoided in a ship at sea, the other being religion.

The tureen was removed, to be replaced by a whole turbot, with dishes of anchovy and lobster butter, lemons and a tub of horseradish.

'I am agog to hear of the retaking of the *Lady Harrington*, sir.'

'A bloody affair Gould, very bloody.'

The story Barclay told was succinct, very noticeably and unusually so, for naval officers were not noted for brevity when recounting tales of actions in which they had participated, this explained as he concluded, 'You will forgive me, Gould, for not covering all the details, but my dear wife has heard it all before, and the casualties were heavy.'

'I noticed the absence of several persons on coming aboard, sir, but one does not like to remark on such matters.'

'Quite.'

'Lieutenant Roscoe lies in the surgeon's berth,' added Emily. 'We pray to heaven that he will come back to full health.'

Barclay's voice suddenly became angry. 'That damned Frenchman humbugged me, Gould, not once, not twice, but three times.'

Seeing Emily frown at the sudden bitter tone, Gould interjected to lighten the mood. 'But it ended successfully, sir, did it not?'

'Aye. But the losses bear down heavily upon me.'

'Your attitude does you credit, sir.'

'It is hard to see it so,' snapped a surprised Ralph Barclay, for he had been meditating on how such losses could affect his career, not on the actual people who had suffered injury and death.

Emily Barclay immediately stepped in to change the subject. 'Captain Gould, you are I believe from Wiltshire.'

Discussions of family, localities and the foibles of locals kept the conversation flowing through the courses that followed, which were of a consistently high standard; a fricassee of sweetbreads followed by a leg of mutton with currant jelly, onion sauce, salad and potatoes. Likewise the wines were splendid, a fine white burgundy from that bucket of cold seawater to go with the fish course and a very decent claret with the meat and cheese, that followed by a Château Y'Quem to accompany the sweet plum pudding which Emily Barclay was keen to inform their guest was entirely the idea and creation of the ship's cook. It was a meal fit for an admiral.

The cloth was drawn, and Emily, who knew her place, rose from the table to leave the men to their affairs.

'That was a damn fine dinner, Mrs Barclay,' said Gould, half out of his chair. 'Had I known you were such a dab hand at provender I would have engaged you to provide my own stores.'

'Have a care of your purse, Captain Gould, for my wife is a dab hand at disbursement too.'

'I thank you for the compliment, Captain Gould,' said Emily, her face set. 'I have to admit to a certain amount of nerves, this being the first occasion on which Captain Barclay and I have entertained. Such a pity that I did not get to know so many of the ship's officers before we lost them.'

'Then I am flattered,' Gould replied, aware that there had been a rebuke to her husband in her words.

'If you will permit, husband, I think I will go and sit with Mr Roscoe.'

'My dear.' Both men half stood as she left, Barclay saying as the door shut, 'She reads to him out loud, but I doubt the poor fellow can hear.'

'If anyone can stir some life in his breast, sir, I am sure it is Mrs Barclay.'

'That's an odd notion, Gould. Personally, I put more faith in the surgeon, though he is such an odd fellow I would be forced to qualify any confidence. Now, let me oblige you with a more fulsome account of the action.'

Which Ralph Barclay did: but it was not the truth, it was a version highly edited to flatter him and his actions, while at the same time diminishing the activities of anyone else, especially a pressed seaman called John Pearce and the useless midshipman, his wife's nephew, Toby Burns, an account he could never have delivered with Emily present.

The maindeck fell silent as she emerged, book in one hand, nosegay in the other, each sailor stiffening in whatever pose he held, except those immediately encountered, who all touched a forelock as she passed. Emily had, she knew, to move slowly, so that word of her presence could spread ahead to the areas of the ship that were very much the preserve of the crew, this to avoid embarrassment to men who might well be partly or wholly undressed, or indulging in some activity they would not want her to see. It had been explained to her by other naval wives who had sailed with their husbands as the blind eye, a quite conscious attempt to avoid embarrassment, not confined to women but used by officers to avoid inflicting an endless stream of punishments for minor infractions of the far too comprehensive regulations which governed life aboard ship.

Sailors diced and played cards, both forbidden; sometimes they fought, well out of sight of anyone in authority, or got together in combinations to discuss grievances, and that left out women smuggled aboard and practices never mentioned in polite conversation. Petty officers who lived in close proximity to their fellow crewmen had authority over them, but had to show sense in how it was applied, for it would never do to be over-zealous when a body thrown overboard at night would be lost forever. Strictly speaking, her own presence aboard was forbidden, but admirals had been captains once and knew what to see and what to ignore. A ship was a world apart as soon as the anchor was fished and catted, governed officially by the Articles of War, in truth presided over by her husband, who had much say in how such rules were applied. The only plain fact, explained to her, was that they could not be applied in total at all times, otherwise the captain would have more of the crew in chains than he would have left to sail the ship.

The smell of the forward maindeck, sweat, unwashed clothing, the animals in the manger, with trapped flatulence added to the stench of the bilge water, was one Emily knew she would never get used to; not even the nosegay she pressed to her face could overcome it. The odour grew overpowering as she made her way down to the white-painted orlop deck, to where there was barely enough air to keep lit the flickering flames in the lanterns. The surgeon's sick bay was a screened-off space only big enough for a cot and a stool to sit on, the lantern slung close to both providing the only illumination.

Lieutenant Roscoe lay there covered by a blanket, pale of face, eyes closed, breathing slowly but regularly. He had suffered from an affliction of the face before being wounded, which gave him, because of half his features being immobile, a palsied look. He had also expressed himself in an abrasive manner, though that was in part due to the poor relationship he had had with her husband. In repose, hovering between life and death, that had disappeared, to be replaced by a look of serenity, and it was possible to see the child he had once been.

But she could never look on his face without recalling the cockpit on the night of that raid on Lézardrieux. So many wounded had come back, and she had elected to aid the surgeon and the gunner's wife in treating them. Emily was no stranger to death; in the company of her mother she had visited enough blighted hovels in her native part of Somerset – a duty imposed on her by her station in life – to be upset by the sight of a cadaver. In her time, she had seen innumerable dead bodies; women expired in childbirth, or parents prematurely aged by toil and deprivation, and had come to look on them, if not without emotion, as least with some sense of equanimity. Children were harder; little wasted bodies, some yet to reach a first birthday, always evoked tears.

But the cockpit had not been like that, had not been silent grieving. It had been blood-soaked and noisy, with men screaming in pain, and the surgeon Lutyens shouting to the sailors holding them to get a grip as he set to with razor sharp knife and toothed saw to amputate a limb, an act he was able to carry out in under a minute, be it a shattered leg or an arm. More quietly he had worked on those, like Lieutenant Roscoe, who had been wounded by musketry, picking gently at the cloth taken into the wound by the ball, using a clear spirit which smelt of herbs to cleanse the wound. It was only an interlude, for even a comatose body reacted to the long probe he inserted to seek and remove the lead, with Emily required to keep the hole clear of the flowing blood so that he could see what he was about.

The world of quiet prayer over a deceased soul had no connection to such mayhem, yet it was pain and death just as it was in a household struck by cholera or the misery of a still birth. As ever, before she began to read, Emily said a quiet prayer for the recovery of the man on the cot.

'Mrs Barclay, you are here again, your sainted self.'

'Hardly that, Mr Lutyens, just a captain's wife doing what she sees as her duty.'

'May I offer you some coffee?'

'That would be most appreciated.'

Lutyens exited, to instruct his assistant, the loblolly boy, to have made and fetch back some coffee from the gunroom, then re-entered his sickbay, looking down with an acute degree of concentration on the lovely face of Emily Barclay. Unlike everyone else aboard, his interest was not carnal; he had a lively curiosity about most things, but most particularly about the project which had brought him aboard the vessel; his desire to study sailors in conditions of both normality and extreme stress, to discern the motives by which they lived and accepted the privations of the service, their attitude to death and discomfort, in short to compile a survey on what made sailors the kind of people they were.

Unlike most medically trained men, he found the

physical side of his occupation dull, one amputation much like another, a dose of pox cured repetitive, the wrenching of a tooth boring. What interested Lutyens was the mind, to him the seat of all activity and emotion. He had come aboard this frigate because the size made close observation possible. In his coat was the book, one of a number, in which he scribbled what he saw, every detail of shipboard life and how each member of the crew felt, what they said, and how their words differed from their true emotions. There were notes on Captain Barclay and his officers, and there were observations on Emily Barclay too; the way she had interceded on behalf of the pressed seaman Pearce, caring little for her husband's wrath. What had caused that; was it a sense of justice or something more primal? He longed to know, but he was astute enough to be aware that asking would get him no information. Not that it mattered; Lutyens worked on a different set of principles, believing that human beings often told you more by what they omitted to say, than by the words they uttered.

'Captain Barclay is regaling Captain Gould with the story of the recent action.'

'I daresay it is already embellished,' Lutyens replied. The frown that engendered pleased him, for it was not entirely disapproval, more an acknowledgement that what he said was bound to be true. 'You did not wish to stay and hear it told?'

Emily looked at her book, to avoid the probing eyes of the surgeon, made uncomfortable by his all too obvious scrutiny. 'I daresay I shall have ample time in my life to hear it.'

'I cannot help but feel the role of Pearce and his fellows will diminish in direct proportion to those of others aboard the ship.'

He meant her husband, but did not say so, and was pleased at the almost infinitesimal reaction, a tiny jerk in her frame at the mention of John Pearce, for he had suspected he had seen her, on the first day she could have observed him, openly admiring him. What would happen if he told her what he knew about the man, the secrets regarding his parentage which Pearce had spilled when drugged with laudanum, of the letter he had written to aid his cause once he landed in England? It was tempting to speculate, but that was all it could be, for the oaths of his profession bound him to silence. The arrival of coffee broke the mood, and as he poured for her he observed the look of pity that she gave to the still comatose Roscoe.

'I believe your father is a chaplain to the Royal Family?'

Lutyens let her change the subject; doing so confirmed how uncomfortable she found the previous one. 'He is, but only in the Lutheran faith, which the Queen, being German born, is wont to practise more than His Majesty. Even if he were to desire it otherwise he must be seen as the committed Anglican.'

'Surely there is not much to choose between them?'

'You're right, but do not ask me to enumerate what those differences are. I'm afraid I find the whole subject of religiosity and its variations baffling.'

'Would you think me too bold if I said that many wonder at your being aboard such a ship as HMS *Brilliant*.'

Lutyens smiled, well aware of the curiosity his presence had engendered. 'You mean with my connections?'

'Not many surgeons can boast of proximity to royalty.' She looked at Roscoe again. 'I'm sure he would be grateful if he knew.'

'Perhaps, though I think the notions of a King's power to heal untenable, and my connections too tenuous to be worth much.'

'Will he live?'

'The longer he stays as he is, the better his prospects.' Then Lutyens tapped his head. 'But really the answer lies here.'

'Surely the answer lies in his heart, not his mind. How can it be when he is comatose?'

'Are you a student of Rousseau, then?' the surgeon asked,

his countenance amused.

'Not a student, Mr Lutyens, but I have read him. I judge from the way you posed the question that you have too, and that you do not agree with him.'

Lutyens just smiled; to explain, to dispute Rousseau's romantic twaddle and site other philosophers in his arguments would mean advancing too many of his own personal theories, and that in turn might alert this lady to the area of his interest.

Ralph Barclay perused the log of HMS *Firefly* with a growing sense of gloom, and thanked the Lord that he had sent a well-oiled Gould back without them in his own barge – he had insisted that his junior finish the port – so that he was not obliged to have the author sitting opposite him as he read. Where Barclay wanted equivocation there was clarity, but at least, even if he had raised questions about the business of the *Lady Harrington* the man had not actually damned him outright in ink. Notes were made so that his own log would bear some relation to what he was reading, for just as he had a right to demand Gould's log, Ralph Barclay would face the same demand from the admiral commanding at any station where he dropped anchor.

Chapter Five

HMS *Griffin*, on deck, was little different from below; there always seemed to be too many bodies for the available space, made more so by the rigid division that the quarterdeck was the preserve of the ship's officers, the only exception being the men at the wheel. To give such a grand name to such a pocket handkerchief of space, and to determine it as the dividing line between officers and men, was a joke.

'We needs the numbers,' Latimer explained, ''cause the buggers we come up against have likely got even more aboard. Hangin' off the gunnels when they set forth, light on stores, an' never out for more'n a two week, looking for easy pickin's. Best time to catch 'em is when they have taken a few, for having crewed a capture or two they are down to bare bones thesselves.'

Latimer, being right chatty, was a source of useful information, so Pearce sought as often as possible to work alongside him. Engaged in blacking the largest cannon balls allowed time for talking, and the sound of others chipping the rust off those being made ready to paint made such a conversation discreet. 'Dozens of the sod there are, weighing from the likes of Dunkirk and St Malo.'

'And they make enough captures?'

'Must do, mate. Stands to reason or they would give it up. I ain't sayin' that sometimes they don't return home empty bellied, but this stretch of water be the busiest in creation what with the number of deep hulls a'carryin' trade up to London, an' the Navy only has so many barkys like *Griffin* to try and stop 'em. And they ain't fussy about neutrals neither. They'll heave the crew into a boat and tell them to whistle for any redress, the buggers. Ain't like us, hamstrung from the outset, wi' the captain liable to be had up for layin' a finger on a ship that ain't French.'

Pearce did not want to hear about that. 'Must be chancy then, if you come up on the privateers well manned.'

Latimer paused in his blacking to grin at Pearce, using one hand to pat the squat cannon by which they were standing. 'They ain't got what we've got, mate. Pop guns is what they carry, like most of the cannon we has aboard. But this here beauty and the other three like her, are serious meat an' no error.'

Pearce looked under Latimer's hand at the squat weapon. The carriage was fixed to the deck and the trunnion had runners for the recoil instead of wheels, the whole turned sideways on to the bulwarks to increase the deck space. The short barrel and bulbous shape made the whole assembly look innocuous.

'Our friend here is called a carronade. She don't fire a ball very far, but as you will see by what you has in your hand they be big buggers, and of a weight that can tear the guts out of anyone we encounter. Not that we want to rip them asunder mind, not much in the way of prize money to be had from a ruined hull. Let us get close enough is all I ask, and one shot from this bugger, placed right in a spot that does for the riggin' or a nice slice of bulwark, will see them cut down their flag damn quick.'

Gently, trying not to be too obvious, Pearce steered the conversation to time spent at sea, the home port and what lay beyond it. Latimer answered his questions without seeming in any way to discern the reasons Pearce had for asking them, that was until the last one, when having provided the information, the sailor added, 'So now you know all you need to run, I reckon.'

'I...'

'Join the rest of the crew, mate. We all has thoughts of that from time to time, never met a tar who didn't, and nowt that has happened on this commission has gone a way to rooting them away.'

'Bosun,' called Colbourne from his precious few feet of quarterdeck, 'pipe the hands to dinner.'

'So John boy,' asked Michael O'Hagan, 'how are we faring?'

This was said as he squeezed an elbow past Pearce to get

at the food on his plate, a question, the import of which, the man on the receiving end well understood. The others lent forward eagerly, but a flick of Pearce's eyebrows indicated Littlejohn. He was too much of an unknown quantity to talk in front of openly, so Pearce waited until he had finished his dinner, at which point he moved away to find the more congenial company of proper seamen. Gherson, bored by the continued silence, followed in his wake, forcing his way into another conversation.

'Notice anything about the food we've been eating?'

'It's good,' replied Rufus, a youth who seemingly had no palate, quantity being his sole criterion for satisfaction. At least the Navy could not be faulted on that!

'Not good,' snorted a more discerning Charlie Taverner, 'but at least it's fresh. The bread is yet to go mouldy green.'

'This tub has been out of harbour less than a week.'

'So?' demanded Michael, with palpable impatience. It was one of the traits in Pearce he least appreciated, the way he strung out his answers to simple questions, and he allied that to the honesty to say so. 'Will you give over with the flippin' teasing?'

Pearce was not to be rushed, for he was thinking as well as talking. 'What room do they have aboard for storage, Michael?'

'Precious little,' the Irishman replied, using a powerful elbow again to ease himself some space, 'seeing as they don't have room for us. Sure it's a ship for leprechauns.'

'No manger, either, no chicken coop on deck, and no real depth in the holds, that with a crew that is twice the number this ship would carry in a time of peace, which added together means they cannot stay at sea for any great time with so many mouths to feed.'

'How long?' asked Charlie, quick to see the logic.

'According to Latimer three weeks out will put us on short commons,' Pearce replied, moving forward to whisper.

'Where do we touch land to revictual?'

'Place called Lymington. It is a port at the bottom end of the New Forest.'

The blank stares that greeted that remark reminded Pearce that none of his fellows had led the truly vagabond life that he had endured, trailing around with his father. Michael had travelled a bit, digging canals and the like, but Rufus knew only his native Litchfield and the bits of the capital he had seen as an apprentice leather worker and an absconding one. Charlie had never been outside the parts of London were he had made his living on the edge of legality – the rookeries of the city and the string of roads that led west to the Strand and Charing Cross, where the chances of finding a flat were greatest, a country bumpkin who could be parted from his money.

From what he knew of the South Hampshire forest, which was not a great deal, it was pretty barren and uninhabited, a place that lived mainly off its timber and provided space for hunting. That was what Pearce had been thinking about as he talked; a wooded expanse sparse of people that, given the very nature of its resources would have shelters in which woodcutters and hunters could lay up, and game in abundance to feed their bellies, as well as the kindling to cook it. He could only hope that once they were away from the shore they would be safe and he did know for certain that the forest stretched north to a main road between the west and London. There was a double attraction; it was a place he could possibly part company from this trio, somewhere they would be safe, and allow him, alone, to go about his own affairs.

Quietly, in a whisper that could not be heard outside their tight little circle, he explained all this, before concluding, 'It wouldn't be easy to get there but I think once deep in the forest we would be hard to find.'

'You're hugger-mugger ain't you?'

Latimer stood, or rather stooped, over their table. Pearce felt a flash of annoyance and he knew the others shared it, for this was an unwelcome intrusion, but the sailor was smiling, and the words he used took the sting out of the mess tables' resentment.

'Mind if I sit with you, 'cause I can't stand any more of that Gherson cove. Had to come away.'

'Take a seat,' said Pearce.

'Where does that lad get off with his tale tellin'?' Latimer asked, as he perched on the barrel that Littlejohn had vacated. 'Anyone would have him for a prince if they were to believe half what he says. Friend to this great man an' that, an' even closer to their wives, with a purse so bulging he would struggle to close it tight. Now I is for story tellin' misself, an' I ain't too fussy about it being right true, as long as it satisfies in the article of amusement or interest, but that Gherson's tales are too tall to be borne.'

'Did he tell you how he came to be pressed?' asked Charlie.

'He did not, though he insists it be an error that will be put right as soon as someone in authority gets to hear of it.'

'He was chucked off London Bridge.'

'Now you be tellin' tales.'

Rufus nodded. 'You don't know that for certain, Charlie.'

'He did come from the bridge.' Pearce added, 'and he was lucky to land by the boat, because he can't swim.'

Charlie was quite indignant at his honesty being put in question, the usual defence of a practised deceiver. 'Who needs to be certain when a fellow comes flying off the bridge, without his shoes or coat, in nothing but a shirt long enough to hide his shame? That's my part of the world, Rufus. Someone chucked him, and knowing as I do the nature of the bugger it were no robbery. More'n like it was someone he'd dunned settling a score. If he ever had a full purse, as he said, it was never come by honest.'

'Sure it matters not where he came from or where he got his coin,' Michael interjected, 'but he is not to be trusted, and that is a fact I have a mind to make plain.'

Latimer nodded his deeply weather-beaten head. 'Good to know that, mate. Not that I was inclined, but someone

who knows the sod a'sayin', well that's better. I'll pass the
word if there's no objection, cause that silver tongue of his
will take in some with wood in place of brains.'

'Tell the world, friend,' Michael replied.

'Sail ho.' They all lifted their heads at the sound, though
not with much in the way of interest, for it was common
enough to spot a ship in these waters. They heard the
stripling, Midshipman Bailey, call out in a squeaky voice,
'Where away?'

As the reply came down from the tops, the canvas screen
at the rear of the deck was flung open and Lieutenant
Colbourne, still chewing, hurried towards the companionway ladder.

Latimer snorted. 'Can't even have his vittels in peace.'

'There's no panic surely?' asked Pearce, who well knew
by now that any sail sighted must be twenty miles away.

Latimer grinned as Colbourne rushed past and up the
ladder to the deck. 'Believe me, mate, you would panic if
you had to leave the deck to the likes of Bailey and Short. I
ain't ever come across such a pair of useless buggers.'

Pearce was right about there being no need to panic,
especially when the sail was identified as a British 74-gun
warship. Back on deck, once she was close enough to make
out her features with the naked eye, she was quickly identified by several of the crew who lined the side to watch her
approach. Pearce was struck by the laxity with which
Colbourne allowed the men to put aside all thoughts of
work so that they could observe this event. Again it contrasted so much with Ralph Barclay's style of captaincy –
the crew of HMS *Brilliant* idly staring over the ship's side
would have sent him into a choleric rage. But there was
another thing; a keen sense of anticipation in those eyeing
the approaching warship, almost like a longing, which he
put down to just being at sea, where the sight of another
warship, especially a friendly one, was welcome.

'That's Billy Ruffian,' called Sam, who had hauled himself
up onto the bulwarks for a better view. 'My brother Brad

and I sailed on her as boys in the Spanish Armament.'

'Billy Ruffian?' asked Michael.

'*Bellerophon*,' Latimer added. 'if 'n yer callin' proper.'

'Slayer of the Chimaera.' Pearce said.

'What?'

'The chimaera.'

'And what, in the name of creation, is a chimaera?'

'A fire breathing monster, part lion, part serpent, part goat.'

'Sounds like the bugger snoring next to me last night.'

'The story is told by Homer in the *Iliad*.' A reference to the great poetic saga of ancient Greece did nothing to remove the looks of ignorance from the faces nearby, but Pearce was aware that he had attracted attention; several of the sailors close to him had turned to look. 'Bellerophon rejected the advances of Phaedra…'

'Who's he,' Sam demanded?

'She was the wife of the Proetus, King of Argos, a beautiful woman, but no better than she should be, while Bellerophon was young, handsome and brave.'

'That's what we all need mate,' called Blubber, 'a women no better than she should be.'

Sam was quick, and got a laugh from the crew when he responded, 'Happen you get one, Blubber, if you weren't old, fat, ugly and shy as hell in a fight.'

'Don't call me old,' Blubber replied with mock irritation.

'Trouble was,' Pearce continued, 'Bellerophon rejected her advances, so she denounced him to her husband who determined to kill him in revenge.'

Pearce had never actually seen a man shudder in the way Gherson did at those words – his whole frame shook from head to toe and the blood drained from his face. He could not know that it had been a cuckolded husband, or more truthfully some ruffians he had hired, who had chucked the man in the Thames with the full expectation that he would drown. He did not linger to wonder at the reasons for Gherson's reaction, because it was clear that those watching the approaching ship with him wanted to hear the tale. On such a poky deck, with a steady but light breeze wafting *Griffin* along, it was impossible to speak in anything above a normal voice without being heard by nearly everyone, and he was aware that he had attracted lots of attention, including that of the two midshipmen. Colbourne was studiously looking through his telescope, but could not hide the impression he was listening too.

So he carried on with the story, telling how Bellerophon was sent off by King Proetus to his father in law, a neighbouring King, with a written message demanding his death, but the neighbour declined just to kill him outright, it being impious, so he was given impossible tasks designed to ensure his demise, all of which he carried out and survived. There was a lot more he could have said, for it was a good story, about Bellerophon's magic horse Pegasus, how he upset the Gods and was driven mad, and challenged to explain what made him say what he did at the end, Pearce could have only replied that it was instinct.

'Which just goes to prove that you can't trust kings and the like, because they might just be trying to get you killed for their pleasure as well as their purse. Daresay you've all met a captain or two of the same hue.'

A few heads nodded, most looked confused and Colbourne finally spoke, his voice even, as if he had heard nothing untoward. 'Mr Short, prepare the signal gun to fire a salute. The rest of you get about your duties. Mr Bailey, to the masthead and tell me if *Bellerophon* shows any sign of shortening sail.'

An exchange of salutes followed as the 74-gun ship of the line bore down on them. Pearce had to admit she was a fine sight, with a full suit of pale brown sails set on three towering masts. Her black hull carved through the sunlit sea, slightly heeled over by the wind but making good speed.

'Any sign, Mr Bailey?' called Colbourne.

'None, sir. Looks as though she going to sail right on by.'

Colbourne, who had obviously been anxious, seemed to

visibly relax, as he said to Short, 'Take the deck while I finish my breakfast.'

'Aye, aye sir.'

'He seemed a bit tight,' said Pearce.

'Captain of that bugger is senior by a mile. Could strip out half the company and take them on board and there's not much Colbourne could say to stop him, an' it can't cheer him to know there's hardly a man jack aboard wouldn't swap this smelly bugger for a 74 now that we know our chances of makin' a bit of coin are low. At least there's enough space aboard to sling your hammock for a proper night's rest. An' I know, come a blow, which I'd rather be on.'

As if to back up his words, and for no apparent reason, the ship's timbers emitted a loud crack. With the few seconds it took Latimer to say those words Pearce evolved the notion of a secondary course of action. If this was not a happy ship, what would happen if it became even less so? The idea was a compound of many things; the attitude of the men to being on a cramped and seemingly unsafe vessel, which had so far been unsuccessful in the duty to which it had been sent: Colbourne's tolerant style of command, allied to the uselessness of the two midshipmen; but paramount was his own need to do something rather than just wait for opportunity to strike. Where it would lead he was unsure, but it was a fully formed notion by the time he had made his way below.

Sailing a ship might be hard work for everyone aboard, but that still left time, provided the weather was not too foul, for yarning. Sailors, tale-tellers *par excellence* themselves, loved to listen to a story as well as relate one, which had Pearce searching his memory for tales to tell; be they fables, truths or legends of the ancients, that all had in common the themes of tyranny and betrayal. Having lived a couple of years in Paris, he was well versed in the crimes, real or imagined, of the late King Louis and his Bourbon ancestors.

Being an entertaining storyteller made it easy to hold the

attention of his shipmates, and he was surprised to find that
he had learned more of that skill from his father than he had
realised. How and when to slightly raise his voice, the time
to go deep and serious, as well as the need, regardless of the
gravity of the tale, to make his listeners laugh, even if it was
as often as not accompanied by a groan for a poorly executed pun. If proof were needed of the effectiveness of his
method, it came from the rapt attention paid to him not
only by strangers but by his fellow Pelicans.

He alluded often to the slavery needed to build the
Pyramids, of Pharaohs marrying or murdering their own
siblings over the bones of countless slaves, somehow man-
aging to make them the precursors of modern day naval
captains. From Ancient Greece came the tales of heroes and
capricious Gods, and in the human sphere of good men
such as Alcibiades allowing fame and military success to go
to their heads, until the Athenians threw a man aiming at
tyranny out of the city – the moral being that even a seemingly good man could go bad. Robert the Bruce, even if he
had been a King, was evoked from his native Scotland to
show the virtue of patience in the face of seemingly insu-
perable odds, for he had triumphed over the greater despot-
ism of Edward Ironside.

Spartacus became a favourite – a story to be told more
than once – for John Pearce relished the tale of the slave
general who had taken on and beaten several Roman armies,
a man with nothing making the mighty tremble. Even the
fact that he lost in the end was put down to treachery rather
than military weakness, but most compelling was the
French Revolution, so recent that everyone aboard knew
something of it, albeit that many of their recollections were
skewed by falsehoods and exaggerations that had grown
grotesque in passing through the triple loops of news journals, rumour and bias.

Pearce knew more about that than most, having sometimes heard the truth from the lips of the very men who had
carried out the overthrow of the monarchy, though he

inclined it towards his own needs. His King Louis was not a weak, vacillating bankrupt, but a bloody oppressor; the twin estates of clergy and nobles were wholly instead of only partly corrupt, every lord and prelate determined to hang on to all their privileges and keep the poor and powerless in their place. Praise was heaped on the Parisian mob, a body Pearce detested consisting as it did of opportunist rioters, goaded by rabble rousers leading, in seemingly permanent revolt, the dregs of the French capital's slums.

The Paris he described was a land of milk and honey, of hot chocolate laced with cream to be enjoyed at the Caveau in the Rue Royale, instead of a place where the fear of denunciation had become prevalent and anything like a luxury hard to come by. He spoke of the happy inhabitants of the Faubourg St Antoine in glowing terms, of their honesty, friendliness and political stability, which was the diametric opposite of the truth; they were uncouth, lazy opportunists, the main constituent part of the rioting mob which had stormed the Tuileries Palace and brutally murdered the thousand strong Swiss Guard. Added to that, since it was recent enough for everyone to know the story, he speculated, as every sailing man had done, about what had happened to Fletcher Christian and the crew of the *Bounty*, the mutiny itself a tale known by all since Bligh's account had been published only three years previously. Being about sailors, the story had rapidly spread through the naval and merchant fleets. If he started by doubting their survival, Pearce always ended by painting a picture of not only that but of a life of plenty in all the areas sailors cared about; food, drink and compliant women, never forgetting to add that in a France liberated from tyranny, and not too far off from the position in which they lay, all three of these commodities were freely available.

Such stories, delivered quietly, could be just as effective as the best rabble-rousing speech of the kind for which his father was famous, especially when those listening were already dissatisfied, and not only inclined to listen but willing to be swayed. The cramped space between decks was an aid, creating a tight, dimly lit space where softly spoken words could be heard and where an atmosphere of conspiracy was easy to fabricate. He imagined Colbourne and the midshipmen, behind their screens, straining to hear his words, while wondering what effect they were having on the crew.

It surprised even Pearce, the speed with which his line of thinking hit home – before a week was out he was sure of the effect he was having. It was helped by the steadily worsening weather; it did not take much on a ship like *Griffin* to make a life that was uncomfortable, nearly intolerable, and as the height of the waves and the strength of the wind steadily increased, so did the sense of deprivation. It was not terrible, the kind of blow that threatened the very existence of the ship, but *Griffin* was a cork on a calm sea, a ship that could not meet a wave without letting all aboard know of its existence. As the sea state deteriorated she pitched and yawed alarmingly, her groaning seams opened with the strain, leaking enough water to require the hard physical work of regular and continuous pumping, this while the men were deprived of hot food, for the cook was not going to ignite his coppers on heaving planking lest he set fire to the ship. Added to that they saw nothing but ships they were forbidden to touch. Stop them they could, so that Colbourne, following on from a wet and damned uncomfortable half hour in an open boat, could examine their papers. Hold or take them they could not, and each hull let loose again was the object of resentment from rowers soaked to the skin, as well as subject to a calculation of what she would have been worth had she been a prize.

Jocularity, the staple of getting through hard toiling days, was replaced by endless moaning at whatever task the crew were asked to perform. The quiet acceptance which had existed when the Pelicans came aboard was replaced with sullen resentment, as Pearce acted on the existing natural grievances to make the whole seem like a plot by those in authority to do the men on HMS *Griffin* down, the execution of that conspiracy carried out by an uncaring Lieutenant Colbourne. It was made easier by the very fact the crew had gripes aplenty that had nothing to do with the ship on which they sailed: they applied to the whole Navy. Poor pay, slow to be delivered, that had stayed the same for over a hundred years, since the time of the second King Charles, food rotten in the cask served up as fresh, punishment seen as arbitrary and an Admiralty that was distant and uncaring. Every man aboard, being a volunteer and a previous member of the King's Navy, had a story of some hard-horse captain who flogged for fun, or of a scheming purser who had robbed them blind. Pearce was quick on that, with Colbourne acting as his own purser, and he made sure the captain garnered to himself the opprobrium that always went with that office, till there was not a man aboard who trusted his scales or wondered at the size of their grog ration or the weight of their tobacco.

Tale-telling on its own, Pearce knew, would not be enough. Dissent was usually sullen and inactive; he needed to ratchet that up, to test the lieutenant's tolerance and force him into a reaction, to create a sense of unfair and arbitrary treatment on this ship that had existed on the last one. Colbourne being no friend to the lash helped, for Pearce would have been wary of baiting a captain who would flog him for his misdemeanours, for that would have meant a permanent station at the grating. At worst, according to those he quizzed regarding punishment, he faced the stoppage of his grog, or extra time on the pumps, while at the extreme he could be gagged or stapled to the deck, though none of the crew had suffered such a fate up till now. Yet the lieutenant seemed reluctant to even impose that sanction, despite the provocation.

Being slow to obey an order was easy, even slower to acknowledge anyone's rank with a sir, quite natural, but Pearce set himself to be a nuisance. Every time Colbourne tried to make his way to the deck when Pearce was off duty

he found the man blocking his path, giving him a belliger-
ent stare and taking time to move aside. If Pearce could col-
lide with his commanding officer or jostle another into his
side, not impossible on such a small deck, he did so, and
Colbourne had to keep his wits about him when walking
the deck to avoid the rope that might trip him or a bucket
of water thrown to windward that would come straight
back inboard.

The Pelicans became almost professionally cack-handed –
in the case of Rufus Dommet it was natural – dropping
things, failing to lash off the falls properly, spilling the lead
based blacking on the deck and trying to ensure that any
collective act like hauling on a rope was messy instead of
smooth. After any such task, Pearce would look aft, only to
see that Colbourne was paying him no attention whatsoever. It was frustrating the way the man failed to react,
almost as if he knew what Pearce was about and refused to
be drawn, and in truth what he was up against was petty
rather than serious rebellion.

The shot coming loose from its deck garland could be
blamed on no one, yet it was odd that the only feet it
threatened to damage as it rolled noisily over the planking
were those of Colbourne and his mids. Pearce felt his best
game was the night, a pitch black moonless one, when he
sneaked one of the smaller cannon balls below with him,
and having got his hammock rigged where he could get out
of it on one side, he climbed the ladder, eased up the hatch
cover, and let it go on the deck before dashing back to his
cramped bed space. If he had been observed by the watch
on duty, men who were dozing where they could, not a
word was said, which was encouraging.

This he had been told was the classic sign to the ship's
officers of impending mutiny. With no moon or stars, and
only a dim stern lantern to give those on watch any light, it
took them time to find it as it rolled across the deck, sound-
ing like thunder before it thudded into the bulwarks, a second before the ship pitched and sent it rumbling again. By

the time it was recovered every sailor below, off watch or on, a bunch who could slumber for the nation, was wide awake.

As the days went by he became more and more aware of Gherson. The man, who had always been wary of him, now seemed never to take his eyes off Pearce, watching him wherever he went, with that suspicious look that was so habitual, making him feel he was being sized up for a coffin. If he was on deck, so was Gherson, the same below, indeed he was not sure that he was unobserved when he went to the heads to relieve himself. The mutual animosity between them was palpable, and had existed almost from the first day he had had words with him. Gherson was selfish, unscrupulous, a coward who found betrayal natural and he openly resented the natural leadership that Pearce exercised over the men he had been pressed with.

'He's watching me like a cat looking at a meal, Michael.'

'A rat more like, John boy. Sure, the devil has a hold on his heart, and he would do you harm if he could, but I cannot see what that would be.'

'It's uncomfortable.'

'Jesus, Mary and Joseph, is the whole ship not that, thanks to you?' Pearce responded with a grin. 'And where will all this be taking us?'

He could not answer, for he had no clear idea where his plan was leading. Did he want to provoke a mutiny? If he did and succeeded, what then? To sail to France was a nice idea for him, but he reckoned on that being a step too far for the rest of those aboard, for he had been told by more than one soft, concerned voice that the Navy always found men who had deserted to the enemy and always hanged them. Had the Navy not sent a frigate all the way to the South Seas to hunt down the Bounty mutineers? Had not three of them found on Otaheiti been hanged less than half a year past?

The idea had occurred that he and the Pelicans might get off the ship some dark night, close to the French shore in a stolen boat, with either active aid or total indifference of the rest of the crew, but even given the most benign set of circumstances that was a very long shot indeed. What he would not admit was a known truth; that he could not abide to be passive, he had to do something, even if it did not, in the end, advance their cause one jot.

'I intend to make our presence so troublesome to Colbourne that he will be glad to see us off the ship.'

'Sounds to me like you just thought of that, brother, which I seem to recall is your way.'

Michael was grinning as he said that, but it was one of those expressions designed to take the sting out of a truth. The Irishman was the only one aboard who knew the real nature of Pearce's predicament.

'I have got to do something Michael. I can not just wait.'

O'Hagan laughed out loud. 'Sure, I have seen that in you since the day we met, John boy, and I would only say this to you that it is not always wise.'

'I don't know why you think I have wisdom, Michael. Charlie and Rufus are the same, and even that scrub Gherson. You all wait for me to decide on a course of action...'

'I don't recall you waiting around to hear another opinion. In truth I think that ordering folk about comes to you very naturally. Happen you should be wearing a blue coat instead of sailors' slops.'

'God forbid.'

'So?'

'What I want is for us to get off this ship, Michael, and to not be too vigorously pursued. That will suffice. But if I have to...'

'It is us?'

The look the Irishman was giving Pearce now was serious and uncomfortable. Pearce did not want to lie, to admit that he had thought of how much easier things might be if he was alone, responsible only to himself and no other, but it was the prudent thing to do, even to a man he considered close.

'My actions are for the good of us all, Michael.'

'You there, you men.' Midshipman Short glared at them, to very little effect. 'Enough idling, get on with your work.'

By now the pause before complying was natural, both men waiting till the midshipman swelled to yell at them before replying, 'Aye aye sir.'

Chapter Six

As the deck heaved again, Pearce wondered how they stayed afloat, and prayed that they would continue to do so as he struggled to keep a foothold on the continually flooded deck. At the same time he was hauling on the rope that would bring round the topsail yard so that the ship would be brought on to the larboard tack, albeit with only a scrap of reefed canvas drawing. With the crash of the waves hitting the ship's timbers and a rain-filled wind that was deafening, thoughts were all he could sustain, for so all-consuming was the roar it placed him in near isolation to those within touching distance. Only a shout of the very loudest would convey words from one to another.

The storm had come screaming in from the west at a speed that amazed the Pelicans, who had never seen it happen. One minute they were sailing with a near intolerable level of discomfort, the next the wind had increased ahead of a slew of black clouds, that accompanied by a sudden rush to shorten sail, and secure anything loose on deck. The shore, a strip of white cliffs to the north had disappeared as if some great hand had drawn a curtain over them, and within no time at all HMS *Griffin* was pitching and rolling in a mad dance. It was not uncomfortable now– it was hellish.

Off the bows lay another labouring vessel, two-masted, of much the same size, one they had spotted and begun to close with before the weather worsened, under a similar scrap of canvas, the rare sight of which, as it rose, fell and yawed, exactly replicating what was happening to the one beneath his bare and frozen feet; he had wondered what this tub would be like in a really heavy sea – now he knew, it was awful. That Colbourne could even contemplate a pursuit in such weather was amazing, all to close on a vessel that had failed to identify itself as friend, foe or neutral, and Pearce was sure that could the lieutenant come up with his intended quarry, he would want his guns run out to demand that she do so, or take the consequences.

The man ropes they had rigged were taut life savers, something to keep a grip on as the deck canted and pitched, tipping the bowsprit into a wall of icy green water that turned white as it was smashed asunder by the prow, sending a mass of flecking foam into the faces of those manning the deck. The tap on his shoulder from the sailor Littlejohn, followed by the jabbing finger, was an admonition that he should get below out of the wind and water till the call came for another change of course. Pearce was about to follow when he saw the powder monkey go by on the opposite side, a boy practically crawling, one hand using the man rope to make progress, the other clutched to his shirt to keep dry the cartridge he had stuffed inside. Looking to where he was heading Pearce saw a gun crew struggling to lever round one of the forward cannon so that, when *Griffin* tacked once more, instead of pointing towards the empty sea, it would be aimed in the general direction of the chase.

Curiosity overcame any discomfort – not that there was much comfort to be gained on the lower deck amongst a crowd of dripping, shivering souls – the only benefit being a momentary release from the wind's howl which assaulted their ears, precious minutes before they would be called on deck again to once more change tack. How in the name of perdition could they even contemplate firing a cannon in such a sea, with so much spume, let alone the scud of the sea itself swirling around their feet? Arm hooked round the stay, eyes slitted to keep out the stinging salt water, Pearce watched as the men worked with their levers, jamming them under the trunnion wheels and pushing to gain an inch at a time, then holding hard as the deck pitched and threatened to undo their efforts.

Colbourne had also made his way past on the opposite side, not a blue-coated popinjay now, but swathed from head to toe in oilskins and foul weather hat, head down and canted forward, that being the only way he could make progress, and never once without a hand to secure himself. Pearce saw the nods and jerks of communication even if the words were lost to him, saw the gun captain cradle the cannon touch hole to protect the powder in the quill, ready for the charge that another rammed home down the barrel, the ball and wad following quickly to act as a barrier to the seawater that would surely invade. His wonderment as to how they proposed to spark the flint was met by the knowledge that somehow, someone had got a length of burning linstock to the gun.

He did not hear the orders, but all his companions had been called on deck again. Michael was beside him to throw him a bewildered glance, and Littlejohn was slapping each of them to take their place on the rope they had so recently secured. Now they would need to hold it steady once it was released, paying it out, working in tandem with those on the other side of the deck as they hauled, so that it came round steadily, with enough restraint to ensure it was not blown uselessly away. There were no games to play now – things had to be done right or they would be in serious danger. Leaning backwards as the rope slid round the cleat, Pearce saw the gunport opened, watched as the gun crew used the forward pitch of the deck to run the cannon out, tried to follow the track, which was surely coming close to aim as Colbourne, arm raised and bent over, looked down the barrel seeking the point at which it would bear. Something was whipped off the touchhole, perhaps a piece of oiled and waterproof canvas, the quill full of dry powder jammed into the slot as the lieutenant's arm dropped and he jumped sideways. The slowmatch had to be cupped to keep it dry, the man applying it relying on the mates who had hold of his clothing to keep him on his feet as he carried out his task. As soon as he touched he too jumped back out of the way.

The crash and subsequent loud bang were enough to overcome the howling wind, that followed by a cloud of black and acrid smoke that swept back along the deck. Pearce strained on tiptoe to see where the ball, now just visible in the air, would land, only to be disappointed when it merely disappeared into a mass of water so disturbed as to kill off any chance of a spout. It had no effect on the quarry except one. Pearce heard the faintest of booms, and saw black smoke envelop the stern of the chase. He assumed they too had fired off a cannon, but they got a result, as carried on the wind the ball sent a spout of water up into the air well off the larboard bow. Also, from being an unknown quantity it suddenly became something else as a flag flew to the masthead. It was not one he recognised, certainly not a tricolour, but the gesticulations from those around the cannon left him in no doubt that it was not a neutral.

The gun was run in and reloaded, though in a fashion far from swift or smooth; in fact it was as if the crew and the officer directing the affair were intoxicated, so much did they stagger around, continually seeking handholds in between the duties they had to carry out to fire the ordnance. Pearce knew what they were doing was extremely dangerous; a nine pounder cannon and its trunnion, which must weigh well over a ton, was enough to crush any flesh and bone with which it came into contact. The only thing that was stopping that from happening was swift jabs with the levers that had about them an air of desperate reaction as the sea state played upon the ship, the rise and fall far from regular, that made worse by some kind of cross sea forcing the bows to yaw, this while on the quarterdeck half a dozen men fought the ship's wheel to keep the rudder where it was required.

The curtain of rain lifted just as the cannon fired its second ball and a break above showed some white in the clouds, increasing the light and rendering much more clear the scene before them, though it was not enough to show where the shot landed. The ship they were chasing was much the same size, now identified by a Latimer shout as a 'Gravelines bugger', which was rendered as more of an insult than a description. Given that it had aloft only enough canvas to give the thing steerage way there was no way to tell much else about it except that she was struggling more than *Griffin* to deal with the conditions, tacking in the same fashion into the wind. The gain Colbourne was making was imperceptible, but gain it was.

This time Pearce went below with the others to find Latimer was crowing about being right, this while he, like everyone else, was shaking himself to get some of the sea water off his body. So much had come down the hatch on them or with them that Pearce was standing inch-deep in slushing water, which would work its way down to the bilges from where it would have to be pumped out.

'Spotted the sod right off, knew it's lines like the back of my hand, a Bilander, which ain't no surprise given the bastards are half-Dutch.'

'You been in an' out of Gravelines a few times then, Latimer?' asked blond Sam.

'Happen,' Latimer replied, suddenly more guarded.

Blubber called out next. 'Come on, Lats, open up and tell for how much you have dunned Billy Pitt.'

That set a few voices going, with comments that Latimer was 'a rich bugger in secret', and 'that he had a coach and four, an' only came to sea with the Navy for the fresh air.'

'What are they about?' said Michael, looking at John Pearce.

He could only shrug. Where the ship was from, or its type, meant nothing to him, apart from the vague recollection that the port of Gravelines was in Flanders, and had been one of the places he and his father might have gone when they fled England. In fact he was ruminating on the very obvious fact that, even soaking wet and freezing cold, heaving about in these cramped surroundings, all it took to alter the mood of these men was a slim prospect of a prize and a bit of money. The men fighting the wheel and rudder were probably the same and that led him to the conclusion that he was probably wasting his time in his efforts to undermine Colbourne's authority.

It was Littlejohn who answered Michael's question. 'Gravelines is the port the East Coast smugglers make for to pick up their goods. The town lives off such trade and it's castle pennant is known to all.' He then called to Latimer. 'Reckon she stuffed with brandy and lace, do you?'

'Not this far down Channel, mate, when there's a crossing to the Kent coast that can be done in a night even on a headwind. No, she'll be armed and prize hunting, and if she's new out she'll be crammed to the gunnels, so let's hope she is not fresh for if she is, we'll have a right fight on our hands.' If that was intended as a warning of possible tough times ahead it had no effect. 'Mind,' Latimer added, 'if she can stay out of range till nightfall, which will come early given the cloud, she might just get clear.'

'Then it be best we crack on and bring her to,' called Blubber.

'God forbid with this wind,' said Littlejohn quietly.

The hatch above Pearce's head was lifted and Midshipman Bailey's voice rang out. 'All hands to make sail.' That was followed by another stream of cold green seawater.

'Christ Almighty! Make sail,' crowed Blubber, as jolly as ever. 'Old Coal Barge must have heard me.'

There was an eagerness to the way the crew ascended the companion ladder that had been lacking this last week; clearly nothing that anyone said would puncture their love of a fight. Colbourne was back on the quarterdeck, speaking trumpet in hand, to direct things as the Pelicans found themselves, soaked once more, hauling on the falls to bring round and hold the upper yard so that the topmen could get on to it from the shrouds, this while the rudder was eased to allow the ship to fall off on to the wind. If the weather had changed, apart from the lack of teeming rain, Pearce could not detect it; the wind seemed as strong as it had been previously, so loud through the rigging that it was a permanent, near-deafening whistle.

The topmen went aloft with all the assurance on which they prided themselves, acting as if the ship was on a mill pond, making John Pearce grateful for his lowly, landsman rating. Even running before the wind *Griffin* was heaving fore and aft and what he felt on deck would, he knew, be exaggerated ten times aloft. Spreading out along the yard the topmen lent over and quickly, on command, they undid a set of knots to let a reef out of the topsail, that followed by a command to those on the falls to sheet it home. The effect of that was immediate as the bows, pressed so much harder, went right under the first wave they met, washing aft two of the gun crew, who had been left at their post, leaving the rest hanging on for dear life. One was brought up by a second cannon, the contact so painful that his scream could be heard clearly above the noise of wind and rigging. The second had good luck, missing that same obstacle by a whisker and being washed towards the open hatch from which the crew had just emerged. A desperate hand got hold of the edge and brought him to, while others grabbed for his hurt companion to hold him from pitching toward the bows as they dropped into a trough.

'Topmen down,' Colbourne yelled.

As soon as that order was obeyed, with those sailors still on the shrouds, he ordered the yard braced round and the helm ported so that they could come back into the wake of the chase. Not that anyone could see a wake; in fact as soon as the they hit the base of the trough all they could see was a wall of water, into which disappeared the bowsprit, followed once more by the bows, deeper than they had been hitherto.

'Saints in heaven,' Michael screamed, 'The bastard wants to drown us.'

Pearce heard his friend, but his eyes were on the faces of those men who knew more about seafaring than he, and the look of doubt they were displaying did nothing to reassure him. Charlie Taverner had his eyes closed and was praying silently, young Rufus had his wide open, and he looked as if he had just seen the Grim Reaper. Slowly the ship began to heave over, the deck beneath their feet falling alarmingly and the other bulwark rising. Pearce was sure he could see the unused cannon straining to break free from their lashings. Unmistakable was the plight of the men who had got hold of the injured member of the bow chaser gun crew, hanging on to him with one hand while the other sought to keep them on their side of the ship. Down they dropped, Pearce feeling his stomach rise and his foothold begin to give, so quick was the motion.

The mast seemed to be right above his head, and with the men still on the shrouds laying near-flat it seemed as if it would never stop, that the ship was going to be driven under by the force of the wind on the sail, and for all the danger he was in Pearce felt the bile rise in his throat; they were going to die because Colbourne wanted to take a prize. The thought stayed with him as the deck ceased to fall and slowly began to right itself, and Pearce heard, with relief flooding through his being, Colbourne give the orders to ease the falls, for the topmen to get back on the yard and clew up the offending sail.

It was a long chase and an uncomfortable one of tack upon tack, soaking upon soaking, with precious little time to go from that to being merely very wet in the meantime. There was no chance of food, though Colbourne did manage to get distributed an extra tot of rum. The effect of that, on men with empty stomachs, was a higher level of inebriation, and that in turn led to an increase in bellicosity that threatened to come to a head below decks, and might have done if they had not been called back up, this time to remain so, for the chase was in plain view now, and slowly but surely coming within range.

The starboard bow chaser, the one most likely to stay clear of the scudding water, was firing regularly now, though Pearce thought it more in hope than expectation, for he had no notion of how anyone, however skilled they professed to be, could take aim from such a moving platform, while the 'Gravelines bugger', wisely, was not even trying to retaliate. Just as he was sure Colbourne, who was doing that aiming, was wasting his time, a shot struck home, slicing through the crown of the nearest bulwark and the rigging lashed to it. The topsail yard of the chase swung abruptly, the falls holding it cut through, and Pearce could see it swing abruptly and uselessly. The crew would be running to get it under control as those on the rudder paid off to keep the ship before the run of the sea; not safe, but safer.

The damage done by Colbourne's lucky shot, and the time taken to make it good, brought the enemy to within hailing distance, but that was the point at which they restored way on the ship and tried to haul off again. Once more *Griffin* was in her wake, this time close enough to make the chance of another lucky shot really tell. One removed a bit of the stern, though at a deflecting angle that saw most of the power, along with a goodly bit of the taffrail, go into the sea. Elevating his cannon, Colbourne tried for the rigging, and though one shot went clean through the topsail, it seemed to have little effect on the chase.

Another hour passed, on deck, off deck and on again, tacking every time to gain the precious inches to overhaul the chase, this while darkness began to encroach, for though the clouds had lifted somewhat it was still an overcast day. Now the talk below was less excited, it being more about the possibility of a missed chance, that made telling by way the effect of that tot of rum wore off. Again they were called on deck, and the crew ascended the companion ladder with much less enthusiasm. They were tallied off to release the maindeck cannon, including the carronades, which were eased round so that their muzzles pointed out through the now open gunports, an act which increased the amount of sea water that swilled across the deck. Midshipman Short took station behind the battery to control the fire, as the gun captains started to fit their

flintlocks, each covering them to keep them dry, this before
powder monkeys appeared with their leather cartridges, and
the process of loading began, slow, because the ship was still
heaving back and forth, with a good yaw in between as she
began to crest a crossing wave.

Touch holes were cleaned so that the quills which would
set off the charge could be easily inserted, the cartridge of
powder rammed home followed by ball and wad, and as it
was completed each gun captain, with a raised arm, pronounced themselves ready. Was Colbourne, who stood
looking straight ahead, staying silent to heighten the tension? Pearce was sure there was a moment of theatricality in
the way he waited while everyone on the deck, still obliged
to keep hold of something to maintain their feet, looked
aft.

Then the trumpet, slowly, went to his lips; even with this
he had to bellow to make himself heard. 'We are going to
bring this fellow to, lads, who seeks to avoid us and is even
declining to fight, and we are going to do it in the next half
a glass, for if we don't it will be dark and he might elude us.
So, when I give the order, it is to fire as your guns bear. I am
going to fall off to larboard and swing us round. The
oncoming wave will raise us and I want you to fire on the
crest. The sea state and the wind obliges me to come right
round, so once your guns are housed I want you back on
the falls to bring the ship into the wake of the chase again.
Once we have closed again, I will repeat the manoeuvre
until we get him somewhere vital. Carronades, I want you
firing at maximum elevation, for if one of you can hit him
once he will be done for regardless of where it strikes.'

If it was meant to be rousing it failed to do the trick; if
anything the men looked disgruntled, while once again it
was garrulous Latimer who, mouth pressed to Pearce's ear,
supplied the reason. 'A carronade ball hits that barky
foursquare and there'll be nowt left to take.'

'Stand by,' Colbourne yelled. 'Let fly.'

It was as if he had given an order to the enemy as well,

who could no doubt see what was taking place on the British deck, for the chase bore up as suddenly as Colbourne did, in a copycat manoeuvre, the side of his ship erupting with cannon fire a spilt second before *Griffin's* foremost gunner got off the first shot. Most of the enemy shot whistled through the rigging doing little damage, cutting the odd line before sending up spouts of water off the stern. The other effect was twofold, to close the gap between the ships, and to present to the rest of the *Griffin* gunners a much juicier target.

'Daft bugger,' Latimer shouted.

'He ain't daft,' added Littlejohn, his voice high in pitch. 'He just don't know what's coming. He thinks our guns be the same as his own.'

The two carronades bore on the target and fired together. There was no time or distance to watch the flight this time, they carried it in seconds. Only one of the rounds hit home, but that was enough, for the side of the enemy ship below the quarterdeck just disintegrated as the heavy ball smashed through the scantlings, and when the smoke and debris cleared there was no one left to hold a wheel and no wheel to hold. The rest of the shot from the five forward cannon did little damage, bar one which glanced off the mainmast, gouging out a deep piece of wood.

'Reload,' Colbourne shouted, giving an order that was unnecessary, for the gunners had anticipated the command. HMS *Griffin* swung round onto the wind, taken half way and near broached by a wave. Somehow Colbourne, or the men on the rudder, got the head round to fall off on the wind, and by the time they had way on the ship once more, the gunner captains had raised their arm to tell the commander they were ready to fire. More orders followed to bring the ship round into the wind again, to face an enemy that was wallowing and in some distress.

'Stand by to give her another drubbing lads.'

'What is he about?' demanded Latimer. 'She'll strike without another shot being fired.'

If Latimer was trying to advise his captain, he was not listening. Again he ordered the sheets eased, and again they came round broadside on to its quarry.

'Fire.'

The side disappeared in a second cloud of smoke, blown away as swiftly as the first. This time more shots struck home, three of the forward cannon and both of the carronades. The destruction was appalling; it seemed as though half the side of the enemy ship had been blown away. The deck was clear of people; there was no one steering and the way she was heaving to and fro it looked as though she might just roll over and go under.

'Sheet home. Helmsmen bring me alongside. Master at arms get the cutlasses and clubs issued and stand by to board. I want her lashed tight to us to keep her afloat. Mr Short, as soon as that is achieved, bring us round before the wind for safety.'

'Board,' spat Latimer, close enough to Pearce's ear to be heard, as he saw Colbourne's steward hand him his cutlass and his hat. 'There's bugger all left to board and precious little left to float.'

By the time *Griffin* came alongside the carnage was obvious, for the deck had been just as heavily manned as her opponent; probably the whole crew had been employed, and as a consequence they had all suffered. Ropes snaked out to lash both ships together and they jumped across to a deck where there was no one left to fight them. Those not wounded or killed by cannon fire had been downed by splinters or crushed under guns that had broken loose, while the rest who had survived unscathed had fled below. Where the wheel had been there was just a mass of bodies and splintered wood. Given that was the point from which the ship would be commanded it seemed certain that there was no one to surrender her, so Colbourne stepped towards the mainmast, weak and creaking because of the shot that had gouged it, and swung his hanger to cut the halyard and bring down the Gravelines flag.

'Mr Bailey, a party below to secure any prisoners. Give me a report on the state of the hull. See if she is making any water.'

A stream of orders followed: to house the loose cannon and gather the shot that was rolling all over the deck; to see to those wounded and get them below. Others were set to rigging repairs and Colbourne ordered that the *Griffin's* carpenter be sent for to assess the damage, the whole carried out by a naval lieutenant who was obviously high on excitement. Bailey came back on deck to report that there was a break in the scantlings through which she was making water but not so serious that pumping would not hold it.

'Good,' Colbourne replied. 'I want her made sound enough to be taken under tow, and then we can work to render her seaworthy again.'

'Are we taking her into port, sir?'

Colbourne's eyes flashed. 'Yes, Mr Bailey, we are. And I daresay I shall be invited by the Commodore to partake of a glass of his best brandy when he sees we have a prize.'

Not everyone aboard the prize had been killed, though few seemed entirely whole and given the mass of repairs to be carried out, shocked as they were, they had to be pressed into service, and Pearce found himself working alongside them. The quality of the French he spoke surprised them more than the questions he asked, not that they were able to tell him about anything that was going on in Paris. He continued to speak to them long after he realised the futility of asking them anything about the present state of their country, until he realised that, occupied as he was, he had not seen Colbourne get close enough to hear him talk. Loudly, he reverted to English, unsure whether his previous conversations had been overheard.

Chapter Seven

'It's not a dead loss, mates. There'll be gun money and head money to share, but that ain't no comparison to a ship whole.'

Blubber was talking to the Pelicans, but there were enough close nearby to hear and murmur assent, with the general opinion being that while Coal Barge might expect to lord it in the port commodore's chamber and sup claret by the pint, they, and he, had been dunned out a goodly sum because the prize was so damaged that it would fetch little when sold. Latimer was especially scathing.

'Smashed quarterdeck, with the cabin below like match-wood, bulwarks caved in, a bloody great dent below water and a mainmast that the carpenter says will need to be taken out and a new one put in. The Prize Master might buy her in to sell on as a coastal trader, but you can bet if he does, it'll be for a song.'

'Happen the commodore won't be happy to see his eighth so blasted.'

'He won't know no different, mate. All he'll have to go by is the report he reads and that will flatter Coal Barge no end, lest someone tells him otherwise. His despatch will tell of a desperate battle where only luck an' better guns saved him from like damage.'

'It's not fair he gets more than we do,' whined Gherson. 'An eighth share and he wasn't even there.'

For once Pearce backed Gherson up, which got him an odd look. 'There will be plenty of lords and the like dipping into your money if they get the chance.'

'That's the way it is,' said Latimer, though with a look that told John Pearce he was as unhappy about it as Gherson. The collective growl that followed showed that old mariner was not alone. 'Flag officer's get their eighth, captains get two, lieutenants, warrants petty officers and mids get two and we gets the rest.'

'Hope the price of a whore ain't risen while we've been out then,' Blubber moaned.

'You never spent more'n twopence in your life mate,' said Latimer.

'That's is 'cause I ain't never met a woman in my life worth more'n the price of a good meat pie.'

Matt had his say. 'God help you, Blubber, if we ever do take a decent prize. You'll explode yerself in a week.'

'Can you imagine the coach and four he'd need,' added Sam. 'There's not a spring made to hold him.'

Blubber's face took on a look of virtue. 'Once I's rich, it'll be bread, water and the odd bit of leaf green for me.'

'You starve yerself,' Latimer scoffed. 'That I'd like to see!'

Pearce cut in, on an opportunity too good to miss. 'Did I ever tell you the tale of the time there was no bread in Paris, it was in a state of near riot, and the Queen, when someone told her said, "can they not eat cake?"'

'I bet she had as much cake as she could scoff.'

'She had bread, mate,' Pearce insisted, 'and meat, fowl and fish, with pies by the cartload, as much as she wanted and so did the King and those who served him. It was the ones with nothing who had nothing.'

'Tell us that Spartacus tale again Pearce,' asked Matt. 'I likes that one, an' we've got time afore we sight land.'

'Capt'n wants to see you Pearce.'

The demand was so unusual that it killed off the normal banter that would have attended a fellow sailor thought to be in trouble, and at this very moment it was the last place Pearce wanted to be; he wanted to be on deck, to examine the approaching shore and harbour, looking out for opportunity. He had denied himself that to avoid engendering suspicion, for there was not a man jack aboard would not be rendered curious by a sailor choosing, on a cold and windy night in late March, to be on deck when off duty, rather than snug below.

Was he in trouble? It did not seem so; the summons to

attend upon the captain was not delivered by anything approaching sourness – indeed Colbourne's steward, a stony-faced bugger called Teal, had looked as curious as the rest, meaning that he himself had no idea what it portended. There was some satisfaction to get beyond that double canvas screen, one that Pearce had glared at so often, to actually see for himself how an officer in command of such a vessel lived.

The gunner occupied half the small space between them on one side, in a cubicle crammed with everything he needed to see to his tasks. At the rear was the hatch to the powder room, set in the even more cramped hold, a special heavy screen fitted with a pane of glass stitched in so that the gunner could see to load his cartridges by the same lantern that illuminated his work and sleep space, the flame safely kept apart from where powder might ignite. On the other side, behind the steward's pantry, lay the berths of Midshipmen Short and Bailey, which given its dimensions had Pearce guessing that the poor buggers had to sleep near upright. That there was a marine in between, sentry to the inner sanctum, was risible, as if one such fellow could stop a crew determined to get at the man who lived beyond. The sentry cocked an eyebrow, to impart the fact that the summons, to him as well, was a mystery, before he called out Pearce's name, and pulled back the flap to admit him.

Colbourne was seated at a tiny desk covered in papers, as far forward as he could manage, this to avoid the sweep of the rudder arm which would traverse the entire cabin and brain him if he was standing. Another canvas screen ran fore and aft on the starboard side, creating a sort of triangular lean-to, which Pearce surmised hid the cot on which the lieutenant slept. Three lanterns guttered away in what was a place of no natural light or air, so that, concentrated as it was by the cramped surrounding, it seemed even more malodorous than the berth occupied by the crew. At least some of the stink they created escaped up through the hatch. Pearce had to put a hand out as the much-damaged prize, being towed, jibbed, stretching the cable that joined the two vessels and checking *Griffin*'s progress.

'Sit down, Pearce, on that barrel under the lantern.'

Colbourne continued to scribble away, the quill scratching across paper, thus allowing Pearce to take a really good look at his quarters. No space was wasted, even the gaps between the deck beams were used to house his sword and a dagger, hats, a pair of telescopes, a sextant and all sorts of odds and sods that could be secured by a couple of well placed hooks. The racks holding the ship's muskets and boarding pistols were behind Colbourne, chained off, as if his own body was defence against unauthorised distribution. His desk, dented and scratched varnish, was of the kind that would break into three parts and no doubt there was a space allocated to it should action demand removal. If Colbourne was sat on a chair it was one without a back – more likely it was a cushioned barrel like the one on which Pearce was propped, that or the Lieutenant's sea chest. Having finished his examination, and having decided that there was precious little advantage, barring privacy, to be had from commanding such a tub like HMS *Griffin*, he was left to look at the top of Colbourne's head.

'We will be anchored within the hour,' the lieutenant said, as he sanded the last of his writing. The ropes controlling the rudder creaked slightly as the man on the wheel made some minor adjustment to the course, probably to accommodate the tow.

Pearce did not bother to reply. The heavy book Colbourne had been using was lifted, and the sand blown with some care onto the bare desktop beneath. Colbourne, having put the book in his desk, took the top off his sanding pot and with one hand gathered that which he had spilled into a pile, then eased it to the edge and inside. If he had wanted to hint at straitened circumstances he could not have done better – the man was so poor he could not bear to waste a bit of fine sand.

Colbourne finally looked at him, elbows on his desk,

leaning forward, a direct stare, almost challenging. 'I daresay your mind is full of plans to desert.'

Pearce replied, with an arch look. His eyes ranged around the cramped space. 'Would I not be a fool to seek to abscond from such plenty.'

The smile with which Colbourne responded, wry with a trace of bitterness, made acknowledgement of the irony unnecessary. 'You are an educated man Pearce, are you not?'

'Educated enough to know on which side my bread is buttered.' The pause, before he added a 'Sir' was just long enough to let this man know how much it meant.

Colbourne sat back, so that his whole face was in light. He looked weary, hardly surprising given the tasks he had to perform which allowed for little in the way of uninterrupted sleep. 'You have every right to be cautious, Pearce, but I am not here to probe.'

'It is I who am here and wondering why?'

Colbourne sighed. 'There are few advantages to be had from commanding a ship like *Griffin*.'

There was an insistent thought in Pearce's mind, telling him to let the man speak, to say nothing, because even the most innocuous words could be revealing. Insistent it might be, but his anger overrode it. 'There are more than there are for a common seaman.'

'Common seaman? You may be many things, but assuredly you are no common seaman.' Colbourne looked him in the eye, as if inviting him to confirm that statement with some supporting fact. When it did not come, he added, 'If anything you are a supremely uncommon one.'

Pearce responded with the faintest nod, for there was little sense in denying something so obvious.

'Your mode of speech marks you out as something of a gentleman, which I recall I noticed from our first encounter. You can read and I even heard you speak French to some of the men we captured in that privateer, good French, easy French, the kind that tells me you are comfortable in the language. My own knowledge of that is too limited to be sure of what you inquired, but I did hear the word Paris mentioned more than once.'

'Given the fact that we are at war with the Revolution, and the seat of that government is in Paris, what else would I ask them?'

'I doubt that any bunch of sailors from the Flanders shore could tell you much.' The silent stare was enough to impart to Colbourne that anything that had been said was his to hold. 'I am glad you don't deny your skill in the language.'

'Why?

Colbourne's tone changed, the weariness was gone and it was now quite pointed. 'It would disappoint me to have you tell me a lie.' Getting no response he added. 'My saying that does not make you curious?'

'I cannot help feeling, Lieutenant Colbourne, that I am not the one in this cabin who is curious.'

'*Touché.*' Colbourne's brow furrowed, which told Pearce that the sparring was over; that the man was about to come to the nub of why he had called him in here. 'You know, Pearce, when you and your companions came aboard, this was an ordinary ship. I would not say a happy and contented vessel, it has too many faults for that, but no more fractious than most on such a duty. There were grumbles, there always are, and there is little point in my rehashing them for you know well what they consisted of. Then there is the added burden associated with a ship's captain acting as his own purser, which always doubles the opprobrium in which that particular breed of individual is held.'

'Every man aboard is convinced you are raking in a neat profit from the office.'

'Oh yes,' said Colbourne in a bitter tone. 'Believe me, it is not a duty that I sought, it is one forced on me by the size of the ship. And as for profit, I am making so much I cannot spare a bit of sand to dry my ink. I sometimes think I would still be held in low esteem if I gave them their baccy and replaced their clothing for nothing.'

Why is he being so revealing? That thought was mingled with a strange twinge of sympathy, for in his face, manner and words Colbourne was letting show the loneliness allied to the crushing responsibility that came with command. Limited knowledge of the Navy did not extend to ignorance of the price such an institution extracted for failure. The Articles of War that Colbourne had read out to them when they had been forced aboard applied equally to him, plus a whole load of expectations not placed upon those for whom he was responsible. He had to be diligent, brave and clever, none of which would guarantee success – that took luck as well, which was probably why he cared nothing for the damage he had inflicted on the prize they were towing in; success was more important to his chances of advancement than money.

He could not be very well connected or he would not be here; people with powerful patrons did not end up in command of an armed cutter. It was a revelatory thought that, if anything, Colbourne had a greater desire to get off this ship than he had himself. The man craved promotion, while being well aware that such an outcome could only come from some action in which he must risk everything. Pearce had a momentary temptation to admit that he understood both those burdens, and the anxieties of running a naval ship of war, to allude to the increase his campaign to undermine discipline had engendered. The moment passed, for he could not let natural empathy interfere with his aims.

'Which,' Colbourne continued after a lengthy pause, 'is what you have been intimating I should do. How easy it is to convince a man deprived of much that someone with a little has an abundance.'

'I have done nothing that falls outside the laws under which we both labour.'

'You have, I think, but not in my sight or that of anyone who would report you to me. No, the real damage has been done by your tongue. Thanks to you and your tales of the ancients, of tyrannical Kings and capricious Gods, I now have a crew that goes about its duties with a scowl, that deliberately talks every time I or my subordinates open our mouths to issue a command, that a few weeks ago went about those same duties with...' Colbourne waved his hand searching for the word.

'Ignorance?' said Pearce, suddenly aware of the smell of coffee. It was time for the captain's once a day luxury; his ritual. He had caught the smell before and been envious.

'I wonder, does making a man wiser make him any more content?' Since Pearce declined to respond Colbourne carried on. 'Was it you who let loose the roundshot the other night, or was it one of your Pelicans?' It was the word Pelican that surprised Pearce, and much as he tried to disguise that it must have shown somewhere in his reaction. 'I know all about your little coterie. Telling tales is not an activity on which you hold a monopoly. I know where and how you were first taken up.'

Gherson, thought Pearce, fighting to keep the certainty of that thought out of his expression. The slimy, ungrateful toad would sell his mother down the river for an extra tot of rum. No, that was not true; Gherson would do it for nothing.

'I have thought long and hard about you, Pearce. How to deal with you, for I must do something if I am not to be brought to nought. You have done everything you can, inside the Articles of War, to try to raise the ire of the ship's crew. It is not too much to say that I suspect you are intent on fermenting mutiny. If that happened, my career in the Navy could be in ruins, and I doubt the two midshipmen who depend on me would fare much better.'

The canvas screen between them was pulled back and Teal poked his head through, that followed by a tray bearing a coffee pot and two cups. Two cups? The tray was placed on the deck, Colbourne nodded his thanks, and the steward disappeared, leaving Pearce with the thought that there, very likely, was another well-tapped source of information for the captain. Gherson was not the only one, but at least the steward could not be accused of betrayal; he owed the Pelicans and John Pearce nothing, Gherson owed them his neck.

'I take it you like coffee?'

The advent of that pot and those two cups had thrown Pearce, and he was uncomfortable with the knowledge. What was Colbourne about? He should not be here, in the cabin, chatting away. The whole notion of his plan did not include such a scenario; him at a grating as an extreme possibility, yes, taking the lash perhaps, more like gagged with a piece of wood tied to his mouth, creating the kind of grievances that would, he hoped, tear apart what little loyalty the crew retained for Colbourne, King and country. And he felt weakened by the certainty this man now pouring him coffee was showing. It was like the boot was on the other foot, with the ship's captain knowing exactly what he was about and John Pearce being in total ignorance.

Colbourne sighed and looked around the cramped space. 'How did I end up here?'

He passed over a cup and saucer, two fine china objects which, in this setting, were exceedingly incongruous. Pearce accepted more to cover his perplexity than anything else. The first sip seemed to clear his mind, and he suddenly knew that Colbourne was trying to seduce him with kindness; to deflect him from his actions by creating an intimacy.

'I am supposed to be grateful for employment when so many of my fellow lieutenants are on the beach. And I am grateful, you know, for that would be worse.'

Pearce could see what was coming; the sort of confessional chat that would seek to suck him in, to show that Colbourne was not so very different from those he commanded, that he too was at the mercy of forces over which he had no control. Let him proceed; the coffee was pleasant if not spectacularly tasteful, an inexpensive blend that went with the lieutenant's impecuniosity, but neither it nor the coming tale would deflect Pearce from his goal.

'And yet, sometimes when I sit here, or curl up in yonder cot, I wonder if I have not deeply offended someone, a senior officer or some politician who has the ear of the Admiralty? It could even be a malicious clerk, someone in the bowels of the building who spends his days poring over the logs and muster books, and yet still has to deal with importuning letters from unemployed sailors. Did I badger them too much? Is there something in my past of which I am unaware. I worry, Pearce, that I will be stuck in this ship, condemned to plough my way up and down the English Channel until Doomsday. Forgotten by all in authority, fetching in the odd not very valuable prize, patted on the head and sent back to sea again, while men who serve aboard flagships, or with powerful patrons, proceed effortlessly past me to their post captaincy, without having ever seen an ounce of action.'

Pearce was subjected to a look, one that sought some notion of the effect of these revelations. 'I detect no sympathy in your demeanour, nor should I expect any. It is a cruel world we inhabit, and that to which I am being subjected is a minor scourge compared to the lot of most of my fellow men. But you can see my case, can you not. I need promotion, but how can I achieve that?'

Pearce could not resist it, being presented with such an opening. 'Getting half your crew killed should do the trick.'

Colbourne actually grinned, something Pearce had never seen before, and it took years off him, making him look boyish. 'If I do that, I stand a very good chance of getting myself killed, or even worse, so badly wounded as to render further service impossible.'

'The notion would not stop you.'

The grin had gone, to be replaced with that look of determination that was more familiar. 'No it would not, but I would not take this ship into action on the grounds of personal gain, and I hope you believe that.'

'I think it is more important that you believe it.'

'But to return to you. The one thing that would sink me

without hope of salvation would be a mutiny, and that is what you are intent on causing.' A hand came up to stop Pearce responding, an unnecessary one since he had no intention of admitting what was tantamount to guilt. 'I know of many captains who would have had you gagged to silence your tongue, some who would even have you seized up to the grating a long time ago, and who would have flogged you daily if necessary to stop your seditious tale-telling. They would have made your life a misery and enjoyed the experience. Me? I fear I am too weak a soul for such methods. I know I should employ them, but I shrink from the actuality. In short, in the article of commanding one of his Majesty's ships, I am irresolute.'

Intended to make Pearce feel like a scrub, it was partly successful, for he found it hard to completely dislike this man. He was half-inclined to tell him so, to let on just how often he had thought that what he was doing was unfair, but it was enough for one person in this place to be confessional.

'Yet I must do something about you, Pearce, for the reasons I have outlined. I do not think I am an unpopular commander, and I know that you have not portrayed me as such. I know that you have taken the Navy, the Government and a cruel world as the hooks on which to foster discontent. Odd that you have a power to command men that I actually envy. Not everyone, of course, but you have so suborned a substantial portion of my crew that they look to you before they look to the natural authority that I represent. So, what to do?'

'Let me and my companions off the ship.'

'Which you are well aware I cannot contemplate.'

'Leave?'

'We will not be in harbour long enough to justify the granting of it, and what would be said when I complained of being short-handed, if I was known to be giving men leave of absence?'

'We are willing to desert.'

'Complicity in such as that, if it were ever exposed, would harm me more than a mutiny and what makes you think you would not be caught. The port we are about to enter, as well as the forest behind it, is teeming with rogues who make part of their living from selling deserters back to the Navy. You may think you can outwit them, but look at you, in your sailors' ducks.'

'I have a change of clothes.'

'You do, but that will not suffice. What about your hands, Pearce, look at the tar that has become ingrained in your flesh from hauling on ropes. Try telling some gang of crimps that you are not a sailor. They will nod, Pearce, then they will laugh, and then they will bind you tight and frog-march you to the nearest officer of the Press and collect their bounty. I am tempted to ask,' Colbourne continued, 'what you intended to do once you had caused your mutiny. Having gained control of the ship, where would you take her? To France, perhaps?'

'You will not be surprised if I do not answer.'

'You don't have to,' said Colbourne, pulling from his desk a letter. 'There are many things you don't have to tell me for they are all in here.'

Colbourne pushed it towards him, but he knew it to be Lutyens' letter before it was in his hand. Under the influence of drugs he had told the surgeon of HMS *Brilliant* everything about himself and his past; the letter had been the surprise result. Addressed to the man's father it was a plea that the Pastor of the Lutheran church should use his influence with royalty to get lifted the warrant for sedition that kept Adam Pearce out of Britain, a reprieve that would grant freedom to John Pearce as well. How in God's name had he got that? Gherson's name and face sprang into his mind again. Why had he ever gone to the bother of saving the bastard's life?

'I return to you your property, with a sincere apology for reading what was, quite obviously, private correspondence. Believe me, I did so from the best of motives.'

'Would that be self-preservation?'

'You are angry, and you have the right to be, but it will not surprise you to know that I have the right to do what I have done and in reading it I have discerned your purpose. It may seem strange to you to hear me say that I am a happier man knowing who you are, in knowing that I was right about your dissimilarity to your fellows.'

'So now all your problems are solved.'

'They could be. I could have you in chains, then hand you over to the port authorities to do with what they wish. I hope it comes as no surprise to you that I would find such an action unpalatable.' Colbourne grinned again and picked up the coffee pot. From above their heads both men could hear the sounds of a ship about to moor. It was a telling notion of how much Colbourne feared Pearce that he was not on deck to supervise it.

'But that does not answer my dilemma. I cannot let you, a common seaman, off this ship, and I cannot keep you, an uncommon one, on board. I will not, in all conscience, hand you over to the authorities, because I, like the fellow who wrote your letter, do not believe a man should be condemned to prison for merely speaking his mind. I am reluctant to gift you to some other captain, for they would be bound to ask me why. Imagine if they were told, and took you, how they would react to your behaviour? I doubt you'd survive a month.'

'There are laws against killing people, even sailors.'

'And there are captains who know how to circumvent them. It is we who write up the story Pearce, and no Admiralty clerk is going to overly enquire about a name that says beside it in the log, "died in the execution of his duties".'

Pearce was wondering what price Gherson had extracted for his thieving, but he would not ask, because he knew that Colbourne would not tell him. 'I'm grateful for the coffee, and for the return of my letter. I daresay you wish from me a promise that I will desist?'

'I would like it, but somehow I doubt I would get it and it is the measure of the respect in which I hold you that I would be disappointed if you made it, for to return to where we started, it would be a lie.'

'Then why all this?' demanded Pearce, lifting Lutyens' letter. 'The coffee, the intimacy.'

'Well, it is pleasant to have someone of equal wit to talk to.' Colbourne saw Pearce's colour rise as he became angry and he spoke quickly to subdue him. 'You need to get ashore, do you not?'

'More than that.'

'Tell me.'

Pearce waved the letter. 'There's not much that is not in here. My father is sick, he is in a country going from bad to worse. I need to get him out. The rest will have to be taken care of when that is accomplished.'

'Then I have the solution.'

'Which is?'

That grin again. 'I intend to rate you as a midshipman.'

It was amazing how, in those few simple words, the case was altered. All the things that would damn Pearce ashore, the gait of a man new from the sea, those ingrained hands black with tar, the way the weather had coloured his face, would become part of his defence against crimps, all for the addition of a simple blue, midshipman's coat.

'It is one of the quirks of the Navy,' Colbourne added. 'that I am allowed, within reason, as many midshipmen as I want and that it is I who appoint them. Of course it is not, in the true nature of things, a rank, it is merely a courtesy title for a youngster learning his profession, but it does mean that he is free to come and go from ship to shore much as he pleases, albeit that he would have to have his captain's permission.'

'Why?'

Pearce asked the question because it was an outcome that had surprised him. In all his imaginings – in all those extrapolations of possible scenarios he had conjured up as a means of getting safely ashore, this one had never even been considered and it was clear that Colbourne knew it, for he was now grinning like a Cheshire cat.

'I thought I had explained, Pearce. I have a choice. I must, for my own sake, not yours, either beat you into submission or get you off this ship. You have been trying to get me to flog you for your minor infractions almost since you came aboard, so to do so would only play into your hands and alienate an already disturbed crew. If I remove you to another captain will that magic away the harm you have done to relations between them and I? No, it may even make it worse. It would be seen as unjust and you know how much sailors love to dwell on such things, be they real or imagined. We have taken a prize, we are coming into harbour, and right now the men are less disturbed but I have no illusions about the *Griffin* or her capabilities. It may be sometime before fortune favours us with the chance to catch another enemy vessel. I do not, therefore, anticipate, a contented crew.'

Pearce could not help himself, he had to ask. 'Did Gherson come to you, or did you engage him to spy for you?'

'I needed to know about you and your motives, he is by nature curious. Let us say that our needs combined.'

'And his reward?'

'Oddly enough, he did not ask for one.'

'That is against his nature.'

Colbourne gave him a knowing look. 'Can you not contemplate the notion that he hates you, Pearce?'

There was no arguing with that, even if he suspected it was not enough. 'I wonder if he will be surprised at the outcome.'

'Why should he be surprised. He has no idea of what is in your letter.'

Pearce was sure Colbourne was lying now. Gherson was not the type to meekly hand over such a thing and not want to know the contents. Very likely he had read it, which explained the close attention he had been paying the subject the last few days, but the result had been the opposite of that which he had sought. Pearce half wondered if he should feel aggrieved, for Gherson, no doubt encouraged by Colbourne, had broken one of the most profound tenets of shipboard life; he had interfered with the possessions of one of his shipmates. Trust, in a crowded ship, was essential; caught, he would have been lucky to survive the daily beating the rest of the crew would have administered.

'It was something of a relief to find that your actions were not personal.'

Pearce was sure, as much as he was sure of anything, that had swayed the ship's captain. He was also sure that to acknowledge that act of generosity would be unwelcome. Colbourne wished to be seen as clever, not kind.

'It will not surprise you to know that I do not have

aboard a mids uniform that would fit you. That must be purchased ashore.' Colbourne paused then and looked hard at Pearce, who quickly smoked the reason.

'I have money to pay for such things.'

'Good.'

'Or at least I had. If Gherson has been rummaging in my belongings I may not have everything that I once possessed.'

'I doubt he's a thief,' Colbourne replied, looking away, then busying himself in his desk. That told Pearce he knew about his purse as well; if Gherson had not actually shown him then he had told the captain, but that too must remain unsaid. As for Gherson being light-fingered, of that there was no doubt; if the purse was still intact it would be because Colbourne has insisted it be so.

The patter of feet above their heads, the muffled shouts of command, were the sounds of the ship being secured to a buoy, while an anchor splashed over the stern, men hauling on a rope to pull them in to their mooring, which would make taut the anchor cable, this while others clewed up the sails. Soon the crew would be prettying themselves up for the traders, whores and tricksters who would come aboard to relieve them of what little coin they had, perhaps more on this visit than the last, for those who preyed on the Navy would observe that, however battered she was, HMS *Griffin* had taken a prize, just as they would know, almost to the last farthing, long before the Prize Court pronounced a sum, how much, with its guns and men, it was worth.

Colbourne had a folded piece of parchment in his hand, which he flicked open. Even from the other side of the so-called cabin, in the dim light, Pearce could see the seal and ribbon affixed to the bottom, could imagine perhaps the florid signature which surmounted it. Should he offer Colbourne money to pay for the document, for parchment was expensive?

'I have here a letter appointing you as a gentleman volunteer, a midshipman to this vessel. In it you will see that I require you to come aboard properly equipped, with all the necessary equipment to carry out the duties you will be required to perform.'

Colbourne handed it over. Pearce took it and tried to look at the words neatly written on the page, the opening line saying *"By the power vested in me…"* but he could not, for his eyes had filled with fluid. He was not crying, but he was, being overcome with such a compound of emotions, close to it.

'You are now, officially, Mister Midshipman Pearce, a young gentleman, and I wish you joy of the elevation.'

The inkpot was pushed forward, and the sanding pot reappeared along with a sheet of paper. 'I now require from you a letter asking to be allowed to go ashore to pursue a personal matter. I have already composed my written permission. You will need that if any zealous Press Gang or recruiting party questions you.'

'Crimps?'

'Won't come near you in a midshipman's coat.'

'You were so certain I would not refuse.'

'Yes, very certain.'

Colbourne stood up, or rather crouched up, and grabbed his hat from the nail above his head, and his cloak from another driven into the hull. 'And now I must go up and see if your fellow mids have made a decent fist of berthing both our ship and the prize. Once I have done that I must go ashore to report to the Commodore's office. You will accompany me.'

'Will I be coming back?'

'The choice is yours, Mr Pearce, not mine.'

The lower deck was deserted, with all hands on the upper deck securing the ship, carrying out that multitude of tasks necessary to make Colbourne happy. Many would have noticed Pearce's absence; they had last seen him go into the captain's quarters. What would they make of it? The more imaginative lot would have a vision of him skewered with Colbourne's sword, lying in a pool of blood, or lashed to a chair awaiting a file of marines to take him to the naval prison. The likes of Michael would be worried while Gherson, no doubt, would be pleased with himself.

His possessions, when he gathered them together from the hold, did not amount to much, being the same clothes in which he had originally been pressed. The coat that had once had a high collar, since ripped off, was musty from being folded for so long. A count up of his money established that it was intact, nearly thirty guineas in total. If Gherson had helped himself to a golden coin, then he would have been welcome to it, for despite his malicious motive, Pearce knew that he had been the instrument of his release. His cambric shirt and thick winter breeches were musty too, for the lack of being aired, and there were his buckled shoes, greenish now, but of good enough quality to buff up once a little spit, blacking and oil was applied.

'Are you sound, John boy?'

Pearce looked round to see Michael O'Hagan crouched down on the ladder, his wide Irish face concerned. They were still working on deck, where he too should have been and the joy he felt turned sour. How was he to tell this man, a friend now risking punishment out of concern, who had done everything in his power to aid him in the suborning of the ship's crew, all designed to get the Pelicans off the ship as a group, that he had the means to depart, but alone.

'More than sound, Michael.'

O'Hagan's eyes did not meet his; they were fixed on the empty ditty bag and at the clothes he had extracted, all laid out as if Pearce was about to change into them. It was clear that the Irishman was trying and failing to make sense of it.

'It would be a kindness to be after telling what's going on?'

Elation at the prospect of release had made him forget about not just Michael, but Charlie and Rufus as well. In truth, Pearce was somewhat stunned by the turn of events and had had no time to think matters through, especially as it related to the Pelicans. To have to explain now was bad, but he was aware that in his excitement he could have walked off the ship and into Colbourne's boat in a continued daze, without a word to his mates, and the knowledge that he might have done that made him feel like the lowest form of life. A scrub he might feel, but that did not alter the fact that he had an opportunity to fulfil his deepest wish, one that he was sure, if he explained, would be understood by Michael and the others.

'Gherson stole a letter from this bag.'

'The bastard,' spat Michael. 'He'll feel my fist.'

'Leave him be, for the sod has done me a favour. He gave it to Colbourne.'

'Mind out, fat arse,' said a voice behind O'Hagan, identifiably Blubber's, a remark that would normally get a jolly retort from the Irishman. Not this time. Pearce could not see his face because he spun round to take on the insult, but he could hear him.

'Is it an early grave you be seeking, bastard?'

'Hold on Michael,' said another voice, which Pearce recognised as that of Latimer, 'he was only making a joke.'

'Michael,' Pearce called, indicating he should vacate the companionway. The crew was obviously finished on deck, and eager to get below for their grooming. That was another thought that had not occurred to John Pearce in his elation at Colbourne's action. It was not just his Pelicans who would wonder at his departure. They, so lately wound up like watch springs to a near state of mutiny, would hardly take kindly to what would look like an act of selfish personal advantage.

Within a minute the lower deck was as crowded as it had ever been, filled with a buzz of noise so loud that Pearce would have had to bawl to tell Michael, now standing beside him, but not looking at him, anything at all. Colbourne came down the ladder, which killed off the noise, while doing nothing to make it any easier in the article of explanation. Head bent he stopped in front of the pair.

'Are you ready to go ashore, Mr Pearce?'

He could not reply, as Colbourne, in a way that assumed agreement, went towards his cabin.

'Mr Pearce! What in the name of Holy Mary is that about?'

Every eye was on him now, and few of them were friendly. Those not glaring at him were like young Rufus, confused, while Charlie Taverner was actually shocked. The problem of what to say was stopped by the reappearance of Colbourne, ship's books and papers cradled in his arms. No fool, he sensed the atmosphere right away, and in truth it would have been impossible not to, given that it was so laden you could cut it with a knife.

'Mr Pearce, you must make haste if you wish to go ashore, for I will not wait for you.'

In the jumble of thoughts that filled John Pearce's mind then, one of them told him that Lieutenant Colbourne had been exceedingly shrewd. How long had he had that letter? It could have been days, yet he has waited until they were berthing to have his interview, waited until Pearce, offered the thing he wanted most in the world, would have no time for explanation, no time to ask permission of his friends to accept. His walking off the ship now would be seen as an act of pure betrayal, killing two birds with one stone. Colbourne was not only ridding himself of a pest, but undermining the message which had made the crew so fractious. He had, in truth, already done so, for even if Pearce declined his offer, in two one-sentence exchanges what trust he had built up among the men on this ship was broken. Colbourne's words in his cabin had been soft soap, designed to get to just this point.

He turned to speak to Michael, but the Irishman turned his back. 'I never thought the stink on this barky could get worse, my boys, but it has. It's not just the timbers that are rotten.'

Was Colbourne smiling? Under his hat, which shaded his face, it was impossible to tell for sure, but Pearce had the distinct impression that it was so. Knowing that he had been out-manoeuvred made no odds, he had to make a decision whether to stay or go, to fulfil one duty, the one he had to this crew, or another to his father. There really was no choice; this lot, barring shot, shell and the pox would survive. Pearce jammed his clothing back into his bag, and as Colbourne passed him he followed the lieutenant up the companionway ladder.

In the seething mass of emotions that assailed him as he hit the cold fresh air, there was only one moment of relief. Gherson had not come below with the others, being one of those assigned the duty of hauling the prize alongside to be lashed off. When he saw Pearce trailing Colbourne, carrying his ditty bags, his face showed momentary triumph, then confusion, given that Pearce was not under restraint. That turned to fury, as Colbourne said, 'New to your duties Mr Pearce, you will not be aware that it is the custom for the senior officer to be last into a boat. So, as you are a midshipman and I a lieutenant, after you.'

The journey across the anchorage was horrible. He faced the men rowing the boat, who had seen him clamber down the side, ditty bag in hand, and had heard too that last exchange and now there was one of their fellow crewmen, and a landsman to boot, not hauling on an oar as they were, but sitting in the thwarts with the captain, for all the world like an officer. The desire to challenge Colbourne, to get him to admit that he had set out not only to get Pearce off the ship but to undermine him, was powerful, but having been truly humbugged once, he decided against it, for he had a very strong feeling that if he was to try and hold a conversation that would be overheard by the nearest men on the oars, the lieutenant would turn it to his advantage.

So he sat in silence, avoiding the eyes that were fixed on him, listening to Colbourne's coxswain issue soft orders that turned the boat left and right though the shipping that filled the anchorage, unable to hear the whispered exchanges between the oarsmen, all of which he knew to be about him. Jumbled thoughts went from anger to despair, the former an attempt at justification which demanded to know why it was he who had to lead men to something they should aspire to and achieve themselves, the latter the certain knowledge that human nature was not designed that way; men needed to be led for good or ill. He had set himself to do just that and walked out on the responsibility he had created.

It was a relief to reach the shore and to step on to dry land for the first time in six weeks, even if the earth seemed to move beneath his feet. Colbourne was standing, legs well spread, showing the way to adjust. 'Take your time Mr Pearce, give it a moment, otherwise I assure you, if you seek to walk right off, you will take a most ignominious tumble, and that would never do. We can hardly have the ship's crew cackling at you, can we?'

Damn the man, he is laughing at me.

'Your ditty bag, Mr Pearce.'

The turn to take it from one of the boat crew was executed slowly. He reached out a hand for the canvas sack, which was released a split second before he grasped it, falling to the ground with a soft thud. Pearce started to bend down, only to hear Colbourne's voice once more.

'No, Mr Pearce. You have a certain station now, so it behoves you to demand that sack be picked up and placed in your hand.' Pearce did not stop, and picked it up himself. Colbourne added, as the sailor dropped back into the boat. 'Insubordination comes so very naturally to you, does it not?'

No reply came, so Colbourne continued. 'My first task is to report to the Commodore's office and hand in my logs and papers. I daresay, since Mr Short has brought in that capture, small and damaged as it is, the great man will oblige me with a glass or two. Normally I would ask you to wait here, but I fear under present circumstances that would be unwise. Like as not I would return to find you floating face down in the harbour.'

'You have had your fun, Mr Colbourne.'

'A simple sir would suffice, and as for fun, Pearce, I think you have had quite a deal of that at my expense this last two weeks. Now let us be off. You will be quite safe outside the naval buildings, which will give you plenty of time to plan your next move.'

'You could hand me over now, couldn't you?'

'Yes, I could, but it may surprise you to know that I meant some of what I said in my cabin. I too have taken part in discussions on the nature of liberty. I have even corresponded with people who have attended meetings where your father spoke, and they would, no doubt, tell me that he is an estimable man who does not deserve to be proscribed merely for holding radical sentiments, just because madness has replaced sense across the Channel. As for the ship and my career in the Navy, I have done what I had to do, and if I seemed to have taken pleasure in it you must allow me that, for it is no more than a release from a period of anxiety that both those things were about to be taken from me. I will not betray you, for I was brought up to keep my word.'

'Thank you…sir.'

Back aboard *Griffin* the mood was sombre. The men changed into the best shore going rig, even although they would not set foot on land, but they did so in a muted way, with none of the joviality that normally attended such an occasion.

'He's gone and left us high and dry,' said Rufus, 'ain't he?'

'He has that Rufus,' Charlie replied, 'and after all we's been through together. I never thought I'd live to see the day.'

That brought a halt to the thoughts that Michael O'Hagan was harbouring, a mixture of hurt and anger. As a man he reckoned himself too trusting, but had decided long ago that it was better to be that way than forever suspicious. That trust had been abused before, but he could recall no time in the past when he had felt as let down as he did now.

In the few weeks he had known John Pearce he had come to think of him as a close friend, the kind he had not had since childhood, and right now, because he knew the reasons he was so desperate to get off the ship, there was room to forgive him for going. But there was no room to forgive Pearce for not explaining. Damnation to the rest of the crew, but he should have told him what was afoot.

'Just goes to show,' Charlie added, 'that in this life it don't do no good to trust anyone.'

Michael glared at him, and recalled that as a customer in the Pelican he had not much liked Charlie Taverner, and that was for his smarming ways as much as anything else. On top of that was the fact that Charlie, like the rest of his mates, rarely had any money, and he was always trying to part from their coin those who had some. Michael worked hard all day, a sinker paid good money to dig deep ditches and shafts, often up to his knees in freezing mud and slime, and at night he drank what he earned. If he woke in the morning with nothing left in his pockets it made no odds, for another day's work would set him up again, but he did have difficulty in recalling what had taken place the night before, and he suspected that sometimes Charlie had taken advantage of his inebriation. On top of that, there had been a serving girl called Rosie that Michael was sweet on, a girl Charlie was always trying to steal away.

'There's a reason,' Michael said.

''Course there is, Michael. He got the chance to look after hisself and he took it.'

'Why don't you tell them?' asked Gherson, who had come close enough to hear. 'Tell them that your sainted friend is a man who has betrayed his country as well as his friends.'

Michael's huge hand shot out and grabbed the man by the throat, lifting him, gasping, until his head hit the deck beams. He then moved in so that his face was right in that of Gherson's, his voice a quiet, menacing hiss. 'Don't you talk of betrayal, or I'll be after telling our shipmates what you get up to when no one's looking. Now you will say nothing and nor will I, but if I hear you have opened your big gob and split, you'll be the loser.'

'Belay Michael, for the love of Christ,' said Latimer, grabbing at his hand, for Gherson's pretty face was going blue. 'You're choking the life out of the bugger.'

Michael let go and Gherson dropped like a sack of peas, in a heap on the planking, his hand rubbing his throat.

'You heard me Gherson, did you not?'

That got a rasping noise and a nod. Charlie, who had always been wary of Michael O'Hagan, not least because he had felt his fist one night when the Irishman was drunk, had taken a couple of steps back, causing those he disturbed to curse him.

'You said there was a reason, Michael,' asked Rufus.

'There is.'

'Is it a good enough one to leave us in the lurch?'

It was a gentler Michael who put his hand on the boy's shoulder. 'To tell the truth, Rufus, I don't know, for what is reason enough for one man, can be seen as little to another. I need to think on that.'

'Are you going to tell us what it is.'

'When we're back at sea, Rufus, then I'll tell you.'

'It won't do for me, whatever it is,' said Charlie Taverner.

That got a chorus of agreement, not much of one, for those who had been offended by Pearce's blatant self-interest, had turned to other more pressing needs, like getting their pigtails greased and decorated, and airing their shore going rig, anything that would make them look good, this despite the fact that the brutes they were going to service would have had them in sackcloth as long as they could pay.

Chapter Nine

Emerging from the gates of the naval yard, John Pearce entered a world more familiar to him than that of any ship; the narrow streets were bustling, with people hurrying to unknown destinations, weaving between carts drawn by hand or horse. The smell was the sweet pungent odour of the manure that covered the cobbled roadway, driven into the gaps between the stones by a constant succession of wheels; of smoke from chimneys too sooted-up for real safety and a general whiff of corruption that went with humans in the mass. There were hawkers and traders in canvas covered stalls filling every available wall space, the odd drab of a whore who would strut in what she supposed to be a seductive way whenever anyone emerged, too poor to do anything but offer her services in an alley, for the folk that emerged through these gates had coin, be they Navy or dockies, and perhaps some of the latter were going home to an abode where what the emaciated whores could give them in a two minute tryst, for a two pence piece, was not available in the bed space of their own home.

Even if Colbourne had not surreptitiously pointed them out, Pearce would have spotted the sharp-eyed men lounging in various poses that allowed them a clear view of the gates, crimps and sharps, always on the lookout for a mark. No doubt they were familiar with the shore workers, the storemen and the Navy clerks, and one or two would have an eye out for the signal that told them these men had something to sell, something they had purloined from the Navy. The largest industrial enterprise in the land was a rich source of almost anything of which a thief could think. Failing that, even if the gate was an unlikely place of exit, they would be on the lookout for men who had no right to be where they were, which would have applied to John Pearce without a uniformed lieutenant walking a pace in front of him. Others would be hoping for some youngster in a blue coat who might have money from which he could be parted, either by guile, or if it could be done without retribution, by force, and that too would apply to any tar allowed ashore because his captain trusted him not to run. Not that either would be approached sober; let them drink first, and copiously, for in their dulled state they were an easier victim.

Odd to think that Charlie Taverner had been one of that kind, something which Pearce had learned from those who knew him rather than from Charlie's own lips. He could imagine him in this setting, hat tipped back, sandy hair showing and a smile on his face, seeking by a welcome look to entice some stranger into his orbit. Pearce doubted, without any evidence, that Charlie was one to club an unfortunate once he had filled them with drink, more the kind to use sweet words and flattery to part them from their money, keeping himself fed in the process before perhaps extracting a small loan. That was how he had worked John Pearce on that first acquaintance in the Pelican, which led him to wonder what inroads Charlie would have made into his money if the Press Gang had not intervened. Pride himself as he might on his prudence and wits, he knew that the likes of Charlie Taverner had means of parting any man from the contents of his purse. Clearly it had not worked on at least one occasion, the law-breaking being what confined him to the Liberties of the Savoy, where Charlie could walk the few streets bounded by that sanction, and work if he could find any that paid.

The scene before him was a tableau which could be seen in every town in the land, and not for the first time Pearce was wont to wonder how many people tried to make their living, by fair means or foul, as parasites feeding on the body of a paying enterprise. It was not just dockyards that attracted such people, you could find them outside any manufactory where the workers received regular pay, in the centre of any market town where those with the means came to buy and sell, people hovering on the edge of life, trying to sustain themselves off the scraps of those who only had a little more. This had been the grist to his father's radical mill, the gap between rich and poor in a world where a man would not have to look too hard to find someone expired of starvation only yards away from the gates of houses full of fat merchants and numerous servants. Walking behind Colbourne, he felt a faint tinge of the resentment that had so animated his father at such injustice, while at the same time reminding himself of something he had learned in Paris: that when it came to change it was not those at the bottom of the pile who effected anything, but people who had full bellies, time and inclination. The only role the dispossessed were given to play was usually destructive.

The shop they entered was dark and low-ceilinged, and the man who responded to the tinkling bell almost a carica-ture of the lowly tailor in the way he was bent and obse-quious, with a long tape measure round his collar, a man able to smile at Colbourne and frown at John Pearce in what seemed to be the same look. There was a whole playlet in the fellow as he examined, in a fleeting second, the coat Pearce was wearing: the sneer at the torn off collar, a slight change of expression as he realised that, despite the way it was marked and creased, the black cloth was of very good quality. The look did not last long for this was a man who also knew a customer from a servant.

'Lieutenant, how may I be of service to you?'

Colbourne indicated Pearce. 'I want a midshipman's coat for this fellow, not a new one. In fact quite well worn will do.'

'Ah!'

Colbourne ignored a reply obviously designed to impart that such a matter was far from easy. 'I know you keep such things, since I was obliged to purchase a used garment as a working coat myself, not two months past.'

The lips pursed in a fleeting show of distaste; this was a man who enjoyed dealing with Post Captains who could

afford a twenty guinea gold-edged broadcloth, took some
pleasure from lieutenants buying new, if plain, but had little
patience with impecunious midshipmen and could barely
bring himself to be civil to anyone seeking second hand. He
approached Pearce and stood under his chin.

'Size will be a problem.'

'You will look.'

The shrug was eloquent if non-committal, but before he
turned to go a finger and thumb were used to feel the edge
of the coat Pearce was wearing, one that had been bought
for him by a woman in Paris, keen that her young and
ardent lover should look like a gentleman, perhaps that her
beauty should not be diminished by his less than perfect
attire. It made him think of the hat that went with it, and
the fine breeches and buckled shoes, as well as the beauty
and accomplishments, both social and private of Amelie
Labordière, the person who had gifted them to him. A week
after the purchase of that garment she had fled Paris with
her husband, who had been a tax farmer under the old
régime, to avoid arrest by the latest group of politicos to
take charge of a revolution descending month by month
into increasing chaos. Pearce recalled with some amusement
how his father had disapproved mightily of both the giver
and the gifts, but what son paid any heed to a parent where
matters of love were concerned?

'Who gives up midshipmen's coats to be sold as seconds?'

Colbourne did not look at him, too busy examining a
captain's uniform on a dummy, complete with the twin
epaulettes that denoted three years' seniority. 'Any number
of people. Imagine how many youngsters quit after one
taste of a mid's berth.' He stopped and looked at Pearce,
before adding. 'You would not know what that's like.'

'It cannot be worse than what I have already experienced.'

'It is, Pearce, believe me. It is home to all manner of
thievery and debauchery, a place were the dreams of the

inexperienced meet head on the misery of the failed. There are boys who have become men, creatures who will never pass for lieutenant, stuck in such places, bereft of any other place to go, too proud or incompetent to take a lesser rank.'

Pearce had a fleeting recollection of the mid's berth aboard *Brilliant*. 'Yet they are always full.'

'Of course. It is a way for a boy with limited prospects to progress…'

'To wealth?' Pearce interrupted. 'Just like every sailor I have ever encountered, ashore and afloat.'

Colbourne ran a finger over one of the epaulettes, his voice taking on a mildly wistful tone. 'When you are a nipper, Pearce, it is glory you dream of, not wealth. Of battles won and honours earned, of superiors amazed at your daring, even a levee at Windsor with the King ignoring admirals and generals, eager to hear of your exploits.'

'Something achieved, I imagine, by one in a thousand.'

'Less. But it is that which makes tolerable no privacy, certain tyranny for whoever is the new boy and never enough food. I cannot ever recall my time there without my stomach rumbling.'

'Most people ashore have more cause to worry where their next meal is coming from. Just outside that door there are boys of the same age as your mids who will starve if they don't steal.'

'We do not live in a perfect world, I'll grant you, but I wonder, does culling the rich, as they are doing in France, make life any better?'

Any reply Pearce might have given to that was stopped by the tailor emerging from his storeroom, several coats over his arm, that followed by the ritual of trying them on. The man, as befitted his trade, had a good eye, and if some of the garments were tight, they were close enough to a fit to be serviceable. The one Pearce would have chosen, almost new and of good quality was discarded after a quick and silent shake of the head from Colbourne. He nodded when Pearce tried on a worn coat, not by any means the worst, not quite shabby, but slightly too small, that cramped him under the arms. Next came the hats, rigid naval scrappers that sat fore and aft on Pearce's head. Again Colbourne assented to one which was not perfect, a bit rat-nibbled around the rim and Pearce, who liked to dress well, was obliged to defer to his choice. Next came the haggling over the price, pitched too high as a matter of course by the tailor, beaten down by both men until a stalemate was reached.

'Of course, if you were to leave your old garment, I may be able to make some alteration to the price.' That got a raised eyebrow from Pearce as the tailor continued. 'It is of decent quality and by the stitching has been run up by a very good craftsman. It is also, of course, French.'

'You can tell?'

The tailor shrugged, in that open-handed gesture that was such a characteristic of his trade. 'To a man in my occupation, the cloth and the cut, but more especially the stitching is to you what a face would be. It tells me a great deal.' Suddenly aware that he might be praising it too much, the tailor added. 'Not that it has full value. A great deal of work, in cleaning and repair, will be needed to make it saleable.'

Pearce emerged under a hat and in his tight blue coat the lighter by near four guineas, to be told that the garments had been chosen because it was best not to look too prosperous. 'For half the sharps round here will be after you before you get way from the port. Wouldn't take long for men like that to smoke your true rank.' The look Pearce gave him produced a small laugh before Colbourne continued. 'These men know their trade, and it is fair to say they know ours.'

'Yours,' insisted Pearce.

'And they are not just here around the ports. They could be anywhere, looking for a running sailor to turn in. Best to look poor.'

Pearce suspected that was not the real reason; Colbourne

had diminished him in the eyes of the ship's crew, dressing him like a near tramp was just another way to take him down a peg. The next purchase was a sextant, and like his coat and hat it had seen better days.

'This is like a badge of office, Pearce. Anyone seeing this and the coat will know you are Navy and elevated enough to be ignored.'

'As long as they don't ask me to use it.'

That purchase completed, Colbourne took him to a large, bustling inn called the Angel, in what was the main street of the town, a wide, uphill thoroughfare of a kind that John Pearce had seen all over England – tall narrow dwellings above shops, red brick and grey stone, well proportioned and redolent of the ordered society that had created them, with the odd medieval structure of timber framed wattle and daub sitting incongruously in between. Civic pride and prosperity had seen the High Street cobbled, with pavements of York stone for those on foot. The Angel was a fairly new construct, meant to look imposing, with large windows and gas lamps to light it at night. Chalked on a board outside the arched entrance to the stableyard were the times and destinations of the various coaches that came and went from the town.

'I leave it to you where you go, that is none of my concern.'

Pearce put out a hand to be shaken, but Colbourne, who had been reasonably friendly throughout the various transactions that had got them to this place, declined to take it. His response was, in fact, quite blunt and aloof. 'I think not, Pearce. It would imply that we are equals and that is not an estate I would want anyone observing us to suppose.'

The message that John Pearce was going to ask him to pass on to Michael O'Hagan died on his lips, and he was forced to mouth the words 'trust me' to the back of a man walking away from him without a backward glance and without even the slightest hint that he wished him well.

The journey across southern England, first to Winchester, then on to the London coach, was far from comfortable. It was not just to save money that Pearce elected to sit on the roof of both, it was also to avoid intimate conversation. The turnpike roads were reasonably smooth and the conveyances well sprung, but it was a rocky ride nevertheless. Even inside, the noise of the iron-hooped wheels on the metalled road surface and the constant blast of the horn meant that any verbal exchange had to be carried on at a high pitch. Yet talk there would be, for taciturn silence would be frowned upon, social intercourse being the only thing that made such travel bearable, the kind that strangers always indulged in. A midshipman's uniform coat was a standing invitation to say which ship he served on, how long he had been in the Navy, what action if any he had seen, and to whom he was related or acquainted.

Pearce fancied himself a manufacturer of tales, but a tissue of lies, which he was bound to impart, was a difficult thing to sustain for two whole days. Best to take an outside seat where, while the coach was in motion, an exchanged shout was the maximum level of talk, and that was usually about the thing that concerned those passengers most: the weather, for rain soaked them, the wind buffeted them and the jostle for an inside seat, where bodies on the rim kept out some of the elements was a game of musical chairs at every stop to change horses and allow the passengers to stretch their legs. He played the taciturn young fellow early on, one who kept away from his fellow passengers in the inns at which they took sustenance, so in the main Pearce was left alone with his thoughts; what life had he led to get him to this point, for it was a fact that it was not one of his choosing.

Would things have been so very different if his mother had not died when he was young? Would his father have become such a peripatetic preacher of social change if he had had a stable family life to maintain? Perhaps he would, dragging along his wife as well as his child, for Adam Pearce was a driven man who believed that, with one more push, the world of equality for all that he sought would come to pass. He was as convinced of that in the same way that the religious saw a beckoning paradise, and his conviction was so deep it made it hard for anyone, least of all his son, to point to the flaws in his contentions.

So they had traversed the length and breath of Britain, with no discernable pattern to their travel, on foot when funds were scarce, in a comfortable carriage when Adam Pearce could find a well-heeled sponsor decent enough to be embarrassed by his prosperity, spreading his brand of gospel, often to willing ears, sometimes to hostile crowds. They called him the Edinburgh Ranter, but Adam Pearce did not rant at all; he often spoke so quietly that those listening had to strain to hear, his words far from bellicose. Neither in speech nor in the many pamphlets he published did he employ venom to challenge the existing state of affairs. He used wit and irony to debunk the present social order, in which a few had plenty, while the rest lived in near starvation. He portrayed it as a farce being played out against the interests of the mass of people, who were fobbed off with the excuse that if things were as they were, that was the way God willed it.

Adam Pearce was most vocally not a religious man, though if pushed he would agree that some kind of superior being must exist, for to imagine otherwise was to take too much of a leap into the unknown. But he subscribed to his old friend Davy Hume's contention that, just because there was a God that did not make him either benign, competent, willing or able to intercede on behalf of humans seeking succour from the grind of everyday existence. Organised religion he hated; the church in all its guises for the way it took money from the poor and superstitious to sustain priests, ministers and vicars, though his true venom was reserved for the Pope and Bishops. Landlords he castigated for the rents they charged, judges for their endemic hypocrisy, monarchs and their offspring for being no more than a superior form of thief, and politicians for being more concerned with lining their pockets than making better the lot of their fellow man.

In his early years, like any son, John Pearce thought his father infallible, this made more potent by the fact that they spent almost every waking moment in each other's company, and though it was skewed by his own ideas, Adam Pearce made time every day, when schooling was impossible, to see to his education. On the rare occasions that they did stop for an extended time, usually a winter spent under a sympathetic roof, proper schooling would be arranged. That was never easy; the making of new friends and the identification of new enemies, usually a fight or two to establish that he was not feeble and could hold his own.

That was coupled with the heaviest burden of all, having to take in the received wisdom of organised schooling that said there was an all-powerful God in heaven, a near divine King on the throne, that England, Scotland or Wales, wherever they happened to be, was a country singularly blessed by the Almighty, that the true task of the budding citizen of this world was to support the present order in all its glory, and to fight and kill the nation's enemies. In fact, the antithesis of everything his father had raised him to believe.

The philosophy Adam Pearce propounded was not going to be challenged by a child too young to argue, nor did constant repetition of the same refrain produce boredom. He saw the world through his father's eyes, and it was not until his fourteenth year, after the publication of a particularly uncompromising pamphlet and they had been taken up by the law and slung into the Bridewell prison that John Pearce seriously began to question his father's philosophy. Locked in a barred chamber with near a hundred other offenders, everyone of whom was vocally innocent, John Pearce had seen life at its most raw, and applying his father's principle to that place, he had found them sadly lacking.

He had never thought that the poor and dispossessed had natural dignity, but exposure to the lowest elements in the mass dispelled the notion that they had any at all. From the warders to the smallest urchin most of those with whom they shared a prison qualified in every way for the soubriquet "dregs of humanity". In fact that was one commodity they did not have at all; grossly ugly, slatternly females, who evinced no shame in public copulation, who saw soap and water as a danger to health and who were wont to relieve themselves where they stood; the men and boys who were no better, displaying ignorance in the mass, a stupidity backed up by the absolute certainty of the rightness of their obtuse opinions. For such people the filthy straw on which they were obliged to sleep was what they lived with all their miserable lives. Few had any hope of release, in fact John had soon learned that freedom was not sought with much vigour; these were folk content to live in such squalor because, damp, filthy and stinking as it was, it was marginally more secure than life outside.

No person was safe from thieving fingers, and providence was most unkind to those prisoners who were solitary souls from a decent background. At least Adam Pearce and his son, who had roughed it in their time and had even been at risk of robbery before, could take turns sleeping, so that one was always on watch to keep what few possessions they had to themselves. Not that they kept them for long since they had to be traded with the warders for small privileges in the article of food and the ability to keep clean, or for paper, wax and quill to send out letters to friends and supporters. These asked for assistance to get them released or moved to one of the more comfortable parts of the prison, on the floors above the ground that did not flood with human waste when the rains fell heavy; where proper beds and privacy could be bought for a price, as could decent food fetched in from good local hostelries. There were few things John Pearce dreaded in life, but a return to that was one of them. He was sure, had the men who pursued him that night caught up with him after he had sought refuge in the Pelican, he might have killed them to avoid being incarcerated in such a place again.

He left the coach at a leafy village called Ealing, and walked the rest of the way through open countryside into London, for to go all the way to Charing Cross was too dangerous; it was a place where sharp eyes were on the lookout for debtors, thieves and anyone who had good reason to hide from the law. Inside his coat he had the letter Surgeon Lutyens had written, detailing the circumstances of the Pearce case, and his first stop was at the Lutheran church that was home to his father.

'I think my son has a notion of my influence with court than is more than the case, Mr Pearce.'

Pastor Lutyens, as he fingered the letter, looked like an older version of his son, with thin grey curly hair, once ginger, that failed to hide a pinkish scalp. He had an upturned nose, pale, almost child-like skin and eyes that, especially when showing surprise, reminded John Pearce of a fish. His accent, guttural and Germanic, was pronounced, his speech imperfect, which explained the way Surgeon Lutyens spoke English; clearly, but with a precision that made it sound as though it was not his native tongue.

'He was most sure that you would help, sir.'

'So shall I, Mr Pearce, for apart from Charles-Heinrich's request I speak, it is Christian duty to do so. All I say is I see the King on few times, and I have been most strong advised not to trouble His Majesty with little things. His health, as I sure you know, is delicate.'

'I was given to understand he was cured of his ailments.'

'The problem lurks, Mr Pearce, ready to come back to haunt. Everyone, his ministers and his servants and equerries are at pains great never to excite him, though what we witness from across the Channel, a King murdered and his wife, children and family treated like worst kind of felons, an even state of mind is hard to keep, Ja!'

'The Queen?' Pearce asked, for the Pastor, looking wistful, seemed about to launch into a discussion of the state of affairs in Paris.

'Comes to me more often, and I am many times called to Windsor to converse with her in native German and listen to her concerns for her soul and those of family. Her sons and daughters give her great worries. Children can be sore trial...'

Pearce coughed, to stop him wandering on to that subject too; the male royal princes were a debauched nuisance, living evidence of the soundness of his father's ideas on monarchy. The girls he knew nothing about, except that they were unmarried.

'Will she be well disposed?'

'I talk with her. And as I often remind good lady what a Christian should do, there is some hope that she will see plea to her husband for clemency as duty, not favour, as my dear son implies.'

'Can I ask what you think the chances are, sir?'

'How I say? I do not have strong rights to King's ear, and do not know how dangerous your father is seen in Court circles, or you. Nor I a reader of such writers as he, but the King is a kind man and listens to Queen. I think he might consent raise warrant that threatens you and your father for an assurance no further incitements will take place.'

'I doubt my father has health enough for that.'

'Then you must leave with me, young man.'

'I must ask for some form of time, sir, since the state of my father's health is most pressing.'

The pastor shrugged. 'If your father believe in God, he would know such matters lay in his hands.'

This was no time for a theological discussion, so John Pearce just said, 'I must trust you to do what you can, and I assure you I am grateful.'

'How I contact you if I have any news.'

'I shall contact you, sir.'

'If you need a place to lay head, I will be happy provide it.'

'That is most kind.'

'Then you could me tell how my fool son is faring at sea.'

Seeing the look of curiosity on Pearce's face, he added, 'Perhaps you not know his competence. It far exceeds the needs of Navy, that a place where barbers pass for surgeons, yet he chooses to throw all his prospects of an excellent position.'

'All I can tell you sir, is that he seemed happy in his station.'

'Indulgence, Mr Pearce, selfish indulgence. I despair of boy.'

The house he was watching was the same one from which he had so nearly been nabbed on his last visit to London, a narrow yellow-brick residence which sat on the end of a terrace of three-storey abodes in Clerkenwell. It was home to John Horne Tooke, one of the men who had founded the London Corresponding Society, in reality a debating club, the first of many to spring up in the aftermath of the Revolution, a society specifically dedicated to effecting the kind of change they saw taking place in France. 1789 and the fall of the Bastille seemed like another age, yet it had happened less than four years previously; hard to recall now the joy with which that event had been greeted, and not only by those who felt the present system of government in Britain corrupt. Even members of the administration had greeted the upheaval in Paris as the overthrow of a tyranny, while writers and poets had poured forth a stream of prose and stanzas to celebrate the event.

To Adam Pearce it was like a vindication of all he had argued for, though he was wise enough to see that part of the euphoria in the upper echelons of society was brought on by a sense of relief at the humbling of a long-time foe. They had been at war with France, with few breaks, since the time of Louis XIV, so a Briton could never think of that country without thinking of an enemy. In the last hundred years the list of conflicts was long; the War of the Spanish Succession, the Austrian Succession, Jenkins's Ear, the Nine Years War, the Seven Years War, the American War of Independence, those interspersed with alarms and excursions as some slight on either side, real or imagined, led to an expansion of the army and the fleet.

Even in the periods of peace the people of the British Isles felt threatened by the one nation left that could match her genius for trade. France was the great commercial rival to be fought in Bengal and the Carnatic, Canada, the West

Indies, the South Seas, in Belgium, the Rhineland and in any
distant outpost where rivalry was endemic to plant the flag
of possession. A country larger by far, more populous in
the mass, who alone in the world could build a navy to
match the Wooden Walls of England. France, a great
Catholic nation, could threaten invasion; it was their support that had kept alive the notion of a Jacobite rebellion
and the hope that some still harboured of a Stuart restora-
tion. Prior to France the great enemy had been Catholic
Spain; she had been humbled by the defeat of the Armada,
never again to threaten the British shore.

The French Revolution was seen as a like event in the life
of the country, the laying to rest of an anxiety that the collective imagination had lived with for several lifetimes. No
great battle had been fought to bring about a hope of
lasting peace, instead the steady drip of war had bankrupted
the monarchical tyranny of France. Britain, and her
Parliamentary system, rooted in her control of the King and
their Protestant faith, had triumphed.

Adam Pearce was suddenly sought after; a man who had
spent years preaching a message of equality, who was held
to have a greater understanding of the forces unleashed by
the events across the Channel, was much in demand. The
hand to mouth existence his son had known all his life was
gone. No more was he obliged to traverse the streets of
some town or city crying out that all should attend to listen
to his father, or to pass the hat round a gathering in some
rural backwater, a weather eye kept out for the local youths
who would certainly rob him of the few pennies and odd
sixpence he collected if they could. At the same time he had
to take the temperature of the reception, for more than
once he and his father had fled a likely spot with sod turfs
flying past their ears.

Meetings became publicised events rather than ad hoc
gatherings, with agreed fees put up by men of means eager
to hear where this new world order would take them, for
there was not a soul born who did not think that events in

Paris and Versailles would impact in Britain. Change would come here too, reform that seemed long overdue to the mass of thinking people in the country. It was part anxiety and part hope that made those with much to gain or lose eager to hear what might come to pass. On top of that it seemed every printer in the land wanted the ideas of Adam Pearce in a pamphlet, with money paid per word, and the Edinburgh Ranter was only too happy to oblige, for, carried along by the euphoria, he too was sure that radical change was coming to sclerotic arteries of British life.

It did not last and it was not just what happened in Paris that altered the mood. True, the humbling of Louis and his Queen evoked sympathy, just as the constant drumbeat of revolution gave alarm to those who believed in order. London was suddenly full of émigrés, and they too were looked on with pity, those who extended that to them seeming to quite forget that all their lives they had been part of a system that had trod on the necks of the poor to keep alive their privileges. Yet it was more the alarm of the established order and those who supported it that brought about change. King George, his family and court worried that they would share the fate of Louis and the parasites of Versailles. What great landowner could look with anything other than a jaundiced eye at reports of moves to break up the great French landed estates. The Bishops saw that their silk-lined livings would disappear, just as they had for their Catholic counterparts in France. The commercial interests, the great trading monopolies and the money brokers of the City of London knew that instability was inimical to profit, and the one salient fact emerging from France was that the box of revolution, once opened, was hard to close.

The tide did not turn suddenly; it was gradual. Within a year speeches damning the excesses of revolution, which would have been howled down twelve months before, were listened to in respectful silence. Clever men like Edmund Burke alluded to the disorder in France, and contrasted it with the settled peace of England, and asked how any good could come of such mayhem. So the rich had been humbled, but had the labourer suddenly become their equal? Was such a thing desirable? Had France really changed, was she no longer a rival to be feared – was she not the same old enemy in another guise? Siren voices played on the fears of the nation. The curse of the papist religion, which Bourbon Kings had determined to force down the throats of Protestant England, was replaced by the fear of no religion at all, for the men leading things across the Channel were Godless creatures.

In that changing climate, Adam Pearce had composed one pamphlet too many, and one too radical. As the French parliamentarians stripped their King of even more power, the Edinburgh Ranter had called for similar measures here. There was nothing new in what he said, he had been saying it for years, but now his voice carried some weight, enough to instil alarm in those who feared his influence. The charge of sedition was invoked, a warrant issued for the arrest of Pearce *père et fils*. One sojourn in the Bridewell was enough prison for any man so they had fled, first to Holland, then to Paris, where Adam Pearce, soul mate to the Revolution, had been welcomed with open arms.

John Pearce shivered, for, standing so long, and thinking these thoughts, the chill had reached to his marrow. The smoke had been coming out of the house chimneys for a while now; the servants would be up and at their duties, lighting fires in cold rooms, heating water for their betters to wash, cleaning and polishing muddy footwear and feeding themselves a breakfast before seeing to the needs of their master and mistress. Several boys had called to deliver post, which indicated that Horne Tooke was still active. The problem Pearce had was how to get to see him without being observed, for it was approaching that self same door that had nearly seen him nabbed the day he had been forced to flee, ending up in the Pelican. There would be people watching the house now as there had been then, men who knew the faces of those wanted by the law.

It was another boy delivering a letter that gave him the idea, and reasonably familiar with the area in which he was walking he quickly found a coffee house on the edge of Smithfield market in which to sit and compose a note, paper and quill provided by the owner. A Penny Post man was engaged to deliver the note and Pearce, ensconced in a deep booth, sat on a cushioned bench, could think about food and, hard by the London meat market, he could not deny himself a succulent beefsteak. Warmth seeped through his body as the food and the heat of the room drove out the chill. He would have dearly liked to sleep a little, for he had left Pastor Lutyens' manse well before dawn, but he dare not. Fortunately the coffee, as well as the continuous babble of those using the coffee house, helped to stave off that desire. There were papers to read, the latest edition of the *Morning Post* and the new *Observer*, and they had despatches from France telling of the latest moves in the National Assembly, plus a list of those newly proscribed by a revolution intent on eating its own.

'You will look in vain, young fellow, for news of your father.' The voice, deep and adult, was behind him, and Pearce felt a frisson of fear run through his body, which subsided quickly as he rationalised that anyone wanting to take him up would have just come and got him. 'I decline to sit with you for reasons that require little explanation.'

'Horne Tooke.'

'The same.'

'You are watched?'

'Every waking hour, and I fear even during the hours of sleep. I observed as I entered that you were reading a newspaper. Hold it up so that your face is covered.'

'You will do the same?'

'No, young John. I have a better way. I talk to myself all the time when out of doors, in the street, sitting in a coffee house or tavern, anywhere I think I can be observed. Sometimes I even wave my arms as if engaged in heated argument. Those who watch me think me touched by madness, I'm sure, but they do not seek another body just because my lips are moving.'

'Do you have news?'

'It is not good news. Your father is in prison, put there I am told for his refusal to keep quiet about the activities of the Revolutionary Tribunal. He was denounced for an article he wrote in the National Assembly by a deputy called Fouché, a Jacobin, but he was not alone in the motion. Nor was your father the only one proscribed that day, though Tom Paine is still at liberty.'

'He has been more circumspect, no doubt.'

They had a lot in common, Paine and Adam Pearce, but they virulently disagreed about one thing. Paine saw the way the Revolution was going as a necessary catharsis on the way to a better life for all; John's father, who had originally held the same view, now disagreed, and was vocal in his belief that it was nothing more than the acts of unprincipled men lusting after power.

'Your note said you left him in poor health.'

'Incarceration will not improve it.'

'Turn the page of your newspaper,' said Horne Tooke before continuing. 'He still has friends, I'm sure. Perhaps they have done something for him, a private room, food and the like.'

Pearce could have said that such things were of the past, that the prisons of Paris were now too full for private apartments and bought-in food. But it was the other dangers that concerned him most. 'I was in Paris last September.'

'Yes, a most deplorable event. It made life very difficult for those of us on the side of the Channel who seek to change things.'

There was a temptation to say how much more difficult it had been for the victims of the September massacres, to put Horne Tooke's discomfort in perspective, but he decided that using irony would not at this stage be helpful. Hundreds had been killed, their bloody heads paraded through the streets on pikes, slaughtered by self-appointed tribunals who had set up drum head courts in the prisons themselves. Few hauled before such arbitrary justice had managed to successfully plead innocence or have someone with power intercede to save their life. Most had been brutally murdered out of hand by madmen lusting after the blood of the rich. Only it was not the rich they were killing; certainly the odd aristocrat had been a victim, but the Revolution had, by that time, lost any reason. Some of the victims had been at the tearing down of the Bastille and things had continued, if not at the same pace, with the same result. A farce of a trial before the Revolutionary Tribunal, with condemnation a near certainty, that followed incarceration and the daily thought that the next tumbrel to the guillotine would be yours.

'There must still be people he can appeal to,' the younger man insisted, 'those with the power to get him released.'

'Certainly such people exist. Danton, for one, might intercede and right now he is powerful and getting more so. Marat, we know, once admired your father's writings, and he might be able to use the power of his paper to change minds.'

That made Pearce wonder just how in touch Horne Tooke was; Danton had sanctioned the murderous storming of the Tuileries, and Marat, in his inflammatory writings, had encouraged the behaviour that led to it. He and Adam Pearce had fallen out months before and he doubted relations with Danton were much better. Both seemed set on a path to ever more bloodshed, not less, and if they were going to intervene, they would have done so to quash the imprisonment.

'What are his chances of avoiding arrest if he comes back to England?'

'Slim John, very slim. He would be required to publicly recant and that is something I doubt he would do.' Pearce thought of Pastor Lutyens words, that old Adam would have to be silent. That would be hard enough to guarantee; to demand he deny his beliefs was to ask the impossible.

'But, here we could certainly see him imprisoned in comfort. The Society has funds for just such a purpose. We could get him a private chamber and pay for any medical assistance he may require.'

'If I could get him to Holland...'

'Then the Society could support him there.'

'You sure you could carry this?'

The voice dropped to a deeper tone, adding sincerity to what Horne Tooke said. 'Your father was a spiritual founder of the Corresponding Society, and he, along with Paine, was one of the leading lights whose beacon we followed. He is therefore a charge upon our conscience, and I assure you no voice would be raised to deny him what he needs. And we do have some influence in Paris. If you wish, I will raise the matter at the next meeting.'

'No.'

'But...'

'If you have men watching the outside of your house, you will also have some inside the Society who are not what they seem.'

Pearce could feel the resentment through the wood at his back as Horne Tooke swelled with indignation, and he spoke quickly to head it off, for he needed this man and all like him. Besides that, having lived in Paris and talked with those men who were now running the country, he knew just how much influence the London Corresponding Society had in the councils of the Revolution; precisely none. To men of action, who had toppled a King and removed his head, had torn apart the way a country was run and were struggling to put it together again, who were engaged in a war to the death with Austria and Prussia on the side of the forces of reaction, people who did nothing but talk were more derided than admired. Any intercession in that quarter from men derisively referred to as *les bavardiers d'Angleterre* might lead to his father being more tightly guarded than released.

'I do not doubt your good offices, sir, nor those with

whom you founded your movement, but it would be naïve of us both to assume that the government had not taken steps to find out what you are about, if only to gather evidence against you.'

'We are careful, young man, very careful.'

John Pearce put as much sincerity into his reply as he could, not only because it was necessary but because he meant it. 'I do not doubt it, sir, but care is not always enough.'

'Then what is to be done to aid him?'

'I must go to Paris and get him released.'

'I trust you jest.'

'No.'

'Then I count you as mad.'

'Please understand, sir, that I have lived in that city. I know it well. I cannot be certain that I still have friends there, but I am sure there must still be some.' What he said next was more to appease Horne Tooke than any belief that the man mentioned would aid him. 'I have met George Danton on more than one occasion, and I have some hope that he will remember me.'

'And Marat. He is riding the crest of a wave right now, having been arraigned by the National Assembly. The mob love him.'

'Which is why I do not. Who is this Fouché you mentioned?'

'An ex-seminarian, very nearly a priest. He is described as dry and humourless, but a fanatical Jacobin.'

'Powerful?'

'Was not particularly so, but who knows how the sands shift in Paris?'

That was said with gloomy resignation, and it evoked some sympathy. Men like Horne Tooke were personally committed to change at some danger to themselves. What they would not countenance was violence to achieve their aims, convinced that such behaviour was un-English, foreign, French and Papist in inspiration even if the perpetrators denounced the Holy Trinity. They were upright Protestant burghers, who held in common with most of their countrymen that they lived under a vastly better system than those across the Channel had ever enjoyed, and had done so since the Great Revolution of 1688. They were patriotic at the same time as they sought to undermine the present way the country was governed, a paradox that made life very difficult indeed.

'I will need help. Can I ask you for it?'

'Name it.'

'My first task is to get to the coast, somewhere safe, and I will need funds, for alone I cannot use force to free my father and if I cannot persuade someone in power to help then I must resort to bribery.'

'There is nowhere truly safe, but I suggest you head for Sandwich in Kent. There is a residual sympathy for Tom Paine there for he lived in the town, and Conway, the local vicar of the Church of St Peter's is, I know, sympathetic to our aims.'

'A radical clergyman?' exclaimed Pearce, with a palpable degree of surprise. 'That is unusual.'

'He is singular certainly, though wise enough to hide his light under a bushel, for there are not many of his more prosperous parishioners who would appreciate his sentiments. I have an address you can go to there, and Sandwich has boats in abundance and easy access to the sea, while the hand of the Excise is, I am told, light.'

Pearce had the feeling he might not be the first to use the suggested avenue of escape; Horne Tooke and his friends had helped others evade the clutches of government men; either that, or a route had been set up with the leaders of the Corresponding Society in mind, arrest for them being a constant possibility.

'I must reluctantly ask again. Funds?'

'That is one thing I am happy to say we are not short on. I will write to our friend in Sandwich, and enclose a draft upon which you may draw up to fifty guineas.'

'Will there be that much money in a small seaside port?'

'It is a smuggling town, John, and one of the things they smuggle most is gold. Our friend the vicar will provide you with the funds you need and arrange your passage across the Channel. You will, I assure you, find him most resourceful.'

'This note might be intercepted.'

Horne Tooke responded with an exasperated tone. 'Do give us some credit, young Pearce, for knowing what we are about. We have a private code which we use in our letters. Myself, you will not see again, for to be observed once more in proximity to me might bring about that which you least desire.'

'I might be followed.'

'Aye. When it comes to the wherewithal to keep the lid on dissent, the government has a seemingly endless supply of men and money.'

'Thank you, sir, and I hope, one day, I will be able to have my father say that to you face to face.'

'Tell me, young John, this Navy garb you are wearing. How did that come about?'

'It is a long story, sir. Too long for an occasion such as this.'

'Perhaps another time?'

'Providence willing.'

'Wait till I have been gone ten minutes before you leave. I have pencilled a note for you to take with you and set it inside a copy of the *Gentleman's Magazine*, which I will leave on my table. Goodbye and good luck.'

The wood between them creaked again as Horne Tooke rose to leave. John Pearce folded his paper and slid out to take it back to the pile that sat on a central table, catching a quick sight of the man's broad back as he exited through the door, and heard him very volubly talking to himself. Quickly he grabbed the magazine and followed him stopping just away from the window that stood to one side of the door. Over the rim of the *Gentleman's Magazine* he watched the scene unfold as two men in heavy coats and big hats which obscured their faces detached themselves to follow him.

He thought about what he had said; that there would be at least one spy in the organisation Horne Tooke headed. He hoped the older man would hold his tongue about their meeting, but had to acknowledge that there was no point in him worrying about it, for it was beyond his control. He must get to the Kent coast, and as quickly as he could. That meant another long walk to the Old Kent Road, to an inn where the coaches going to South East England made their first stop to change horses after Charing Cross.

Rain began to fall as he walked, and he cursed it, for the short jacket he was wearing was not much to keep out the wet and the prospect he faced, of once more sitting on the top of a coach, was most unwelcome. On this occasion it was more than ever necessary, for the road went by way of the River Medway, and that debouched onto the Nore anchorage, the place where he had first been taken aboard HMS *Brilliant*. He recalled the mass of shipping, including 100-gun ships-of-the-line that filled the estuary, thus there was a good chance that some of the coach passengers would have connections to the Navy.

A haberdashers shop at Blackfriars, close to the bridge across the Thames, was happy to sell him a cloak, disappointed, given the state of his other garments, that they could not oblige him with a whole new outfit, but his determination to bargain got him a scarf thrown in.

Chapter Eleven

The cry that there was a ship in the offing did nothing to stop the flogging of Devenow, the ship's bully. Ralph Barclay knew him of old, a man who harboured his grog for a true blow-out. He had got drunk and had started to fight, or rather, since he was a huge man with big fists, to beat up his messmates. The fact that he had a broken jaw, not properly mended, did nothing to inhibit either the drinking or the fighting. So Devenow had to have his Monday dozen, and since he was not much loved by the rest of the crew, the bosun's mate was laying to with a will; Devenow's back showed the scars of previous floggings, but no sound escaped from his mouth, though he bit hard on the leather strap placed there.

'Punishment complete, sir.'

'Cut him down, Mr Sykes,' he said to the bosun, before adding wearily, 'Let that be a lesson to you, Devenow. It is my earnest wish never to see you seized up to the grating again.'

'Fat chance,' said Bosun Sykes, under his breath.

'Mr Lutyens, he is all yours.'

Devenow went below to the sick bay, trailed by the surgeon, stiff in his gait, but without aid, determined to show all aboard that he could take his punishment as well as he took his drink, this while Henry Digby gave the orders that would get the deck cleaned up. Ralph Barclay took a telescope and trained it on the horizon.

The vessel beating up towards the convoy was quickly identified as a warship, a frigate of much the same size as HMS *Brilliant*. Both Ralph Barclay and Davidge Gould were on the threatened side by the time she was hull up, staying in that station even when the pennant at the foremasthead identified her as a British warship under the command of a Vice Admiral of the White Squadron. With the convoy sailing majestically on, Ralph Barclay ordered

Firefly back to her station, awaiting the arrival of the vessel which, going astern of him, came up smartly on to the wind and set a course to come alongside. The voice, once they were sailing in parallel, speaking through the trumpet, boomed over the intervening water.

'*Amethyst*, Captain Blackstone at your service.'

Ralph Barclay's first thought was that this Blackstone was his junior; he knew every name on the captain's list and how they stood in relation to him and it was comforting to know when he shouted out his ship and name that the other fellow would know that in a situation requiring a face to face meeting, it would be he who would be obliged to lower a boat.

'I have orders, sir, from Admiral Hotham, who is presently anchored at Lisbon.'

'I am under Admiralty orders, Captain Blackstone.'

'I am aware of that, sir, but Admiral Hotham has sent me out expressly to meet escorted south bound convoys and assure those in command of King's ships that between here and Gibraltar the seas are clear of any enemy vessels and are being heavily patrolled by our Spanish allies. Given his shortage of frigates and sloops, the admiral is somewhat blind to matters pertaining to the Mediterranean, where he is bound once his fleet is assembled. He therefore requests that you accede to his orders to leave your convoy and join him forthwith. Naturally written orders will be made out to cover you from any censure.'

Ralph Barclay knew he did not have to accede to such a request; he was within his rights to refuse. Against that he and Davidge Gould would be joining that fleet as soon as he had delivered his convoy and it would be a bad idea to start off in bad odour with Admiral William Hotham, the present commander, who would probably take it very amiss that what he had asked for had not been granted. That would be doubly true if the eventual head of affairs became Admiral Lord Hood, presently the senior naval lord on the Board of Admiralty, but certain, from what he had heard before he weighed, to take over the Mediterranean command. That was someone with whom Ralph Barclay already had a strained relationship; to be in the black books of both the proposed commanding officer and his deputy was madness.

'I'm sure you understand the nature of the request, sir, and the service you would be doing the nation by agreeing.'

Raising his speaking trumpet, Ralph Barclay replied: 'I am minded to agree, sir, but from your words am I to understand you wish to strip the convoy of all of its escorts?'

'That is the admiral's wish.'

It was damned uncomfortable having this shouted conversation, something everyone on both crowded decks could hear, for Ralph Barclay was forming a notion that would aid him in another way, namely the chance to detach himself from Davidge Gould and HMS *Firefly*. He could not be sure that the simultaneous examination of his and Gould's logs would not set off an inquest into his recent behaviour but if he could stagger their joining, with Gould doing so after he had reached Gibraltar, that possibility would be diminished, if not actually killed off. And if Hotham wanted frigates and sloops in the Mediterranean, there was not much point in Gould raising the Rock then coming all the way back to Lisbon.

'Captain Blackstone, you may have observed that we took a prize on the way south, a French barque. I am loath to leave the convoy entirely unprotected, so I will order Captain Davidge Gould, who has HMS *Firefly*, to stay with her, and I will set a course with said prize for Lisbon, once I have given the requisite orders.'

'Admiral Hotham will be most grateful, sir, and may I wish you joy of your capture.'

'You may, sir, you most certainly may.' Then Ralph Barclay turned to the master, Collins, and ordered him to work out a course for Lisbon. 'Mr Digby, signal to both escort vessels to close with *Brilliant*, if you please.'

Henry Digby was as happy as his captain, for what was

being proposed offered the prospect of adventure. Convoying merchant vessels was dull, frustrating work, made doubly so by the cantankerous, nay downright perverse, behaviour of the people they were tasked to protect, the merchant captains.

'Lisbon,' said Lutyens, who had been invited to take coffee in the captain's cabin by Emily Barclay. 'I daresay we shall take some pleasure there.'

'Dry land will be a pleasure.'

'Amen to that.'

'And,' Emily added, carefully pouring a second cup for the little surgeon to avoid spillage due to the swell, 'it will do Lieutenant Roscoe no end of good to be ashore and still, will it not?'

Lutyens smiled, for Emily was, he knew, teasing him. 'I had not forgotten Mr Roscoe, Mrs Barclay, and you are right. And just so I am aware of what you are truly thinking, it will also do him good to be under the care of more competent medical practitioners.'

'I thought no such thing,' protested Emily, loudly.

'What?' asked her husband, entering the cabin and removing his hat.

'Mr Lutyens was being unfair, husband.'

It was a very jovial Ralph Barclay who responded. 'A flogging offence if you are involved, my dear.'

'I merely alluded to the better care that Lieutenant Roscoe would receive in Lisbon, sir.'

'No, sir,' said Emily, jabbing his arm in a coquettish way that betrayed her youth. 'You did not, sir, you made a most cruel allusion that I thought you incompetent.'

'Then in the face of such dire punishment I must withdraw it, unreservedly.'

'Coffee?' asked Ralph Barclay, who followed that with an irritable look at Lutyens. The surgeon quite mistook it, not knowing that the captain was thinking that if he had removed one fly from the ointment of his career with the notion to detach Davidge Gould, then he still had one firmly stuck in his sick bay.

'It was a jest, Captain Barclay.'

'Of course,' Barclay replied, aware that he was frowning. 'Forgive me, I have many matters to consider.'

Complex, thought Lutyens, looking at Barclay's slightly puffy, broken-veined face, now relaxed and smiling as he took the small coffee cup from his wife. His uniform coat gave him an air of command, but his fluctuating moods tended to diminish that. Her I can read, for she is all innocence, but her husband, that is a man with many strands to his being. If they anchored at Lisbon his workload would decrease – the wounded would be sent ashore and for the rest, the crew would be too busy trying to catch the pox for him to worry about treating them. This would allow him time to collate the observations he had made so far on this voyage and begin, perhaps, to draw some conclusions. Not enough to begin to write a paper, but pointers to which way his research should proceed. The title of the eventual dissertation he had already decided upon: *An Enquiry into the Stresses of Life at Sea for the Seamen & Officers of His Majesty's Navy and certain conclusions on the mental heath thereof.*

'Perhaps it should be officers and seamen.'

'Sorry?' enquired Emily.

Lutyens had spoken, inadvertently, out loud, a trait that he would have to watch. It would never do to let on that he was researching the crew of HMS *Brilliant*. All in all, his decision to join this vessel was working out to his advantage. With no way of knowing if the crew were typical, he had nevertheless observed the application of discipline and its limitations, had not only watched as men went into a fight but had dealt as a surgeon with the consequences. He had seen men pressed and the way they reacted to that, many of those who had come aboard at Sheerness now seemingly resigned to a life in the Navy, just as he had seen the strivings of the likes of John Pearce and his ilk to get off the ship. That last thought made him wonder where Pearce

was now; ashore probably and using to full advantage the
letter, he, Lutyens had written to help him in his cause.

That made him look at Emily Barclay because, although
he could not be certain, he had felt that she had been fascinated in some measure by John Pearce. Perhaps for the reason that he was so different from the run of the fellows her
husband had pressed from that Thameside tavern; he had a
bearing about him that made him stand out, yet there was
always the chance that it was more than that. He would
never know, for to ask would only offend, but it had added
to his study the effect of a captain having his wife aboard,
and the difference that presence made to the way that same
captain went about his duties.

'So I escape my flogging after all?' joked Lutyens.

'For the moment, sir. I would not wish to deny myself
the right for eternity.'

'Surely you would never flog the surgeon, husband?'

Ralph Barclay laughed, for he knew, as did Lutyens, that
he had no right to do so. 'You have my word, my dear, that
he is safe.'

Lutyens, thinking of the man whose back he had just
treated, said, 'You would not extend that to the rest of the
crew?'

It was a damned uncomfortable question to pose with his
wife present, and Ralph Barclay had to fight to stop himself
from saying so. There was a fundamental disagreement
between him and Emily about shipboard punishment; she
was horrified by it, he knew the need of it. Lutyens must
have realised that it was a maladroit question too, for he
flushed slightly.

'I recall a little rhyme that covers my thinking on the
matter, Mr Lutyens:

*Tender handed stroke a nettle, and it stings you for your
pains,*
Grasp it as a man of mettle, and it soft as silk remains.
*Tis the same with common natures – use them kindly, they
rebel,*
*but be rough as nutmeg graters, and the rogues will use you
well.'*

'It is an interesting notion to see your men as plants.'

'Believe me, sir,' replied Ralph Barclay, looking at Lutyens but really speaking to his wife, 'there are men aboard this vessel who would aspire to the sense innate in a plant, and fail to achieve it. Now, let us move on to more congenial topics, like Lisbon.'

They raised Cape de Roca just after dawn the following day, making a southing before coming up nor, nor east to enter the mouth of the Tagus. Hotham had anchored his fleet opposite the city, in the Pietade Cove – half a dozen line of battle ships, including the 64-gun *Agamemnon* – and it gave Ralph Barclay some pleasure to know that Horatio Nelson, who commanded her, would have his eye on the barque in his wake, with the red ensign above the French Tricolour, denoting that she was a prize. He hoped and prayed that Nelson, along with all the other ship's captains, was deeply jealous.

Almost immediately he secured his anchorage, the flag-ship made his number and that required him to go aboard with his logs, his exit from the ship coinciding with that of the still comatose Lieutenant Roscoe, who was sent into a boat strapped to a piece of planking lowered from a whip on the yard. There was a moment when Ralph Barclay stepped through the entry port of HMS *Britannia*, to be greeted by stamping marines and a flagship lieutenant with his hat raised, when he imagined himself coming aboard such a 100-gun vessel as its captain, and that was only a short step from the notion that one day he might be greeted as the commanding admiral. He was years away from such a rank, but this war might last and take a few of those ahead of him on the captains' list out of commission. Ralph Barclay felt no guilt at contemplating the death or serious injury of his peers; he assumed they thought likewise. Each and every one was fired by ambition for rank and wealth, not necessarily in that order. In truth he was sure all of them would forgo the former for the latter any day. Better to be rich than merely gilded.

That he was kept waiting, after such a peremptory summons to come aboard, came as no surprise; admirals liked to
keep captains waiting, it reinforced their sense of superiority. That he did not have to wait long, Ralph Barclay put
down to his having taken a prize. Not that Hotham would
make a penny out of it; being under Admiralty orders there
was no flag officer grasping for an eighth share. Relieved by
the admiral's clerk of his books and papers, he was invited
to sit opposite William Hotham, reprising, as he did so,
what he knew of the man. Reasonably successful, Hotham
was short, pink of face and good looking for his age, a sailor
who had done quite well out of the American War, but that
was only part of the reason he was here. The man had connections sufficient to make him hard to refuse and since he
was not utterly incompetent he had been gifted what was a
most important post, albeit that he would soon be super-
seded by Lord Hood. There was a bowl of fruit on the table,
mainly grapes, and one of nuts, evidence that one thing he
had heard was true: that the man cared much for his belly.

'I see a pretty little ship in your wake, Captain Barclay.'
Hotham sat forward slowly, selected a grape with great care,
then sat back and put it in his mouth. 'Am I to assume you
have enjoyed some good fortune?'

This was said with studied indifference, as though it was
of no account whatsoever. Hotham was near to lounging in
his chair as he added an apathetic stare to the question,
which made Ralph Barclay think that he did not like him.
Mind Hotham was not alone in that; Ralph Barclay had little time for admirals as a breed, the only one he would
speak of with deep respect had been his patron Lord
Rodney, and he was dead.

'Yes, sir, we took her off Finisterre, she being out of La
Rochelle. Her present name is *Chantonnay*.'

'I daresay you wish me to buy her in?'

'Captain Blackstone did say you were somewhat short on
vessels for long range reconnaissance.' And, you black-
guard, he was thinking, if you were due an eighth of the

value, you would not hesitate. 'I would suggest that being completely sound, we took her without a shot being fired, she would be ideal.'

Now it was the turn of the other bowl, and time was taken to crack a walnut. 'I will think upon it.'

Ralph Barclay knew he had an ace up his sleeve, and he played it straight away. 'I have, regretfully sir, to report some losses, particularly of officers.'

The eyebrows rose slowly. 'Without a shot being fired?'

'This was a different affair, sir. After an engagement with another French privateer, this time off the coast of Brittany, I lost my second lieutenant, though the Premier is still alive, albeit at death's door.'

'Explain.' Hotham said abruptly, sitting forward, his chewing stopped. He stayed in that listening position as the tale was recounted, the filleted version that put Ralph Barclay in a good light.

'My losses in crew I have made up from the capture of that barque, though I would be obliged if I could distribute them through the fleet in exchange for other seamen since I take no comfort sailing with so many Frenchmen aboard.' Hotham nodded, and Ralph Barclay knew he would sail on with a full complement made up in the main of proper British tars. He then added, his eyes firmly fixed on the admiral's ruddy and handsome face, 'But in the article of officers, sir, I am of course at your disposal for advice.'

Hotham did not beam, he was too experienced to react, but his visitor knew he would be damned pleased. Of the eight lieutenants aboard *Britannia*, a high proportion would be there because of some connection to him, for William Hotham was the surest route to promotion. Lieutenants on flagships nearly always got first pick of anything going. Then there were captains in some of the anchored ships who had a claim on Hotham's good offices, and they would have what they saw as lieutenants deserving of promotion. An admiral gained prestige from his ability to advance his followers and their dependants – not just commissioned officers but those holding warrants as well. So early in a war the twin creators of opportunity, sickness and death in battle, had yet to take effect, so by offering him the chance to fill *Brilliant*'s vacancies, Ralph Barclay was gifting the admiral a real favour.

'Who have you put into the prize?'

'The Premier of my fellow escort HMS *Firefly*. She is commanded by Lieutenant Davidge Gould.' Giving Gould his true naval rank sent a message to Hotham, who hardly needed it. Gould being only a Master and Commander, not a Post Captain, could safely be ignored in whatever calculations were being made in Hotham's mind. 'That vessel too is mainly crewed by Frenchmen, though I hope a redistribution will take place at the Rock.'

'We will see to that, Captain Barclay, if it is not so. Too high a proportion of Frenchmen on any vessel is hardly conducive to fighting efficiency. And who knows, some of them may elect to be taken to a prison hulk rather than serve with us.' Hotham popped a quick grape, then added, 'Do you wish me to give you a list of available candidates for promotion?'

'I doubt I know them, sir, while you do, or at least the captains who serve under you do.' And you have got three plums to give out, Ralph Barclay was thinking, which will ripple right through the fleet and do you no harm whatever; quite a bit of good fortune before Hood arrives. 'I am therefore willing to be advised.'

The nuances of what Ralph Barclay was saying were clear to Hotham, he was sure of that. If he knew anything about *Brilliant*'s captain, he would know how much his career had suffered by his attachment to Rodney. Not only was the late admiral dead, but he had caused many a scandal when alive – not a problem to the likes of Ralph Barclay, who saw it only as the flawed side of genius – but meat and drink to those who loathed everything Rodney did and stood for, one of those being Lord Hood, who was close to being implacable about Barclay's old mentor. Given the serious disagreement he and Hood had had before HMS *Brilliant* weighed from the Nore, first over the appointment of the frigate's officers and then in regard to manning, with him coming out to command, Ralph Barclay was in need of some protection from Hood's ill-will.

Hotham nailed the point, though the face, including his deep brown eyes, was a study in forced blandness. 'I seem to recall you served with Rodney?'

'I did, sir. I owe to him my rise within the service. He arranged my examination for lieutenant and it was on station in the Caribbean that he exercised his right as a commanding admiral to raise me to Post rank.'

'You were with him at the Saintes?'

'In a frigate, sir, not in the line of battle.'

Ralph Barclay had a vision then of the channel between Guadeloupe and Martinique, and the Isles de Saintes which had given that encounter its name. The hot Caribbean sun, the sparkling sea, the din and smoke as the great ships clashed, the sudden shift in the wind that had given George Rodney his opportunity, which meant that when it was all over he had smashed the enemy, taken five French line of battle ships, and Ralph Barclay and the other frigate captains were picking dead Frenchmen out of the warm sea, not their own countrymen.

'It was a fine victory. The nation owes the late admiral a debt of gratitude.'

'Naturally, I agree, sir.'

Hotham sat bolt upright. 'I shall recommend some officers to you. Please, if you object to any one of them, say so.'

'That is handsome of you, sir.'

Hotham nodded at what was a rather obsequious remark. 'My only question is this. Do you wish to retain whoever it is who is acting as your Premier, for that will have some bearing on my choice?'

'Lieutenant Digby is too junior to retain the position, sir.'

'But?' Hotham asked, because Ralph Barclay was frowning in a way that implied that this presented a difficulty.

It did, for Digby deserved something, having carried out his duties with efficiency. He was too junior to be made up to First Lieutenant, but Ralph Barclay could imagine that his wife would be far from pleased if he got nothing. They were friendly, too damned friendly, but quite apart from that Digby had been witness to the events off the Brittany coast, as well as those to do with that pest John Pearce. Left in place he could prejudice the men Hotham promoted against their captain. The fact that Digby, like Roscoe, had been foisted on him by Samuel Hood clinched his resolve to be rid of him.

'Might I suggest, sir, that his lot would be improved enough by a place on the flagship?'

Hotham rubbed his chin then, the slightly bulbous brown eyes looking away, his hand toying with another walnut. It was an easy request to grant; *Britannia*'s captain would be a fool to disagree, but convention demanded he made it look like a difficult one. Finally he nodded.

'So be it. You will have a new suite of lieutenants, Captain Barclay. I will arrange for you to meet them this afternoon, when you come to dinner.'

'One more thing, sir. I have my wife with me.'

'A little more female company will brighten up my cabin, Captain Barclay.' Sensing the curiosity he added. 'There are other ladies coming, so by all means fetch your wife along. Who knows, we might name that barque you brought in after her.'

That finished the bargain, as Ralph Barclay knew it would. Hotham was going to buy in the prize and gift it to someone else he wished to advance, yet another officer who would know to whom he owed his good fortune, and one who would in times to come, act accordingly. But most important of all, he had signalled, without actually having to say the words, that Ralph Barclay no longer lacked for influence. He had been, if the word was not inappropriate, adopted. In time Hotham would repay the debt he owed, and work hard to promote the officer before him into a bigger and better ship.

Emily Barclay had no need to be nervous, but she was, as her husband's cutter took them to the flagship. Again he was piped aboard, saluted by a file of marines coming smartly to "present arms", she receiving a very deep bow from the receiving lieutenant. Nelson's boat came alongside before they departed, so introductions were in order.

'Captain Horatio Nelson, my dear.'

'Mrs Barclay,' Nelson said, startlingly blue eyes wide, before bending over her proffered hand. 'I last saw you dancing in Sheerness.'

Yes, Emily thought, looking down at the top of the bared head, and the thick, rather untidily tied blond hair. You sneaked on me to my husband, telling him what a good time I had and implying, no doubt, that I was being flighty.

Nelson stood to receive what was a cold stare, her husband, standing to one side, unable to keep the amused smile off his face at the confusion the glare caused. He was not fond of Nelson for many reasons: though not far ahead of him on the captain's list he had a ship-of-the-line not, like him, a frigate; his connections were sound and included Barclay's *bête noire*, Sam Hood. Then there was the sloppy way he ran his ships, the fact that he could not hold his drink, but most of all for the way that the pint-sized little sod always behaved to him as though they were friends, which was the exact opposite of the true state of their relationship. Mind he did that with everyone, and Ralph Barclay was sure he was cordially disliked because of it.

'I think we should go on up, my dear. We must not keep the admiral waiting.'

They left Nelson standing, which was a snub, for the proper thing to do would have been to insist that they ascend the companionway together. Seemingly feeling rather foolish, Nelson followed in their wake.

'He looks too small to be a naval captain, husband,'

Emily whispered. 'Indeed he is more like a boy than a man.'

Her husband replied in kind. 'I think I said to you before, my dear, that he is best avoided. The man is a bore, who is convinced he is a genius. He also holds some absurd notion that he's attractive to the fairer sex.'

'If you count me amongst them, husband, let me assure you he is not.'

Ralph Barclay was not really listening, he was looking instead at Hotham, who had straightened himself to gain a good inch at the sight of Emily, and there was a flash in the man's eye that spoke volumes. 'I think I can safely say the admiral grants you that station, my dear.'

Hotham came forward to greet Emily warmly, immediately insisting that he was going to place her at his right hand. This occasioned a bit of shifting of the place cards, for it had not been planned until the admiral saw that she was a beauty, not some broad-faced, horse-hipped harridan. Those shifted a place away from Hotham, the consort of the Ambassador and several ladies, wives, sisters and daughters connected to the British merchants who lived in Lisbon, tried hard not to let anyone know they had noticed, or were in any way put out by this, but there was much sharp flicking of fans and glares aimed in Emily's direction. Ralph Barclay, who declined to change his own place, was content. Such people meant nothing; let the admiral drool over his wife, for it was another part of the cement that would adhere him to Hotham.

The lieutenants were introduced, three rather stiff young men called Glaister, Bourne and Mitcham, who would be seated well below the salt. Their new captain bid them come aboard the following day, making a mental note to send Digby in the other direction before they arrived. Then it was time to be seated, to partake of a meal that underlined the admiral's love of good food, and allowed Ralph Barclay to acquaint himself with some of the officers and personages who would be part of the same fleet as he.

Whoever had arranged the menu had clearly given some

thought to local dishes; they had freshly caught sardines grilled over open coals, beefsteaks baked in wine with bacon and capsicums then soused with vinegar so that they sizzled when served, while the main fish dish had been wrapped in vine leaves and came with a strong sauce of anchovies. The wine was from the north of the country, heavy and much stronger than claret, which had several officers drunk well before the cloth was drawn, the ladies departed, and the port and brandy decanters were set out. Nelson, particularly, was affected, growing more garrulous and noisy with each bumper he consumed, but he had always had a light head, and it was not helped by the heat of the crowded cabin.

Ralph Barclay himself took the temperature of the other naval guests. Word would have got round the fleet about the promotions Hotham was arranging and men as experienced as he would have drawn certain conclusions, one being that the captain of HMS *Brilliant* might be a man to cultivate, for he clearly had the ear of the commanding officer and if he did not, they only had to look to the centre of the top table to see that his pretty young wife had the admiral's undisguised admiration.

'I like your admiral, Captain Barclay,' Emily opined, as they waited for their boat to come alongside, 'not least for the praise he heaped upon you. I could not dislike any man who calls you, in such a fulsome way, a gallant officer.'

'Perhaps he will consent to dine with us before he orders me away.'

'Do admirals eat in lowly frigates, husband?'

'They do when they are to be hosted by someone as beautiful as you, my dear.'

Emily, who had her husband's arm, squeezed it. He was not often given to that kind of flattery, being too stiff in himself for raillery, and it was true that the one he had just uttered was due to the fact that he had drunk quite copiously, but it was welcome nevertheless. She too, though nowhere near inebriated, had a warm glow from the wines she had consumed. Let others doubt the wisdom of her marrying a man so many years her senior, and yes there had been an element of family duty in it, but she was determined to make it work, and that was so much easier when husband Ralph was in such a benign mood.

'What was it Nelson said that so upset everybody, by the way?'

'You saw he was drunk?'

'I could hardly fail to, since his voice went up with every glass, but I did not hear what he said that had everyone close to him looking away in embarrassment.'

'He said, in reference to the marriage vows, my dear, that every man is a bachelor east of Gibraltar.'

'How crass.'

'Quite.'

'If you do invite the admiral to dine, don't invite him.'

'I wouldn't dream of it, my dear.'

Henry Digby watched the departure of HMS *Brilliant* with mixed feelings, unsure whether his new station was a promotion or just a sideways move. Life as an eighth lieutenant aboard a 100-gun flagship had its compensations; space in the wardroom, decent food, and the knowledge that as those above him were promoted into other ships he too would eventually be shifted out to another vessel, but it had many drawbacks in the sheer numbers aboard, over eight hundred souls of a lower rank than him, so that the intimacy of small ship life, where you would get to know everyone by name, was lost. Such service was at some stage necessary; he could not expect to spend his life in frigates, but it was the prospect of immediate battle he would miss; ships-of-the-line fought vessels of the same size in fleet actions, and they were rare events indeed.

After only four days to revictual and make good his supplies of wood and water, Ralph Barclay was glad to be away. Lisbon was too tempting a place for a crew with a bit of prize money in the offing, to his new officers who seemed addicted, once the duties of the day were completed, to the whorehouse, but most especially his wife, who could not help but see a bargain in every tiny emporium; lace, furniture, cloth for clothing and drapes, copperwares, functional if not decorative porcelain, in fact everything that in England cost five times more, so that below decks there were dozens of filled crates lined with straw. What was doubly galling was that his frowns of clear disapproval at such expenditure had no discernable effect, which made him wonder what had happened to the creature he had known in England, before and after their nuptials, who had meekly fallen in with whatever he wanted, whether he stated it or not.

There were positives; his crew now had a decent balance between British and foreign hands and he had his full complement in all respects, most notably in the article of proper seamen. Emily had charmed Hotham and most of the senior fleet officers, made manifest by the renaming of the captured *Chantonnay* as HMS *Frome* after the Barclay's home town, while the way he himself had made clear an attachment to the admiral had got him what he wanted most, the dream of every captain, an independent cruise.

He had also made contact with several dealers in specie, and should he be fortunate enough to touch at Lisbon homeward bound, he had been assured that he could count on a cargo of gold and silver to take home with him. Like taking his wife to sea, it was forbidden for the captain of a King's ship to carry private ventures, but the latter was ignored more comprehensively than the former. Gold and silver came in to the Iberian peninsula from the southern Americas, but only realised its true value when shipped to the capital markets of the north, the greatest of which was London. The dealers liked their bullion to be carried in heavily armed vessels, preferably swift sailors and were happy to pay a one and a half percentage fee for carriage of the cargo. Naturally, when these could run into a quarter of a million in value, naval officers queued up to oblige. The number of homebound warships forced to stop at Lisbon for essential repairs might be scandalous, but it was one that was generally treated with a 'blind eye'.

Having cleared the mouth of the Tagus, Ralph Barclay set a course for Cadiz, to drop off a despatch for the officer liaising with Hotham's Spanish allies, an attempt to coordinate the entry of both fleets into the Mediterranean. He would be there long before them, with a ship in good order, a full complement of officers and crew, the comfort of his wife and opportunity begging. He was a happy man.

John Pearce was far from happy; the weather in the northern part of the English Channel was bad, and it had taken a heavy bribe just to get a local fishing smack to put to sea, a far cry from that which the professional smugglers used in these parts. They employed lightly built, twenty-four oared galleys the best of which, he had been assured, could make the twenty five mile crossing, on the right tide, a calm sea and with a following wind, in close to two hours. This was nothing like that; he was on a boat that was really built for inshore fishing, one which made the *Griffin* seem stable, so they were heaving around in the dark, with their passenger locked below and having no idea if they were making any headway, this while he cursed himself for his impatience in not waiting for the weather to moderate. All he was aware of, as he tightened his scarf and wrapped himself in his new cloak, was the stink of long dead fish which permeated the wood of the hull and the constant motion that had no rhythm to it. To top it all, he had been seasick for the first couple of hours, something he had not experienced before and that made him silently promise never to makes jokes at the expense of those afflicted in future, for it was a damned uncomfortable sensation.

He also knew that the boast the master of this tub had made was likely to be just that; he was no real smuggler, only an occasional opportunistic one, and it had been Pearce's money that had persuaded him to put to sea at a time when getting a decent catch from fishing, with the weather foul and likely to remain so, was difficult. The Reverend John Conway, who had arranged matters, had turned out to be a most surprising cleric. He was not only a radical thinker, but had demonstrated a fine talent for forgery. He had produced for his guest a set of papers that looked truly official, a large and very convincing tricolour cockade, as well as the means to pay for both his passage and what difficulties he would meet once across. In the process of trying to get him a boat the divine had introduced him to some of the men who lived off the contraband trade; hard, gimlet-eyed and reserved fellows who said little except to politely refuse a request to carry him to France, whatever the proffered fee. Right at this moment Pearce would have offered a King's ransom for a calm sea state and the right crew and vessel.

'First hint of dawn is on us, friend,' said a voice from a raised hatch above his head. 'Happen we'll get a sight of the coast.'

Pearce bit back the temptation to say, 'Yes, but which one?'

'Hope there's no revenue men around, 'cause they's bound to wonder what we's doing out here in this weather.'

That was a hazard not previously mentioned, and it got Pearce to his feet. Damn the spray that would soak him, cloak and all; if there was any danger he wanted to see it for himself; he also wanted to know if they could get away from it. Quickly he tied his scarf round his hat to keep it on his head and climbed up through the hatch. The north east wind bit into him as he emerged, so icy cold he could easily believe it came all the way from Russia, whipping up short vicious waves that drove under the keel of the fishing smack and lifted it with ease. But that wind had one advantage; it meant clear skies so that there was some visibility from a three-quarter moon, and dawn came with speed, turning the inky sky blue, so that any danger that threatened would be seen at a distance. Soon chilled to the marrow, he looked around him at a deck no more than ten feet in length, with nets rolled at the side to slow the water that ran through the scuppers. There was a single mast well forward, with gaff boom running aft to make the triangle of the main sail and a bowsprit for a small jib. The scraps of canvas were well clewed up and four men, the whole crew, were on the tiller, while another stood, arm wrapped round a stay, in the prow, hand over eyes, searching the horizon. Every one of them had been up all night, for he had occupied the crew quarters alone, yet he had no sympathy; for the money Conway was paying they could go without sleep for days. As the sun rose in the east, Pearce went to join the fellow forward, realised it was the master, and yelled in his ear.

'What chance a revenue cutter?'

He felt the man's warm breath on his ear as he got his reply. 'A fair one, 'cause if'n my reckonin' be correct, we is right on the route to Gravelines, an' that be the main smuggling port on the coast.'

There was temptation to say that he was aware of the name, as a way of letting this man know he was no stranger to such matters, but he decided the effort was too great, and besides, the less this fellow knew of him the less he could blab to others. Pearce stood for a good twenty minutes, watching the sun first edge the earth's surface, and slowly tear itself clear, changing from a fiery red to gold as it did so, and all the while the master kept his vigil. That he did so was a worry, and his next question was put to ease his concern.

'Will they bother to demand we heave to?'

'Never met a nosey bugger of a revenue man that wouldn't.'

'Then let's hope…'

His passenger never finished the sentence, for the fisherman's arm shot out, to a point to larboard of the small prow, and yelled 'Sail'. Before Pearce could respond the man was gone, hurrying down the pitching deck to the wheel, where he could be seen jabbing his hand. That had two men on the ropes that worked the single mainsail, raising it to expose a bit more canvas, while the captain joined the others to push the tiller round on to a more southerly course, the boom immediately adjusted and sheeted home for the new course. Looking to where the man had pointed he saw for himself, as both the smack and the other vessel rose on their respective waves, the point of a cream coloured sail.

There was no way of knowing what it was and even he, who still considered himself a lubber, knew they were on one of the main trade routes of the North Sea, for the Royal Navy depended on the northern states of the Baltic for half the things needed to keep their ships at sea. The Hanse ports of the North German shore constituted one of the great seaborne cartels in the world and Russia, Sweden and Denmark likewise traded on this route, which carried hundreds of ships a week, so the chances of the sighted sail being a threat seemed to him remote; that it did not to the fishermen was obvious. Whatever course and sail plan he had decided on was now in place, for the master came forward again to shout into his ear, asking him to come below. Back in the cramped and stinking crew quarters, so small they were almost nose to nose, they could at least speak. The master hauled off his foulweather hat to reveal a ruddy, gnarled, ugly face, and, as he spoke, a mouth without a single tooth.

'We're going to try and make the beaches off Dunkirk. It's not where I had in mind to drop you off 'cause you'll have a right old tramp to find a road, and if there be any patrols out they's bound to haul you in.'

'With respect, is this not a little premature?'

'How so?'

'You have yet to positively identify the ship you see as a threat. It could be a merchant vessel or even another fishing smack.'

The jaw rammed shut, the lower lip in such a toothless mouth nearly touching the master's nose and his eyes left Pearce in no doubt that he had been tactless. 'Allow that I can see a topsail for what it is, sir. Now it might be a Hollander warship, or even one of our own, but whoever heard of a merchant captain having his high poles rigged at dawn. No sir, never in life. They is set up for a chase if they sights owt, and I take leave to suggest that if I can see them from my deck, then with lookouts aloft they'll have no trouble, no trouble at all, in seeing us with the sun full on our own canvas.'

'Do we need to run? Even if they are revenue and they come aboard, there's nothing to find.'

'There's you, sir, and I ain't asked you, 'cause it's no part of our bargain, what you are about that needs such a fee to get over the water.'

'I could disguise myself as one of your crew.'

The empty mouth opened in an exaggerated burst of laughter. 'What do you take revenue men for, fools? They know the measure of my boat an' all the others, and they know the crew numbers if not every face. You wouldn't pass for a fisherman in a month of Sundays, for all you have a bit of tar in your palms, even if we could clothe you in someat right. Now you tell me it makes no odds if you're taken back to Sandwich and I'll alter course to close with the buggers, but I take leave to doubt that a man so secret about his travel wants that to happen?'

'Can we outrun them?'

The master nodded, for the question answered his own. 'Depends on our true position, sir, and that is more reckonin' than certainty, but I was hoping to spy a line of dunes as soon as the sun rose enough to light them, so we best get back on deck and see if'n I is right.'

Both emerged and looked east, peering harder as the smack lifted on the swell. The master grabbed hold of one of the hoops that ran up the back of his mast and began to climb, this while Pearce looked at the threat to the north, and saw that it was much closer, not just the highest sails now, but the mainsails below them were visible on the rise.

Halfway up his mast the master stopped and pointed again, his voice carrying to Pearce in spite of the wind. 'Just as I had it.' Then he looked at the sail to the north, before clambering down to put his warm and smelly breath into Pearce's ear. 'It'll be too close a thing to set you ashore without your feet getting wet. We don't draw much water under our keel so I will take us in as close as I dare. Thank Christ the wind is off the land and the tide is falling, for I'd never have got you beached if it were a lee shore.'

'How close in can you get?'

'I doubt you'll have to hang on to your hat, but I don't think you'll get much comfort from your breeches till you find a fire.'

It was an unpleasant thought, wet breeches, a freezing wind and sand, but the alternative was worse, for he would have great difficulty in explaining himself to anyone from the revenue. Indeed, with the clothes he was wearing under his cloak, midshipman blue, he might be taken for a spy. For certain he would be taken back to his home shore, there to be questioned and Pearce doubted if whatever tale he came up with would stand up to much scrutiny. He felt lonely then and wished that his fellow Pelicans, particularly Michael O'Hagan, were around to share his plight. Michael would be as stalwart as always, even useless Rufus would be someone to talk to, and Charlie, when it came to escaping the clutches of the law, had more experience than he. Whatever, he could talk with them, and give some clarity to what was, at this moment, a whirl of confused thoughts in his mind.

The master had gone to a locker by the wheel, and he came back with a battered box that contained a pistol, a powder horn and a small bag of lead balls. 'Do you know how to load this.' Pearce nodded, so the man continued. 'Then you'se got to keep it dry, and fire off a shot at us once you'se on land, and it would be right handy if they was close enough to see the powder from the muzzle. Then I can say you came aboard by surprise like, and forced us to take you to France. It was that or a ball in the guts.'

It was thin, very thin, and the next words the master used underlined that. 'They has to prove we's liars, for we'll all stick to the same tale and you being armed and taking us unawares, we's not likely to know your name. I'll have to say you was in naval garb, that you knew more'n enough to tell us how to sail our boat, and that it was you who set the course. My guess is they will not believe a word of it, but they'll let us go after a bit of chest poking.'

The ship closing with them was hull up now, and, as Pearce, back to the wind, prepared the pistol for firing, the master confirmed it was a revenue cutter, crewed by customs officers who would be afire to take them, for they had a lean time against the men who plied the contraband trade. Those who traded illegally across the Channel knew the waters like the back of their hands, which way the tides ran and the effect of every fluke of wind and if they were in a galley, unless the sea was rough, they could show them a clean pair of heels anytime. Added to that nearly every citizen on both shores was an enemy to them, either selling smuggled goods or trading them to England. There was scarce a house on the East Kent or Essex shore that did not have a hiding place for contraband, and there was not a soul would spit on his neighbour to say what was hidden there. Even the quality were in on the trade, often financing the cargoes, and no faith could be placed in the local magistrates; they were more likely to aid their fellows than some busybody that threatened to bankrupt them. Try as the revenue men might, they rarely found smuggled goods, and it was a red letter day if they made a capture.

The wind had dropped slightly, the rising dunes that were now in plain view taking just the edge off it. The beach ran north and south for miles, and Pearce, once he had confirmed his intention to head inland, questioned the master about what lay beyond.

'There's a highway that runs up the coast, not too far in, but my advice would be to get across that and use the fields to get to the outskirts of Calais, 'cause it's a military road and it is bound to have patrols and barriers manned by them new-fangled National Guards. Beyond that, I don't know.'

Pearce declined to tell him that he did, for he had come to this part of the coast on his way to England less than two months before. He would miss out Calais and head inland for a coach stop at the little village of Ardres, a place that was less likely to be under observation than the main port for cross channel traffic. The shore was close now, the waves breaking across the beach and carrying them south. The master did not seem too worried about this, more concerned to keep his rudder and sails in a position that would prevent the smack from grounding. His last words to Pearce were simply that he could not do more than back his sail to take the way off the boat and that only for a moment. Then he must get away, and tack towards the revenue cutter, to underline the tale that they had all be taken under coercion. Pearce had removed his boots and the captain, having put the now loaded but cocked pistol in one, with a tiny wad of tow between flint and cap, and the powder horn and spare lead balls in the other, tied them round Pearce's neck.

'Roll up your cloak and wrap it round your shoulders, for it will foul you in the water left loose.'

'My ditty bag?'

'Put your hat in it and toss that ashore, is the best way.'

'Thank you,' Pearce said, and the look he added told the master that it was for more than the given advice. 'I have not even asked your name.'

There was just a hint of embarrassment in the reply. 'Nor should you, for I never had a hankering to know yours. As for the passage and the revenue, friend, we can't have anyone saying that Sandwich Town fisher folk don't abide by a paid bargain, that would never do. Now get yourself set, chuck your dunnage and jump when I say, and may God speed you to wherever it is you're in such a hellfire hurry to get to.'

The single sail flapped as it was hauled round, the rudder put hard over to bring the smack up into the wind, then it was a hard tap that told John Pearce it was time. The bag, weighed down by the sextant, flew through the air and he followed, jumping over the side into the icy water that came right up to his lower chest, which made him gasp. At first being in the lee of the smack meant he was under no pressure, but the sail was reset quickly and they were heading offshore which exposed him to the waves. It was a blessing that they pushed him shoreward, but he could feel the undertow that tried to drag his lower half back out again. He came ashore in a series of jumps more than a walk and made it to the flat, sandy beach.

Letting go of his cloak, he turned to look at his saviour, now clawing off with ease, driven by the wind that jagged at Pearce's back. The revenue cutter was in clear view now, the forepeak crowded with men as it raced towards the shore, all sail set. Pearce, not rushing, pulled out his hat and Conway's cockade, which he fixed to the brim. That on his head, he took out the pistol, and after carefully removing the tow while keeping a strong thumb on the hammer, aimed it out to sea and fired. That it was a wasted shot in terms of a threat was obvious; a musket ball would have done no harm to either vessel, let alone a pistol, but there was a satisfying crack and a belch of visible smoke, which was what was required. He just hoped that it would suffice.

With that he put the pistol in his waistband, picked up his boots and turning, headed inland, trying to get himself to think in French, so that if challenged by anyone, he would reply in that language.

Chapter Thirteen

It was easy, trudging across fields on the flat and barren landscape between Calais and Ardres, with what houses existed visible for a mile or more, to forget the upheavals that had gripped France in the last four years, turmoil that would eventually affect even the most isolated farmhouse. No doubt there would be those this far north and west that were unaware of what had happened in Paris; having been exposed to deep rural stupidity all over his homeland, John Pearce had no doubt the same depth of ignorance existed here. Not that the tenor of their lives would be upset by knowledge if they had any; they would likely worry more about the seasons than any Legislative or National Assembly, think more of the health of their livestock before that of a beheaded King or an arraigned aristocrat.

Though cold because of the wind, it was not unpleasant due to the clear blue skies and the sharp sunlight, and given time to ruminate, John Pearce surmised that the two nations were probably not so very different, much as the opposite was trumpeted. The French were Catholic and held to be deeply superstitious, while they were also at the mercy of rapacious abbots, bishops, and feudal lords; was it so very different in Britain? He had witnessed as much foolish belief in demons and evil spirits in shire counties as would exist in any Papist country; most vicars lived very much like French country priests prior to the Revolution, hand to mouth, needing several livings to make ends meet, unlike the princes of the French church who had amassed wealth beyond the dreams of avarice; indeed it was the sequestration of that and the land the church held which had sustained the public purse following the Revolution.

While not as rapacious, neither John Pearce nor his father Adam had ever met an abbot or a bishop in England who was not sleek and well fed, while around their monasteries and palaces people lived on the verge of starvation, and having attended both High Anglican and Catholic liturgies he was at a loss to see much of a difference. He and his father had, on the odd occasion been admitted to the great country estates of Britain's elite, Adam Pearce the radical orator having a certain cachet as a house guest for the outrageously wealthy. The British aristocracy, to his mind, needed no lessons in acquisitiveness from their French counterparts. At some point he stopped his mental condemnation and, with hunger rumbling his belly, he reminded himself that he was being a hypocrite; he liked good food, wine and clothing, interesting conversation, the company of intelligent and beautiful women and right now he would sell the soul he doubted he possessed for a carriage to carry him to Paris.

He had had disputes with his father's friends in the spring and summer of the previous year, about the course events had taken, no longer the dutiful son who agreed with everything Adam Pearce stood for, but a person growing to manhood with his own opinions. How many people had to flee or be proscribed to guarantee the safety of the Revolution? The rise of the good men who had clipped the wings of monarchy had been eclipsed by the subsequent elevation of demagogues who competed with each other to satisfy the dregs of the city, the so-called *enragés* who whipped up the passions of an out of control mob who had come to be called *sans-culottes*. It took time for his father's certainty to waver; Adam Pearce was not about to surrender a lifetime of ideas – which had seen him trudge the length and breath of England to preach – to the reality he saw all around him.

Then, in early August came the butchery and mutilation before the Tuileries Palace, this followed by the September massacres. That was when Adam Pearce, who in between these two events had been offered and declined a seat in the new National Assembly, had spoken out regarding excess, and he had committed his views to paper, arguing against Marat's call in his journal, *The People's Friend,* to engage in

"A merciless struggle with the enemies of the Revolution". He found that the new rulers of France were no more inclined to accept critical opinions than their confrères across the Channel, found that his stock as a long time radical who had suffered for the cause of freedom counted for a lot less than his unwelcome views.

John Pearce mourned for the Paris of the year '91 when freedom had been in the air and yet still there was an atmosphere of elegance and excitement. It was a time when young John, in the salons of the knowledgeable ladies who ran such things, had attracted attention for his youth, manners and fine bearing in a society famous for the laxity of its morals. It was also lax in the matter of hierarchy, so John found himself ordered to amuse the likes of Germaine de Staël or a famous wit like Talleyrand, while they, without condescension, openly sought the views of a young man who was not French, and knew something of the outside world. He thought of the restaurants and cafes where glittering minds and beauty congregated; Ramponneau or Le Tour d'Argent, the exciting cuisine of *Les Frères Provençaux*; there were tableaux, theatres, balls and the great festivals celebrating freedom.

Dozens of encounters surfaced from his memory as he trudged across the muddy unploughed fields, of meals consumed and wines drunk, sometimes to excess, of beautiful women and opportunities both taken and missed, the warmest being of Amelie Labordière, the lady, ten years his senior, who had become his mistress, though he recalled that he had been the victim of a seduction rather than the initiator. Her husband was too busy with his own liaisons to care that his wife had taken a lover, nor did he mind that she spent some of his money on presents that turned a gauche young man into a bit of a dandy. It was too good to last; he had watched those salons thin out and cease; it was no longer sensible to openly debate the rights and wrongs of the regime, or to show even a hint of wealth, grace and good manners. Then Amelie and her husband had disappeared, saying nothing to anyone; one day she was there, laughing, sensuous with delightful vulgarity, the next, like so many others, she was gone. Where he did not know; all he could hope was that her escape had been successful.

The Paris he was going back to was a place of caution if not downright fear, of food riots and increasingly authoritarian government. The thought that came to him then, as he approached the hamlet of Ardres, was that this was the simple part of his journey, alone with only the odd distant peasant to observe his passing; from now on it would get more difficult until he reached the capital itself, at which point it might become deadly. Yet nothing outlined the difference between Britain and France more than what lay straight ahead. He had crossed half of southern England at risk only from his own loose tongue; there were no barriers or officious busybodies demanding to know his name and his reason for travel. He was less than ten miles inside France, and that obstacle, the first of many he knew he would encounter, stood before him. But he had to go through it, had to get off country fields and on to the road, where he could take a coach from the local auberge, which lay just beyond, it being a regular stop for a change of horses on the St Omer to Calais road.

The scruffy quartet of National Guardsmen who manned the Ardres crossroads, crowded round a flaming brazier, watched Pearce approach, and he could almost feel them, as they looked him up and down, assessing his worth. The cloak which he had acquired was of reasonable quality, but had fortunately, like his shoes, suffered from the cross country mud and the need to force his way through hedgerows. He let it fall open to reveal the poor quality of his short blue naval coat, so faded from the original deep blue as to be unidentifiable in terms of which nation he belonged to. The canvas ditty bag he carried over his shoulder likewise pointed to a young man in straitened circumstances.

His tale was ready, and, thanks to the Reverend Conway

and his skill with pen and paper, as well as the language, he had papers to show that he was a French sailor heading home. He had the advantage that he was heading inland, not towards the coast, so he was unlikely to be an émigré fleeing to safety, but most of all, as he examined the men manning the barrier that stretched across the road, and saw the threadbare nature of their once bright uniforms, he had in his palm a gold coin and he was sure that would, in the event he could not persuade them otherwise, see him through better than any explanation.

'Bonjour, bon soir,' he said, as the men straightened into some semblance of a military posture. The one in charge, a portly fellow with a substantial moustache over a fat face held up a hand for him to stop and demanded to know if he had any papers. Pearce pulled Conway's folded letter from his pocket and presented it, with an imposing anchor-shaped seal over a three strand tricolour ribbon of the same material that made up his cockade, that surmounted by a florid signature. Very likely it would not stand up to too rigorous an examination, but one advantage lay in the fact that in the many changes of government there were no papers of the kind that existed in monarchical times, so that made up documents could rarely be nailed as outright forgeries. If the fellow could read, which Pearce doubted, he would see that *Capitaine de Vaiseau*, Henri Dumont, had given permission for *sous-officier* Jean-Louis Martin, a good Republican, to leave his ship and proceed to Paris to attend to his dying father. The blue coat, the tricolour cockade he had fitted to his hat, and the sextant poking out from his ditty bag all proclaimed his profession; the letter gave good reason for his being away from the sea.

The guard grunted as he read, trying to give the impression he understood every word, but merely confirming Pearce's suspicion that he was illiterate. What the man said next, about the necessity of the holder of this letter needing to wait until his officer came on duty, underlined that. When Pearce enquired, only to be told that the officer

might or might not come by next morning, he began, first
to plead, then to sob, informing all the guards of the par-
lous state of his father's health and of his deep need to see
him before he expired. It was a telling tale to a Frenchman,
for Pearce knew how they felt about family; that they had
an almost mystical attachment to blood relations and a pas-
sion, almost amounting to morbidity, regarding attendance
at the point of death. Taking his interlocutor a little away
from his fellows, Pearce explained that there was an inheri-
tance to protect as well, working on the other subject for
which the French had a mystical regard. It was hardly surprising, in the light of such a thing, that he was willing to
pay to avoid being delayed, and the expert way the National
Guardsman palmed the half-guinea coin from Pearce's hand
was sound evidence that it was not the first time he had
accepted a bribe.

   The barrier was lifted without further ado and John
Pearce, passing a rather limp and forlorn liberty tree – that
symbol of Revolution imported from America – walked
through to the low, thatched inn that was the Auberge d'
Ardres, where he could eat lobster and wait for a coach,
leaving the quartet of guards to split his *douceur* and laugh
at the way they had dunned their officer.

Public travel had to be given up when he got close to Paris;
Abbeville had been tricky, Amiens worse, for all the talk on
the coach and at each stop was of trouble in Lyon and a
Royalist uprising in the Vendée, so suspicion, never far
away, was heightened. Now, near the capital, there were too
many stops, too many interrogations, too many officials
with sharp eyes and the temperament to hold him up indef-
initely until his papers could be checked. So he first saw the
windmills that covered the hill of Montmartre from the
back of a farm wagon, having cadged a lift from a farmer
heading in to the vegetable market to sell his produce, winter greens that had that smell of over-used and never
washed stockings. Hat, cloak and coat buried under the
produce, and grimy from three days of travelling, he looked

and felt like a peasant. The driver was a garrulous soul, who wished his passenger to know that he had a wife he hated, a useless sod of a son and two daughters he would gladly give away if he had the money for a dowry. This chatter suited his passenger, who wanted to avoid thinking of his reasons for being here.

Almost the whole three-day journey had had him gnawing at the conundrum of how he was to effect the removal of his father and get him home. A second note from Horne Tooke, delivered in Sandwich, had told him that he was in the Conciergerie, an old medieval royal palace on the Ile de la Cité that had been a prison for four hundred years. The place had been over-crowded before John had left and was hardly likely to be less so now, well guarded because it held the supposed enemies of the Revolution. The easiest way to get him out of there was intervention by a higher authority, the other way, a bribe, would need to be so massive it was probably beyond his means to pay; indeed he wondered just how much he would have to expend just to get to see him. If he occasionally toyed with the idea of a daring rescue it was only that; he knew the place too well, towering as it did over the river, and plainly visible from the opposite bank. Tell himself as he might that continual deliberating on it would produce no solutions, that he would have to wait until he was actually in the vicinity to decide, did not stop him from doing so, and the closer he got to the city gate, the worse it became.

The walls of Paris, surrounded by endless rows of housing, looked imposing, but they were of another age. Yet they still preserved their function, and the Porte de St Denis was no exception; it had a full complement of National Guards, properly uniformed and armed, and imperious in their authority, none more so than the officer who commanded them, a choleric looking individual, with an outrageous cockade in his hat, who strode around with his sword scabbard slapping his highly polished boots, all to create the impression that he was ensuring the men under his command examined properly anyone who wished to enter or leave the city. At least Pearce did not have to guess this time; he knew for certain just how venal this lot were, knew that like every fellow who manned the numerous gates that surrounded Paris, the high coloured officer had probably paid a lot of money for this posting, funds which could only be recouped in one way. This was not the National Guard of the now fled Lafayette, but the successor, manned by rapacious rogues, not honest citizen soldiers. They were on the Belgian border or the Rhine, fighting the Prussians and the Austrians.

So every trader paid their dues, and passed the cost on to the citizens of a capital that seethed with fear of speculators. Quite likely émigrés, should there still be any, could get out of Paris as long as they had the funds and made the proper arrangements in advance, the sum based on their need and their implied crimes, which was why the men who now ran France, and suffered from the delusion as to the number of their enemies, tried to make sure they were locked up before they could escape. Enemies of the Revolution entered Paris even more easily, for the *fonctionnaires* who manned the gates saw it as no part of their duty to protect anything other than their investment. There was a risk; every so often they would ostentatiously apprehend some individual, almost certainly someone without the means to pay a bribe, and march him off to the nearest prison. Guilt or innocence mattered less than appearances; the gatekeepers of Paris had to be seen to be doing their duty.

Pearce got through for a bundle of paper *assignats*, the heartily disliked currency of the Revolution, money which went down in value on a daily basis, a stack of which he had exchanged for one golden guinea in St Omer. Another couple of guineas had got him some pre-Revolutionary coinage, which he needed to buy food, and was useful where an inducement, most in his case, was not worth the expenditure of more than silver or copper. His vegetable grower lost two boxes of cabbages from the back of his wagon, and though he cursed the robbing bastards who taxed him, he did so in a very soft voice that they could not hear. In fairness, Pearce gave him some of his *assignats* to alleviate the loss.

Near the vegetable market, still north of the Seine, he retrieved his garments from their hiding place and parted company from the grateful farmer, disappearing into the maze of narrow streets that constituted the Marais section of the city. From there he made his way down the Rue du Temple to the river, and looked with a creeping sense of despair at the walls of the Conciergerie, at the constant stream of people coming and going through the great gate, before crossing the twin parts of the Seine by the Pont Neuf, past Notre Dame, and heading for the Quartier St Généviere behind the University of Paris, where he and his father had lived for two years.

At the house which contained the apartment his father had rented, three floors up in the Rue St Etienne de Gres, he found a broken lock on the street door, with whatever the place had contained, furniture and possessions, looted. The two lower floors, occupied by a maker of coach lamps and his plump wife, had been comfortably furnished, better than that with which he had endowed the floor he rented. Now, what had not been taken had been smashed or wrecked, not that there was much of that, some broken chairs, torn drapes and the shards of a mirror; they looked as if they had suffered in the rush to steal rather than been left for lack of value. Up the stairs he went, knowing that he would, likewise, find his own and his father's possessions gone.

It saddened him to stand at the open door and survey what had become of the place in which he had so recently lived. It had been cold in winter and too damned hot in summer, but it represented the only home he could truly say he had shared with his father, for in Paris their travelling existence had stopped, and even if Adam Pearce had things to do, he was, for the first time in many years, free from responsibilities. Regardless of what was happening outside the cracked panes of glass on the windows it had been a place from which a youngster might come and go knowing that there was some constancy in his life. Right now it was too painful to look at the bare floor boards stripped of oil-cloth, the empty grate of the fire by which his father was wont to work in winter, oblivious to the smoke which never ever wholly made its way up the chimney or the missing desk by the window, which was flooded by daylight when the sun shone.

Pearce turned, went back downstairs and secured the front door, jamming it shut with a sliver of broken timber, wondering about the owners. Had they fled, or been arrested, denounced for a trade that served the wealthy, or worse, caught up just because his father had been arraigned? Whatever, they were gone, so he had a place to lay his head, albeit on a bare floor with nothing but the rags of those torn drapes to cover him. The well in the backyard still functioned, a scoop still in the bucket. There was broken timber for a fire to heat water in, so using the shards of mirror he was able to wash and shave and that completed, and having hidden his pistol and other possessions in the rear courtyard, he set out to see what he could find. The result was depressing; most houses he called at were either empty or occupied by grubby strangers, who were happy to imply that the previous owner was *sans tête*.

Others, people who had been friends to Adam Pearce in the past, refused to open their doors to the son of a man in prison, lest some sharp eye spotted the connection and denounced them. The church house in Cluny where his tutor, the Abbé Morlant, had lived, was a gutted, burnt out shell, with no one passing willing or able to tell him why or how it had happened. The old Abbé had, of course, refused to take the Oath to the Constitution demanded by the state, and had thus earned the dubious honour of becoming what was called a non-juring priest, a man loyal to Rome, not the Revolution. He crossed the river to the Hotel de Ville to see if he could find anyone who might intercede, only to find his way blocked by a crowd of supplicants, all with a grievance, a complaint or seeking a favour from the men who held the power in Paris Commune.

It was impossible to miss the fear that permeated the entire citizenry. Paris had been a city of laughter, the streets as full of costermongers, jugglers, fire-eaters and hucksters as it was of beggars, pickpockets and thieves. Now it seemed full of the destitute. Nowhere was this more obvious than around the Palais-Royale, home to the one-time Duc d'Orleans, now the self-styled Philippe Egalité who had voted for the death of his royal cousin. The colonnaded passages that surrounded the palace had been home to all sorts of whores and pimps, pornographers, writers of scurrilous pamphlets, silver and goldsmiths, purveyors of luxury goods, and charlatans passing off everything from useless patent medicines to false religious relics. It was from the Café du Foy that Camille Desmoulins had started the riot that led to the fall of the Bastille.

The Palais-Royale had not only survived the fall of that Royal prison, it had seemed to thrive on it, its cafes and restaurants and walkways filled to overflowing. Only the pornographers were left now, selling tales old and new of the supposed debauchery of the Queen and the ladies of the court; they, the whores, the pimps and the vendors of the dozens of news sheets which flooded the city, spewing forth bile. Most had long since ceased to be purveyors of news if you excepted listing, as they did, those who had been condemned to the guillotine, and had become organs for the various ranting editors. Denunciation stood at the core of their polemics, of anyone remotely tainted by their own less than objective standards, that and demands for more radical reforms to the way the nation was run, in reality a plea by those who penned them to be elevated to a station where they could put their ideas into action.

Further on along the Rue de Faubourg St Honoré lay the

Jacobin Club and Pearce stopped to look at the message
above the door; a mockery, for there was no *Humanité,*
Indivisibilité, Liberté, Egalité or *Fraternité* that he could
feel, only the kind of naked power that reduced the people
to beggars after justice. He turned away from that, momentarily debating the worth of making for the National
Assembly, housed in the Tuileries Palace, when a voice
addressed his back.

'Young Monsieur Pearce, is it not?'

John froze, turning slowly, not knowing whom he was
about to encounter. The man looking at him had a handsome if somewhat florid face, thick red lips and, as he
placed the name, a dark colouring that betokened his southern upbringing. He was well dressed, almost dandyish in
burgundy silk, which seemed a dangerous thing to be in
such times when black was the colour of choice, but he also
seemed to have an assurance that such display, in his case at
any rate, was acceptable. The lips were smiling and there
was no animosity in the dark brown eyes.

'Monsieur de Cambacérès.'

'Indeed.'

He had met Régis de Cambacérès many times, because he
was a man who frequented the same salons as those which
welcomed young Monsieur Pearce, though John had always
tried to avoid too close an association with the man,
because, although interesting in a firebrand sort of way, he
was a well known and quite open pederast. That he had
gravitated, in those salons, towards a handsome young fellow and engaged him in conversation was to be expected,
but it was under no circumstances, however enlightening,
to be encouraged.

'I was given to understand that you had left Paris.'

'You know about my father?'

'Sadly, yes.' That was examined for hypocrisy, but to
Pearce it seemed genuine, as Cambacérès added, 'Walk with
me. It does not do these days to be seen standing and talking in the street. Suspicious minds, of which we have an

abundance, see conspiracy everywhere, even in innocent conversation.'

'You have come from the Jacobin Club?'

'I have,' Cambacérès sighed. 'I swear the place becomes more tedious by the day.'

As they began to walk, John remembered a conversation he had had with his father about this man, with old Adam wondering how the one time deputy to the Legislative Assembly had survived when so many of his contemporaries had fled. Régis de Cambacérès had been an original electee to the States General in '89, had taken the famous oath in the Tennis Courts, had been, if not at the forefront of the Revolution, a leading light. Vain, highly intelligent, not given to holding his tongue when he saw political chicanery, he had become a member of the National Assembly as well, voting openly for the death of King Louis, yet not afraid to denounce those who shared the odium of that ballot if he felt they were less than true to the revolutionary purity he saw as essential. The man, in short, was a survivor.

'It was unwise of your father to publish his views.'

'Nothing would stop him,' Pearce replied. Cambacérès obviously detected the slight weariness in that reply, for he looked at his young companion keenly. 'It has been his way all his life, and at least he has been in prison before.'

'I doubt even an English jail would prepare him for what he faces now?'

'What does he face?'

'It is small consolation,' the Frenchman said, avoiding the question, 'to observe that he is in excellent company. I daresay with the quality of mind that these rabid dogs have incarcerated, the highest level of debate in Paris today is in its prisons.'

Pearce thought it not the sort of remark you made at a time like this if you wanted to be safe. Indeed it was exactly the kind of expression of opinion that had probably seen his father arrested. 'Are you still a member of the Assembly, monsieur?'

'I am, and of the Committee of Public Defence, which is supposed to be the guardian of the Revolution.'

'Can my father be got out of the Conciergerie?'

Cambacérès stopped, and looked at the younger man. 'You are asking me if I have the power to intervene?'

'I am.'

'Alas, I fear not. Indeed at this very moment Danton and my pretty young friend St Just are conspiring to edge me off the aforesaid Committee, since they find the way I disagree with them so frequently unpalatable. They are in the process of forming a new body, of which I suspect I will not be a member.'

'Who then?'

'Danton could do it, but you must understand, young Jean, that he has Mayor Pache and the beasts of the Paris Commune at his heels, watching his every move, who want to cut off the head of everyone in France with either blue blood or a brain. Quite apart from that the air is full of treachery. No one trusts our generals not to surrender to the Austrians or Prussians, Lyon and Marseilles refuse to accept the writ of Paris, and there is a full scale effort to restore the monarchy in the Vendée.'

'I believe he was denounced by a man called Fouché.'

The reply was non-committal. 'Was he?'

'Could I appeal to him?'

'He is not in Paris. Fouché has been sent to Lyon as a Representative on Mission.' Seeing the look of confusion on John Pearce's face, Cambacérès explained about this new revolutionary office. 'They carry with them the power of the Committee of Public Defence, soon, I believe, to be renamed Public Safety, and they have the power to impose the Revolution by whatever means are necessary. But I am bound to say, even if he was here, he is a loathsome creature, to whom I doubt any appeal would be successful.'

'I need help.'

'I can offer you hospitality, food, a place to lay your head, but not more. I desire to keep my head on my shoulders and pleading for someone denounced by a fellow member of the Jacobin Club, however odious, is not the way to achieve that. There are too many voices in the Assembly looking for victims, so that they may prove the purity of their own revolutionary credentials.'

'It is kind of you, but no.'

The slight smile on Cambacérès' thick red lips was wet and unattractive. 'You fear for your virtue?'

Pearce did not want to offend this man, it being a bad idea to do so when he had no notion what tomorrow would bring. 'Let me just say that, with all the other things I have to worry about, I would not want to add that to the list.'

'Politely put, young man,' the Frenchman replied with good humour. 'I recall you had a deft turn of phrase. The offer stands, if you should need it. My home is just along from the Jacobins in the Rue de Faubourg St Honoré. It is open to you should you need it, and you have word that hospitality is all I will offer you.'

'Thank you,' John replied, 'now I must go and see if I can visit my father.'

'Then I wish you both good luck.'

Chapter Fourteen

Dispirited, he made his way back past the Louvre and along the banks of the Seine, crossing the Pont Neuf once more to westernmost point of the Ile de la Cité, a walk around the Conciergerie depressing him even further. The walls were thick, the windows – heavily barred at ground level – were small, the gates massive, closed and well guarded. Eyeing the place provided no solutions as to how to get someone free, but the escorted tumbrel that came out of the massive gate on the far side, with six miserable looking souls stood up in it, two women and four men, hands tied behind their backs, provided an even more telling reason to do something, though a quick search of the faces relieved him of the worry that his father might be amongst them.

As soon as the passers-by spotted them, they reached for some of the abundant filth that lay in the streets and began to pelt the prisoners, and the names they used to denigrate these poor unfortunates left Pearce in no doubt as to their station or their fate; they were condemned souls, being taken across and along the bank of the river to le Place de la Revolution, where a gathering crowd and a guillotine awaited them. With a sinking heart he watched them as they rattled over the cobbles, only the bonds that lashed them to the cart keeping them upright, drums playing as their solemn escort marched them to their death. One woman sobbed uncontrollably, the others looked straight ahead in studied defiance. The men had their heads bowed and all were in filthy rags that had once been fine clothes, evidence of long incarceration. Who where they, what had they done? Probably little, and certainly nothing to warrant the loss of their heads. He fought a morbid desire to follow them; he had seen enough of executions before he left Paris nearly two months before, including that of the King.

Yet the sight of that tumbrel gave urgency to his needs and he made his way to the Café St Florien, which lay

across a short bridge to the Ile St Louis, the place where
those with business at the Conciergerie took their refresh-
ments. If food was short in Paris, there seemed no evidence
of it here; everyone seemed to be able to eat their fill as long
as they had the means to pay. It was busy with noisy advo-
cates, who were determined not to confine their arguments
to a court of law, of men with hooded eyes who looked like
functionaries of the state, they who would execute the warrants issued by the demagogues who now ruled France, and
who looked at him as if measuring him for arrest. There
were, too, sad-eyed looking individuals, men and women
who, no doubt like him, had relatives behind the massive
walls that surrounded the nearby prison. It was they who
identified for him the men he must talk to, as they sought
favours from the *gardiens* who manned the world beyond
the gates, and who used this place to trade for the right to
either news of a relative or a visit.

One seemed more approachable than the rest, a heavy-
jowled fellow in a leather waistcoat and a grubby cap of liberty, with a stomach so huge that it defied gravity, that surmounted by a thick belt which had on it a ring for the keys
he had left behind. He approached him once the others supplicants had finished, to be greeted by a raised eyebrow and
a cynical sneer on a near round face that spoke volumes.
Here was a fellow who knew he was cock-of-the-walk, a
man who could demand and get obeisance from those to
whom he might formally have had to grovel. His love of the
power he wielded was so obvious that Pearce had to stifle
the temptation to clout him and wipe that smirk off his
face, his body shaking with the tension that emotion produced. It was doubly galling that the trembling seemed to
be evident in his voice, which was taken by the *gardien* to
represent fear.

'I want to go in to the prison.'

A flick of the head preceded the reply, given in the kind
of gutter French from the eastern part of the city that
would have been incomprehensible to anyone who had not

lived in Paris, and the smell of his breath was redolent of garlic and stale wine. 'There be one or two here'll take you in if you so desire.'

John deliberately juggled a number of coins in his hand, the dull sound of which made the man narrow his eyes, which led Pearce to wonder how often he was offered real money instead of *assignats* or goods in kind. Clearly he knew the sound of gold from that of copper and silver.

'My father is in there.'

Suddenly he was all concern. 'Then keep your voice down, for those same men will have you up. Blood relative to a prisoner is enough. What is his name?'

'Pearce, Adam. Not French.'

He looked at him keenly then, to see if the name made any impression. There were a lot of people in the crowded prison, probably well over a thousand, that he knew, but someone not of French nationality should stand out. Nothing in the blank expression obliged.

'A foreigner?'

Pearce nodded, 'I assume it is possible.'

'It is, if the fee be right,' then, annoyingly, he smirked again. 'Seein' as it has to get you out again.'

'English gold.'

That was a risk, but one he had to take. The man did not even blink. 'As good as any?'

'One in, and another when I come out.'

The heavy jowled cheeks shook slowly. 'Two to go in and out, paid here and now.'

That was steep, but being in no position to bargain, Pearce nodded, yet he did wonder at the sense of what he was doing, knowing that he might himself never get out again. Not for the first time since leaving Colbourne's ship he was conscious of being alone, without support, so he added, 'I will want to visit him more than once.'

The *gardien* nodded to indicate he understood the message; that there was more gold to come and Pearce resolved that after he had seen his father, he would ask this turd how much of a bribe it would take to get the old man out. He might not have enough, there might not be a sum that was enough, but there was no harm in knowing. Before they left he bought some bread, cheese and a straw-covered flagon of wine. Having been incarcerated before, he knew that they would be welcome.

Let in through a heavily guarded postern door that opened onto the Rue du Palais, John Pearce was glad he had not given much consideration to a daring rescue. There had been escapes from the Paris prisons, but that had been in the early days of proscription, before those in charge got their regime properly organised. Walking beside the stout, waddling *gardien*, Pearce surmised he had been a royal gaoler before he had become a revolutionary one; he had that air about him of a man long in his occupation. Nods were exchanged at the next gate, silent looks that no doubt told his fellows warders that there was a share of something good for letting them through. It was how they made their living, that and fleecing the prisoners for every favour granted. They were cast from the same mould as the Bridewell warders he and his father had had to deal with in London, and while one part of Pearce saw that they had little choice if they were to eat, he could not fathom what sort of man would choose such a life as an occupation. The last postern gate led into a vaulted guardroom and the *gardien* took him through a side door from that.

'Can't use the Great Hall,' he said. 'Tribunals sitting.'

'What tribunal?'

As soon as he said that Pearce cursed himself for an unguarded comment, for it had the potential to engender suspicions in the *gardien*'s mind which he would rather not raise. The Paris he had lived in before was daily awash with rumours of plots and daring rescues, mostly of the royals. Few, if any, were true, but that did not stop the mill of rumour fabricating and disseminating them.

'Where you been, the moon?' the *gardien* sneered. 'The Revolutionary Tribunal, that God willing, now that it is sitting permanent, is going to chalk the doors and clear some of the folk out of this place, 'cause I tell you no lie when I say it is bursting at the seams.'

'I have been away from the city.'

'Then you missed them doin' what should have been done this last year. Stands to reason you can't just keep takin' traitors up without the sods going somewhere, not that a few don't die right here. The tribunal will do the trick. Drag 'em in and if they're innocent, not that there's many of those, they're free. If not, then it's straight out the door to execution and good riddance.'

These words echoed off the walls of a series of dank, dimly lit corridors, which finally brought them to a court-yard surrounded by high walls and windows, crowded with humanity, the hub of noise dying as all eyes fixed on the pair just come through the last postern gate. With a shock John Pearce realised that the look on their faces was one of terror, not curiosity. They feared the call to that tribunal the *gardien* had talked about, to be followed by the tumbrel and the blade, and this is how it would come to them, except it would be a man with their name on a piece of paper.

'One sandglass, then I'll come back for you. Be waiting for me, for I shan't wait on you.'

As he moved forward, the crowd parted, no one, given they had no idea who he was, wanting to make eye or bod-ily contact, in case he was the representative of the Grim Reaper. In his cloak, hat and his bold tricolour cockade he probably looked like one, and he would have removed the latter so as to appear less threatening if he had not been clasping the provisions he had bought. Scanning the faces, looking for his father, he could not help but notice how much faded grandeur there was in the person and clothes of some of those who looked away, of the same sort as he had seen in that tumbrel. Once beautiful women looking hag-gard, their dresses turned to rags, men of all ages in *ancien régime* coats that had once been bright but were now dun coloured and dirty. Those who had once been fat now had folds of skin hanging off them in the same manner as their now too large clothes, and it took no great insight to see that everyone here was close to starving.

He would have asked where they slept and where they eased themselves if the stench and the bundles of untidy straw that lined the outer walls did not make that unnecessary and he surmised that each morning some of the bodies that huddled against that wall at night would not move, would not wake to the new day. They would be carted out, to be thrown into a common grave somewhere outside the walls of Paris; the régime had more ways to dispose of its enemies than ritualised decapitation. It was common knowledge that there were dungeons below his feet, *oubliettes*, so dank, cold and perennially wet that made this courtyard a place to value.

A series of large chambers, equally crowded, lay off the courtyard; no cleaner than outside they at least had the virtue of shelter from the elements. From one he heard the sound of singing, a sweet young male voice intoning the phrases of a hymn, that in itself, in this place, seeming like an act of defiance. Pushing his way through a watching crowd, John found the source, a young man in a straw-coloured wig that had once been dressed white and a coat that had once been fine, rendering his *chanson* to an audience rapt with attention, most with their eyes closed, no doubt seeing behind those lids the better life than the one they lived now. Behind them rose a set of stone stairs that led to the landings above, the space between each riser seemingly the home of one prisoner. The landings and tiny cell-like rooms on the upper floor were just as crowded, each enquiry he made met with mostly slack-eyed indifference, at best a slow and weary shake of the head.

He found his father eventually, after many enquiries, in a cot in one of those cells, propped up by a roughly made pillow of straw wrapped in cloth, his appearance shocking, the green coat with pale silk facing he had been so pleased with when new, now just as dull as those of everyone else in this place. The already lined face was now skeletal; sunken eye sockets, prominent jaw bones and a mouth that was slack from the loss of muscle. Taking his cold hand and leaning close John heard mumbled words that were familiar, the same tirade now whispered against all the things the Edinburgh Ranter had opposed all his life; kings, courts, obsequious lackeys, rack-rent landlords and the stupidity of those who maintained them by their refusal to risk change.

'Father.'

It took several shakes of the hand, and repetition of the word, to open the eyes, and there was a moment when it seemed there was no recognition. Then just a flicker of the bright blue eyes presaged a ghost of a smile, and, as the squeeze was returned, he said, 'Laddie.'

About to say that 'he had come to take him home,' John stopped. How was he going to get him out of here in this condition? He needed to be fed, needed a doctor, for there was little likelihood that the affliction that had kept him in Paris had abated. He felt a flash of anger then. Why had he not been silent? Why had he continued to bait people with the power to do this to him? It did not last long, for John Pearce knew that if his father was stubborn, a man who refused to bend, then it was a trait he had inherited.

'Who are you?'

Pearce turned to face the gently posed question, to find himself looking into another skeletal face. 'I am his son.'

'Ah! He has spoken of you often, with much pride I might add.'

'Do not all fathers praise their sons?'

'No, young man, they do not. Most curse them roundly as wastrels until they have sons of their own. Only then do they become indulgent.'

'Do not argue with the Marquis, laddie,' croaked his father, feebly trying to raise himself, 'look what he has reduced me to.'

'You should remain still, Adam, as I told you. You know how movement causes you pain.' As he spoke, John Pearce was looking at the face of this Marquis, and what he saw there was genuine concern; indeed, if John had not been there he was sure this man would have come forward to help his father, for he smiled as he said, 'You will observe he has not lost the power of disobedience.'

'He will never lose that, monsieur…?'

'De la Motte,' the Marquis replied, 'at your service.'

John Pearce, as he turned back to his father, had the vague sensation that he had met this man before, but he could not place him. Not that such a thing was unusual, for Adam Pearce had been much fêted when he came to Paris by those who had read his writings. Even men who wished only to curb the power of the monarchy, and found his republican ideas too radical, sought out the new arrival.

Old Adam was smiling, albeit weakly, which lifted his son's spirits. 'He's a good man, laddie, even if he has some auld fashioned notions about the way the world should be run. I had nothing but a wee space in the courtyard when I came in, but he brought me to this cell, and gave me his ain bed.'

There was a terrible temptation to ask his father what he thought of the Revolution now, but it had to be fought. This was no time for debates. Instead he asked him how this had come about. 'I had a few things to say to the Jacobins for no' standing up to those who called for mair bloodshed, laddie, and that turd Fouché denounced me in the assembly.'

'I know nothing of him.'

'A shit o' the first order. If there's ony blood in his veins it canna be seen. Religious one minute, then bloodthirsty the next. I tell you, them that has been priests, or near to, are the worst. Purity they call it, when whit they mean is cut off the heid of ony man who dissna' agree.'

The eyes closed and the head lolled back a bit, as though the effort of speaking those words had drained him. 'I have brought some food,' John said, producing the cheese and wine, and half turning to include the Marquis. He did not respond, but there was a great deal of shifting from the two other occupants of the cell.

The reply was soft, a whisper, and a slight movement to cut sight of himself off from Adam Pearce. 'You brought that for your father.'

'You know he will share it.'

'There are too many hungry mouths in this place to make any share worthwhile. Feed him, and perhaps it will restore some of his strength.'

A sudden groan made John spin round again. His father had his hands clutched over his lower belly, and the bony face was screwed up in deep pain. He had seen it before, and in the past had eased it with laudanum, before calling a physician. John pulled the stopper out of the wine bottle, and he put the top of the flagon to the thin, pale lips, easing it down his father's throat. It was not laudanum by a long way, but it might help.

'Monsieur, I do not have much time, but I have already indicated to the warder who brought me in here that I would return. I will bring with me some laudanum to ease his pain, but I would enquire is there any way of getting him some medical attention.'

'There are doctors and surgeons in this prison, and if you were to ask them they would say to you what they have said to me. His only hope is to be put under the knife, to be opened so that the source of his agony can be explored.'

'It might kill him,' John replied, not adding the other thought he had that if the affliction did not, the surgeons, in whom he had little faith, would.

'What he has now will kill him anyway.' The Marquis saw the pained reaction of John's face and once more dropped his voice. 'And that says nothing for those ghouls in the Great Hall who sit in judgement on us.'

'That was not in existence when I left.'

'Things change by the day. I fully expect my door to be chalked any day now.' Seeing the look of mystification in the younger man's eyes, he added, 'It is how they select you for their travesty of a trial, in what we already call the Room of the Doomed, for few come out of it to go anywhere but to their death. A chalk mark on the door is a signal to the guards to take you there. They will condemn me for my rank, and my hatred of everything they stand for, even if I helped to bring about the end of the Bourbons. It comes to us all, and it is when we need our faith in a merciful God the most.'

The voice of Adam Pearce was stronger, clearly the wine had revived him a little. 'Don't listen to him, laddie. He will corrupt your brain with all that superstitious babble.'

John stood quickly, for he feared he had been in this place too long, and it might just be that the man who had let him in, if he delayed, would not be there to let him out. 'I must leave. I will be back tomorrow with more food. Please, Monsieur, use what is already here, for you know as well as I do that if it is not consumed it will be stolen as soon as you are both asleep.'

Then he lent down and retook his father's hand. 'Drink the wine, eat the food, get your strength back. You will need it for the journey home.'

'Home, laddie? I don't think we ever had one.'

'How much to get a prisoner out?' he asked the *gardien*, as they emerged into the falling darkness.

The answer was depressing. 'However much money it takes to replace a head and bring a dead man back to life?'

'Surely there is a way?'

'How many times a day do you think I am asked that? And who do you think it is who sends these folk to this place and sits it judgement on them in the Great Hall. They ain't fools, and neither, young fellow, am I. A bit of coin for a favour is one thing, but taking a gift to get you in for a visit is pushing it as far as I dare.'

Pearce thought about a request for extra comfort, but realised that it too was probably beyond the ability of this man; the place was too crowded. So the only thing that presented itself as a possibility was to plead with those who had the power to get his father out. This Fouché being out of Paris would help, and he had good reason to hope that Cambacérès would aid him in getting to the likes of Danton.

As he looked for somewhere to eat, he weighed the odds and felt more comfortable for doing so. What could they possibly hold against old Adam? If they wanted, he would write a recantation under his father's name. The reputation of the Revolution was odious enough, it would not be helped by the judicial murder of a foreign national and one with his father's reputation. He was no threat to their safety or that of the state; the men who ran France now had to be of a practical bent, and that meant they would surely see that Adam Pearce was harmless. Such thoughts were helped by a bottle of good wine and a proper meal, so that by the time he wrapped himself in those torn drapes to try and get some sleep, he was reasonably confident that he could get his father out of Paris and France.

Chapter Fifteen

Doubts surfaced with the dawn, to replace the sanguine notions that had comforted John Pearce as he went to sleep and that followed on from troubled dreams of storm-tossed ships, rising and falling steel blades, the contorted face of his father making rabid speeches or screwed up in pain, which were directly related to sleeping on a hard floor and a level of discomfort that made him long for a hammock. The walls of the Conciergerie loomed larger and thicker in his imagination and the previous evening's practical politicians became, in his mind, blood-soaked demagogues, so that by the time he was washed and shaved, he was in a far from optimistic frame of mind. Taking extra care, he resolved to find a coat and hat that would be more presentable, for he would need to look as good as possible if he were to face members of the Committee of Public Defence. That posed another problem – he only knew three of the names, so he must find out the rest.

Buying better clothes than those he was wearing was not difficult; as he had seen the previous day there were people on the streets so desperate to find the funds just to be able to eat that they were selling anything they could find that another might buy; chips of stone, supposedly from the destroyed Bastille, ribbons and tricolours, bits of string and used brown paper, of crockery and cutlery, most of which had seen many better days, cracked looking glasses, strips of cloth, clothing in abundance, some of it better classed as rags, domestic and trade artefacts of every description, and that took no account of those selling themselves, either girls or grown women offering their bodies, or men of all ages offering themselves as menial labour, they only outnumbered by the outright beggars. He returned to the Rue St Etienne de Gres with a black coat and breeches, plus a tall hat more in keeping with the present French fashion. That he wrapped in the kind of tricolour band he had seen the previous day when watching the comings and goings from the Jacobin Club, the whole making him look like a man committed to the cause.

Changed, with his discarded garments hidden away with his pistol and ditty bag, and well aware he was in for a long day, he made sure of a good breakfast, a pigeon pie washed down with a *pichet* of red wine, and it was while consuming that he first heard, then read, about the new committee that had been set up. Marat's news sheet *l'Ami du Peuple* hailed the inception of the Committee of Public Safety to replace Public Defence. What difference it made to the people of France Pearce could not fathom, and he was too well versed in ways of revolutionary slogan-making to pay much attention to Marat's screaming polemic regarding the threats to the people, the movement, the number of traitors waiting to stab the Revolution in the back, the criminals in the Vendée and the other major cities who were standing in the way of a New World Order, or the need for vigilance on the frontiers of France and more arrests here in Paris. The ugly little swine had been saying the same things for years; to him, perusing the names, it did make one major difference; Cambacérès was not a member.

That was a problem he would have to deal with later; the time had come to visit the Conciergerie with more food and laudanum, which he bought on the way. The *gardien* worried him by being late, though he did raise an eye at the changed appearance. That was followed by a grinning allusion to a busy but fruitful morning, which was sickening, for it implied that another batch of unfortunate victims were off to the Place de la Revolution. He then taxed Pearce's patience in the way he dealt with the other suppliants for his favours, seeming to deliberately take his time as he accepted small parcels, probably mostly of food, for those inside. Eventually he came waddling towards Pearce, with his huge belly and thick thighs, his hand twitching at his side to indicate that payment must be made before anything else. The coins were slipped into his sweaty hand, and

Pearce followed him out of the door, heading for the same set of gates by which he had entered the previous day, just in time to see a distant and full tumbrel turning left along the banks of the Seine, its iron-hooped wheels making an audible death knell sound on the cobbled pavé.

The route was not the same as before; this time the *gardien* led him through the Great Hall, a huge chamber in which their footsteps, under a high, vaulted timber roof, echoed on the flagstone floor. The walls were lined with armorial decorations, swords, long spears and shields arranged in patterns that were medieval in appearance, with one wall excepted, that covered by three huge drapes of red, white and blue. Set before these was a long table, strewn with papers, the seats thrown back and empty for, as he was informed, the Revolutionary Tribunal had done their work for the morning, and would not again be sitting till the afternoon. In the middle of the hall was a stall, slightly raised on a plinth, which was no doubt the dock where the accused would stand, and passing it, Pearce picked up the smell of human evacuation, caused as the victims voided their bodies on hearing their fate. It was a double indignity that few people would lie under the guillotine blade who had not already soiled themselves in a state of sheer terror.

Done up to look like a man of the Revolution, Pearce caused even more of a reaction as he entered the courtyard, the door closing behind him with the same admonishment about time and attendance, with those present seeming to shy away from him. It did occur, too late, that such a costume might be unwise in this place, once the *gardien* went back through the postern gate. With the inmates mistaking him for one of their persecutors, they might well tear him limb from limb, so it was with head held defiantly high that he made his way through the throng, packages of food and medicine held in plain view. There was no singing, and Pearce thought he detected an even greater air of listlessness than he had the day before. Retracing his steps up to the landing, he stopped abruptly when he saw the great slash of chalk marked on the door to his father's cell, and by the time he got to the doorway, and saw the empty cot, his heart was in his boots, the parcels dropping out of his hands.

The Marquis was on his knees on the stone floor, silently praying, while one of the other inmates who had been present the day before sat huddled in a corner looking wretched. There was no time for ceremony, no time to wait on another man's devotions and Pearce grabbed the penitent by the shoulder and hauled him round, to look into a face streaked with tears and eyes full of despair. A cry came out from those damp lips, an achingly sorrowful sound and John Pearce found himself looking down at the balding head of a man who had put his arms round his knees and was, in a mumbling way, begging forgiveness.

'Tell me?'

'They came for me…they chalked the door for me… but I was not here, and when the guards demanded the Marquis de la Motte…' He stopped then, too upset to go on. Pearce wanted to strike him, because he knew what was coming and it made him boil with anger. Instead he patted the man gently to encourage him to speak. 'Your father answered to my name.'

The wretch huddled in the corner mumbled. 'He said, let them take a man who is dying anyway.'

'This morning?'

The head at his knees moved slowly, and Pearce had a vision of that tumbrel rattling over the cobbles and disappearing round the corner of the prison. There was no way of saying that there was only one cart in that batch of the condemned, there could have been several, but he had a horrible feeling that he had, unknowingly, watched his own father on the way to the guillotine. He pushed off the weeping Marquis and he rushed out of the cell, his thoughts in turmoil. Could he get out before the appointed time; had the Marquis, on discovering the mistake, taken any steps to rectify it, or had he merely sunk to his knees to pray to

God? What for, deliverance or another man's soul; what was his father thinking about? Him possibly, the idea that his son might get himself killed trying a rescue. Or was it a last act of defiance? Was he dying? There was no certainty of that. Outside, with proper medical attention, he might have recovered. Maybe they had found him innocent and set him free. Was he now wandering the streets of Paris in a daze? Could he get to the Place de la Revolution and stop the execution if he had been pronounced guilty?

With these questions rattling round in his brain he rushed across the courtyard and banged on the postern door, suspecting that it would be useless. How many of the people listlessly watching him had done that in the past to no avail? But he pounded on nevertheless, even when one or two of the prisoners started to laugh at his efforts, they were soon joined by others that raised the level of hilarity to such a pitch that, echoing off the high walls, the curious *gardien* came to investigate.

Pearce was through the door before the man had time to ask for an explanation and the way he grabbed and tried to drag him away brought forth a string of curses. The breathless explanation did little to enlighten the man, who was determined to stand on what dignity he thought he owned, fists on hips, great belly protruding. Pearce wanted to kill him there and then, but he forced himself to calm down, still breathing heavily as he gave a garbled account of what had happened. The falling face, the look of sadness on the fleshy jowls, had nothing to do with his father's possible fate, more to do with a realisation of a lost source of income, so that it was with no great hurry that he locked the postern gate and led Pearce out, again going through the empty great hall, where the vision of his father, standing in that dock, was seared into Pearce's mind. It was tempered by the certainty that Adam Pearce would not have sobbed, would not have soiled himself. He would have looked them in the eye with the boldness that had been the hallmark of his whole life and sneered at their sentence.

It seemed to take forever to get to the outside of the walls. Hat in hand, Pearce ran like a demon for the Pont Neuf, slowing to a walk as he got clear so as not to alarm those who guarded the crossing looking for suspicious souls. He had to walk across to the Right Bank, his heart pounding, his mood swinging from hope to despair and back again, until he was off and heading for the square that had once been named for King Louis XV, but was now the place of execution. He heard the faint roar of the crowd a long way off, abreast the Louvre, and knew that the blade had dropped and another head had been held up for the *canaille* who spent their time watching men and women die whom they hated without ever knowing. He heard it twice more before he was past the great open space in front of the Tuileries, and he wondered if, in the building that housed the National Assembly, those representatives of the people could hear through the walls the results of their bloody deliberations.

The Place de la Revolution was packed, this now a daily diversion for the dregs and perverse of Paris, and trying to elbow his way through the crowd was like swimming in molasses. His size and desperation helped, that and the look in his eye that told anyone who wanted to contest with him that they would have to do so with violence. In his ears another roar, and jumping up he had a vision of a female head held aloft for the edification of the crowd. This was followed by another roll of the drums, the signal for a new victim to ascend the steps, that drowned out by the crowing of the yet to be sated crowd.

John Pearce was still only halfway to the guillotine, with the crowd even thicker close to, when he heard the voice. His father had always had the ability to command a crowd and the bellow he let out silenced them for a moment, though perhaps his son was the only one present who understood the few words he was allowed to say before he was silenced. Where he got the strength from, not only to stand away from his escorts, but to produce such a stentorian cry was a marvel.

'You who have condemned me will in turn die like me. You have betrayed your principles for your life, but that will not save you. I...'

He never got to say Adam Pearce, which was what his watching and desperate son thought was coming next, for he was seized and thrown down out of sight on to the sliding plank that would take his head beneath a blade already dripping blood. John froze, knowing he was too late, knowing too that even earlier there would have been nothing he could do. He watched as the angled metal began to drop and closed his eyes as the audible thud declared that it had done its work. His eyes stayed closed, fists clenched, body screwed up in despair as the swine around him cawed their triumph at the sight of another severed head. Then he turned, and with no strength whatever, tried to make his way out to a place where he could breath, and finding himself in the open spaces of the Champs Elysées he leant against a tree and wept.

Régis de Cambacérès came to his own door as soon as his servant told him of the despairing young man, the look in his eye, as he saw both the identity of his visitor and his state, a clear indication that he could guess what had happened. In the Paris in which he lived, that took no great leap of imagination. Taking an arm, he led John Pearce in to a comfortable if fussily over-furnished room and sat him down on a chaise, then went to pour him a brandy. Sitting down himself, he took the young man's free hand and squeezed it gently.

'Your father?'

The story tumbled out, not clear in its order, a mumbled and disordered version of what had happened that morning, much self-castigation mixed with curses at the régime, the prisons and even once his own father for the way he had behaved. The reassuring noises that Cambacérès made, to the effect that he should not blame himself, were wasted on John Pearce, who was sure in his own mind that when he had originally left Paris on his father's instructions it had been as much for his own good as to fulfil any filial obligation.

'You must, young Jean, see it as an act of great courage. If, as you say, your father was convinced of the imminence of his own death he has granted life to another, and who knows in the confusion of the world we live in, how long that will last?'

'I want to bury him.'

Perhaps it was the brandy, perhaps the soothing words, but Pearce was aware of a mixture of feelings, self pity as well as grief, and it being in his nature to honestly examine his own emotions the notion that he might be feeling sorry for himself as much as for his father was disturbing.

'That will not be easy.'

'Will you help me?'

Without letting go of the hand, Cambacérès sat back a bit and examined the young man beside him, aware that from under lowered eyelids he himself was likewise being scrutinized. The florid, heavily patterned silk morning coat that went all the way to the floor was the most obvious signal of the Frenchman's proclivities, but it was in the cast of his features and the movements of his body as well, a softness allied to an arch quality that was most evident in his face; blue, slightly protruding eyes, clear, well cared for skin, but most of all the sensual, almost feminine lips.

'Will you?' Pearce repeated.

'I am wondering whether you like me?' That made Pearce look away. 'I doubt that you approve of me, yet you come in your hour of need to seek my help. Why?'

Pearce raised his head, to look Cambacérès right in the eye. 'I come because I know of no one else to ask.'

'And in return you offer?'

'Nothing.'

Had he said that too quickly, too emphatically? Was the shocked look on the Frenchman's face real or mock, for there was an affected quality to the man? All Pearce knew was that he meant it; he had nothing he was prepared to give this man in return for his help, except gratitude. Cambacérès stood up and going to the mantle rang a bell, before turning and smiling.

'Well, at least you are honest, which is, in itself, a rare commodity these days.'

'I know you are no longer...' Pearce stopped. He did not know how to say what was in his mind.

'No longer powerful? Is that what you were going to say?' In the absence of a reply the Frenchman continued. 'I wonder, my young friend, if I ever was. Let us find out shall we? He went over to an escritoire and began to write. Then the quill stopped abruptly and he turned back to Pearce just as his servant entered. 'I am sorry, I must ask this, what was your father wearing?'

John had to put his head in his hands then, for what Cambacérès was asking was obvious; that while it might be possible, even easy, to identify the severed head, there was no way to match it to the body without some description of his father's clothing. In his mind he saw him, standing to harangue the crowd, his look defiant, and there was a surge of pride mixed in with his other feelings as he replied.

'A green silk coat, with lighter facings.'

What Cambacérès said to his servant John Pearce did not hear. The man was gone, and he had another brandy in his hands without knowing how it got there. This time Cambacérès sat opposite him, in silence, just looking at him. 'I think you are weary, my young friend. I suggest that until my man returns you should lie down.'

The look John gave him then made him burst out laughing, and it was full of humour, not contrived and oddly appropriate, even to a grieving son. 'You have a lot to learn, young Monsieur Pearce, about some of your fellow men, but you may rest knowing you will learn nothing today.'

John Pearce had lain down knowing sleep would be impossible, so it was a surprise when the door opened and a servant bearing food and coffee entered, and he realised that it was nearly dark. He wondered where he was momentarily, until the events of the day came flooding back. He felt the bile rise in his throat, the feelings of hatred for this city, its inhabitants and the men who ruled France. What had his father done but question them? So what if he had taken the place of another, he had still been imprisoned, perhaps he would have lost his head anyway. There would soon be another exodus from Paris when word got round, this time of foreign sympathisers who had come to support the original Revolution.

'The master's compliments, Monsieur,' said the servant, who had been patient. 'He said to tell you that matters have been arranged, and that once you have partaken of this he will be waiting for you in the salon.'

The brioche and coffee he wolfed down, yet, eager as he was to find out what matters had been arranged, he looked in the mirror to check his appearance, realising that his face was streaked with grime from earlier in the day, the rivulets where he had shed tears, now smudged tracks on his cheeks. There was a jug of water and a basin, so he washed that off and adjusted his garments to try and take out the creases that had come from sleeping fully clothed, wondering why he cared so much.

Cambacérès, fully and elegantly dressed, was waiting for him. He looked keenly at him then nodded when he saw that, while still grieving, the face was also set with grim determination.

'We have recovered your father's body, and separated it...' Now it was the Frenchman's turn to stop abruptly, for that, in the circumstances, was a malapropism.

'Thank you,' Pearce replied, to relieve him of his embarrassment.

'I have also arranged for it to be taken to be buried in the cemetery of the church of St Germain de Prés and I have a trap waiting to take us there now.'

'Hallowed ground in a Catholic church. I'm not sure my father would approve.'

'Let him argue with God should he ever get there, or the devil if he does not.'

The trap was covered and once inside Cambacérès pulled down the blinds to ensure complete privacy. As they rattled across the cobbles, and took the bridge over the Seine, Cambacérès talked of the new committee, from which he had been excluded, which helped to take Pearce's mind off the reason for being here.

'We go on, because we cannot go back. King Louis had to die, for if he had not then the threat to those things we have gained would be lost. But the Queen, she, with her children and relatives should be sent back to Austria. I daresay in arguing that, I ensured I would not be asked to sit on Danton's Committee of Public Safety.'

'I am unclear what anyone has gained.'

'Mayhem now, and it may get worse, but France will never again be under the untrammelled power of a King. After all, we have the example of your own country to follow.'

'Where will it end.'

'In peace and prosperity, my young friend, as it always does, but not soon. Like England we will probably have to find a man with a sword, a Cromwell to make the world respect us and leave us alone.'

'England got a King back.'

'Yes, but one subject to the power of the people.'

'My father wanted more.'

'Perhaps one day it will come, like America, but I doubt France is ready for such freedoms yet.' The trap stopped, and Cambacérès pulled at the blind. 'We must be discreet, as all the others are.'

'Others?'

'What is said and what is done are not the same thing. This night there will be funerals going on all over France, even many here in Paris, with non-juring priests carrying out the rituals by which the people were raised. It takes more than debates in an assembly and grand ideas to drive out the religion by which we were all raised.'

'The zealots, the enraged ones?'

'Will not come near, lest they find themselves hanging from a rope.'

The church, which had suffered much from those zealots, was in darkness. Cambacérès led John past the altar and in to the presbytery, where a pinewood coffin stood on two trestles. The trouble the man had gone to was immense, for Adam Pearce lay with his hands folded across his chest, eyes closed, his neck wrapped in a scarf so that it appeared his head was still joined to his body, that he was still whole. His face was tranquil and in repose, waxy pale but somehow natural and if the shock of his decapitation had registered that had been made good by the men Cambacérès had engaged to see to the body. John went close and leaning over, a wave of sadness physically running though his body, kissed his father on the forehead, murmuring, not a prayer, just a goodbye. As the lid was screwed on his mind was full of images of the times he spent in his father's company, of the travails, the laughs, the perils and the arguments.

The grave was dug and ready, the body lowered into it by the light of a single lantern. John picked up a handful of earth and threw it on to the coffin lid, took another substantial clod and placed it in his pocket, then turned away as the men engaged to fill it in started shovelling.

'Can I ask you Monsieur Cambacérès, why you have done all this?'

'Yes, you can,' he replied, looking at the shovelling gravediggers. There was, in his mode of speech, a wistful note, as if he was seeing his own tomb. 'I hope that, should I share your father's fate, someone will carry out a similar service for me.'

'My father spoke of you once. He said you were a survivor.'

'Let us hope he is right.'

'Would you see a stone erected so that people will know

he lies here?'

'It will take time, but yes.'

John went back to the graveside, now nearly full, and gave the diggers a coin apiece for their labours, then followed Cambacérès back to the trap.

'You will stay at my house tomorrow. Then I will give you papers that will get you out of France, swiftly and in safety.'

'I thought you had no power?'

'I have the power to forge Danton's signature, and I still have the seals to make it valid. If I date it yesterday, then the committee on which I served was still in existence.'

Before retiring, with the promised *laisser-passer* safe in his coat pocket, Pearce had a servant fetch him quill, ink, wax and paper. He wrote his thanks to Cambacérès and left the note with most of the contents of his purse, to pay for a headstone and to reimburse a man whose kindness could not have come cheap, keeping for himself only what he thought he needed to pay for his passage to get back to England, something that was not a heavy expense, given that he could take a coach and then the cartel that ran, war or no war, between Calais and Dover. In another piece of paper, folded over into a package and sealed, he placed the earth he had taken from the graveside, in his mind's eye imagining the day he would make that bastard Fouché choke on it. The packet in his pocket, he left the house as dawn broke, without alerting any of the occupants.

He stopped at the Rue Etienne de Gres to collect his other possessions, and there was a moment, toying with the old battered pistol and the means to load it when he considered the idea of immediate revenge. Who to kill, and would one victim be payment enough or end the descent into chaos which Cambacérès saw coming? Even if he succeeded, all he would do would be to share his father's fate. He wanted vengeance, but it had to be more satisfying than that.

With no clear idea of how that might be achieved he made his way on foot to the Place de Valenciennes, the square from where the coaches to the North departed, with a last look at the Conciergerie on the way. Cambacérès signature and the florid seal of his now defunct committee got him through the Porte St Denis without difficulty, and John Pearce left Paris with heavy thoughts and much doubt, journeying across the northern part of France with a heart that grew harder with every league.

Chapter Sixteen

Sunshine and Mediterranean warmth made working up the crew of HMS *Brilliant* so much easier. Stripped to the waist, they were not encumbered by clothing, and just out from port, still full of fresh food, Ralph Barclay could say they were happy. So was he; with a full complement of proper sailors, no outright troublemakers and a set of officers so eager to please him that all his previous problems seemed like a distant memory. Off his larboard side, sailing on a parallel course, lay HMS *Firefly*, Davidge Gould obeying his orders to exercise his guns, each vessel supplying a target for the other to aim at in dumb show. He would fire one broadside to keep the men happy, but that would come at the end of the exercise, just before they were piped to dinner and would send them away happy. To fire more meant accounting for his powder and shot, and he was disinclined to do that, since he would not know who would first examine his logs, a superior who approved of and lauded gunnery practice, or one that preferred a deck without the grooves drawn by much used cannon.

He was without hat or coat, walking the deck with his watch in his hand, cajoling and encouraging his crew as they ran the guns in and out, in between going through a mime of loading. Some were quicker than others, all were quicker than Devenow; despite his strength the huge bone-headed bully was a sore trial on such occasions, being cack-handed and getting in the way of his fellows manhandling the twelve pounder. That he saw himself as a follower to Ralph Barclay, and had hurried to join HMS *Brilliant* as soon as he heard of his patron's commission, was a trial that his captain just had to bear.

He set the men to their task again, noticing that one of the maindeck cannon was run in, reloaded and run out much quicker than the others. He also noticed that one of the crew, and not the man in charge either, was urging on his companions to greater efforts.

'That fellow in your division, Mr Mitcham, he is working with a will.'

'Name of Walker, sir. I believe he declined a chance to go aboard that merchant vessel you sent back to England.'

'One of my London volunteers?'

Mitcham blinked; he had not been aboard long but he knew just how that section of the crew had 'volunteered'. 'Yes, sir. A good man and enthusiastic, I would say, a quick learner who has taken to his new life with gusto. He is working like a real blue-water man, and as you have seen he is keen to persuade the fellows on his gun crew, even his gun captain, that they could do better.'

'Fetch him to me.'

Ben Walker was close enough to the two men to have heard the entire exchange, but he made no move until he was ordered to do so. He did not like Ralph Barclay and, albeit that things had eased aboard since Lisbon, he still saw him as the tyrant so described by John Pearce. At moments like these he wished he had gone with them, stayed one of the Pelicans, because Ben hated to be out of the crowd, feared that he might be asked why he had chosen to reside in the Liberties of the Savoy from which he and his mates had been pressed. A man did not live in that part of London unless he had a secret. Ben's fear of being singled out stemmed from the fact that he had a great deal to hide.

'Walker?'

Ben knuckled his forehead in the regulation manner, while Ralph Barclay saw before him a man of slight but wiry build, with bright bird-like eyes and something keen in his expression, an intimation of a degree of intelligence. It was very much part of his duties to spot such people, to separate them from the dull and hidebound herd who would make up most of a ship's crew, and see if they could be brought to a higher pitch of usefulness.

'You are rated landsman, at this time. Is that correct?'

'Aye, sir.'

'Mr Mitcham, I know he is a member of your division but, being of the build he is and eager, I wonder if he would not be better employed as a topman.'

'I would say, sir, he would be an asset in that department.'

Ben Walker was thinking they were talking about him as if he did not exist, and it made him angry.

'In that case, Walker, I shall rate you able, and I will have you report to the Yeoman of the Sheets after we have finished this exercise. Carry on.'

'Obliged, your honour.'

Ralph Barclay was satisfied; he had done a good thing, rewarded effort and taken a man from one station to another where his skill would expand, and so would his usefulness to the ship. As he walked back to the quarterdeck he spied his marine drummer, a boy called Martin Dent, and noticed the eruption of spots of the lad's face, that and the fact that he was growing out of his red coat. Time to transfer him as well and, seeing he was nimble, he could likewise go to the tops. No ship wishing to be called a crack frigate could have too many topmen.

'Right, Mr Glaister,' he called to his new Premier, 'let us have one more go, and see if we can't knock a few seconds off our time.'

'You starts on the maincourse, what'll give you plenty of practise, an' I can see how you fare.'

'Bugger that,' said Martin, his voice a breaking croak. 'I can get to the masthead quicker than any sod aboard.'

The Yeoman of the Sheets, who had charge of the topmen, just grinned, for he knew the boy well. A sea-brat, Martin Dent had never really had a father, and outside the Navy never really had a home. He was cheeky, a bit of a tearaway, but liked by the crew and it seemed that the broken nose he had got just before they weighed had helped to make him look more like a man. But he needed to be put in his place if he was going to work aloft, where there was no room for skylarking, for that got folk killed.

'Happen you can, Martin, but you'se an unruly bugger, so

you will start where I say an' do as you're told. An' you can look after Walker here. If he falls and spreads his guts on the deck, an' the captain hauls me up, I can blame you.'

The pair of new topmen eyed each other with deep suspicion. Martin had been part of the press gang that had raided the Pelican. John Pearce had broken his nose that night and the boy, seeking a settling of scores, had come close to maiming him more than once. Worse, in seeking out Pearce he had brought about the death of one of the friends Ben had worked and lived with; to say he did not trust him was to underestimate the dislike he felt. That the lad had behaved better later on, in fact had gone out of his way to be friendly, had not laid the ghost of his first transgression.

'I ain't no wet nurse,' Martin growled.

'You are what I tell you you are,' said the Yeoman, 'and you stay that till I tell you otherwise. Now get up them shrouds and let me see what you make of them.'

Both ran for the shrouds, Martin besting Ben by a whisker. He also climbed quicker, but that did not bother Ben, for he watched his every move and swore to himself that soon he would beat that boy, and become the best topman on the ship. He had decided to stay for one reason; he had never found a better place to hide from his past than this. Compared to the Navy, the Liberties of the Savoy did not come close.

'And who, Mr Glaister, first got you into the service?'

The Premier, golden-haired and blue-eyed, rested his knife and fork, as if the moving of those and answering a question were mutually exclusive actions. That was in the nature of the man; a West Highlands Scot, he was measured of speech, never hurried in his movements, but efficient in a quiet way. Sandy-haired, all skin and bone, with thin high cheekbones, he looked fragile enough to break, but had shown himself to be tougher than he looked, and pleasing to the man who had posed the question who hated to see laxity in the pace of any other; a slow sailor, when Glaister was on deck, could expect a knotted rope on his back.

'Admiral Duncan, sir; though he was, of course, Captain Duncan then. My mother is a first cousin to his wife.'

'Then he has seen to your career in the proper manner?'

'He has shown me nothing but kindness, Captain Barclay. When I passed for Lieutenant, at a board he had the kindness to arrange, he got me a place with Captain Elphinstone. He, in turn, made representation to the captain of HMS *Britannia*, to get me a berth on the flagship.'

Damned Scotsmen, thought Ralph Barclay. They're like a second tribe of Israel, they get everywhere and feather each others nest! 'Do you still write to Admiral Duncan?'

'I do, sir.'

'Then I hope you will mention your new berth.'

'I will praise it, sir, and not only for the worth of the ship and its commander.' Glaister nodded to Emily Barclay then, 'but for the added benefit of the delightful company at table.'

The table had become a daily affair, a proper dinner with at least one of the ship's officers and mids invited to join them. Farmiloe, not unlike the Premier in looks and colouring, but better built, was at the far end, the space between his mouth and his plate something of a blur. The other officers were below, in the gun room, eating more common fare bulked out with their private stores.

'I do hope the food will get a mention, Mr Glaister.'

'Excellent as it is, Madame, it does not compare with the kindness of the hostess.'

'Harrumph.'

The noisy clearing of the throat had the knife and fork back in Glaister's hands, and food to his face to cover his embarrassment, for he had allowed his attraction to get the better of his manners. Lutyens, the other guest at the table was wondering what Ralph Barclay expected. He had an exceedingly attractive wife, he was on a ship with only one other female, the 'broad as she was long' gunner's wife, and a group of one hundred and forty souls deprived of that which they wanted most in the world, something they suspected he was enjoying on a daily basis. To react to compliments to Emily, to express such an obvious pique, was foolish.

'I am told that your part of the world is a place of great beauty, Mr Glaister,' said Emily.

'It is sparse but it is a wonder, high rolling hills, deep glens and sudden sparkling lakes. If you are fond of weather, Mrs Barclay, there is no better place in the British Isles. I swear on one day I have seen every combination of snow, rain, mist, and sunshine imaginable. You can sit down to your soup in brilliant sunshine and be bound in by mist before the bowl is half done. By the time you are finished it has rained and stopped and the snow is falling through sunshine.'

'Sounds damned uncomfortable,' said Barclay.

'It is home, sir, and does one not always hanker after that?'

Ralph Barclay had a vision of his own home town then, and it was not an entirely comfortable one, beautiful as Frome was, nestling in a deep Somerset river valley. It had been a place where he had for several years, as a half-pay naval captain, been forced to stretch his credit to the limit to keep up the standing of himself and his sisters. The way trades people to whom he was indebted assumed a acquaintance that hinted at equality was enough to make him shudder every time he thought of it. But there had, of course, been Emily, and a wedding he could hardly have dared to hope for.

'What about you Mr Lutyens. Do you hanker after home?' he asked.

'I am more attracted to the idea of experience, sir.'

'Yet you have given up much to be here, have you not?'

Lutyens knew that Barclay was probing again. It had become a tedious habit since his wife had instituted these dinners; the captain was fascinated with anything to do with the life of the Court, and would swing the conversation round to that regardless of what the surgeon tried to do to avoid it. Best to take it head on and get it over with.

'I have given up tedious journeys to Windsor, that is true, that and standing with my father in a draughty audience chamber waiting for a monarch who has a poor sense of punctuality, and is parsimonious to the point of being a miser in the article of firewood.'

'Is that not *lèse-majesté,* Mr Lutyens?' asked Emily with a devilish smile.

'It is the truth, I regret to say. When he does attend his *levee,* the King is wont to bark at whoever he is addressing. He has a most bulbous set of eyes and he fixes his quarry with those as if expecting to be misled. With his sons, he is sure of it, and they rarely escape without a tongue lashing for their dissolute way of life, embarrassing to them and to all who are obliged to overhear it. The most annoying thing is when King George fails to turn up at all, and we are left standing around shivering as the fire dies out.'

'His health?'

'Is never mentioned, Captain Barclay. To the nation he is fully recovered from his malaise and in total command of his faculties.'

'Would you, with your connections, not know the truth of that?'

'My father may pray with the Queen, sir, and even occasionally with His Majesty, but if he has observed any recurrence of his madness, he has not told me, and I think you would agree, neither should he.'

'Of course,' Ralph Barclay replied, trying, and utterly failing not to sound thwarted. 'Mr Farmiloe,' he barked, bringing the boy's head sharply up. 'When I invite you to my table it is to engage in social intercourse, not merely to stuff your face with food. You are supposed to be a young gentleman, so it would behove you to behave like one.'

Some of that food escaped his mouth as he replied. 'Forgive me, sir.'

'Come husband,' said Emily, with a warm smile aimed at Farmiloe, 'let him feed. He gets little enough in the mids' berth.'

She's done it again, Ralph Barclay thought, checked me publicly again! The other thought he had centred round his own inability to remind his wife of her place, and looking at her, masking his ire, he did not see that he was being observed by an amused Lutyens.

'Sail drill after dinner, Mr Glaister. We will have an hour before the sun begins to set.'

'Aye, aye sir.'

All the officers were on the quarterdeck by the time Ralph Barclay emerged, each hat lifted to acknowledge his arrival. He made his way to the windward side, his preserve as the captain and paced back and forth for several minutes, head bowed as if in deep thought. In reality he was enjoying the demonstration of his power. Nothing could happen till he said so; his officers, the Master, Mr Collins, the new marine officer and all his midshipmen were waiting on his command. It was the sweetest part of his office. He looked over the bulwark, to the south were Africa lay, smelling the wind that was coming off that continent to see if he could pick up any of the burnt scent of the land. Though not perfect it was steady, and it would strengthen slightly as the heat went out of the day, and he had a mind to see what his ship could do. Then as if he had made a sudden decision, he snapped his head round and went to stand by the wheel.

'Quartermaster, ease off a few points. I want the wind playing on our sails to best advantage. Signal Captain Gould to hold station on us. Mr Glaister, all hands on deck to make sail.'

The whole ship had been waiting for that, warned in advance to expect it, so the crew rushed on to the deck in record time. In the main it was not done to please their captain – many heartily disliked Ralph Barclay – but they had a sharp eye for their own comfort and they knew that if he was content then their lives were eased. Make him unhappy, which had already happened on this commission, and they all suffered in the backwash.

'T'gallants aloft please, Mr Glaister.'

The Premier raised the speaking trumpet, for once his measured way of doing things irritating, and called out the requisite orders. The topmen had gone to their stations and ropes appeared from the main and fore yards, ready to haul up the topgallant yards once the lubbers below had hauled them out and bent on the sails. They were hauled aloft, chained, and on command let loose, to be sheeted home on the lines that ran to the cleats on the deck. Immediately, as the wind took them HMS *Brilliant* heeled.

'Mr Farmiloe, my compliments to my wife. She should get my steward to secure anything of a fragile nature, since we are going to heel more as we continue.'

The sky sails and an outer jib followed the topgallant, and the deck canted a few degrees more, the blue water of the Mediterranean bursting white and fairly creaming down the leeward side.

'The log, Mr Glaister, let us see what we are making, and let us have out the studdingsail booms ready to be sent aloft.'

By the time the sun began to set in their wake, Ralph Barclay had everything set he could, and he began to play with the tension on the sails to improve the way they all drew. Mr Collins, the master, whose department this was, agreed with every suggestion he made, for he had come to have much fear of his captain's temper, and the man's uncanny ability to expose his weaknesses.

'They'll he taking it all in ten minutes from now,' said Martin Dent. Ben Walker just nodded, as the boy continued. 'You ever been right up at the masthead, Ben?' That got a head shake. 'It be grand up there, best spot on the ship. What say we go up and have a look see.'

'Yeoman said we was to go no higher than the main yard.'

'Stuff him, mate, what does he know. I'm going up to watch the sun set. If you ain't game to follow me, so be it.'

Martin had reached the bulwarks before Ben reacted. He had to go, for it was like a challenge and he knew he had a flaw in his nature, in that he could never pass up on one. So he followed Martin up to the maincap, eschewing, as the boy did, the lubber's hole, and carrying right on to the next set of shrouds. They passed to the tops in the same fashion, Ben climbing in Martin's wake until they reached the top-gallant yard, where the boy slipped along, hooking his arm round the smooth pine of the mast.

'Take the other side Ben, an' look around you. If we was to stay here long enough it would be dark on deck and still light up here, and there's a wonder of the world, even if I say so.'

In truth, there was nothing to see but that setting sun and an expanse of water turning from blue to grey, but Ben was exhilarated nonetheless. Then he looked down and the case was altered. Swaying forward he could see the dip of the bowsprit into the water, watch the trails of the accompanying dolphins criss-crossing the bows, and see the flash of their wet backs as they took their leap.

'Ben.'

'What?' He had to look at Martin Dent, for the tone with which the name had been said demanded it.

'I need you to know that I is sorry for what went before. I never meant no harm.'

'Martin, that ain't true. You meant harm to another.'

'Then I regrets it, do you believe that?'

Ben Walker was about to say no when he remembered his own past deeds, things he regretted with every ounce of his being, actions which, had they not occurred would not have seen him in the Liberties, nor pressed into the Navy. Perhaps the boy was genuine, and like him.

'I wants us to be friends, Ben, true messmates, an' if you will grant that I can live with my errors.'

'They haunt you?'

'They do, Ben. An' I can see no way out, since all the others on the edge of my harm have left the ship. But for you to forgive me…'

Ben looked hard at the boy, at his pleading spotty face.

'Do I have the power, Martin?'

'Can't think of another that does.'

'Then you have it,' Ben said, wishing in his heart that forgiveness for his sins could be brought about by a similar absolution.

'Mates,' said Martin, holding out his free hand. 'I'll look out for you, an' you look out for me, through thick and thin?'

Ben put out his hand and said, 'Mates.'

They heard the commands from below as Lieutenant Glaister gave out the orders to take in sail, that followed by an angry shout from the Yeoman of the Sheets. 'You two buggers, what in Christ's name do you think you are about. Get down out of there now!'

John Pearce watched HMS *Griffin* anchor with mixed feelings. He had no affection for the vessel, but a great deal of regard for the Pelicans on board, and a feeling that he owed the trio a great deal. Every time he recalled the looks he had received on departure his heart contracted with shame, forcing him to remind himself for the thousandth time that he had had no choice. Coming back to this place was something he had to do, maybe just because staying in London had been impossible.

Having informed Pastor Lutyens of his father's demise, he had then asked Horne Tooke to send the information to the various journals that came out daily in the capital, to be disseminated all around the country. He read them all in a coffee house over the following week, to discover that to most it was a footnote in the great drama being enacted across Europe. Some saw the story as due and divine retribution on a well-known troublemaker, others a further disgrace on a Revolution that had lost all claims to legitimacy, even the odd writer who reckoned it a slight to the nation. None gave Adam Pearce his due, nor praised any of the tenets by which he had lived. How the world had changed in under four years!

The only good news was that the warrant on his father, which had included him only as an accomplice, had lapsed with his demise, leaving him free to travel openly. Changing back into his midshipman's uniform, he had sold the clothes he had bought in Paris for more than he had paid, which gave him the means to eat plain, if not plentiful, on the way. It had been a long and slow journey from London back to Lymington on foot, on the back of a cart where he could beg relief, the whole carried out with an utter lack of real purpose, given that the aims that he was pursuing were exceedingly vague, if not downright confused. That had not changed on arrival, as he stood looking out over the narrow estuary that led out to the Solent.

Colbourne's boat put off almost before the ship was tied off to the buoy, as he knew it would, he being obliged to hand his papers and his revictualling requirements in to the Commodore who, no doubt, saw it as part of his professional duty to be impatient. He felt a strange sensation in his gut, brought on by nerves at what he knew was going to be a difficult encounter and he moved back from the edge of the quay to a point where those manning the boat could not see him, to a point where he could meet the ship's captain face to face and in private. Another very public humiliation was the last thing he wanted.

'God in heaven!' the man exclaimed, as Pearce stepped out in front of him. Clearly he felt threatened, for he held out the oilskin case containing the ship's logs and papers as if to defend his body.

'I wish to speak with you, sir.' Pearce was careful to make the "sir" sound like a remark between equals rather than an acknowledgement of the man's rank. 'If you will indulge me.'

'What about?'

'The possibility of rejoining the ship.'

'Damn you, Pearce, you are not short on effrontery.'

'Or need. I ask for a few minutes of your time, to plead my case. Then you can say yes or no.'

'I do not have the freedom to indulge you. The Commodore has made my number and right now will be examining his wall clock and wondering why I am taking such a devilish long time to obey his orders.'

'After you have seen him?'

'Why should I?'

There was no choice but to be an open supplicant, much as Pearce hated the idea. 'I need your help.'

Much as he tried to mask it, Colbourne was intrigued, and Pearce could see that his instincts were at odds with his curiosity. Clearly, he had not heard of his father's murder, hardly surprising given he spent almost his entire time at

SHOT ROLLING SHIP 235

sea.

'Go to the Angel. I had intended to take breakfast there.'

'May I ask how long?'

'It is pointless asking me, Pearce. If you really want to know you should make enquiries of the Commodore.'

'I will wait for you outside.'

Standing outside the Angel exposed the truth that was the underbelly of the seeming prosperity of the place. There was not a space in any English town that was not occupied by layers of desperate people and Lymington was no exception. Poor souls hung around the Angel Inn, hoping for something, anything, like the chore of catching hold of the horse traces as the Post Chaise arrived. Having seen to that they would grovel for the right to carry a traveller's luggage, and someone leaning against the wall, a stranger in a cloak, fit, strong and clean, might steal from them that job. Even the urchins who hung around hoping for a note to carry looked at Pearce with suspicion, wondering if he was a rival for the coin that task would earn.

The crossing sweeper, who kept the road in front of the inn free from dung, got very busy, for he would be questioning if his job, one of the lowest in the pecking order, was being eyed up, with good reason, for there was always a desperate cove who would go to the owner and offer to do the job for less than the scraps of food he was given to eat and ullage he received to drink, spilt beer gone flat that would otherwise be thrown away. The beggars, even ones supposed to be blind, were cursory in their examination, for he was too whole and well set up to threaten them, likewise the raddled whores peeping out from the alleyways who would prance and display themselves when a conveyance, or any one prosperous, came past.

The one who decided to enquire after his purpose reminded Pearce of Charlie Taverner; a sway in the walk, once-good clothes just too far the down side of worn, the big insincere smile and the hand inside his coat which could well be holding on to a cudgel.

'Waiting for someone, friend.'

'I'm minding my own concerns.'

'That be sharp of you, brother. It never does a man to do otherwise, I say.'

Pearce pulled the cloak open, to reveal the worn midshipman's coat and the man's eyes opened in mock surprise. 'Why you'se Navy, and here's us wondering what you was about?'

'Who was wondering?'

There was a clear glint of avarice then, the smile broadened, and the hand came out, empty, from under his coat. 'There's one or two round here it would be unwise to trust. Happen you need a bit of help to see what's going on around you, mate.'

'And you're just the fellow to oblige?'

'Tom Watts at your service. There's many a sailor boy been pleased to have me show them the ropes.' Watts laughed out loud and repeated his pun. 'Show them the ropes, sailor boys, do you smoke it?'

'Tom, I am standing here waiting for someone because I am too poor to go inside. Should I do so I would be obliged to purchase something for which I lack the means to pay, so I think that you might be wasting your time.'

'Now that offends, friend. An offer to help is just that.'

Said with mock anger, it nevertheless hit home, for Tom was already moving back.

'As you say, Tom. But I think we would both profit more from being left alone.'

That little exchange brought home to Pearce once more what little he had in the way of prospects, and certainly he had no means of elevating himself to become the kind of person who could take revenge on those murderers across the Channel. It was all very well entertaining a fantasy of rising to become a powerful man, but that was all it would stay; being the son of a radical orator did not fit you for much; in fact it positively debarred him from certain routes to the kind of goal he sought. He had something of an

education but, besides being incomplete, in what? A smattering of Latin and Greek, an incomplete knowledge of the
classics, the ability to ride well and wield a sword was hardly
the basis of any kind of career, and certainly not enough to
equip him to apply for a profession. The law was too expensive, and he would require a high degree of learning, which
he did not possess at present and lacked the means to
acquire in the immediate future. Medicine held no appeal,
although he was convinced that even totally ignorant he
could probably get by as a doctor, given the number of
charlatans who passed themselves off in that field.

Teaching was another option; he had enough learning for
that, especially in French, but quite apart from the fact that
they earned a pittance, he had bad memories of the schools
he had attended and the kind of people that taught in them;
miserable sods who were sore-headed in the morning,
drunk in the afternoon, and very fond of the birch cane as
a teaching aid. He could follow in the parental footsteps –
the name Adam Pearce would open certain doors – except
he had none of the conviction that had sustained his father
over the years.

Besides that, he longed to clear himself in the eyes of the
only friends he felt he had in the world. Right now
Colbourne was the sole person who could provide him with
an avenue, however tenuous, to do that, for they were on
the ship and might never be allowed ashore while the war
lasted. Maybe the Navy would assuage that desire for
revenge he felt by giving him a chance to strike back at the
French in some small way. He had no mind to be a soldier;
that was known to be worse than being a sailor, unless you
were an officer, and that required the means to buy a commission. He had even thought about the idea of a sum of
prize money that would set him up, before reminding himself, as he had sought to relay to others, that such notions
were in the realms of a pipe dream.

These depressing thoughts ceased as the Lieutenant came
up the High Street from the Commodore's house, head

thrust forward, trailing the usual following of grubby boys, cupped hands out, one persistently asking for a penny, another for a halfpenny, the most desperate for a farthing. He almost felt a kindred spirit to them.

'Even if your return is fortuitous, I have no real notion that I want you back aboard my ship.'

They were inside now, sat at a table, waiting for the food that had been ordered, each man with a flagon of cider in his hand. Pearce, who had failed to mention that he could not pay, longed to ask why his presence was fortuitous, but he sensed that would not help his cause. 'I will come back aboard as a common seaman.'

'You will not!' Colbourne exclaimed. 'If I allow you back on board at all it will be in the rank with which you departed, that of a volunteer. Then at least the Navy won't have to pay you, and nor will you get a chance to undermine the crew.'

Hope thought Pearce; he is thinking of agreeing.

'If that damn fool Bailey had not broken his leg I would not even consider it.' Colbourne responded to the enquiring look. 'He fell out of the rigging, fortunately from not too great a height. So you see I am short of a body, even a fairly useless one, to run the ship.'

Pearce posed his next question with some trepidation. 'I was given to understand that a queue of boys existed who would do anything to get in to the Navy.'

'Not aboard the *Griffin*.' Colbourne snapped. 'I even asked the Commodore for a suggestion. He said, and I quote his attempt to be jocose, "that he could think of no person he disliked enough".' Then he looked hard at Pearce and asked, 'Why?'

'I will not lie to you, I am at stand and the way I left *Griffin* still makes me uncomfortable.'

'The notion that you are stymied makes me content. In fact I can recall the moment you allude to and the fact that I thoroughly enjoyed it.'

Pearce felt his opinion of Colbourne shifting, though in

truth it had been dented on their last parting. He had seen him as rather soft, easy-going, perhaps with a sense of humour, but experience had shown that he had his own way of dealing with things, and a devious mind to boot. And there was an air of malice in his responses that Pearce had never thought to see.

'Might I ask if the crew is less disgruntled?'

That touched a nerve, for Colbourne spat a reply. 'The crew will do what is required of them.'

Perhaps things have not settled after all, Pearce thought. Would telling him the story of how his father had died and how he had witnessed it provoke sympathy, enough to aid the case? It was possible but he did not want to reprise it; he had dreamt about it too often these last two weeks, woken from his nightmare to curse himself as a coward for not even endeavouring to attempt a rescue. He should have tried and died in the process, and that he failed to do so would haunt him for the rest of his life.

'In truth, Mr Colbourne, at this moment, I have nowhere else to go and it pains me to tell you that I do not even have the means to pay for the food we have ordered.'

That quite visibly surprised the Lieutenant, who suddenly covered the lower half of his face with his cider tankard, holding it there longer than the time taken for a gulp.

'I can pay for your dinner.'

'Thank you.'

There was another pause, of the kind that all men make when faced with a decision they would rather avoid. Then Colbourne allowed himself a slight smile, as though he had just had a notion that amused him. 'I will grant you one voyage. In that time you must show me that my kindness is not misplaced. You must also show me you have the ability to command those men who were your former shipmates.'

Pearce could not resist the thought that Colbourne was toying with him once more, and he would have liked to have declined; but since he had no choice, he was forced to say. 'Thank you, again.'

'The correct form of address, Mr Pearce, is thank you, sir.'

The looks he got when he arrived at the quayside almost made his prior action worthwhile, which felt very much like grovelling. In no position to say anything, the boat crew had to look at him once more, this time their faces blank masks, to let him know the opposite of what was the truth; that they were near-dying of curiosity. Alongside *Griffin* a flat-bottomed Hoy was pumping fresh water aboard, this while a barge disgorged bundles of wood to feed the ship's stoves and the cook's coppers. Off the stern another party was hoisting in sacks of fresh bread, dried peas and oatmeal, and barrels of beer, salt beef and pork, these being lowered though a hatch to the holds. The cry of *Griffin* from the coxswain, to let those aboard ship know that their captain was coming aboard, did little to disturb the work. The men necessary to see Colbourne aboard, the quartet of marines and Midshipman Short, had changed from working clothes to proper uniform the minute they had seen the boat put off from the shore, this told to them by a ship's boy set at the masthead for that purpose.

Pearce had no idea who it was who spotted and identified him, but all labour ceased in an instant, every eye on the approaching boat, with several hands outstretched and pointing fingers. The roar of a petty officer's voice, heavy with cursing, got them working again, but not at the previous pace; every action was made in the light of the need to keep an eye on John Pearce. Colbourne was piped aboard to the stamp of marine boots, and Pearce, as he followed, was gifted the sight of Midshipman Short's lined old face in deep shock, this while his jaw worked to find the words he should say. Finally, taking his hat from his head, they came out as a croak.

'Welcome aboard, sir.'

Colbourne lifted his own hat to what passed for the quarterdeck, an act which had Pearce doing the same, as he recalled that it was what officers did on coming aboard ship. A ripple of exclamation, gasps and damnations swept the deck, that followed by another bellow from the petty officer to get working.

'Mr Short,' said Colbourne. 'As you know I rated Mr Pearce as a gentleman volunteer prior to his departure from the ship.'

'Sir.'

'He is now rejoining to replace Mr Bailey.'

There was obviously an enquiry in the Captain's look for Short responded. 'Shipped ashore, sir, to the hospital. I have been told to expect him to be unable to resume his duties for some six weeks, and he has asked me to ask you if he has permission to go home and convalesce with his family.'

'Six weeks, Mr Pearce. You might last more than one voyage after all.'

It could not have been staged, but it certainly felt like it, for those words were, as usual, heard by everyone. It was almost as if Colbourne was telling the crew to give him a hard time. Pearce remembered that slight amused smile before Colbourne consented to take him aboard. He thought now he understood it.

'Please return to your duties, Mr Short, while I outline to Mr Pearce his. After all, he is a complete novice. I will write Mr Bailey's permission to go home. It can go ashore with one of the supply vessels.'

All trooped below, Short and the marines to change back into working gear, Pearce trailing Colbourne to his so-called cabin. The captain stopped between the two layers of hanging canvas. 'You may put your possessions, such as they are, in where Mr Bailey berthed, and treat it as your own. I am sure he will have no objection to you using those things he has left behind. The most important will be his books on seamanship. I suggest you make a deep study of those.'

In his 'cabin' Colbourne continued, sitting himself but not inviting his new Midshipman to do the same, so Pearce was forced to stand head bowed, legs well spread and uncomfortable. 'Once we sail you will share watches with Mr Short, four hours on, and four off. I will take the deck at dawn each day, and I will wish the ship to be cleared for action just before that. You will keep the ship on the course I have set and do no more than alert me should you sight another vessel, apprehend any threat, or feel that the state of the weather requires my presence on deck. Now, I suggest you go on deck and supervise some of the loading of stores.'

Pearce put as much effort into his 'Aye aye, sir,' as he could. Probably futile, he was determined to show Colbourne that his petty malice had no effect. Busy getting out the materials to write a letter, the man did not even notice.

Pearce stood at the bottom of the companionway ladder for a moment, looking around what had once been his quarters and half regretting the fact that it was no longer the case, steeling himself for what he knew was likely to be a hostile reception. At all costs he must get Michael O'Hagan alone. If he could explain to the Irishman, and convince him that he had had no choice, then Michael would bring round the rest of the crew. The other thing he determined was that, while he was aboard, he would carry out his duties as scrupulously as he could, giving neither Colbourne, nor the rest of the hands, any excuse to regret his being there. Taking a deep breath he began to climb.

There was banter on the deck, there always was when this kind of duty was being performed, as one tar would jocosely insult another for laziness, looks, the pox, or some other perceived fault. It died completely, as did the work, the moment Pearce's head emerged from the hatchway. More telling was the fact that no one looked in his direction – any inadvertent eye was quickly turned away – that and the quiet manner, as opposed to the previous shouts, by which they were told to resume the proper level of labour.

Pearce headed for Short, who was, in all probability, his

superior. He would have to share a berth with him, albeit they would rarely be *in situ* at the same time. 'Mr Short, where would you like me to be?'

The look on that preternaturally aged face, and the glare that went with it, was as good as the man saying hell, but he had responsibility, and that overrode his personal desires. 'They are loading victuals aft. Take charge of the party there and see to it that what is sent below is properly stowed.'

Pearce heard the rumble as he made to oblige. Even in harbour the ship pitched on a slight swell, and whoever had dislodged it had timed it well, for as it grew louder he had to turn to look. Then he had to jump, quick, for the cannon ball was very close to his ankle, rolling by to come up against the rim of the hatchway. Slowly Pearce bent down and picked it up, turning and holding it in his hand. Not one eye was aimed in his direction, everyone was busy. Then, slowly he walked towards the bows, looking for the garland from which it had been taken, seeing one missing from the nine pounder furthest forward. Carefully he placed it back where it belonged, and as he straightened he caught the look of one of his shipmates. It was that of Michael, and it was a look filled with what appeared to be a deep loathing.

Chapter Eighteen

The very tactic that Pearce had visited on Lieutenant Colbourne was, on that duty, now being applied to him. In charge of loading the rest of the stores he would issue an order and it would be obeyed, but at a pace designed to show him just how he stood in the estimation of the crew. It did not help that he had to ask advice regarding the proper storage of the casks, which led to a string of derogatory remarks, all loud enough to reach his ears. Any hope he had of talking to the Pelicans was nullified by the fact that they stayed as far away from him as possible, working on the deck of the store ship rather than their own.

As the hands were being piped to dinner, he made his way below, passing through the crew quarters to get to the screened-off den that was now his, which exposed him to hissed curses and no shortage of jostling. Charlie Taverner and Rufus Dommet refused to meet his eye, not something Michael was prepared to do, though given the look Pearce wished he would. The dinner he ate was no better than that he had been given before, and in Short he had a companion who, either from suspicion or dislike, was good for no more than an occasional grunt in conversation, this in a berth so cramped that he almost longed for the crush he had known previously.

Then it was back on deck to complete the victualling of the ship, this work carried out with more of a will. That had nothing to do with Midshipman Pearce and his ability to issue orders, more to do with the fact that the boats would be coming out from shore again, and the men were keen to pretty themselves up for the visit. Colbourne clearly had no notion to witness the debauchery, for he called for his boat to go ashore. He would have to come back, for he was obliged by standing orders to sleep aboard, but he would, no doubt, time his return for when things had quieted somewhat. Short, once work was completed and they were back below, did actually speak to him on the matter of the forthcoming arrangements, nothing more galling than his assumption of agreement.

'You will appreciate, Pearce, that Bailey was too young to have an interest in the fair sex.' Pearce just nodded, having a very good idea what was coming. 'That would not, of course, apply to you, would it?'

Pearce looked up from his seat on Bailey's sea chest; not very far up for sitting, he was nearly the same height as his new messmate, conjuring up as he did so an image of the whores he had seen ashore, which did nothing to cheer him, for it would be they or their ilk coming out to service the crew tonight.

'I do have an interest in the fair sex, Mr Short, but it is not an appellation I would apply to the females who are presently going to come aboard. In them I have no interest whatsoever.'

That brought an expression to Short's face which could only be described as thwarted, and it was with some feeling that he said, 'Beggars can't be choosers.'

'Then I am happy to admit to not being a beggar.'

'It is the question of room, Pearce,' Short insisted, looking round their hutch. 'You do understand that a fellow has needs, and a degree of decent privacy is necessary when they are...'

He could not finish the sentence, but then he did not have to. 'If I had somewhere else to go, Mr Short, I would oblige you. But as I do not, and as I have no desire to share the pleasures you no doubt anticipate, I intend to sling a hammock and try to get some sleep.'

Short's little old face screwed up with frustration. 'That is damned unco-operative, Pearce. I should think that someone already in bad odour with the crew...'

'Would conclude,' Pearce interrupted, 'that it makes no odds if that is extended.'

The look Short gave him, just before he spun round and made his exit, was deeply malevolent, and Pearce wondered if he had been wise to be so intransigent, for he would, very likely, need advice from this dwarf if he was to carry out his duties. That was until he reminded himself that he really did have no choice, apart from spending the night on the open deck, hardly an enticing prospect since, given the over-crowding aboard, that was likely to be a scene of much car-nal activity.

His few possessions, sextant, shaving implements, flints, he placed on the available shelves, including a small tin he had purchased to hold that paper-wrapped earth he had taken from his father's graveside. Then, on second consid-eration, he decided to keep the tin on his person, to remind him of the cause he must pursue. In his pocket he could touch it constantly, and perhaps draw from it resolve, if not strength. When he did rig his hammock and climb in he found himself, with so little space, staring at his own knees. At least when he opened Bailey's copy of *The Seaman's Vade-Mecum* it was resting in the right place to read, that is if the light from the guttering lantern had been any good. He heard the scrape of boats coming alongside, and feet on the deck as the tribe of money-grasping nocturnals came aboard. That was the least of the noise, which increased in pitch as time wore on. There was a fiddler scratching a tune, probably for a penny, of which he was unworthy, squeals of female laughter mingled with screams, some happy, others angry and vicious, and he tried to blot from his imagination the scene beyond the screen at his feet, and what was hap-pening above his head on deck. The canvas that cut him off from the passage to Colbourne's cabin was hauled back more than once, and he found himself looking into faces of supreme ugliness, of whores who were still looking for a trick, or eager to service more than one tar. Finding that a polite refusal was insufficient, he roared at them to get out, which they did, leaving behind them aspersions on his man-hood and his probable inclinations.

Sleep did come, but not quickly and only through sheer exhaustion, and even that was disturbed by a drunken Short

trying to rig his hammock and the noise of the captain coming back on board. So it was a very groggy John Pearce who
stood to, as ordered, at dawn. That being the point at which
the tide favoured a departure from Lymington he had
another task to perform, to get the women off the ship, and
to ensure that no illicit drink was left behind, which was not
an action to raise the standing of even a popular officer. It
was also an occasion when he found out that dealing with
harpies made the most truculent sailor look easy; they
screamed, they cursed, they tried to bite, scratch and hit
him, that was when they were not trying to grab him in the
crotch and inviting him to slip into a hammock and enjoy
himself.

With the last of the spitting harridans over the side, it was
time to unmoor the ship. The attitude of the crew was the
same as the loading, this not aided by the state of their
heads, for every one of them had been very drunk the night
before from banned spirits brought aboard by the women.
The fact that he was merely relaying instructions from the
captain made no odds, and Colbourne, who could not fail
to observe the way he was ignored, declined to intervene,
except to embarrass him further.

'Mr Pearce, you really must get the men about their
duties. Establish your authority, for heaven's sake. You have
my permission to start any man who is tardy.'

There was nothing he could say; he was damned if he was
going to become a tyrant, and he lacked the means to persuade, so he had to fall back on the only course left open to
him, to do things himself, which would have been fine if he
had known what he was about. Apart from a bit of gun
practice and shroud climbing all he had ever done aboard
ship was haul on a rope or hump a barrel. Certainly, aboard
the merchantman, the *Lady Harrington*, observation had
shown him much, but the Navy was different; everything
must be done quickly, and paying attention to such duties
as hauling in the mooring cable left him unsighted when
anyone sought to goad him.

Stepping back he tripped on a small cask left there precisely for that purpose. He landed heavily, but one hand was put out to help him up, that of the old salt, Latimer. There was no kindness in the look or the words that accompanied it. 'You'd best find yourself another occupation, mister, for we are going to be in deep water soon, and that is no place to be unpopular on a dark and noisy night.'

'Even if I earn your respect?'

Michael O'Hagan, like the other Pelicans, was close enough to hear and reply to that. 'Sure, hell will freeze over first.'

'Why did you ever come back aboard?' demanded Rufus, his young, freckled face looking truly hurt.

'Don't ask him that,' snarled Charlie Taverner. 'He'll only lie to you like he did before.'

'Mr Pearce, is that mooring cable going to sully my deck much longer? Let's get it stowed away.'

'You heard the man, lads. Now you can decline the duty, and happen he will punish you just so you like me a little less.'

'Ain't possible,' said Latimer, but he went on, 'let's get it stowed. Be hard to have our grog stopped just so Coal Barge can bait this bugger. I needs a hair of the dog.'

As they set to, like proper seamen, Colbourne could not resist another jab, little knowing that it was to be inimical to his intention. 'I see you have the measure of them, Mr Pearce. Well done. I think you can come aft and join me on the quarterdeck now, where I am sure we can begin your nautical education.'

It was the sailor called Matt who spoke then, bent over hauling the slimy cable as Pearce walked away, a perplexed expression on his round face. 'Someat' ain't right here, lads. If we'es baiting Pearce, why is Coal Barge at it as well?'

'Who says he baiting him?' asked Rufus.

'Can any one lend this boy a brain, 'cause sure as hell he ain't got one.'

'Could say the ship's at one, mate,' said Charlie.

'Then it'll be the first I ever sailed on.'

'You'se got a point there, Matt,' said Latimer, a look of deep curiosity on his lined, weather-beaten face.

Pearce approached Colbourne and asked, 'Sir, do you think it aids the efficiency of the ship if you undermine me?'

'Mr Pearce, I have no idea what you are talking about, quite apart from the fact that you are at this moment so useless that the greatest threat to the efficiency of the ship resides in your person. Now be so good as to prepare the signal gun. Even you must be aware that it is the custom, on departure, to salute the Commodore's flag.'

The gunner was already there, with his light charges ready and the gun boomed out, to be replied to from the shore, in what to Pearce's mind was just a waste of powder. Then they were beyond the harbour mouth, albeit not yet fully at sea, but the ship began to lift and drop in that familiar way, with Pearce suddenly wondering if the seasickness which afflicted him when he had crossed the Channel in that fishing smack would come back to haunt him. Right now that was the last thing he needed. At least the sun was shining, and it was a clear spring day, as Colbourne put his helm down once they had cleared the narrow estuary and headed south-west down the Solent. Within the hour they were passing the Needles, the pinnacles of weather-hammered chalk standing clear and imposing at the southern tip of the Isle of Wight.

Colbourne stayed on deck throughout, for this was a busy shipping lane, especially for warships standing in for Portsmouth and the Spithead anchorage. Because he was there, and the petty officers were seeing to the various tasks that needed to be carried out, mainly clearing the deck from the mess it had been after the previous day and night to what it needed to be at sea, Pearce could relax. Easy as he was, he listened to every command that the captain gave, watched how he set the sail, took cognisance of the fact that he often went to the ship's side and looked at the colour of the water, making minor adjustments to account for the currents. They passed a patrolling frigate, a vessel that had the unenviable duty of guarding the Solent approaches, a task even less exciting than that on which HMS *Griffin* was engaged.

He had time to think too, the first notion being a question; was he really cut out for this life? The second was more alarming, as he began to understand just how little he knew. There was the setting of sails, the stowing of the ship's stores, blocks and tackles, ropes, knots, navigation, gunnery, all a mystery. He recalled the mids aboard HMS *Brilliant*, how they seemed as ignorant as he was now and presumably both Colbourne and Barclay had started in the same way. They had learned and so must he, and now he had the advantage that at any time, once they touched shore, he could walk off the ship and bid the whole business goodbye.

'Mr Pearce, you must not stand and daydream so. You may not be aware that I can, at any time I wish, withdraw your status as a volunteer and reduce you to a common seaman. So I suggest when you do not have an immediate task in hand you put yourself to study, for tonight you will be alone on this deck in sole charge of the ship.'

It was eerie on deck; not entirely alone, but with only a quartermaster and his mate manning the wheel, on a pitch black moonless night, with the wind steady over the stern to starboard, it felt strange. Colbourne had set the course and it was chalked on a slate under the binnacle lantern, registered on the compass above that and he had no power to change it. Not that he wanted to; he had no clear idea where they were going now, so would have even less of one if it was altered. He assumed that they were heading for the same waters where *Griffin* had taken that privateer, there to cruise in the hope of intercepting another, but no one had bothered to enlighten him. His sole task was to turn the half hour glass, and order the bell to be rung so that anyone awake would know the time. After eight bells he would retire and hand over the deck to Midshipman Short.

Alone with his thoughts, he sniffed at the night air, wondering if he would ever be in a position, as he had heard others claim, to smell the approach of bad weather. What he did know was, steady as the wind seemed to be, it was not constant, that there were flukes of change, slight but noticeable, and there were cross currents in the waters beneath the hull that rendered slightly uneven the pitch and roll of the ship. But the only sound, apart from the whistle of the wind through the rigging, was the creak of ropes as the quartermaster carried out minor adjustments to keep steady the compass needle. Those ropes ran through Colbourne's sleeping quarters, which made Pearce wonder how the man ever got any rest.

Isolated in darkness, with nothing really to do, it was easy to sink into a near comatose state, so the first rumble made him jump. But the dull thud as the cannon ball hit the side was unmistakable, that soon followed by another rumble as the ball was shifted by the pitch of the ship. Peering forward he could see nothing, but he knew it was a problem with which he would have to deal, for if he did not, it would go on and on. It was the kind of noise designed to wake everyone on board – he knew that from his own shot rolling – and it would keep them awake as well. Stepping forward beyond the binnacle it was even darker; he could see nothing at all, not the side of the ship, the shrouds, or the gun carriages, but he could hear the cannon ball, though fixing it by sound alone was impossible.

Pearce suddenly crouched down, hands out in front of him, in a forlorn hope that the damned thing would oblige him by trundling in the right direction. The swift movement of air, just above his head, removed his hat but missed his head, and he heard a muttered curse as he instinctively rolled sideways, ramming into a gun carriage and jarring his shoulder. The pain of that he would feel later; right now he had someone in the Stygian blackness who could seemingly see better than he and was trying to brain him; whatever had removed his hat had been solid enough for the purpose. Safety lay on the quarterdeck, by that binnacle lantern, but whoever had tried to clout him would know that, so he moved slightly towards the prow, which placed his assailant in silhouette. Pearce could not see much, an indistinct shape, an arm raised with the outline of a marlin spike, but it gave him some idea of where to aim.

The temptation to shout out was huge, but he resisted it; would the quartermaster or his mate leave the wheel to come to his aid anyway? He was damn sure no one would come from below for that purpose. There was no clear process of thought, he just knew he had to deal with this himself and using the gun carriage he hauled himself to his feet and kicked out, feeling the toe of his shoe make contact. Now his attacker was right between him and the light, and Pearce belted him with a swift jab to the head that hit bone and hurt his knuckles, that followed up by another kick that landed on something and the silhouette disappeared. That damned cannon ball rumbled again, coming aft and getting louder; if it came quickly enough to hit in the right spot it was enough to break a bone or two and the confusion about what to do gave his assailant the time he needed to get away. There was no more than a sliver of faint light as the hatch lid lifted and dropped, but it was enough to let Pearce know that, barring that rolling shot, he was in no more danger.

'On the wheel there, get a lantern lit and fetch it forrard.' Seeing no movement Pearce lost his temper, and shouted in a way to ensure that any soul who could sleep through shot rolling would wake now. 'Damn you man, do as I say and do it at the double.'

The effect was gratifying, even if, with his anger subsiding, he felt slightly foolish. The quartermaster's mate used the binnacle flame to light an oil lantern and came forward gingerly, it held high above his head, during which time Pearce had got himself, by feel alone, behind one of the gun carriages. It took no time at all once the tiny deck was lit, to find and secure the cannon ball, at which point Pearce resumed his position, with both men back on the wheel, and now that it was quiet again he could think over what had just happened, on the level of that threat and how he was going to have to deal with it.

'The glass, Mr Pearce. It needs turning,' said the quartermaster.

It was sheepish Pearce who replied. 'How many bells? I've forgotten.'

'Seven.'

The way the man audibly sighed as he replied was strangely reassuring, for it indicated to Pearce that he had no idea of what had happened in the darkness beyond the binnacle, and that seemed to imply whoever had attacked him was not doing so on behalf of the whole crew. He might be wrong, of course, clutching at straws, but it made him feel good to believe it, for the alternative, with three weeks at sea, was deadly. The sand ran through the glass one more time before a grumpy and uncommunicative Short came up to relieve him, but he waited for a bit before he made his way to his hammock, for just as the watch changed on deck, so it would below, with half the men being turned out of their hammocks so as to be ready to work the ship should that be necessary. When he did descend the companionway he was forced by the lack of room to crawl under sleeping bodies, every nerve tingling, for all would know where he was going at this time and anyone who wished him ill, either awake or just pretending to be asleep, would have another opportunity to attack him.

He was up with everyone else before first light, in command of the larboard guns as Colbourne swept the increasingly defined surroundings. Not that it was clear, heavy cloud and a grey sea made the point at which the sky ceased and water began indistinct, but it was empty, so the guns could be housed and the naval day could commence with the cleaning of the decks. Pearce was examining every man as they carried out their duties of wetting, sanding, sweeping and flogging, looking for signs of a limp or a bruise to the head. He was also looking for the furtive glance in his direction that would indicate a conspirator. He naturally paid particular attention to his Pelicans, and was relieved that they did not look at him at all. Then he saw Gherson rub his lower leg, and noticed that the bandana he was wearing was tied a lot lower than normal. So perhaps there was a bruise under there.

That, however, set off a train of thought. Gherson was a pest, but he was malleable, a crawler, an easy man to persuade to undertake the task of braining Pearce and coward enough to wait until dark to do it. As far as he knew he had betrayed him to Colbourne for little more than the captain's gratitude and he would do the same for another. That begged the question of who put him up to it, because with his previous behaviour of interfering with Pearce's possessions it could again be Colbourne, a doubtful scenario, for there was no logic in it, but one that had to be considered. So were there others, who had put the sod up to it? Who were they and did they have the intention of making another attempt, this time by somebody more competent?

'Pipe the hands to breakfast,' said Colbourne, at which point Pearce moved close to him so that the exchange would not be overheard.

'Permission to address the crew, sir.'

Colbourne's eyebrows shot up. 'Address the crew, Mr Pearce. I do believe that is a captain's prerogative.'

'I suspected it would be, sir, but I have something I wish to say to them that may well increase the efficiency of the ship.'

'No more rolling shot?'

That was Colbourne's first acknowledgement of the fact that he had heard it.

'More than that.'

'Believe me, Mr Pearce, that is enough. You may address the hands below as they take their breakfast. I will not oblige you by assembling them on deck.'

'That suits me, sir, and with your permission I will close the hatch. I have no mind to let either you or Mr Short hear what I have to say.'

He would listen, of course he would, but he could not say so and the knowledge that he would eavesdrop stopped him from checking Pearce for words that were definitely insubordinate. Waiting till all the men were finishing their breakfast, Pearce slipped down the hatch and closed it behind him, amused because the sound of feet moving forward was clearly audible. He stopped on the bottom rung, as Colbourne had done that first day aboard, and looked at the crew, waiting till they, made curious by his staying where he was, stared at him.

'Right,' Pearce said. 'I am going to say something to you all, and be assured there will be no repetition. I don't expect you to like me...'

'Never fear that, mate,' said a low hidden voice, which he recognised as that of Blubber.

'...nor do I care if you respect me, but I will from now on, when I am on watch in the dark, have close to me a pistol, primed and loaded. So if anyone is thinking of repeating last night's little escapade, be warned, it is a weapon I know how to use.'

His eyes ranged over the group, looking for the reaction, trying to see who they were that would happily kill him, and how many. Gherson was looking at the deck but everyone else was giving him a stare to equal his own, not friendly, but not guilty either, more the look of folk wondering what the hell he was on about, which made him question if he had made a misjudgement; could Gherson have acted on his own?

'Apart from three of your number, I have no loyalty to you, which means I owe you nothing.'

'Is this another story, Pearce?' demanded Latimer.

'If you don't know now what the story telling was about, ask Michael over there, for he will tell you. Or Gherson, who stole a letter from my ditty bag.'

'That's a lie.'

Not a head turned at that, so Pearce had no idea if they believed him or not. 'I did it for my own reasons and for my own reasons I am a midshipman aboard this ship. I am telling you here and now that if I am given the responsibilities of an officer I will act like one. I have no mind to spend the whole voyage either watching my back or getting myself dirty doing the work you are supposed to carry out. I will, if I have to, report you to the captain for punishment.'

'Man turns easy,' said Latimer.

'Don't bait me.'

'Why is Coal Barge at the same game, Pearce?' asked Matt.

'He's enjoying himself. Every time you torment me it gives him pleasure, for that is what I did to him when I was last aboard. Anyway, I have said my piece, and I will say no more.'

Blubber again. 'Thank Christ for that.'

Pearce ignored him, taking it as just a standard reaction. Instead he looked right at O'Hagan. 'Michael, I want you, Rufus and Charlie on deck now. I have something to say to you.' Charlie opened his mouth with the clear intention of saying no, but Pearce cut him off. 'And that, I'm sorry to say, is an order.'

Waiting in the bows, Pearce was never sure what brought them up. Not fear for sure, more likely curiosity, and perhaps the other crew members had goaded them out of the same sentiment. The way they approached was almost amusing, the walk of each trying to send him the message that they were his equal. Michael carried it off with ease, Charlie with a swagger that was too obvious to be anything other than an act. Rufus tried to look as if he was tough, and ended up looking like a fool. Behind them Gherson came on deck, until Pearce called out.

'Go below, or I'll rip that bandana off your head and have a look at what you're hiding underneath it.'

No more proof was required that Gherson was the culprit; he shot below like a scalded cat, leaving Pearce looking at three faces in various expressions of distrust.

'I want to say I'm sorry, and explain.'

'You'd need to be more than sorry,' said Taverner.

'Then I don't know what that is Charlie. Beyond a sorry and meant there is nothing.'

'Talk,' said Michael.

'I would not want you to turn around, but if you did you would see Lieutenant Colbourne staring at us, and I think it won't be long before he asks what we are about. So…'

Pearce wondered as he spoke, not for the first time in his life, why explanations always sounded like excuses, even when they were true. Try as he might to find a tone in his voice that would convey the veracity of his words he could not do it and nothing on the faces of the trio of men before him led him to believe he was succeeding, for their expressions remained blank.

'The trap was sprung on me, and Colbourne was clever in his timing leaving me no margin to include any of you. I had to decide between you three, who faced no threat, and my father, who faced a very real one.'

'We only have your word for that,' said Charlie.

'It was real Charlie. I found out when I got to London that he had been imprisoned in Paris. That is where I have been…'

'Don't tell me, you went and rescued him. The hero Pearce.'

'No Charlie, though I wanted to.'

'You went all the way there?' asked Rufus, his eyes open in wonder.

'He was my father, my only relative living, so what choice did I have. I found him in his cell…'

'Was?'

Pearce, as he looked at Michael, felt the tears well up once more in his eyes, felt again that sensation of not knowing if they were caused by grief or self-pity. 'Ten days ago they took my father, in a cart, from a prison called the Conciergerie in Paris, to a square called the Place de la Revolution.'

Michael was ahead of him and his malice evaporated. He had obviously picked up the catch in the voice, and he could not fail to see the wetness around Pearce's eyes. He put a gentle hand on his forearm. 'There, with a crowd who had no idea of his name screaming for his blood, he was, like a dozen other poor innocents, strapped to a board, and his head was cut off.'

'John boy,' said Michael, 'we need no more.'

'You do Michael, you do, for I was there, in the crowd, and I saw it happen. And do you know Michael, I did nothing.'

'Mr Pearce, I am wondering what you are doing loitering in the bows with those fellows?'

'I will get you off this ship, I promise, all three of you. I owe you that.'

'How do we know we can believe you?' asked Rufus.

It was Michael who replied, looking right into Pearce's eyes. 'I believe him.'

'What about you?' asked Charlie.

'I'll stay if Colbourne let's me. Right now I have nowhere else to go.'

Ben Walker heard the voice above him shout that he had sighted a sail, but bent over the yard, untying a knot, and supported only by his upper arms and a dipping foot rope, he declined to react. Martin Dent, being more accustomed to being aloft, did, but swore he could see nothing.

'Where away?' called Lieutenant Glaister, from the quarterdeck.

'Two sail. Five points free off the starboard bow.'

The orders came to stop the drill, and to set a sail plan more suited to the conditions. Midshipman Farmiloe went past them as they let go of the mainsail, and it was sheeted home by the time he got to the tops with his telescope. Both Martin and Ben Walker were back on deck when he reported what he could see, the shout directed at Ralph Barclay, who had come on deck, happy to leave the mass of paper which littered his desk and the noisy preparations for yet another dinner being prepared by his wife.

'Two ships, sir, one square rigged, the other with a single mainmast, though the mainsail, lanteen-rigged seems over-large.'

'Does it have a colour, that sail?' shouted Barclay, through a speaking trumpet, a question that earned him curious looks, but he, having sailed in these waters before, knew why he was asking.

'Deep red, sir.'

'The other?'

'Three masts, sir, dun coloured sails. I guess it to be some kind of merchant vessel.'

'Mr Glaister, signal to Captain Gould to come alongside. Helmsmen, we will be coming round on a course to close.' That led to a string of orders, while in their wake HMS *Firefly* had cracked on some sail to close. As she came alongside Ralph Barclay called out, 'I daresay your lookouts have smoked those sails, Gould. Close until you can identify them and then let me know what they are. I will be in your wake.' Then it was another shout to the tops. 'Mr Farmiloe, keep a weather eye out. I want to know if they change course.'

'You anticipate that, sir?' asked Glaister, as *Firefly* pulled away.

'Most certainly. As soon as they see we are ships of war.' He pointed to the foremast, where the white pennant streamed out, with the national flag in one corner. 'That should tell them they have nothing to fear, but it will be some time before they can see it clearly.'

'Unless they are French, sir.'

'Take my word for it, Mr Glaister, that they are not.'

His Premier gave a look that encouraged him to disclose his reasons for such certainty, an invitation he declined.

'Ships have altered course, sir, and they have split up.' There was a long pause, before Farmiloe yelled again. 'I think the red sail, sir, is a galley of some kind. I can see what appear to be sweeps hitting the water either side, and she is closing with us. The other ship has held its course.'

'Sails and oars,' said Glaister, eyebrows raised.

Every eye was on Ralph Barclay now, waiting for him to react in some way. All he said was, 'A galley in the name of Creation? I never thought to still see one of them still in use.' He said no more for an age, until he could see the approaching vessel himself, pleased with his own pre-science, for given the colour of the sail he had anticipated the provenance of the sighting, if not the nature of the vessel. 'An old-fashioned Algerine vessel by the look of it. We will hold our course, and see what Captain Gould discovers.'

It was half an hour before Gould did anything, and that was to drop a boat in the water.

Down below Emily Barclay was anticipating her dinner, having by now become reconciled to the absurd naval habit of having it at three in the afternoon. Unfortunately, due to the sighting, she was having to wait, left to look at the four place settings, because today's guests, the marine officer and third Lieutenant, Mitcham, were all on deck with her husband.

'Shenton,' she said eventually, 'be so good as to go and tell Captain Barclay that his dinner is ready.'

Though he complied, that request got her an old-fashioned look, as though it was not done, but Shenton was like that, the kind to forever shake his head and suck his teeth if asked to do anything out of the ordinary. At least he had got used to her presence, and had learned to knock before entering any of the cabins. He was back in a few seconds.

'Captain's compliments, Mrs Barclay, but could he have a plate taken on deck.'

Emily opened her mouth to protest, and to ask what the 'good' captain thought he was going to do about his guests, but that died in her throat. It was unwise to be open with servants about anything that smacked of a family dispute; they might know, indeed they always did, but it was a tenet of respectable life to keep a distance. That stricture was doubly applied on board this ship, where the article of discipline, something she was unsure of, added another dimension. The steward, with his long, doleful face and sad eyes, was looking at her in that way he had, almost as if he had yet to comprehend that she was really aboard. That he was unhappy with the fact was not a secret, much as he tried to cover it, which Emily put down to the increase it created in his responsibilities; not his workload, for he passed most of that on to others.

'Would you go back on deck and ask Captain Barclay if it would be acceptable for his officers to be fed likewise?'

It was with plates in hand that the quarterdeck of HMS *Brilliant* observed Gould's boat, the gap shortening rapidly as the rowers pulled hard to close, and it gave Ralph Barclay cause for disquiet; it was a strange way to behave, and hinted at a message more complicated than that which could be sent by flags.

'Mr Farmiloe, do you see anything of interest.'

'The galley-type vessel is holding it's course, sir, but, coming into the wind, she has clewed up her mainsail. The merchant ship has ported her helm and is heading due east.'

'Armament?'

'Two heavy cannon bows and stern, sir, by my reckoning, but I cannot see what weight of shot they will take.'

'Mr Glaister. I do not want to clear for action, but I would want some of the preliminaries carried out, so that should we have to, we can get our guns out and into action quickly. Alert the gunner and prepare the ladyhole for my wife.'

Glaister, who had just taken a mouthful of beefsteak and oyster sauce, the last of the Lisbon stores, replied with a muffled, 'Mye, Mye thur.'

Emily, alone at the table trying to eat the same dish, was rudely interrupted by a posse of sailors, Shenton at their head, not sad-faced now but actually smirking.

'Sorry, Ma'am, we's got to strike the bulkheads and cabin furniture below and that means crating the plate and silverware. Captain has sent a party to get some seating and a lantern in the cable tier, just in case we get into a fight.'

With that she was hustled out of her quarters, asking in vain for her embroidery, as the wedges were knocked out and the walls of the cabins began to disappear.

'Stand by to get a line to haul in that boat.'

Whoever was coxing that knew his stuff, crossing *Brilliant*'s bow to bring himself onto the lee rail, lower in the water than the weather side of the ship, and he spun her expertly so that she was on the same course, only closing to the side when the bowsprit was past. Lines snaked out from the deck to haul her in, at the same time as boathooks were employed to keep a slight gap between boat and the side of the ship, by which time Ralph Barclay was leaning over the side.

'Captain Gould has identified her as a galley, sir.'

How clever of him, Ralph Barclay thought, testily. Does he think we have no eyes aboard *Brilliant*!

'Reckons her an Algerine pirate, sir, from off the Barbary Coast, and that merchantman a capture. Galley has sent her away and is likely to challenge our right to bring her to and demand answers.'

'Does he think she'll fight?'

'Rather than give up the capture, yes, sir.'

Ralph Barclay was tempted to say, 'well at least we agree on something.' But he held his tongue, disinclined to share the thought with anyone else on deck.

'Sheer off. We will let fly our sheets and get you aboard.'

The order took Glaister by surprise; he thought closing with the galley more important, but Ralph Barclay was not about to explain his reason for not leaving a boatload of sailors in the water when a North African pirate, possibly prepared to be hostile, was in the offing. Having served in the Mediterranean as a youngster, he knew all about them. If it did come to a scrap, he had no notion to leave these men in a position where they might be captured, to end up in a stinking North African dungeon or as a slave rower on the kind of vessel he was about to meet. Another order had the cooped livestock in the boat, before it was let aft to be towed astern. The hoofed animals, the goat, a cow, three pigs and a couple of sheep would just have to take their chances in the manger.

'Sheet home,' Glaister called, as soon as the tasks were completed, and HMS *Brilliant* resumed her course.

Ralph Barclay went to the weather side of the quarterdeck to pace up and down, head down and hands behind his back. It was a telling fact that a galley was at sea at all, for it must be an old vessel, they having not been in use for near a century for any kind of fighting, though still common in coastal trading and port work. Even North African pirates used Xebecs these days, small and fast, if no match for a frigate, but he supposed, with the seas clear of French warships because of the decimation of their navy, and Spaniards who were gathering at Cadiz to re-enter the Mediterranean in force, the way was clear for all sorts of vermin to emerge.

If that galley was a corsair, then he had every right to employ whatever force he needed to stop her activities. As against that, there would be no proof; that, if it existed, was sailing away from him as fast as the wind would carry her. This would be the Algerine's ploy, to delay him as long as possible so that he could not chase the other vessel, which could never hope to outrun a frigate, let alone HMS *Firefly*.

He tried to put himself in the mind of the galley commander. He would come alongside Gould with expressions of cordiality, and keep him occupied till *Brilliant* closed. There would, no doubt, be an invitation to visit, and an offer of food, talk of many things, anything to keep the two British warships where they were. If that was successful and he had taken an illegal capture, it would be near his home port long before they could come up with her. Ralph Barclay could not decline an offer of hospitality without causing offence and his orders obliged him to treat with neutrals carefully, and that included the various Bays and Deys of the North African coast, who could cause no end of trouble to a fleet trying to control the Mediterranean, quite apart from the fact that it was a place to secure supplies to maintain that fleet. The normal tactic was to bribe them to stay out of the way, and leave alone supply ships and merchantmen.

Not one man in a thousand believed the Algerines to be neutral in any other sense than they were not fighting the French. If they came across a British merchantman, bribed or not, they would take her if they thought they could get away with it. Was that fleeing merchantman that very thing, a well-laden Levant trader that had sailed before any convoys were formed or one on the way home, laden with silks and spices? Whatever, it would be worth a mint of money, and Ralph Barclay was minded to secure that rather than leave it to a bunch of sea-borne brigands. In his mind he formed a plan, one that might be profitable if he was right, which would keep him out of trouble if he was wrong.

'Mr Glaister, I want the larboard battery loaded with

powder charges only. Tell the gunner to use his worst leavings, the bottom of the barrel stuff, for what I want is smoke. Let us ease our braces a little and signal Captain Gould to come about and close with us. And ask my wife to come on deck.'

By the time *Firefly* was sailing on her previous station, with Gould, like *Brilliant*'s officers fully appraised of what to do, the deck of the galley was in plain view through a telescope, a clutch of turbaned and gaudily dressed individuals on a raised poop, watching him as they were being watched themselves. They would have observed the two warships resume their previous course and speed, sailing easy, braces not stretched, in the manner of vessels concerned to spare their canvas, no great activity on deck, for that had ceased an age ago on the frigate and had not taken place at all on Gould's ship. To complete the tranquil scene, they would see a captain in full uniform walking the weather rail arm in arm with a pretty young woman.

They were not talking, for Ralph Barclay was thinking, and Emily was obliged to respect that. He suspected that the galley's guns, in both prow and stern, would be loaded and bowsed against her gun ports, an act which would have been carried out long before her deck came in view. He had examined the ship closely while she was further off; what was showing of her well-reefed great mainsail, hauled right round, was not doing much to propel her – if anything it was slowing her progress. Forward motion was being provided by the poor souls pulling on her sweeps below the maindeck, slaves of many nationalities, some bound to be Christians.

But they were rowing easily too; there was no attempt to close at speed for the longer it took the better. Calculation was continuous, as well as futile; he could not tell from looking through a telescope how large was her crew – for instance, did her captain have enough men to put a whole new set of rowers on the sweeps – whether indeed her cannon were loaded, or if the supposition he was making was correct. All he knew was that it made sense.

'What a fine looking ship,' said Emily.

'Over decorated to my taste, my dear, and old-fashioned as a gun platform. For her size too much space is taken up by rowers, as well as her shape, to mount the kind of cannon she should, and as a fighting vessel they are utterly useless in foul weather. Algerine's are the only people who would still use them in the open sea and only then when the weather is calm.'

The galley, once she was close, let fly the sheets on her scrap of mainsail, and raised her starboard sweeps, gliding round in an arc to come between the British warships and what might be her capture. Again that was indicative of a less than honest motive and the sweeps were not boated; they stayed out, there to manoeuvre the vessel and her prow in a way that no square rigged ship could hope to match. Well-trained vessels such as these could turn in their own length, and cock a snook at the wind on an unruffled sea.

Ralph Barclay had to be careful everything on his deck was made to look as if he was really going to heave to, speed slowing and the rudder swinging the frigate so it would heave to opposite the north/south facing galley, all the men on deck seemingly engaged in unimportant tasks. The bang made both him and his wife start, but it was just a brass swivel gun saluting his pennant. Only it was for Ralph Barclay a different kind of signal, that and the fact that he dare not heave to completely, for it would take too much time to get under way again.

'Go to the cable tier NOW Mrs Barclay.' As Emily obeyed this command, her husband said. 'Mr Glaister, if you please.'

The Premier was no slow West Highlander at that moment. The speaking trumpet came out from his back and a stream of orders followed. The waisters ran to the falls and hauled tight those sails already set, while the gun crews were at their weapons, ports opening and cannon run out in a matter of seconds. The helm was down as more sails cascaded from the yard, dropped by topmen who had raced aloft, and with that wind HMS *Brilliant* began to move more swiftly, with the rudder pushed hard over to take the frigate past the stern of the other vessel.

'Fire.'

There was no aiming, without cannon balls it was not necessary. What Ralph Barclay was after was sound, fury and smoke, enough of the first to convince those on the galley's deck that he was firing at them, enough of the second to ensure their gunners kept their heads down for a few seconds, with the third obscuring what was happening on his deck. Trouble was, it obscured the other deck as well, but he could well imagine that the Algerine was spinning round on its sweeps, running out loaded bow-cannon to retaliate. Behind him Gould had come round swiftly on a southerly course to take him past the galley at long pistol shot range, in the hope of avoiding damage from those same weapons.

The breeze whipped the smoke forward off his deck and he could see the oars in the water, biting to bring the galley round and aim its cannon, now poking out through open ports, but he was sailing better now, his bowsprit already beyond the point where the stern had been. And on the opposing deck they would have realised that no shot had come with his own broadside and that would put doubt in their mind. If they delayed the order to fire for half a minute, he would be damn near clear. The cannon were run in and properly loaded this time, for he knew he might need some roundshot, the only nagging thought being that he had no idea how quickly that galley could make way through the water at full tilt. With her great mainsail drawing on a following wind and sweeps to boost her speed, she might have the legs of him.

Aloft Ben Walker, having beaten young Martin up the shrouds for the first time, was very pleased with himself, cackling to the boy that he would have to learn to shift if he was to be an upper yardsman. On the end of the mainmast he was pounding the canvas to loosen and drop it so that it would fully draw. Suddenly the air was alive with round-shot, and a hole appeared beneath his feet, but it was a following ball that hit the yard and, smashing through the timber, blew him off, too fast for the hand of Martin to grab and save him. The ship was heeled over, and had he not been propelled sideways by the blast he would have smashed into the deck. As it was his momentum carried him just past the scantlings and into the deep blue water.

Going under, he was vaguely aware of the coppered bottom of his floating home sliding by, but immersed he did not hear Martin's scream of man overboard. Ben Walker could not swim, so by the time he resurfaced, carried up only by his own natural buoyancy, spluttering and blinded by seawater, the ship was nearly past him. The latticed hatch cover, grabbed by a couple of his shipmates at Martin's shout, and slung as close to him as possible, actually landed within reach of his arm, and with a couple of panicked kicks, Ben got a hold on it. It was from there that he watched the decorated stern of HMS *Brilliant* disappear, the last thing to go past his nose, some ten feet distant and totally unreachable, a boat full of clacking and fearful chickens.

Martin, from his elevated position, could see him, and knew at least, on that hatch cover, Ben could float. But he also knew that Ralph Barclay would not heave to for the sake of one man, for to do so would risk the ship. Instead of going down on deck, as he was ordered, the youngster climbed to the masthead, so that he could keep an eye on a man with whom he had wanted to be friends, paying no attention, as everyone else on the ship was doing, to the attempts by the Algerine to put roundshot into *Firefly*, which suffered in the sails as her consort had done. Nor did he pay attention to the galley coming round sharply on those sweeps, huge mainsail set, to begin a pursuit. His only thought was that with three ships close by, not one had any care for a solitary sailor in distress, who would surely drown if he did not die of hunger and thirst.

It was a quarter of an hour before Ralph Barclay relaxed, sure that he could out-run the galley, and to aid him the sea was getting up on a hot wind coming off the Mahgreb shore; being choppy it was helping him and hindering his opponent. He listened intently as Glaister reported the damage, the end of the mainmast gone, the odd spar carried away and one man lost overboard, in all a very satisfactory outcome and ahead of him was that fleeing merchantman, which he was sure, with he and Gould well spread out to cover a lot of sea, he would catch the next day.

'Are you hungry Mr Glaister?'

'A little, sir.'

'Damn me, sir, I am more than that. My belly is rumbling. I wonder if you could send someone to ask my wife if there are any leftovers from our missed dinner?'

The Algerine gave up the chase long before nightfall, leaving both warships to eat up the sea miles, until four bells in the night watch, when they hauled their wind and reversed their course. The calculation was that the merchant vessel, hopefully unaware of what had happened in her wake, had been told to hold her own course until a certain hour, then come about to rendezvous at a prearranged point, for they had been sailing due south when first spotted, so it was a fair bet, looking at the charts, that the home port they were aiming for was either Oran or Mostaganem, Algiers itself being too far to the east.

Stood to at dawn, they spotted her hull up as the sun rose, and the chase began, not that the outcome could be in any doubt and that was removed completely when the merchantman let fly her sheets. Within minutes there was a boat over the side and a single mast stepped, that followed by a triangular sail. Through his telescope Ralph Barclay watched the men piling into the boat, thought he caught a flash of white, saw them brace their sail tight, and set off due south to the shore which lay over the horizon.

'They have abandoned her, sir.'

'They have, Mr Glaister,' said Ralph Barclay sadly. 'Please ask Mr Lutyens to be ready to go aboard, and Mr Glaister, ensure that while we are alongside, my wife does not come on deck.'

The merchantman, a large fully laden Levanter as Ralph Barclay had suspected, wallowed on the swell, and they approached in what was an eerie silence. The deck itself was clear if not clean, and hooked on he went aboard himself, with Lutyens making a pig's ear of crossing the two bulwarks and having to be aided over by two sailors. Most of the bodies were below, in the crew quarters, their throats cut from ear to ear, and so recently that the cramped space was awash with fresh blood. Clearly they had been kept aboard as prisoners to sail the ship.

The Master, likewise, was dead in what had once been the luxuriously appointed cabin, and he had endured more, his face bloated with bruising, his breeches round his ankles for purposes Ralph Barclay had no desire to think about. In the side cabin there was evidence of female occupation, clothing, a mirror, hairbrushes and the like. That explained the flash of white; it had been a woman forced into that boat. He had a sudden vision of his own young bride and what that woman, probably the master's wife, must have suffered already. She would suffer more, there was no doubt of that, and the captain of HMS *Brilliant*, not a deeply religious or caring man, nevertheless said a silent prayer for her.

'Not one alive,' said Lutyens. 'Why?'

'Death means they are not able to bear witness to piracy. There was a woman taken alive.'

'Is there a reason why they let her live. Surely she can bear witness as well as any man?'

'Mr Lutyens, if she is fair and plain skinned she will be sold to some harem in the interior, never to be heard of again. If she is not fair, she may well end up scrubbing Musselmen floors with a daily beating to make sure she does her work.'

'We could not go after them and rescue her?'

'No. For then they would slit her throat too.'

Leafing through the manifests, he realised just how valuable a cargo this vessel carried, saffron and vanilla, the first the most precious of spices, but many more all the way down to peppercorns, and silks, the whole certainly not less that a hundred thousand pounds in value. But he could not rejoice, and felt it would be gross to even begin to think about his own share of so rich a prize.

Back on deck he called over to his own ship. 'Mr Glaister, sort out a party to take charge of the prize under the command of the Third Lieutenant. He is to take the ship into Gibraltar and hopefully he can pick up the fleet from there and return to us when they join.'

'Aye, aye sir.'

'And tell Mr Mitcham he can borrow the sailmaker for an hour or two. As to canvas and balls to weight the victim's shrouds, I'm sure there is enough aboard for the necessary burials.'

Griffin was cruising off the north coast of Brittany to cover a route that would be taken by St Malo privateers looking for quarry, and was by now settled into a tedious routine of ploughing a box on the charts that would, Colbourne hoped, intercept them either on the way to their hunting grounds or their prizes coming in, sent back lightly manned to the corsair's home port. But as usual, all they had seen for days, apart from one large and intact British incoming convoy, were neutral merchant vessels that were happy to heave to for inspection and, quite naturally, this did not please the men. It was curious for Pearce to listen to the loud and clear moaning of the crew through the canvas rather than to be part of it, and even although it was nothing like the pitch it had been with his encouragement, it gave him some idea of how uncomfortable it must have been for Short, Bailey and the captain.

Other discomforts came from lack of knowledge and constantly interrupted sleep, but by reading Bailey's books on seamanship he began to get some idea of how a ship worked: what was meant by a bowline, the number of points free on a compass a ship could sail into the wind, a better understanding of leeway and how it affected a ship's course, and even the currents of the waters in which they were sailing, tidal flows that changed predictably over the lunar cycles throughout every twenty-four hour period, based on the time at Dover. What was less helpful was the disinclination of either Colbourne or Short to add to that educative process, which left him to find out a great deal for himself, but never before he had exposed his ignorance.

And daily, indeed hourly, he gnawed on the guilt associated with what had happened in Paris, sometimes finding himself near to a feeling of hate for his father for burdening him with such a responsibility, welcoming any diversion that took his mind of the events of that day. If anything had been said about him to the rest of the crew, it had been done so out of his hearing, but the change in attitude was quick. Really, Pearce knew, all he needed was O'Hagan on his side, for although the crew did not go in fear of him – he was no bully – they did respect his prowess with his fists, so were not inclined to dispute with him. Besides that Michael was, quite naturally, a bit of a bellweather for others; people trusted Michael O'Hagan or disliked him, and there were few of the latter. Charlie, for a while, tried to remain distant, as if to imply he was considering before making up his mind, with Rufus, as befitted his nature, dithering one way then the other, but within two days they had fallen into line, not yet chatty and friendly, but not glaring and suspicious. The rest of the crew began to josh him in a gently disparaging way, which Pearce knew was not ill-intentioned merely by the tone.

Apart from his every instruction being carried out in a normal way, the most pleasing thing was the isolation of Gherson. Clearly, feeling deserted, Michael had not let the crew know of the theft of his letter. Just as obviously, with their friendship re-established, he had done so now and the sod was on the receiving end of kicks shoves and much spitting, for there was nothing worse to a sailor than an onboard thief, the irony being that Pearce, if he saw any of this, had to intervene to protect him. The reaction of Colbourne was surprise, which led to a command once more, right after the crew's breakfast, to attend upon him in his cabin.

'You are a slippery fellow, are you not?' Pearce declined to answer, he just met the lieutenant's eye. 'And full of yourself to boot. You dare to try and stare me down, which is insubordinate.'

'It would be of some help, sir, if you could write down what is and what is not an offence, so that I may learn. I cannot feel that to decline to reply to what seems like an accusation can be seen as that.'

'The solution for me, Pearce, is to have aboard inferiors

who know their place.'

'The ability to command the men...'

Colbourne interrupted him then, but he was no longer looking at Pearce, he was looking at his deck, his shoulders set in a crabbed, stubborn way, almost as if he was talking to himself. 'I should have handed you over to the magistrates as soon as I found out who you were. I am too soft.'

'And now, sir, you are too late.'

It was the wrong thing to say, which Pearce knew as soon as it left his lips, for Colbourne slapped the desk. 'Do not talk to me, man, as though you are my equal. You are aboard on my sufferance, in the lowest station a man can hold and still call himself a gentleman.'

'You wish to withdraw that status?'

'No!'

Colbourne did not say so, but it was obvious to both that to return him to his previous rating would be worse than suffering him in his present one, quite literally leaving him be was the lesser of two evils. Pearce was silent too, though there was a lot that he would have liked to have brought out in the open, not least an open admission of Colbourne's plan to pay him back in kind. That had backfired, leaving nothing but the spite with which it had been initiated, but he did remind himself of that to which the lieutenant had just alluded; he could have turned him in after he had read Lutyens' letter, but had not done so. Whatever his behaviour since, Pearce owed him for that.

There was another reason for holding his tongue; he did not want to lose this little bit of rank. In only a few days, even with all the vicissitudes he had faced, he had taken to life aboard much more than he had as a lowly landsman. If his berth was cramped there was some solitude; the food was no better but it was eaten out of sight of anyone but Short, and often even he was not present. He had books to read – not those he would have chosen necessarily, but there was no chance for such a thing in the space he had occupied before. It was, all in all, if far from perfect, a much better existence. Added to that was his promise to the other Pelicans; his blue coat meant he could be much more active in helping them to run.

Colbourne sat back suddenly, his face showing no sign of his previous anger. If anything he looked bemused. 'Tell me Pearce, what future do you see for yourself?'

Was it an olive branch? Pearce could not be sure, but it was such a startling change of tack, both in manner and expression, that he was inclined to take it so. He made very effort to keep out of his reply any hint of arrogance. If it was what he suspected, the best thing to do was to meet it halfway.

'I would be less than honest, sir, if I said I knew.'

'The Navy?'

'Possibly.'

'Then let me enlighten you to some unpleasant facts. You have this berth because of an injury to Mr Bailey, which I will rescind on his return to duty. Will he return to duty? He is not obliged to, being a volunteer, and I have no notion that he took to the life. Quite apart from that, even one so young will have realised that this is no place to be for anyone interested in advancement, so he may seek another ship and another captain.'

Pearce was thinking; six weeks, two voyages, not much time to help his Pelicans desert.

'Maybe I will keep you aboard, but such a thing could be as much a curse as a blessing, for you cannot get anywhere in the Navy without influence. Do you have influence, Pearce? I am on this vessel, instead of a frigate or a ship-of-the-line, because I lack a patron, a senior captain, an admiral or someone with either blue blood or political power to move me up in the service.'

'Yet you are a lieutenant are you not?'

'I had the good fortune to be in the West Indies when I was promoted. That is a station where such things are made to fill dead men's shoes. I have no inclination to believe that my elevation would have happened anywhere else. How can

I complain, my pleas to the Admiralty for employment did not go entirely unheard.' A bitter tone crept into his voice and his eyes ranged around his tiny space. 'Though sometimes, when I look at what I have, I wonder whether someone has sent me to this as a cruel jest. Every time we touch the shore I send off a plea to be moved to another ship. I point out that, ideally, given the length of my service, I should be a First Lieutenant on a seventy-four, and each time we touch again, I have my reply.'

The bitter sarcasm larded Colbourne's voice as he revealed what the replies said, staring at the deck beams above his head as he spoke. 'The Commissioners for executing the office of Lord High Admiral have taken cognisance of your request, but fear, given the level of similar requests they are forced to satisfy, they are in no position to oblige. You are, of course, at liberty to resign your present commission at any time of your own choosing, in the expectation that some other employment may become vacant.'

'You are saying that I should not look to the Navy for a future?'

Pearce never got a reply, for the curtain was thrown back and Colbourne's steward appeared. 'Mr Short's compliments, sir, but the lookout has espied a ship to the southeast, and he begs to give the opinion it ain't no merchant vessel.'

Given the lack of space, Pearce had to go out of the 'cabin' before him, but stood aside to let Colbourne pass on the way up to the deck. The lieutenant immediately took a telescope from the rack and following Short's finger trained it on what had been seen, not difficult as ploughing into the wind on the southerly side of their box the yards were braced right round. Pearce stood, with the southwest wind on his face, just observing.

'All hands,' he said, as soon as he had focused, his voice strained. 'Stand by to come about.'

'Might I ask...'

Short never got a chance to finish his question, as Colbourne barked at him, 'It is an enemy seventy-four, Mr Short, and he has the weather gage, so if you do not desire to spend the rest of your days in a French prison, I should get on with obeying my orders.'

'Sail has altered course, sir,' the lookout called down.

'Mr Short, I want that man in chains,' Colbourne hissed. 'Those sails should have been spotted an age ago. Get a better pair of eyes aloft this minute.'

The little midshipman's old lined face looked aggrieved, as if Colbourne was chastising him and not the man at the masthead. 'I did my best, sir.'

That was when Colbourne blew, his voice was heard all over the ship. 'Then your best, sir, is not good enough and I doubt you know this, but we stand little chance in this vessel of outrunning a ship of the line.' Then the voice softened, as though he was talking to himself. 'Let us hope she is a dog, or a bottom covered in weed.'

The orders were issued and the ship came up into the wind with little grace, HMS *Griffin* behaving as she always did, and Colbourne put her right before the wind, jagging to starboard and larboard slightly to get the best out of her and setting as much aloft as she would bear. Pearce was fascinated by the air of the man, an aura of total competence as he stood rooted to the spot doing nothing but issue one order after another. Now he was training his telescope over the stern, fixed on those high sails, which he knew had altered course on spying the sails of the smaller vessel, first to close, now to pursue.

'Mr Pearce, get the hatches off on the lower deck and men standing by with axes to start the water. Then we will need a party on the pumps, with a relief standing by.'

That party should have included the Pelicans, but Charlie Taverner looked at John Pearce in a jaundiced way that implied he was likely to be unfair, even if that was not the case. They were lubbers, and it made no sense to put a trained seaman to a job that required no brains or ability and some brawn. Thinking himself too soft, he gave his mates the axes, and he detailed Littlejohn to lead them, that as Colbourne issued another order.

'Set up the fire engine as well, and get the hose down to the bilges. It will speed things up. And Mr Pearce, remind anyone slacking of what fate awaits them.'

He wanted to ask questions, not one but several, but it was clear to Pearce that Colbourne would be in no mood to answer. How had he identified the other ship so swiftly, for he could only have seen her sails? If they could overhaul *Griffin* how long did they have? From his reading he had a good idea that they were being swept along by a helpful current, but a picture of the map in his head told him that and the course they were on was taking them in the direction of Guernsey, the outermost of the Channel Islands, which Bailey's book on sailing in these waters had said was a place of powerful tides requiring extreme caution and good seamanship.

After a long flurry of activity, everything went quiet. The ship was set on its course, all that Colbourne required to be done was in place, the crew now free to look themselves over the stern at the enemy seventy-four, though all they could see was the odd tip of a brownish sail topping the horizon and the slight flash of a pennant. Looking at Colbourne, still with his eye to the telescope most of the time, Pearce wondered at his thoughts, even more so when he dropped the glass from his eye, to reveal a face full of perplexed calculation.

'Mr Pearce, start the water, and get the pumps and fire engine going. Mr Short, I want a crane rigged over the hatches to get out our stores. I'm going below to study the charts.'

'Bugger's gaining on us,' said Latimer. 'That's fer certain.'

Pearce heard these words as he followed Colbourne down the companionway ladder, a group of men behind him with axes in their hands, two others with the fire engine hose, the rest left behind to man the pumps which had been rigged on each side of the deck. The next drop was down into the forward hold, damp, smelly and dark. He was not sure he heard scurrying, it might have been his imagination, but he knew there were rats down here.

'Lanterns,' he ordered, 'and get that deck hatch lifted to give us some air.'

'What's Coal Barge looking at the charts for?' asked Rufus.

'If I knew the answer to that I'd be in charge, not Colbourne.'

'He'll be looking for a landfall, mate,' said Littlejohn, 'someplace to run the ship ashore and burn her.'

'Christ!' exclaimed Charlie.

'Anything to avoid being taken.'

'What do we do then?'

'Those that's allowed into the boats can make for home once the coast is clear.'

'And who might they be?

'Prime hands like me, mate.'

'And the rest?'

Littlejohn clearly enjoyed his next answer, he was almost laughing. 'Lubbers like you, Charlie, walk to the nearest town and hand themselves in.'

'Still want to get to France, John boy?' asked Michael.

Pearce suspected he was grinning too, but could not see him in the dark, though he reasoned that if what Littlejohn was saying was true, then he would at least be in a position to help those who would be left behind. It was not a prospect that excited him, just a duty that he knew he would have to perform.

Light first came with the removal of the deck hatch cover, faint, grey and insufficient. The lanterns followed and Pearce surveyed the stacked barrels resting one on top of the other, and thanked the lord they were on an even swell for such things were dangerous in anything else when there was flesh and bone about.

'What's the best way to do this?' he asked.

Again it was Littlejohn who responded. 'Stove in the tops of them you can get at, then once they's emptied they're easy to shift.'

'We'll run out of room in no time. Charlie, get aloft and ask the carpenter's mates to come below and knock off the hoops. We can throw the staves up through the hatchway.'

As Taverner obliged, Pearce took an axe out of Rufus's hand and went for a barrel. Sharp as it was, he was not well balanced and there was no room for a full swing so the damn thing, hitting what was a thin piece of wood, bounced back at him, the blade narrowly missing his shins. The laugh came from Michael, as well as the words.

'Happen you need a real worker for that task, John boy. Step aside.'

Even in the gloomy light Pearce could see that the axe, in Michael's hand, looked like a toy and when the Irishman swung it there was no bounce. It went straight through and as Michael extracted it a stream of water gushed out. Another smack, this time followed by a twist, removed the lid whole, so that the barrel emptied in seconds, and was pushed to one side so they could get at the next. Above their head they could hear muffled shouting, then the sound of running feet but they had no idea what it portended until Colbourne's voice called down the hatch.

'Mr Pearce, belay that, and get the men on deck.'

'Sir,' he replied, before ordering the men out and the lanterns doused. He was last out of the hold, last to get on deck, last to find out why everyone was grinning, to receive the news that there was relief in the offing, that a British warship had been sighted north of their position, one which had yet to be seen from the deck.

'Let that be a lesson to you Mr Short,' Colbourne said, in a voice that was almost happy. 'Only put aloft as a lookout men who have good eyes and the brains to look in all directions. Now hold our course and prepare the signal, "enemy in sight" and have the gunner load a signal gun.'

Colbourne made his way to the shrouds and tucking in

his telescope began to climb, which impressed Pearce. Yet it made sense; if you were in command and you wanted to see for yourself there was no other way. Besides, being at the masthead would add a good deal of time to that which you had to form any plan of action. He was almost tempted to follow, out of sheer curiosity.

Colbourne was up there for a good twenty minutes, sweeping his glass first forward, then over the stern to the still chasing Frenchman, who would be too far off to see the other sail to the north. It was like an itch Pearce could not scratch, wondering what was going through the man's mind. He longed to be up there, making decisions not following those of someone else, however much that person knew more than he.

'Will you be after stopping all that hopping about, Mr Pearce,' said Michael – he was mister on deck and John boy when they were out of officer earshot. 'Sure you'll be wearing a hole in the deck and sinking us.'

That got a laugh from all who heard it, as the man it was aimed at realised that was what he had just been doing.

'Mr Short, send aloft the signal.'

The flags flew up the halyard and fluttered in the breeze, and the gunner, who had been alerted to do so, fired the signal gun, which, if it could not be heard, would attract the eye because of the smoke.

'Helmsman, ease off a few points so the signal can be read.' The ship slowed perceptibly as it came off its best point of sailing. 'Stand by to come about, Mr Short, and close with the enemy. Once we are on our new course you can clear for action.'

There was a palpable air of excitement about the crew as they obeyed that last order and the armed cutter came about with something approaching stateliness. It was that same driver Pearce had seen before – sailors it seemed were happy as long as something, anything, was happening; it was boredom that rendered them cross-grained. Given the traded jocularity it seemed that the men were quite happy to take on a French 74 without assistance if that be the case. It was, of course, nothing but bravado.

Colbourne, back on deck, somewhat spoiled that mood by the way he set a modest sail plan, so that *Griffin*, once more heading into the wind, made little progress. Clearing a ship like his to fight did not take much – canvas screens and hammocks came down easy and the amount of impediments to be struck below were few. It was more the casting off and the preparation of the guns, that accompanied by the swivel gun firing at intervals to ensure that the approaching British warship was aware that there was an enemy in the offing. Once completed, and after an interval of ten minutes when nothing happened, Pearce left his station by the larboard cannon and walked back the half dozen paces to the quarterdeck, to be greeted by a less than welcoming look from Colbourne. The lieutenant turned away, as if confused, raising his telescope to stare over the stern.

'Your station is on the guns, Mr Pearce.'

It took a look back along the deck for Pearce to realise that he had broken some taboo. Midshipman Short was standing rigidly behind his cannon, staring out to sea, and the crews, with the exception of the gun captains kneeling by each piece, and the other sailors were gathered in groups by the falls, ready to work on the sails. No doubt he, likewise, should have stayed at his station, but having failed to do so he had no choice but to ask that which had brought him here.

'Forgive me, sir, but I am curious as to what you have in mind.'

'Are you, by damn!'

'I don't think I am alone in that, sir.'

The telescope came down abruptly, and the hissed reply was soft enough to keep the next exchange just between them. 'You are not suggesting I discuss what I anticipate, or what I hope, with the whole crew?'

'What harm could it do, sir?'

'You have so much to learn about command, Pearce. Officers make decisions, their inferiors do as they are bid. You, no doubt, would be the type for a rousing speech.' The signal gun banged out again, and a rather testy Colbourne ordered that to cease. 'Our consort has acknowledged. Get that signal down and raise our number so he knows who we are.'

Pearce half turned and looked over the bows, to the now clearly visible Frenchman, hull up on the swell and with a full suit of sails aloft. 'It seems the enemy is still closing, sir?'

'He is?'

'So he cannot see that he faces two British ships, not one?'

'No, Pearce, and I suspect he thinks we are bluffing, using that signal aloft to humbug him, saying that there is another warship in sight because we cannot outrun him.'

'What will he do when he is disabused of that?'

'Am I being interrogated?'

Pearce wondered why he was being so tense and uncommunicative. 'No, sir, you are being asked what is likely to happen by someone who has no idea.'

'It is not necessary for you to have ideas. Just do your duty, Pearce, that will be sufficient. Now go back to your station, and take cognisance of Mr Short, who has enough of the officer in him not to have left his.'

There was no choice but to obey, and as he complied the lookout called down, 'Frenchman shortening sail, sir.'

Colbourne was tense, and really talking to himself when he said. 'Now we shall see how the day will progress.'

The French 74 may have shortened sail to slow his approach, but he had not altered course, and it took some time to find out why. As usual members of the crew could recognise their rescuer as soon as enough of her features became visible from the deck.

'*Centurion*, fifty,' said Blubber, now stood by one of the nine pounders and had raised himself on the carriage for a better view.

'Does that mean she has fifty guns?' asked Rufus, from the nearby carronade, which got him a withering look that gave an affirmative answer. 'But that Frenchie has got more.'

'Need twice the number to take us on,' called a cheerful voice from across the deck.

'Belay that,' snapped Short, standing near to five-foot erect. Latimer, who was one of the two larboard quarter gunners, shook his head at that same remark, in a way that told Pearce he did not agree.

'She's no spring chicken, HMS *Centurion*. Laid down this thirty year or more.'

'Which means?' asked Pearce, very quietly, hoping that neither Colbourne nor Short would hear, for if asking his commanding officer questions in a situation like this was anathema, then it must be that in spades with a member of the crew.

Latimer gave him an old-fashioned look that made the same point – blue coats did not ask advice from common seamen – which on that lined dark-skinned face looked really crabbed. The look reminded Pearce that he had been a lot less chatty since he had come back aboard, so he added, 'I asked the captain, but he seems to want to keep everything to himself.'

'Colbourne don't know what's going to happen. He ain't keeping owt to hisself. It'll be the captain of *Centurion* that makes the choices.'

'What do you think he will do?'

'Why you asking me?'

'Because,' Pearce hissed in frustration, 'I don't know.'

Latimer thought for a bit, then relented. 'Was a time that a fifty could stand in the line, not any more.'

'So?'

The older man nodded towards the bows. 'So our friend John Crapaud yonder will know soon enough what he's facing, if he don't know already, know that he has the weight of shot to take old *Centurion* apart, what with her having old and worn timbers. But is he worked up proper? Has he got a crew aboard who knows what they are about? He took a bit of way off so as he could work out what to do. If he comes on, it'll be because he wants a fight.'

'And *Centurion*?'

'Would be well advised haul right round to run, with us on her tail.'

'That's what you would do?'

'Damned right. I have no mind to see the scuppers running with blood. That Frenchie has the wind and we don't, so, providing he has the lads to man the sails proper, he can do what he likes.'

'You've been in battle before?'

Those brown eyes fixed Pearce. 'I have, an' it ain't the lark some of the buggers on this deck think it is.'

'How long have you been at sea, Lats?'

'Can't recall a time I weren't,' the old man replied. Then he grinned, and spoke a bit louder, 'According to Michael there, your old Pa would have had me an admiral, it's been so long.'

'Sure, he would that, Latimer, and a right floggin' old bugger you would be.'

'Signal from *Centurion*, sir.'

So, thought Pearce, people like Latimer knew of his past now; did they know what had happened since? He suppressed the familiar and troubling images that surfaced then, making himself concentrate on Colbourne. Had he made HMS *Centurion* out and knew her size and name before he had come back on deck? Maybe he shared Latimer's view, maybe that was why he had been so tense and terse. He looked aft, to where the lieutenant had taken out the signal book and was leafing through it himself, raising his telescope from time to time to check on a flag. Every eye on his own deck was on him, though they would wait in vain for him to speak. Once he had read the signal he turned stone-faced to look forward.

'Mr Short, Mr Pearce, please join me on the quarterdeck.' When they did so, in the space of a second, he spoke softly, tension very evident in his voice. 'The signal was to engage the enemy more closely, gentlemen.'

'Is it the course you would have chosen, sir?' asked Pearce, which earned him a shocked look from Midshipman Short.

The look on Colbourne's face was totally at odds with his reply. 'I can think of no other.' Then he shook slightly as if to rid himself of his torpor. 'We will act independently. *Centurion* will I think engage the enemy yardarm to yardarm, though that has yet to be proved. Whatever, we must try to get across her stern and use our carronades to sweep her lower deck. That may, if we are successful, give *Centurion* some hope.'

'Meaning she has little hope now?'

'Are you shy of this?' spat Short.

'I don't know,' Pearce replied, just as vexed, 'but no doubt with your vast experience of fighting at sea you will be able to tell if I should be.'

'Enough. We will do our duty and support our consort, and with luck, we will triumph. Now you may wish to pen a last letter, or write a last testament. Once you have done that go back to your stations and make sure, doubly check, that all is as it should be, for I do not anticipate that we will get more than one chance to affect the outcome of the forthcoming fight.'

With no one to write to Pearce just went back to his station, to be greeted by a whisper from Latimer. 'So, what's happenin'?'

'We're going to take our Frenchie on. Colbourne is going to try and get across her stern and use the carronades.'

The 'bugger' was not suppressed, that followed by Latimer saying to those nearby, 'Time to pray, lads. Whoever's got *Centurion* is a glory hunting sod.'

Time went slowly, as slowly as the closing warships, the Frenchman coming down to topsails for the forthcoming fight, both the British ships forced to keep a full suit aloft, to tack and wear as they closed into the wind. All this Pearce learned from the men on his part of the deck, who, with the exception of Latimer, seemed indifferent to the possible fate that awaited them. Pearce doubted they were as sanguine as they appeared. No doubt it was that male attitude of not showing fear in front of your fellows, combined with no real idea of what was coming. He, himself, was quietly grateful for his own ignorance; since he had little idea of what was about to happen he could not be in terror of it, and if it presaged death, then he was in no position to avoid it. You cannot run from a ship at sea and, being little different from those he led, nothing would allow him to show that he cared.

He thought back to his earlier attempt to extract an explanation from Colbourne. He knew nothing about commanding men, but he did know he would have handled matters differently, not least by keeping the crew of *Griffin* informed of what he was thinking, and of what was happening, instead of leaving them to guess. Perhaps Colbourne feared that they would fail to do their duty; did he wonder that he might, for there was none of the fire that had been present on the previous cruise when they had taken that privateer. It was that thought which brought home to Pearce just what they might be sailing into; for a man so wedded to the need for promotion a successful sea fight would be just the ticket he needed.

So for him to be so subdued meant he thought what they

were about was folly, thought that he would be lucky to survive, reckoned that whoever commanded *Centurion* was crazy to take on a larger and more powerful ship with only an armed cutter to assist. That made Pearce angry, for if Colbourne thought that, then he should decline to take part. If there was about to be carnage on this deck it would not be confined to him. Too afraid to be seen to be cowardly, he was doing the one thing that damned him in John Pearce's eyes; he was failing to stand up to authority. He turned to tell him, to say what true bravery consisted of, when the booming sound of a cannon reverberated across the water, that followed by two huge spouts of water just off the bows.

'No fool, our Frenchie,' said Latimer, 'he has a mind to take care of us afore we can even get close.'

'Harken to that, lads,' called Michael O'Hagan. 'Admiral Latimer has spoken.'

'Is it going to be bad, Pearce?' asked Rufus.

Pearce moved to put his hand on the youngsters shoulder, wondering why he was bothering with words of encouragement, wondering if the words he used were addressed to himself rather than Rufus and Charlie. 'All we can do here is our best. There's nowhere to go, so not doing that will likely make it more dangerous.'

'And pray,' added Michael, crossing himself as another two spouts of water shot up from the sea, this time close enough for the spray to drift across the deck.

'Happen it's goin' to get warm,' Blubber responded, 'so getting a good clench on your arsecheeks will help.'

Blond Sam hooted from down the deck, 'Need a rope an' a windlass to close yours up, Blubber.'

'Mr Short,' called Colbourne, 'below and break out a cask of rum. A large tot to each man at their station. No time to mix it, serve it neat.'

'Bugger's human after all,' said Charlie Taverner, who looked as pale as a ghost.

'We've been here before, my friends,' Pearce said,

reminding them of what had happened as members of Ralph Barclay's crew, 'and I know we acquitted ourselves well.'

'You're right,' hooted Michael. 'That there French sod might think he has the measure of us, but he has yet to face the Pelicans.'

Blubber replied, with a huge grin. 'Only thing you got in common with a Pelican, Paddy, is the size of your mouth.'

'Sure, it's scarce big enough to swallow you, you over-larded sod.'

'Take a whale for that,' cawed Matt.

One of the next balls from the Frenchman's bow chasers landed so close to the hull that the ship actually shuddered. Colbourne called for the men set to work the sails to stand by and told the helmsman to bring *Griffin* onto a more westerly course. For once, having a large crew was an advantage; he had enough men for both sail and gunnery duty. The wisdom of his choice was proved as both the next cannon balls landed over to larboard, but worryingly they seemed to be level with the ship, which meant they had the range.

'Let fly the sheets,' called Colbourne, and that obeyed the way came off the ship.

Waiting a minute he ordered them sheeted home again, then braced round to sail on a different tack. He was being shrewd, changing course and speed to confound the enemy, waiting for the larger ship to come up and split the onslaught from those bow chasers. HMS *Centurion* was close now, they could see the men on her deck, though only those close to the bulwarks, given her greater height, but most on the *Griffin*'s deck were more interested in the rum cask and the ladle Short was using to distribute the contents. Neat, with no lime juice to thin it, the rum made even the hardiest tar gag a bit, but there was no doubt it was welcome, a bit of fire in the belly for the coming fight.

The next boom did not come from the Frenchman but from *Centurion*, its bow chasers speaking out to tell the enemy that they were coming into range and that their fire was now to be returned. If the captain had hoped that would spare the *Griffin* he was immediately disabused, as another pair of balls arced through the clear air, one of which removed the top of the mainmast, and the lookout who was still up there.

'Topmen aloft,' Colbourne shouted, adding as they raced up the shrouds, 'secure anything loose, and report the damage.' Then he rushed to the side, searching for the man who had been blown overboard, in the vain hope that he might have survived. 'Mr Pearce, an axe at the double, and cut the line holding the ship's boats. If the lookout can get to them he will have a chance.'

Pearce was moving before the sentence was finished, and did as he was bid, though he could see no sign of the lookout in the water. 'Resume your place, Mr Pearce. God will decide whether he survives or not. We cannot heave to and search for one man.'

'*Griffin*!' The voice boomed over the intervening water between the two British vessels. 'Your name, sir.'

'Lieutenant Colbourne.'

'Captain Marchand, at your service. Let fly your sheets and take station in our wake once we are by you or I fear you will be sunk.'

'Aye, aye, sir.'

The order was obeyed with as much alacrity as Colbourne could muster, with that damage aloft. Once in the larger vessel's wake, following it as it tacked and wore, they became blind to what was happening over the bows, except for the sight of what shot missed, landing in the water to either side. That was until one ball from the Frenchman overshot and, having left a neat hole in the mainsail, landed in the white water of *Centurion*'s wake just a few feet from the bowsprit, which brought all work aloft to a halt, as the topmen worked to secure flapping lines and the blocks necessary to get what was left of the topmast out and a jury one set up.

Then the *Centurion*'s captain was over his taffrail, as
below him men worked to block off the casement windows
of the various rear cabins, issuing orders through his speaking trumpet.

'Mr Colbourne, I intend to try to get across the stern of
the enemy and give him a drubbing, my aim to disable as
many of his cannon and gun crews as possible. If I can get
past him I will have the weather gage. He, I suspect, will
continue to fire into my rigging hoping to disable me and
board. I want you, once we are close, to come out of my
wake and make as much of a nuisance of yourself as you
can, but do not linger in the arc of his larger guns, for I
doubt you would survive it. My advice then is to take station on his bow and play upon his rigging.'

'I will do my best, sir.'

'Of course you will, Mr Colbourne, and your crew I'm
sure. And should we be successful I think we might look
forward to the gratitude of the nation. Why, I would be
damned surprised if you were not made post.'

'Coffin more like,' spat Latimer.

Pearce could see that the man speaking had said just the
right thing to Colbourne. It was almost as if his whole
shape changed, shoulders going back and head lifting as if
to sniff a bright future. But his new midshipman's concerns
were different; if it was going to be bloody, was there anything he could do to survive himself and help those under
his charge to do the same.

'Well it won't do you no good standing there like a
statue,' said Latimer. 'Keep moving up and down, 'cause if
they has muskets it'll be you they'll take aim on. If you
think they are loading grape, lie down. Being brave will fill
you full of holes.'

'Anything else?'

'Pray!' This was no time to say what he thought of that
idea, but he did ask for what? 'That our Frenchie is short-
handed, that his crew ain't worked up right and are not
handy on the guns, that their captain is as thick as the bitts

holding his anchor cable, and that Marchand, or whatever his name is on *Centurion*, gets in a full broadside afore he is shot to pieces.'

Looking past Latimer he saw his Irish friend, eyes closed and mouth moving silently.

'I think Michael is doing enough for all of us.'

'I doubt it, 'cause there is unlikely to be enough prayers in the world.'

The air was suddenly full of booms, so much that Pearce was sure he could feel the pressure of them in the air. Then the waters around *Centurion* boiled, but not all the shot had missed and, as well as several holes appearing, they heard the sound of cracking timber, that followed by screams. The captain had been replaced at the taffrail by a midshipman there to relay his orders, so that it was the voice of a near child that informed Colbourne that it was time for him to alter course, this as the huge rudder on the ship ahead began to swing.

The French 74 soon came into view, having luffed up and fired her broadside at *Centurion*, and was now busy getting under way again to headreach her and give her a second broadside at close quarters, square on to her bows. Whatever damage the fifty-gun ship had suffered did nothing to hamper her sailing qualities, for as soon as the Frenchman was under way, Marchand spun his ship to first run alongside the Frenchman and then with luck to get across his stern. The boy on the taffrail relayed the order for Griffin to hold her course and carry out the previous instructions that had been given by the captain.

Now they were in full view of the enemy, just as he fired a second broadside, this answered by *Centurion*. There was no doubt about the pressure now, Pearce could feel the air movement in his ears, as Colbourne ordered Short to fire his cannon, that followed by an order to the quartermaster to note the time on the slate. So the guns of HMS *Griffin* spoke out, and battle was joined.

Chapter Twenty-Two

Close to, from their lower deck, the enemy was a frightening sight, two long rows of open gunports, empty, but shrouded with the leftover smoke from their broadside, the great masts and topsails high above their heads, with men in the tops aiming muskets, even a swivel gun on the mainmast cap. The shot from *Griffin* did little damage, the balls from nine pounders skidding off the Frenchman's upper scantlings because they had not been aimed high enough to reach the bulwarks. The eighteen pounder carronade balls did strike home but, at the range they were fired, though they did some damage, they did not penetrate the thick planking, and all the while they got closer and closer. Busy reloading, the gun crews failed to see those empty ports fill one by one, dark muzzles poking out, until each contained a cannon. With a clarity that surprised him, Pearce could see they were aimed high, the side of the ship suddenly shrouded in thick black smoke belching out behind the fired shot. Through that smoke came *Centurion's* reply, her cannon balls smashing into the enemy at maindeck level, the clang as metal struck metal reverberating across the water in between. As the wind blew the smoke clear, he could see that two of those French gunports had been blown asunder.

They were closer now, and with better aim *Griffin's* guns did some damage on the second broadside, though mostly just to the top timber near the bowsprit, decorative stuff rather than anything vital. The next broadside came from *Centurion*, quicker to reload than her opponent, but that was only seconds and since the two capital ships had closed the gap between them it seemed that the intervening space was nothing but a maelstrom of death and destruction. So much smoke billowed across the face of the French cannon that those aboard *Griffin* did not see that on reappearing, the forward guns were aimed not at *Centurion* but at themselves. They found out, to their cost, within seconds, as the deck and the lower tops were swept with grapeshot.

Pearce felt the small metal balls whistle past his head, so close he wondered how he survived and he heard the screams from behind of those that took them. With his gun crews reloading, most in crouched positions because of that, it was the men waiting by the starboard guns that bore the brunt, and turning he saw half a dozen writhing in agony, while two or three more appeared to be already dead. Midshipman Short, who had stood rigid as he thought it his duty to do, was lying in the middle of the deck, a pool of blood spreading from his body, one hand clutching at the air as if a grip would give him a hold on life, but it was by the wheel that the worst damage had been done. Colbourne was on his knees, holding a shattered and badly bleeding arm, head bowed, while the quartermaster and one of his mates were sprawled against the side, clearly in deep agony. It was instinct that took over then, and he called to those on the starboard battery who had survived.

'Three of you, get on the wheel and hold our course. The rest get the wounded below, and any not occupied to this side and get your heads down.'

'Cannon reloaded,' shouted Latimer, that repeated by the forward quarter gunner.

Pearce shouted his reply without looking round, 'Fire as soon as you can.'

'Ain't never heard that one afore,' the old seaman replied, as he ordered the gun captains to pull their lanyards. Not paying attention, trying to order the decks cleared of wounded, Pearce had got too close to the recoiling guns, and it was one of the gun captains jumping clear that knocked him clean over on to the deck just as the next set of shot from the Frenchman swept across the deck. This time it was roundshot and aimed into the rigging, and, lying on his back looking up he saw ropes cut through, with blocks blown asunder and a mast knocked out of its chains, so that he had to cover his head as the debris rained down on the deck. Yet he was aware and deeply impressed by the fact that much was going on regardless; powder monkeys still moving towards the guns with their cartridges while they were being swabbed and reloaded; men looking to their fallen comrades without instructions, others going aloft unbidden to see to the damaged rigging.

Rolling to his feet he got to Midshipman Short, taking that still groping hand and using it to turn him slightly so he could see the wound. Eyes closed and in deep pain the little man looked ninety. The shoulder was shattered and blood was pumping out of open veins. He called to two seamen and grabbing a nine pounder wad pressed it against the wound.

'Don't take him below, get him against a bulwark and keep that wad in place. Press hard on it to try and stop the flow of blood.'

Latimer was beside him suddenly. 'You'd best get on that quarterdeck, 'cause there ain't no other to take charge. Coal Barge is still down.'

'Guns?'

'Are being taken care of.'

Pearce got to the wounded lieutenant in three big strides and, kneeling, lifted his head. 'Mr Colbourne?'

'Get me to my feet, Pearce.'

'We must look at the wound.'

The reply was bitter and came through clenched teeth. 'Dammit man do you ever obey an order?'

Being on the side of the wounded arm Pearce had to cross to Colbourne's good arm, with just enough time to glance and see that the way on the ship had taken the *Griffin* clear of the Frenchman's bows. Not that they were safe, for the two bow chasers they had faced earlier were waiting for them, muzzles pointing down right at the stern. Pearce could never understand then, or afterwards, as they both fired, why he threw himself to cover the lieutenant's back, he just did it out of instinct. It was not metal in the air now, it was wood blasted from the stern rail and the deck below it. Pearce's hat went, speared by a sliver of timber and he felt a searing pain across his scalp. Another splinter from the taffrail, pointed like a dagger, embedded itself in the planking right by his hand, shuddering like a thrown knife. Again there were the screams of pain from those who had been less fortunate, not least those men he had put on the wheel, which like them, was smashed, so that the ship was now drifting.

With some effort he got Colbourne to his feet, and watched as the man, holding his shattered arm with his good hand, pulled himself upright, his voice strained by pain as he spoke, and hard to hear over the continuing gunfire that consumed the two larger vessels. 'Report the damage, Mr Pearce.'

'I wouldn't know where to begin.'

The head came up, with a defiant look in the eye, which also managed to convey the fact that he was useless. 'Send the carpenter into the hold to see if we are taking in water. Make sure that any wounded on the gun crews are replaced. We must get men aloft to secure what needs it, and to run lines so that we can reset our sails and come about to re-engage.'

Most of that, short of checking for leaks, was happening without his bidding; the men on the ship knew what to do without orders, but the idea of re-entering the fray, after the damage *Griffin* had suffered, seemed mad. 'The wheel is shattered.'

'The rudder?' Pearce looked round, observing that the stern post looked to be undamaged, and he said so. 'Then we can still, thank God, steer and as long as we can do that we can fight. Get a party below to my cabin and work the rudder from the ropes. You'll need a relay of messengers.' Colbourne tried to turn round, but a stab of deep pain stopped him and his head bowed again, the cracked voice evidence of how much he was suffering. 'How does *Centurion* fare?'

A glance was enough. She seemed to be drifting. The

rigging was a mess, broken masts, tattered canvas, ropes hanging loose, the bulwarks too were full of gaps and it was a fair bet that some of the maindeck guns had been dismounted. What it was like below he shuddered to think.

'Badly.'

'Has Captain Marchand got across her stern?'

'No.'

'And the enemy?'

The Frenchman had swung side on to *Griffin*, and for a moment Pearce had a vision of a full broadside coming their way, but he realised that she was coming round on her undamaged side to engage again with her larboard battery. As a ship of war she looked more complete, with most of the rigging that supported her topsail intact, the most obvious advantage she had that she could still manoeuvre, though ten seconds watching showed that she did not have to do much, since the leeway was slowly taking her towards the *Centurion*'s side.

'We must get back into the action,' Colbourne hissed as he heard what was happening.

'Lift your head, sir, and look along your deck, then tell me we should get back into the action.'

Colbourne did so, and had he been looking with as much attention as John Pearce he would have seen the carnage. Men still not moving, probably dead. Streaks of blood all across the planking, which was covered with a mass of ropes and blocks. Short against a bulwark with two sailors kneeling beside him, the mid quite clearly having passed out. Pearce could feel blood trickling down his cheek, and then he tasted it as it reached the edge of his lips. There was a dull pain in his head, but nothing he could not bear. That was the moment when the man he was holding upright became a dead weight as the lieutenant, too, passed out.

Then two of the Frenchman's cannon took *Griffin* low on the larboard side of her stern. There were no flying timbers this time, just the sound of shattering wood, and Pearce knew that the ship had taken a heavy blow. The question was, where?

'Michael,' Pearce called. 'Help me get him below. He needs a tourniquet on that arm. I think he has passed out from loss of blood.'

Wiping the blood from his own face, his eyes searched for Charlie and Rufus as he and the Irishman carried Colbourne towards the hatch, and he was relieved to see that though both men looked shocked and confused, they were whole. That was when he spotted Gherson cowering right in the bows, and he yelled at him like the most stentorian bosun in creation.

'Move, you scum, or as God is my witness I'll strap you to the muzzle of a carronade and fire you at the enemy.'

'Now which God would that be John boy?' asked Michael, as he took the weight of the lieutenant, and eased both him and his charge down the companionway ladder. Pearce followed him and passed by, heading for the stern, shouting down the hatch to the carpenter to get aft and assess the damage if he could. Standing in what had been Colbourne's cabin he was sure he could hear running water below his feet, but he could also see that the rudder ropes and the tackle that they ran through were intact.

Michael was beside him again, whipping off the bandana he had had on to protect his eardrums, wrapping it round Pearce's head, just as another sailor appeared.

'Carpenter says to tell you he can't get to the stern, with too much in the way of stores to shift.'

'So how do I find out if we are taking in water?'

The sailor looked shocked to be asked, either that or the shock was at Pearce's ignorance. 'You'se got to check the level in the well, to see if it's getting deeper.'

'Make it so,' Pearce replied, thinking that at least sounded like a correct form of words. Looking up, he saw above his head Colbourne's sword, as well as a ceremonial sort of dagger. He grabbed both and, Michael at his heels, he made his way back to the deck, past the men laid out in what had been their living quarters. Midshipman Short had been fetched below as well. He was still in that sitting position, though the wad had been strapped on tight. There was a couple of hands aboard who knew a smattering of how to aid the wounded and they, like so many of the crew, had gone to work without instructions. Not that they were doing much in the way of pain relief, their only medicine being the residue of that rum cask that Short had passed round before the engagement started. They were dulling their patients, not curing them.

'Jesus, it's enough to tempt you to a wound,' said O'Hagan, eyeing the cask.

Pearce grinned, though it was a weary jest that followed. 'Don't get drunk Michael, you might get into a fight.'

'Sure if I'm not in one already, pinch me.'

'Orders, sir?' demanded Latimer, as Pearce's head came through the hatchway.

Orders? He was in charge, and once he had got fully on deck the unpleasant shock of the fact hit home, with any number of men looking at him silently demanding to be told what to do, his Pelicans included. To give himself a moment to think he looked aloft, to where the topmen were still working, securing what they could not repair. Then he realised that the firing had ceased and given the near silence he looked aft and asked the most obvious question, 'Those cannon?'

'Think they have seen to us,' the old man replied. 'Ain't shown since that last salvo.'

It had only been a temporary respite, and the two major vessels, with the Frenchman now stern on to *Griffin*, resumed their battle, with guns blazing and great swathes of smoke billowing up between them. It was obvious that *Centurion* was not giving as good as she was getting, obvious that in the contest, in which her captain had been a fool to engage, she was losing, drifting away from *Griffin*, with the Frenchman doing likewise, though at a barely perceptible, faster rate.

Another head popped up though the companionway, that

of the sailor who had checked the level in the ship's well. 'We're taking water in fast, sir, round an inch a minute. Carpenter's asked for extra hands to get some of the stores shifted so'es he can get a look see, but I reckon the time he will take he might be too late.'

'There's no time for that. Get some axes and stove in the planking astern on the lower deck, see if you can get to it that way.'

'Still need help.'

'Latimer, you know the men, you detail them.'

The old sailor laughed out loud, though Pearce could only wonder at how anyone could see humour in the situation in which they found themselves. 'Rank at last, happen your old Papa was right.'

Mention of his father suddenly brought back to Pearce that whole scene in Paris, that stinking, yelling mob salivating for blood, not just his father's blood, but that of anyone that their damned tribunal condemned. Ever since that day he had harboured a desire to retaliate, to do something to those vipers that would redress the pain and guilt he felt. From indifference he had moved over the intervening weeks to a visceral hatred of the French Revolution and what it had produced, the rule of the mob, the death of the innocent, the traducing of everything his father had worked all his life to promote, and ever since that day he had felt his own life to be worthless, something of no account, his self respect so damaged that he had no care for his fate. Here he was in a sea fight with that same idea; perhaps not the same people, but the dogma they represented. He had felt useless since that day, impotent. Now he had a chance to do something, one that might never recur again.

'Will she answer to the sails?'

'She will,' Latimer replied, 'but not with anything like grace.'

'She never had that, Latimer, but let's try and bring her round.'

'Top hampers gone, so'es you'll need to let fall the

maincourse and set a jib to keep her head steady.'

Pearce smiled at the old man. 'Make it so, Mr Latimer. I will be back on deck before we are round.'

'Mr Latimer,' crowed Michael, 'did you hear that lads. We'll be tipping our caps to him now.'

Blubber could not be kept out of a jest. 'One of those Frenchies gets your friend, Paddy, and he'll be captain.'

Pearce went below again, to kneel by Lieutenant Colbourne, who, still unconscious, lay flat out on the deck. Looking at the arm, with a tight tourniquet on the upper part having stopped the flow of blood, Pearce reckoned it so damaged, with the two ends of bone poking out and trails of sinew, that it would probably have to come off. There was no one aboard with the competence to undertake that; he needed a proper surgeon and casting his eyes about Pearce knew he was one of any number, these thoughts running through his mind as around him the shouts reverberated as instructions were called down from the deck to be relayed to the men working the rudder.

The thought that *Centurion* would have a surgeon was followed by one less welcome; so would the French 74. He could surrender the ship and quite possibly save some lives. That the idea was anathema to him was of little consideration; there were a lot of men aboard this ship which might well be in danger of sinking, and it was, as had already been proved, certainly not of a size to engage the enemy. Really, despite his earlier thoughts of personal revenge, the decision was one for the whole crew, not a notion that the man he was looking at would approve of.

Latimer had got *Griffin* round by the time he came on deck again, though with nothing sheeted home the ship was wallowing on the swell, so it was by looking over the bows he saw the deteriorating situation of *Centurion*. You did not have to be a sailor to see that she was in deep trouble and that was getting worse by the minute. Little now existed above her lower masts, the bulwarks were totally stove in along their whole length and the firing for her remaining guns seemed uncoordinated.

That sailor's head came up again. 'Four foot of water in the well, sir, and still making fast.'

'He should strike,' Pearce said, nodding towards *Centurion*.

'He won't, Latimer replied, 'he'll force them to board.'

'Why!'

There was a wry look on the old man's face as he replied. 'Happen you don't know much about the navy you're in, Mr Pearce, but we's not much given to packin' it in until we're sure we's beat.'

'And our own crew?'

'Same.'

While Latimer had been speaking, Pearce had been examining the situation, his mind strangely clear of all distractions. He felt a slight tremor run through his body, the same kind he had always experienced just before a fist fight. It had happened to him as a boy and as a man, being something seen by him as a frisson of fear, a sensation to be ashamed of. Yet as always it had produced a heightened sense of awareness, the ability to not only see danger but to anticipate it, and with it this time came a half notion of a plan.

'*Centurion* will be taken, will she not?'

'Be a miracle if'n she ain't.'

'How long?'

Latimer thought before replying. 'Half a glass, a whole one at the most.'

'And so will we.'

'Right after, fer certain, if we don't sink afore.'

'Can we get away?'

'Hard to see how, the way we're taking in water. Sinking won't be quick, but she'll sail even slower.'

Surrender? Thoughts of the Conciergerie surfaced again, that and the Bridewell with a similar stench and sewage running through the straw if the River Thames rose. They would imprison him and the crew and that was something he was determined to avoid. Added to that desire to revenge himself it was a heady brew.

'Will the crew fight?'

Latimer looked at him then, in a strange way, as if he had a notion of what Pearce was thinking. 'That's what they're here for.'

'What would make that bastard draw off?'

'A hundred gun ship, which I take leave to doubt will suddenly appear.'

Pearce's eyes were on the eighteen pounder carronades, that and the line of nine pounders, and then he looked towards the stern of the French 74, close enough now to pick out the name, *Valmy*, and some of the words Colbourne had used earlier came back to him. Could it be done, to get the crew of this ship aboard their consort and so disable the enemy as to allow them to get clear? If it was possible it was unlikely, but to Pearce it represented the only hope they had, so it had to be worth a try.

'Let's get under way. I want all starboard guns loaded and run out.' An expression he had heard, one in common usage ashore, came back to him and he added, without really being sure it was the right thing to say, 'Double shotted!'

'It'd be better if you give the orders, not me.'

'Stay here, I will need you.'

Pearce stepped up to the small space that had once been the quarterdeck, now scarred, without a wheel or a binnacle, searching his mind for the words to use. 'Michael, a party on the falls to sheet home. Let's get some way on the ship. Blubber, sort out gun crews for the starboard battery and make sure each has a good captain.'

He looked at Latimer then who said quietly, 'We need a party on the pumps.'

He gave the orders, then added, as he saw the man he so disliked. 'Gherson, you lazy sod, get pumping.'

There was a pause while he thought through what else had to be done, things for which he did not need Latimer. 'I want the carpenter and all his mates on deck with as much of their spare planking as they can get out of the holds. Michael, once the sails are set and drawing take your men below and fetch the wounded on deck. Lay them behind the bulwarks on the starboard side. Stand by with grappling irons and every man who can use a musket and is not otherwise engaged to get one ready for use.'

'Christ, Pearce,' exclaimed Latimer, 'you planning to board the Frenchie?'

'Wait and see.'

The creaks and groans of protesting timber, as HMS *Griffin* got under way, yards braced round to take the now helpful wind, were familiar and somehow strangely reassuring, so that Pearce felt a twinge of something approaching gratification as, with orders shouted below and with the men pulling hard, she answered to her rudder. It was not smooth, there was a certain amount of unwelcome yawing to and fro, but once he had got the course he wanted set, the bowsprit aimed right for *Centurion's* side amidships, he told them to lash it off to hold it steady. Looking over the bows he could see the smoke-filed and narrowing gap into which he was heading. The high-pitched whistling sound was mystifying, until he recalled that he had already heard it twice that day. The *Centurion's* deck was being swept with grape, designed to kill anyone who sought to oppose the act of boarding.

To the front of Pearce the carpenter and his mates were hammering and lashing together their spare planking to make stretchers. One or two completed, the comatose wounded, Colbourne and Short included, were being strapped on before being laid between the starboard guns, others who could walk were shepherded to a place of relative safety, sat back to the bulwarks. Muskets were being primed and loaded, swords, clubs and pikes laid ready, while aloft, on the stump of the mainmast yard, the topmen were rigging blocks with slings to lift those stretchers, so that once alongside *Centurion*, they could try to get them aboard. Pearce had no doubt that few of them would make it unscathed; that applied to every man in the crew if what he planned to do came to pass, but at least it gave them a chance, for there was no doubt in his mind that the last place they would be safe once he had completed the task he had set himself was on this deck. If it worked they might just live. If not? Well that was not a helpful thing to dwell on.

'They's spotted what we're about,' said Latimer, still by Pearce's side, pointing to someone on the *Valmy*'s taffrail gesticulating at them. 'Reckon we'll take a salvo from their stern chasers afore we get under them.'

'Under them?'

'We's low and those cannon are maindeck. Once we's close they won't be able to tip them enough to hit us.'

'That's good to know.'

'By that time,' Latimer said, with wry amusement, 'we should be close enough to the lower deck thirty-two pounders to look like a right sweet target.'

'I was hoping they would think us to puny to care about.'

'Then you was hoping wrong, mate.'

'What do you reckon?'

Latimer's hand went to hold his chin, a sign that what he was about to say was speculation, which reassured Pearce since it matched his own lack of certainty. 'Our deck is about level with their lower guns and they will want the hull if they can get her.'

'We're sinking, you said so yourself.'

'Pity is, they don't know that, and with what they've got, they can take out the bulwarks both sides quick as kiss my hand. But them stern chasers are first to worry about, and I reckon they will pepper us with grapeshot.'

A head came up the hatch and a voice called out, 'Eight feet of water in the well.'

The party on the rudder, and those pumping, were safe from that but that was not the case for others, so he called down those aloft. 'Anyone not manning a cannon, get below. Everybody else, get behind the trunnion and keep your head down.'

'Us an' all?' Latimer asked.

Pearce moved to the rearmost larboard gun and sat on the deck, followed by the older man. Lying there, they heard the whistle and swish as grape swept over the deck, the clang as some of it hit metal, the thud of straight shot and ricochets embedding themselves in wood, but he heard no screams, and that was what mattered.

'Everyone up,' he shouted, getting to his own feet. 'Let's show the bastards we're alive.'

That brought forth not only sailors, but a load of shouted insults and filthy gestures aimed at the French gunners. Pearce went to the bows, then walked quickly back down the line of guns, ordering them elevated so that they would fire as high as they could.

'How are we doing, John boy?' asked Michael.

His tone was slightly jocular, the same as it always was when he asked that question. If the Irishman had any fear of what they were sailing into, he was not the man to show it, nor was he one to give a hint of any doubt about what his friend was doing. It had been the same every time they had gone into a fight before.

The answer was a whisper. 'I feel like a fake, Michael.'

'Don't you believe it. Sure, have I not said before, you were born to be a blue coat.'

'Is we goin' to get out of this Pearce?' asked Rufus, who was not too proud to tremble.

Pearce patted the carronade they were manning, the last on the deck, and spoke with a certainty he did not feel. 'Ask me when this has been fired.'

It was a tense Charlie Taverner who added, looking over Pearce's shoulder to the badly damaged *Centurion*, 'Hope we have breath in us to do it.'

What could he say to them; lay out the choices, tell them they might accept being prisoners but he would not, add that he had only a vague idea of what he was about and it was a hope rather than a certainty that they would survive. They had always burdened him with the making of decisions, now he was making them without considering that they might think differently, and for once, he felt no misgivings about doing so. Perhaps Michael O'Hagan was right.

Behind him Latimer was silently counting off the time

with his fingers, and after he had gone across his hands several times, mouthing the pattern of loading and running out a cannon, he shouted, 'Time to get our heads down again.'

Pearce complied, as did everyone on the deck, just seconds before another load of grape swept over. Apart from balls thudding into the masts there was little sound this time apart from the high-pitched whistle of its passing, until they heard the patter of a mass of small shot hitting the wake of the ship.

The armed cutter, with the wind coming over her starboard quarter, was making less speed as the water filling her holds slowed her down. Closing on the two near-stationary ships the gap was closing rapidly, now barely big enough for *Griffin* to enter, with the faces of musket-bearing Frenchmen leaning over the rail in plain view. Looking across the thirty yards of water he could see the remnants of *Centurion*'s gunners running out what was left of their maindeck battery, and within seconds the air was again full of sound, fury and shot, of breaking wood, of screams, which partly masked the sound as a lead ball hit the planking by his feet. Looking down, he saw how close was the gouged wood, and he knew he had been lucky not to get it in the foot.

'Those of you that have muskets ready and loaded, clear those sods off that rail above our head.'

Pearce went forward again as the guns were lifted, aimed and fired quickly by the marines, less efficiently by the tars, not looking at those returning fire from the enemy poop for to do so would be useless – providence would decide if he was going to take a shot – going to the first nine pounder and standing behind it. Each cannon would fire in turn, and since it was his scheme they were going to try and execute he was determined to be the sole arbiter of when the flintlocks should be sparked. They were under the *Valmy*'s counter now, close enough to touch the gilding on the stern decoration and ahead Pearce could see the first of the lower deck cannon that could do them damage, its black spout, with a wisp of hot smoke lazily exiting its muzzle, waiting for them to come alongside.

'Sam, Matt,' he called to the pair, 'get some wads off the gunner and soak them in turpentine. We need something to set them alight as well.'

'Slowmatch'll do it for turps,' Sam replied, as Matt ran below shouting for help.

Griffin was hardly making any way at all now, and she was definitely wallowing as the bowsprit crept past the Frenchman's stern. It went completely quiet; *Centurion* would not fire for fear of hitting *Griffin* and the Frenchman was just waiting, knowing that the armed cutter was placing itself in between the two fighting vessels in an attempt to save her larger consort, waiting to blow her out of the water and out of the way before completing the day's work. As the first cannon came abreast of the Frenchman's rudder, Pearce pulled the lanyard on the nine pounder and jumped clear of the recoil.

At a range of less than thirty feet it should have been impossible to miss the rudder, but miss he did, the ball flying past to land harmlessly in the water beyond. By that time, having told the first crew to scarper aft, Pearce was behind the second nine pounder, this time more careful and more successful. The ball hit home, but even at such close range it did no more than create surface splintering on what was a substantial piece of timber. On down the line he went, seeing in the corner of his eye Sam with a pair of armourer's tongs holding at arm's length a flaming wad.

'Through the gunport, Sam. Lets give the buggers on those cannon something to think about other than shooting at us.'

The French gunners could have fired at the foredeck, but they must have realised, looking along the muzzle, with the larboard side deserted, there was no one to aim at. So they waited until that first nine pounder came alongside, and assuming there must be a gun crew hiding behind the bulwarks, they blew both that and the gun asunder. The clang was deafening and the nine pounder and its trunnion, all a ton and a half of it, flew across the deck and smashed through the larboard side and jammed there. The balls that had been in the garlands were likewise dislodged and began to roll about the deck making that noise so like thunder.

'This is no time to be thinking of mutiny,' Michael called out, as he stooped to catch one of the cannon balls, a joke that brought forth a laugh from the men, a sound that increased in volume as he threw it hard at the side of the enemy ship.

As the thirty-two pounder was withdrawn to reload, Sam threw his flaming wad through the gap, while Matt followed that with half a bucketful of turpentine, whooping with delight as he heard the cries of panic that his action engendered, for he knew, if Pearce did not, just how much sailors feared fire. Flames shot out of the gunport, and they heard a dull explosion as some powder, possibly a waiting cartridge, blew up. By that time Sam had a second one going and that went through just as Pearce fired the next gun, taking more splinters off the rudder, again ordering the gun crew aft as the second French thirty-two pounder fired a ball that went right through both bulwarks of the ship.

Griffin began to grind along the side of *Centurion*, and proof of how tight the gap had been came when the bow of the armed cutter collided with and bounced off the side of the Frenchman. Already the grappling irons were flashing out, not yet to secure *Griffin* but in readiness for when the order came. Hands were coming out of *Centurion*'s lower ports offering to take the walking wounded, an offer of which Gherson, who seemed not to have a scratch, took immediate advantage. The curse that Pearce wanted to shout after him died on his lips, being pointless. With only a foot to spare the ship ground on, crashing into one vessel then the other, by which time five nine pounder balls had been aimed at the enemy rudder. If they weakened it, the two carronades did the real damage, the first of their heavier balls smashing it near in half, the second removing the lower section so completely that the enemy would be denied steerage way. That was when *Griffin* ground to a halt, finally crushed between the two ships, her bulwarks shattered, and guns dismounted by the relentless fire of the enemy, half the cannon balls on deck rolling into the scuppers. But Sam and Matt had done good service too, since many of the gunports were belching smoke from a fire those behind the scantlings were struggling to contain.

'Lash us off tight,' Latimer called, to those on the grappling lines.

Colbourne and Midshipman Short were already aloft by the time that order was given, hauled by the crew and hooked in to land on the larger ship's deck. Just as they disappeared a rope hit the planking beside Pearce, as the first of the French boarders dropped to their deck, with others trying to get at them from those gunports free of flames. He might had died on the spot but for Michael O'Hagan, who stepped past him to clout, with another cannonball, an enemy sailor raising his short heavy sword. The man dropped like a stone as the Irishman's hand caught his coat collar and pulled him backwards into a line that had been formed without his bidding, made up of all the crew that could hold a weapon. Now it was the turn of the enemy to face musket fire as the men on the *Centurion* fired over their heads. It created a temporary respite, and dropped several of them, before they closed to fight hand to hand.

The men of the *Griffin* began to scrap hard, to contest their deck, their numbers as those below came up, which must have come as a shock to their enemies, initially pushing the French back to their own ship's side. This was not what Pearce had in mind, for in the end there was no way they could hold off what the enemy could eventually throw at them, and there was precious little space on the armed cutter's deck for the assistance that could come from their consort. His idea was to get on to *Centurion* and then hopefully Marchand could get that vessel, badly damaged as she was, away from the *Valmy*. If Pearce had read it right –

and he had plenty of doubt that he had – without a rudder the Frenchman would be unable to chase, and once the British Man o' War was out of range, she could get both her crew and that of *Griffin* to safety. As for the armed cutter, she would no doubt sink.

These thoughts came to him as he was heavily engaged on a deck that, even with the holds full of seawater, rose and fell with the swell. Colbourne's sword might be a bit cere-monial, but it was a weapon with which Pearce was familiar; he knew how to use it to good effect, though it took several blows with the hilt, a jab with the knife in his other hand and a couple of well aimed kicks to deter those right in front of him and create the right amount of space to render the sharp blade dangerous and the thrusting point deadly. To his left he had Michael, formidable with just a marlin spike in his one hand, backed up by a left fist, while on his right he could use his longer weapon to keep those before Charlie and Rufus at bay. They were fighting too, they were just not doing so as effectively as the Irishman.

Not for the first time in his life, Pearce was aware of how much action effectively cleared his brain. He saw things with clarity and was able to parry thrusts aimed at him and return a blow that would wound and discourage his assailants. At the same time he had a clear notion of the problem faced by the men of *Griffin*, as well as those who had come to their aid from *Centurion*. Once the wounded had been taken to safety, matters would come to a danger-ous head, that there would be no time when they would be more vulnerable as the point at which they tried to retreat.

Above their heads the small arms gunfire was constant, muskets, swivel guns and few of the remaining cannon as those on both line of battle ships' decks tried to back up their own side and harm the other, creating between them enough smoke to make Pearce feel he was fighting in a fog, that punctuated by shouts, curses and screams, the occa-sional discharge of a pistol, with men falling and being dragged back out of the action. None of the lower deck guns on either side could fire for fear of hitting their own, and so had been withdrawn, and that was the means of escape for the defenders – through the gunports. Someone on the lower deck of *Centurion* had a brain, for from the side of each port came a couple of pikes, to jab at the enemy through the mass of defenders, while from above came a shower of everything from spikes to fallen blocks, as well as small casks thrown at the attackers to hold them at bay, the whole obviously an attempt to create a space, not a very great one, for a safe withdrawal.

'Griffins, back!' yelled Pearce, hoping that they would obey, for several seemed to have their blood so high up that they were oblivious to the need to get clear. Charlie and Rufus at least obeyed with alacrity, Rufus slipping through a gunport and Taverner diving after him. Michael got to the port and, back to the hull, turned to renew the fight. All along the deck men were doing as they were bid, either scaling the side of the grappling ropes or using gunports and gaps in the scantlings to get to safety. Yet some of the others seemed oblivious to the danger. Latimer might be old, but it did not seem to interfere with his ability to wield an axe. Blubber stood feet apart, two large hands swinging a short naval hanger like a scythe, and doing so with enough effect to keep clear a space in front of his substantial belly. Sam and Matt had abandoned their turps throwing to take up clubs with which they were belabouring those in front of them. It was the sight of that pair that had Pearce searching for the cask they had been using, and he yelled at them to do his bidding.

'Sam, Matt, kick over that turpentine, then throw the slowmatch on it.'

Time stood still for Pearce then, because the two could not easily disengage. He had retreated into the space between two pikes so was now only concerned with the men in front of him, Michael occupied the space that separated him from the next gunport and was going to find it harder to get to safety. Eventually Matt got a boot to the cask, which turned on its side then rolled across the deck, spilling its contents. Sam had ducked down, and only just survived a blow that took off his hat, exposing his bright blond hair, without seeming to do much to the head underneath. The slowmatch tub he just picked up and threw, his attempt to upend it successful so that the burning linstock landed in the spilled turpentine. That took immediately and created a blast of flame on the deck that made the enemy fighters take note, and in doing so they paused for that vital couple of seconds that allowed those opposing them to dive for safety.

Pearce could not go until the last man was clear, and that proved his undoing. Suddenly there was a blue coat in front of him and a fellow with a like sword who wanted a contest, either a lieutenant or a *sous-officier*. It was unwelcome for a man whose sole notion was to escape, especially when he realised that the lines to the grappling irons were being cut, which would allow *Centurion* to drift apart from the *Griffin* and *Valmy*. If he took this fellow on and the delay was great enough he would be stranded on this deck, but he also knew that close as the man was and with the weapon he had, to turn his back on him was to invite a sword thrust that would certainly seriously wound him, and might in fact kill him.

There was no choice but to engage and it was only when the two blades met that Pearce realised how much the level of extraneous noise had fallen. The clash of steel rang out like a pealing bell, that followed by the clear rasping sound of metal sliding on metal. Pearce had one hand to his back now, in a classic fighting pose to aid his balance, but he knew he had a problem in that he could not drive his opponent back, as to do so would take him forward into danger from a swarm of his fellow countrymen. He had no notion that they would hold back from maiming him out a some sense of chivalry – they would kill him as quick as they could. In the corner of his vision he could see that the two jabbing pikes which had protected his flanks were slowly moving back, evidence that the route to safety was going away from him, that indeed he was trapped. For all he was engaged, for all the thoughts of what was happening behind him, he could still see the irony in the fact that even if he killed the man he was fighting, he would be on his own with dozens more and that could only end in one way; that the most obvious solution was to surrender and become a prisoner.

It was that thought, and his own determination not to accept it, that fired his swordplay. Damning the consequences he began to use his blade with more aggression, his lead foot jabbing forward to take his blade with it, the look on his opponent's face leaving him in no doubt that this sudden assault came as a surprise. There was another thing in the fellow's eyes, something John Pearce had seen before, when fencing; the move from the certainty of victory to the possibility of defeat. It was the moment for a swordsman to strike, that spilt second when doubt first surfaced, for that weakened both the arm and the resolve. The swift circle he made with his sword brought forth a desperate lunge for the Frenchman that exposed him. Pearce parried his thrust, flicked his blade to one side, and sliced down immediately, the tip of his sword cutting through uniform and flesh. The shock of that was all he needed for the kill, and those behind his blue-coated enemy knew that. Had he followed through then he too would have died. Instead he leapt back, reversed the sword and threw it like a spear, before jumping onto the bulwark and diving into the sea. Only those on *Centurion*, already twenty feet distant, saw the narrow margin by which he escaped thrusting pikes, thrown knives and discharged pistols. Pearce did not; he was under water swimming to deep security.

When he surfaced, shook the water from his head and eyes and began to swim properly, it was to a rousing cheer from the decks of the *Centurion*, and to an Irish hand held out of a gunport, that of a man strong enough to bodily lift him clear of the water. He was hauled onto a dark, red-painted deck that yet showed many a streak of blood, to be faced by a black-faced lieutenant who took him by the hand and hauled it heartily up and down, creating, as the water ran off Pearce, an impression of a man working a pump.

'Give you joy, sir, that was prodigious.' Then the hat was off his head. 'I lift my scrapper in your honour, sir, and ask the crew to give you three times three.'

Dripping wet and being cheered were, or Pearce thought ought to be, two mutually exclusive affairs.

'Now, sir, join me on deck, and let us see what we can do.'

'You are?'

'Lieutenant Slattery, First Lieutenant, at your service.'

'Midshipman Pearce. Captain Marchand?'

Slattery took his arm and hauled him towards the companionway. 'Is in the cockpit, sir, being attended to by the surgeon.'

'He...?'

'Will survive, sir, I am sure. You are a mid, sir, not commissioned?'

'No.'

'Then that raises your actions to an even greater degree of wonder, sir.'

They came up on to a deck that looked as if it had been swept by some mighty and furious giant. Guns were dismounted, though men were working to get them back in place. Ignorance of rigging did not prevent Pearce from seeing just how comprehensively it had been damaged. There was blood everywhere, though those who had shed it had been removed, and no doubt there had been bodies blown or thrown over the side.

'Now Mr Pearce, let us see what our French dog is about.'

'Running for home, I hope.'

Slattery nearly whooped. 'He would be, sir, if you had not shot away his rudder. As it is, once we get some canvas aloft and steer down on the swine, he is at our mercy. I expect him to strike as soon as we get across his stern.'

'Strike?' asked Pearce, who only wanted to get away from any more thought of battle.

'Certainly, sir. Thanks to you he cannot manoeuvre. I will take him under tow, and pull him into Spithead, where we will not only be fêted as heroes, but line our pockets with a pretty penny.'

Pearce had been about to protest, to say enough was enough, but then he saw the eyes of his shipmates, Pelicans and Griffins, and he knew that they would never forgive him if he did so.

'So be it.'

'You would do me the honour, sir, of demanding he strike, that is if he understands English.'

'There's no need, Lieutenant Slattery. I speak French.'

'Damn me, sir, if you ain't a paragon.'

Hyperbolic in expression the Premier might be, but he was right. A jury rig that would allow them to steer was up within half an hour and they bore down on the struggling *Valmy*. Having tried and failed to steer using *Griffin*'s rudder, he had cut her loose to slowly sink, and she was down to her scuppers as *Centurion* swept by. There was a trading of shot, but the French captain did not wait to see his maindeck swept from stem to stern with shot. As soon as the British Man o' War got across his stern, he struck his tricolour to avoid the carnage which was bound to follow. By that time, the armed cutter HMS *Griffin* was gone.

'Come sir,' called Slattery. 'I invite you to come aboard, and help me take the captain's sword. Dammit, if they don't make me post for this, I swear I'll eat my best hat. As for you, sir, the world is your oyster.'

It was a happy if well damaged HMS *Centurion* that sailed up the Solent towards Spithead, with *Valmy* in tow, cheered from every beach they shaved, for news of the victory had preceded them, brought ashore by swifter sailing vessels eager to be the one to deliver the news. The mere fact of a battle won so early in the war was enough to bring cheer to the crew, but to that was added the calculations being made about prize money. If there was one thing more pleasing than taking a merchant vessel, it was, in addition to the glory, the capture of an enemy warship, especially one on which the damage, though severe, was well worth the cost of repair. The only thing more valuable was the capture of a Spanish plate ship, which might set a man up for life, but a French 74 ought to be good for two whole years' wages to the lowest landsman. There was, of course, the vexed question of the capture being a joint one, which would keep the Prize Agents and the lawyers busy for a while, but there was many a discount house ashore that would be happy to buy the tickets of the crews so they could spend their money before it was actually paid out.

Such joy was not, however, universal. Quite apart from the severity of his wound, which had seen him lose his arm, the question of Colbourne's actual rank had been raised by Captain Marchand. He insisted that Colbourne was not, in the true sense of the word, a captain, and therefore had no entitlement to the full share of his two eighths – he wanted to downgrade him to the sum set for the sea-lieutenants. This would mean HMS *Griffin*'s commander sharing an eighth with a half a dozen others; all the surviving lieutenants from *Centurion*, added to her marine captain, the master and the surgeon who had lopped off his shattered limb. Naturally Colbourne, who saw it as an attempt to rob him, even in constant pain and sometimes quite feverish, had disputed this. He had already written the letter that would be delivered to his Commodore at Lymington. That officer could be relied on to get involved, and likewise dispute with Marchand's admiral at Spithead about a division of the spoils due to superior officers.

Pearce tried not to think about it, for he was in the fourth class for distribution, which meant the gunners and carpenters of both vessels would get more; he was lumped in with the *Centurion*'s mids and the surgeon's mates. Whatever it was, and it would be no fortune, was good enough; he was heading for shore, where he was sure the crew of the armed cutter would be put ashore. With luck, he and his trio of Pelicans could get clear of the seaport and away from the Navy. What he would do then, his promise fulfilled, would have to wait. Meanwhile, having been accommodated in the midshipman's berth, he had to put up with a level of discomfort as bad as the lower deck of *Griffin*. Worse, there was a twenty-year old senior midshipman called Burkett who got on his nerves so much that he wished Short would leave the sick bay, where he was comfortable, and relieve him of some of the burden of dealing with the man.

'I have no idea what sort of thing passes for proper behaviour aboard an armed cutter, Mr Pearce, but on a ship like *Centurion* it is not done to fraternise too closely with ordinary seamen.'

Pearce looked up from the dirty pewter plate that had been set before him by the scruffy servant, aware that the man who had said those words was referring to the way he talked to the men who had just fought alongside him. That was bad enough in Burkett's eyes, but the intimacy he showed towards Michael, Charlie and Rufus really got under his skin, the whole compounded by the way Pearce ensured that the Griffins were not subsumed into the *Centurion*'s muster and put to work as ordinary crew members.

What he saw pleased him even less than what he heard, for Burkett had a high colour, a flaring nose and thin lips over a pinched and unsmiling mouth; the man reeked of disapproval in all he did and said, made worse by his tone of voice, which he used to force home the fact that he was well born. The rest of the table, the surviving mids, four youths of varying ages – for two had been killed – were looking at their own plates. Being scared stiff of Burkett, they were not about to tell John Pearce if they agreed with that statement or not.

'I shall take care not to have any contact with ordinary folk, Mr Burkett, but the men from *Griffin* are anything but that, I'm sure you would agree.'

'I find I cannot, sir. A common seaman is a common seaman.'

'Then I can only assume that you have less than perfect eyesight.' He saw Burkett swell to protest, but added before he could speak. 'And no discernment either, and that means you will probably lack the qualities necessary to make a good officer.'

'Damn you, sir, how dare you.'

Pearce was furious, for this was not the first time Burkett had sought to chastise him, so he took matters to the limit. 'I may dare to repeat it, sir, in public and off this ship, and leave you to decide how to seek redress.'

'Captain's compliments, Mr Pearce, and he would like you to join him in his cabin.'

Pearce thanked the steward who had popped his head in and stood up, waiting for a second to allow Burkett to accept his challenge. The moment passed; he took his leave and as soon as he was out of sight, cursed himself. Why allow a nobody like that to rile him so? In the captain's cabin, he found a pale Lieutenant Colbourne, and a florid-faced Captain Marchand, who seemed to him like an older version of Burkett, a well-connected buffoon.

He had been to dinner in this cabin several times, while Colbourne was convalescing. Marchand, with his arm in a sling, did not impress him at all. He made great play of his need to have his food cut up for him, continually making the same joke about "It being damned hard to think of fishing", one that his own officers, led by Slattery, laughed at uproariously regardless of how often they heard it repeated, their open sycophancy quite sickening. Naturally the captain and officers of the *Valmy* were guests, and Pearce suspected his presence, well below the salt, had more to do with his facility in French than any desire to elevate him above his station. The enemy sailors had no English, and conversation was dull and stilted, good manners preventing any mention of the recent action; it would never do to discuss that in the presence of those who had suffered defeat, even if they were in the eyes of their hosts men who had a dubious claim to their rank, having only achieved it because better men had fled. Pearce did nothing to help; he was not about to tell the enemy either how he had learned their language, or anything about what had happened in Paris, and he made no secret of the fact that he despised them.

'We will moor the ship within the hour, Pearce,' said Marchand, patting the thick and sealed despatches on his desk, one of which Pearce had written at Colbourne's dictation. 'Then these have to go to Lord Howe.'

'Yes, sir.'

'He has already sent a boat, and the officer on board that assured me we would receive a warm welcome.' There was a pause, when he looked questioningly across the table, but since his other visitor did not speak, he added. 'And I have prevailed upon Lieutenant Colbourne that you should accompany us ashore.'

Pearce looked at Colbourne, who refused to meet his eye, which made him wonder at his previous distant behaviour. Visiting him in the sick bay, writing that despatch, he had put that down to the pain of his wound and the uncertainty he might have about his future. Perhaps it was more than that; perhaps with some glory in the offing the last thing he wanted, knowing that he had been unconscious for most of the time, was the presence of the man who had actually secured it.

'Before that, sir, I have a favour to ask.'

Marchand fixed him with bulbous eyes. 'Which is?'

'There are certain men aboard the ship, sir, who were Illegally pressed into the Navy.' He wondered whether to add "as I was myself", but decided against it.

'Is this your tedious Pelicans, Pearce!' snapped Colbourne.

'It is, sir,' he replied, still looking at a mystified Marchand. 'I would want them released.'

'Can they prove their impressment was Illegal?'

'I can swear to it, sir.'

'Then I daresay you can take it up ashore.' Then the captain beamed at him. 'I doubt you will be denied anything for which you ask.'

The only sound of that was Colbourne sucking hard on his teeth.

'A damn fine show, sir. You are a credit to the service,' said Lord Howe, commanding admiral of the Channel Fleet, repeating himself for the umpteenth time.

'Hear him, hear him.'

Pearce was standing in a room full of admirals and captains when the King's Messenger arrived – the place was awash with glittering gold epaulettes. The numerous ships in the Spithead anchorage had emptied so that all the senior officers could be ashore to greet the returning heroes. Led by Howe there was a veritable plethora of Lords and Knights. Marchand was basking in their admiration, Colbourne in their commiserations at his condition, this while they were all at pains to assure him that his unfortunate wound in no way diminished the role he had played; he commanded the *Griffin* and it was to his credit that he had taken aboard as a volunteer a young man of such a stripe as Midshipman Pearce. Under the deluge of such praise, the Lieutenant had mellowed somewhat.

'Well,' said Lord Howe, to whom the message had been given. 'You are required at the palace. This is an order for you, all three, to attend upon His Majesty at tomorrow's levee.'

'Then I suggest,' said another admiral, 'that they best shift.'

Howe looked at Colbourne and Pearce, his rheumy, old man's blue eyes not happy. 'They must make a visit to the tailor first. We can't have them going into the presence of the King looking like tramps.' Suddenly the old man became solicitous. 'Mr Colbourne, are you up to such a journey?'

Pearce had to stop himself then, for he nearly burst out laughing, sure that Colbourne would crawl over broken glass rather than miss such an opportunity. But then did he want such a thing? Given his history, what was he doing even contemplating walking into the presence of royalty. Then he had an idea; it was a golden opportunity to tell Farmer George the result of that warrant, which had placed both him and his father in jeopardy, to tell the King that he had, ultimately, been responsible for the beheading of a man merely for expressing his opinions.

But prior to that he had a request for Lord Howe, one that he delivered out of earshot of any of the others present. The old man listened and replied.

'Leave their names with my aide, and I will see to it.'

If it had been a glittering array of senior officers at Portsmouth it was as nothing to Windsor. The King's audience chamber was crowded with generals as well as admirals, politicians in silks, lords in satins, ladies of all ages, of beauty and aged ugliness, in gowns and turbans of a cost to keep a poor man for life, all trying to look as though the chill from the stone walls of Windsor Castle, and the lack of a fire to warm them, had no effect. John Pearce, dressed from head to foot in new clothing, stood well apart, rehearsing what he was going to say to George of Hanover. Head down, concentrating on that, he was unaware that he had been approached until the smell of expensive perfume filed his nostrils. Suddenly, mentally, he was back in Paris, in a salon a lot warmer than this, surrounded by beauty and brains.

'And who, might I ask, are you?'

Pearce looked up into the face of a very beautiful woman, and automatically gave her a slight bow. 'John Pearce, Midshipman.'

'Ah, the hero of the hour.' It was false he knew; this lady had known who he was before she came close. 'The midshipman who not only saved one warship, but helped to capture another.'

'I was not alone.'

'How delightfully modest.'

'May I ask to whom I am speaking.'

It was Marchand who provided the answer, coming towards the pair. 'Lady Annabel, I see you have met our hero.'

'I have Captain Marchand.' Then she looked Pearce up and down in a way that no lady had done since Paris, the final look leaving no doubt that she was pleased with what she saw. John Pearce felt his blood begin to race as she continued. 'As you know, Captain Marchand, I am having a little dinner tonight, a celebration of your victory. I would be most disappointed if you did not fetch along our young Lysander.'

How old was she? It was hard to tell, but even under a fair degree of finery he could discern a very pleasing figure, and her bosom, half covered with a jewelled necklace, was very inviting. His plan, once this levee was over – and if he avoided being thrown into a cell for insulting the King – had been to make haste back to Portsmouth, to get his friends off the *Centurion*. But one day would make no difference.

'I would not only be delighted to accept, Milady, but I would consider it an honour.'

'My,' she replied, in an arch but amused way. 'Not only brave, but with graceful manners.'

She was gone, with Marchand speaking softly into his ear. 'Best watch yourself there, lad, Lady Annabel Fitzherbert is one to eat up such as you. There's a bit of blue blood in those veins, though on the wrong side of the blanket.'

Pearce was thinking how pleasant that would be – to be eaten up – especially for a man who had been deprived as long as he. The last woman to affect him in this way had been Barclay's wife, Emily. He was rolling her name and the image of her beauty around in his mind when the entrance of the King was announced. It took an age for the monarch to get round to his part of the room, and before that he had seen fit to rail loudly at his sons for their manifest failings, but finally, having spoken to all the courtiers that required a word, he turned to his sailors. He was shorter than Pearce had expected, rather plump, with that Hanoverian nose dominating his ruddy face.

'Well, Marchand, a fine show, what, what?'

'A most pleasing result, Your Majesty.'

'Tell me?'

Marchand was brief. As he had told both Pearce and Colbourne in the coach that brought them to Windsor, the King, whom he had met many times, was not a patient man. Story told, in which he flattered his own actions more than others, he turned and said, 'Allow me to introduce to you Lieutenant Colbourne, the captain of HMS *Griffin*, who so nobly aided me and my ship in the capture.'

The King leant forward and looked into Colbourne's face. 'An arm, eh, Colbourne, a stiff price, what, what?'

'Well worth paying, sir.' Colbourne replied, his voice gruff through nerves.

'Well I shall make sure it is, what, what? Those devils at the Admiralty will find you something to your credit or answer to me.' Then he spun round suddenly and shouted. 'Chatham!'

The man who responded did so without haste, approaching the King and giving him a courtly bow. Stood up again, Pearce thought he looked like a drinker, his face carrying that excess flesh which was a sign, that and his eyes, which were rather watery, as though he had slept badly.

'Your Majesty.'

'I hope you are going to give this poor devil a ship.'

'His commission as captain has already been posted. As soon as he is recovered, sir, I am sure we will find him suitable employment.'

'And this, Your Majesty,' said Marchand, 'is the real hero of the hour. It was he, manning each gun himself, who shot away *Valmy*'s rudder. I doubt we would have enjoyed success without his intervention. Indeed, I must admit the outcome could have been in doubt.'

'Pearce!' This was said before Marchand could introduce him, his voice becoming very emphatic. 'Son of the late Adam Pearce.'

That set a buzz of conversation going, and as the King turned to silence it, Pearce got a view of Lady Annabel, and her lips, slightly parted, seemed to be inviting him, or was it his imagination. Concentrating on that, he failed to control his conversation with the King who, with his back to Pearce, was speaking to Chatham again.

'A lieutenancy would not go amiss as a reward, Chatham, what, what?'

'If the young man has the required sea time, Your Majesty, I am sure it will be a mere formality.'

'Sea time, be damned, sir. Lad's a fighter, what, what, plain as the nose on your face.'

'The service has rules, Your Majesty.'

'The service, sir, is the Royal Navy, and I, sir, am the King.' The voice began to rise as he continued, and Pearce wondered if he was going to lose control of himself. Certainly he had created a few worried faces. 'And if I am the King, sir, and the Navy is Royal, then they are beholden to me, are they not!'

Another courtier stepped forward, his voice emollient. Shorter and slimmer than Chatham, he was younger looking, more elegant, but yet there was a definite likeness. 'If it is your wish, sir, then it will be so, rest assured.'

'Make it so, Mr Pitt, make it so, what, what?'

John Pearce opened his mouth to tell the King about his

father, and damn the promotion, but the monarch had gone, and all he got was a view of his disappearing back. Then he was face to face with Pitt.

'Did I hear your name aright?'

The question was softly posed, there was no rancour or threat in it, which forced Pearce to reply in kind.

'Then let me say I was sorry to hear of the way your father died. It was monstrous.'

'Which is what I wanted to tell the King. If he had not been driven from the country, he would still be alive.'

'Don't be hard on King George, young man,' Pitt said. 'If anyone deserves your anger it is I. William Pitt, First Lord of the Treasury, at your service. I can see in your eyes a flash of hate, which I daresay I deserve. But rest assured if I did anything regarding yourself and your late parent, it was for the safety of the nation.'

'That sounds like exaggeration.'

'It may sound like it, but it is not. How do you think I feel about this war, Mr Pearce, about the lives that will be lost, quite apart from the cost in money. Before you finally decide I am destined for hellfire, ask yourself this. When you felt threatened in that fight that has brought you here, did you think about the men that died so you could stay alive, on both sides?'

'It is not the same.'

'Please do not presume to tell me what I constitute as a threat to my life, my well being and that of the country. You will have your lieutenancy, Mr Pearce...'

'I don't want it.'

'It matters not. The King has wiled and we do our utmost not to create difficulties in that area, since with His Majesty one has no idea where it would lead.'

Clearly Pitt was referring to the King's mental state, which must be more delicate than the nation knew.

'And if you want a place, write to me and I will ensure you get one. It is the least I can do, for although I do not expect you to believe me, your father is on my conscience.

Now, why don't you mingle. It might take that very sour look off your face.'

'Perhaps I can help,' said Lady Annabel, who had again approached unseen. Pitt bowed and walked away. That smile was on her lips again, and the Pearce blood was reacting. 'Promotion? That is something which should be celebrated and here I am asking myself what I can possibly gift you that would be reward enough?'

It was two days before John Pearce could tear himself away from the arms of Lady Annabel Fitzherbert, and if he had felt twinges of guilt at the delay in setting his Pelicans free, he had also enjoyed rediscovering elegant life and the pleasures of the bedchamber. Dressed as a lieutenant, in a uniform bought for him by his wealthy, gracious and sensuous paramour, he coached to Portsmouth alone in one of her husband's well sprung carriages, which he commanded take him straight to the Naval Dockyard. There he requested a boat to take him out to *Centurion*, now surrounded by other vessels and scaffold as her damaged upper works were repaired. He came aboard to be greeted by that supercilious sod Burkett, who when he saw his new uniform coat went puce with envy.

'I have come for my men, Burkett,' he said, gilding the lily slightly as he added, 'on the express orders of Lord Howe, from whom I presume you have had some communication. Please be so good as to send someone for them.'

'Which men?'

Pearce had some pleasure in forcing him to say sir. 'Their names are O'Hagan, Taverner and Dommet.'

'From HMS *Griffin*?'

'Where else, man?'

Burkett looked at the ceiling, but his face belied the words that followed. 'Then I am sorry to have to inform you, sir, that the entire crew of *Griffin* was shipped into HMS *Leander*, which was short handed. They are now at sea, on their way to the Mediterranean.'